Tumultuous Affairs

Uncertain Politics and Unlikely Romance During a Turbulent Time 1964 - 1975

Durham Caldwell

Copyright © 2009 Durham Caldwell
All rights reserved.

ISBN: 1-4392-5396-X
ISBN-13: 9781439253960

To order additional copies, please contact us.
BookSurge
www.booksurge.com
1-866-308-6235
orders@booksurge.com

Dedication

To Carmenceita Jones, who led the fight to end *de facto* segregation in the public schools of Springfield, Massachusetts, and who kept her sense of humor throughout.

To Dr. John E. Deady, who as superintendent of schools shepherded the Springfield school system through a trying period while keeping the confidence of officialdom and the public.

And to my wife, Jean Caldwell, for her lifelong support, her participation in covering many of these stories, and her eagle-eyed proofreading.

Cover Illustration
PAUL FLANNERY

Technical Assistance
NICOLE CHOTAIN

Also by Durham Caldwell:

The House at the Cliffs

*Remembering World War II:
Ludlow (Mass.) veterans of the armed forces
tell their stories in their own words*

*Television Documentaries:
Bishop Weldon, A Look Back
The Sixties
The View from Riverview
POW's, Welcome Home
Springfield Armory, Fight for Survival
The Interrupted Convention
The Man in Blue
Model Cities, Hope or Hang-up?
Pioneer Valley, U.S.A.*

Prologue

Riverbridge, Massachusetts, is a fictional community. But the author has drawn liberally on his experiences as a radio and television news director in the City of Springfield and its environs to present an accurate historical picture of the politics and racial tensions of the times. Any resemblance between the citizens of Riverbridge and real people is coincidental. On the other hand, the characters depicted in the book at state and national levels are drawn from real life and portrayed in situations like those in which they actually took part.

I

Wow! What a dish! Buzz said to himself as he walked toward the back of the plane.

His decision to sit down in the empty seat beside Judy Ferguson had been innocent enough. He was a newsman on the prowl, notebook in hand and tape recorder over his shoulder. She was a freshman city councilor back home—and, early twenties and an alternate delegate, the youngest member of the 1964 Massachusetts convention delegation.

She had spunk. He knew that. An Ohio girl, she'd gotten involved in campaigns in Riverbridge during her years as a political science major at Mount Holyoke College. She had stayed on after graduation and been elected to the Riverbridge City Council a scant year later. In her first day as a councilor, she had given Buzz's old friend Max Feigenson the deciding vote in his quest for the council presidency against the old boy coalition which had controlled the council for a decade. Newspaper columnist Donald Dibble, the old boys' self-anointed champion, wrote an acid column about the "Feigenson-Ferguson coalition, the combination of college girls and shysters who are trying to take over the town." Regular readers knew "shysters" was Dibble shorthand for "Jewish lawyers."

Judy took note of the column in her maiden speech to the council. "Mister Dribble, I mean Dibble," she said, "should rename his column. How about 'Dibble's Drivel'?"

Dibble didn't change the name of his column, but Judy's speech did change the vocabulary at City Hall, in the city's broadcast newsrooms, and even in the newspaper city room when Dibble himself was safely out of earshot. He was no longer "Donald Dibble." He was "Mister Dribble-I-Mean-Dibble" and occasionally "Mister Drivel."

She also had a reputation around City Hall as an insufferable flirt. But Buzz's city government reporter, Happy Hooper, had

Durham Caldwell

chalked that up as a defense mechanism against the kind of attention that an attractive young woman was bound to get.

Buzz didn't really know her—he wasn't covering City Council meetings any more. But she'd entranced him not only with her good looks. Her smartly-tailored business suit disguised but couldn't conceal a traffic-stopping figure, and she was as pretty as his own Elaine. Maybe even prettier, if that was possible. Shorter. Blonde instead of brunette. But, like Elaine, with a smile that could fill a room. She had teased him for only a moment when he sat down beside her and then got right down to business answering his questions.

What really had gotten him in their brief meeting was her sparkling personality and, even more, her grasp of convention issues and of city government issues back home. She'd volunteered that she was concerned about racial tensions in the city, that the mayor's heart was in the right place but that he wasn't moving fast enough to get rid of discrimination in city hiring—there were only a handful of Negro policemen, for example—nor was he pushing the School Committee to correct some bad situations in the schools. She'd even gotten Buzz's agreement to consider a series of TV programs on racial issues. And she'd acted as delighted to talk with this veteran hometown journalist as he'd been to talk with her.

He would willingly have sat and chatted with her the rest of the way to San Francisco, but the wandering delegation members assigned to sit next to her had returned to claim their seats.

What a vibrant young woman, he thought. Yes, that was the word for Judy Ferguson—vibrant! Their brief encounter had stirred up feelings within him that he hadn't experienced since Elaine died—forgotten feelings that he had never expected to experience again.

In the airplane restroom, Buzz took off his glasses and squinted at himself in the mirror. Would he have a shot at a pretty young woman like that? The mirror reflected the gray at his temples and in his sideburns, the crow's feet around his eyes, and the unmistakable hint of a double chin below his square face. Who are you kidding? he laughed. You're old enough to be her father.

Well, he could introduce her to Johnny. Not that he was eager to do his smart-aleck son any favors. But what a great addition this good looking, personable, intelligent woman would make to the Buckley family. The grandson he dreamed of to carry on the Buckley name would be blessed to have Judy Ferguson for a mother.

As Buzz returned from the rear of the plane looking for somebody else to interview, his ruminations about Judy Ferguson were interrupted by a tug on his sleeve and a throaty woman's voice inquiring, "Buzz Buckley?"

He turned around to see an attractive sandy haired woman of about his own age looking up at him through a pair of sparkling gray eyes, a saucy smile crinkling into dimples just beyond the corners of her mouth. She looked vaguely familiar, but Buzz couldn't put a name to the pretty face. He bent over to get a better look at the name tag that she, like most of the Republican women on the plane, was wearing.

"Marsha Antonelli, Fifth Worcester, Alternate. Where do I know you from?"

"Try my maiden name. Marsha Lockett."

"Oh, my God!" She was the girl he had dated when they were both high school juniors—the girl who broke his heart when she turned down his request for a goodnight kiss. She had moved away before the start of their senior year.

"Marsha! I haven't seen you in twenty-five years. No wonder I didn't recognize you."

"Twenty-seven," she corrected, again flashing the saucy smile with the dimples. "Sit down," she urged, moving over to the empty middle seat and leaving the aisle seat for him.

"What a nice surprise!" he said, mentally forgiving her for the anguish she had caused him as a teenager. "You look wonderful!"

She did—even though the tailored suit, which seemed to be the convention uniform for San Francisco-bound Republican women, made it difficult to tell whether her form was as pretty as her face. Remembering her from long ago, he just assumed that it was.

She was now living north of Worcester. Yes, she was active in the party—very active since John Volpe's first run for governor four years ago. Her husband was a dentist, and he'd pushed her to work for Volpe, a successful businessman and fellow Italian-American. They had a college-age daughter. And, besides civic activity, she had just started doing a little feature writing for the local paper, would even be doing some blurbs from the convention concentrating on the local angle. She'd been a housewife too long, she said, and hoped the part-time writing job would lead to something more substantial. She pulled a photo of her daughter out of her purse—a pretty teenager who looked very much like Marsha.

"Now tell me about you," she commanded as she put the picture away. "Have you been to national conventions before?"

"No, first one." He grinned. "I'm here because the network—ABC—needed a Massachusetts delegation reporter. They're paying twenty-five bucks a day on the hotel bill. Otherwise the boss would never have sent me."

She looked reflective. "You married Elaine Whiteside, didn't you?"

Buzz's face turned grim. It was still difficult to talk about. "Yeah," he said, "she died two years ago."

"Oh, Buzz, I'm so sorry." She put a comforting hand on his forearm as she said it. "She was such a nice kid when I knew her." A pause. "Do you want to talk about it?"

"It's hard. She was such a kind, generous person. We went through some rocky times. Family. Job. But she was always there with a smile. And just at the time things were going so well, they found she had a malignant brain tumor. Inoperable. She must've been in terrible pain. But she was so brave. Smiled right to the end. Or at least almost." His voice faltered, and tears came to his eyes, as he remembered especially those last weeks when Elaine had to grope for words but usually managed to find the two most important ones—"Love you!"

Marsha put her hand back on his forearm. "You poor guy. How are you managing?"

He didn't answer right away. He was struggling to regain his composure.

"Burying myself in work, I guess," he said eventually and as brightly as he could. "The job I have—radio/TV news operation, I'm the news director. It's a fun job, and it keeps me hopping. Elaine, I'll never get over losing her. But I'm doing a little better."

He became conscious of a large form in a red dress standing over him. He looked up at a badge reading "Fifth Worcester, Delegate" pinned on the dress's oversized bosom. All the Republican women were not wearing tailored suits after all.

"Young man, I hate to impose on you, but I want to take a little nap, and I'd like to move into my own seat to do it."

Buzz looked at Marsha. "Take a walk with me. Maybe we'll find two seats together."

As she walked ahead of him, he got a better look. Yes, her form was still very nice. Five-foot-thray, eyes of gray, he sized her up, corrupting the brogue of the Irish-American mayor back home to make a silly rhyme out of it.

The two seats they found were next to City Councilor Judy Ferguson, whose itinerant seatmates were roving again. The plane had gone beyond the cloud cover which had blanketed the earth since takeoff and was now twenty thousand feet over the Badlands of South Dakota which stretched out below them all brown and yellow and orange.

Judy was so wrapped up in the landscape that she barely nodded to Buzz and his woman companion. They crowded as close as they could and drank in the scenery peering over Judy's shoulders. Buzz inhaled a subtle but intoxicating whiff of perfume. Those almost forgotten feelings stirred again within him.

Only as the Badlands disappeared in the distance did Judy turn for introductions.

"Judy, this is my old love interest from high school, Marsha..." He took a quick peek at her name tag. "Marsha Antonelli, Alternate, Fifth Worcester.

"Marsha, this is my new love interest, from the Riverbridge City Council, Judy Ferguson."

Judy responded with a big grin. Marsha couldn't think he was serious—this pretty blonde was only half his age—but she wasn't sure. "Your new love interest?"

Durham Caldwell

"Wishful thinking," he conceded.

"Hey, sometimes wishes come true," Judy said good-humoredly. The two women had fun getting acquainted with each other, sharing their limited political experiences, and making predictions on the convention outcome.

"I don't think we can stop Goldwater," Judy admitted, "but we'll make a fight of it as long as we can. If Romney and Rockefeller had gotten out and Bill Scranton had gotten in early on, we might have been able to do it." George Romney was the middle-of-the-road Republican governor of Michigan, Nelson Rockefeller the liberal governor of New York. Scranton, the governor of Pennsylvania, had been the last-minute entry of Republican moderates when Rocky and Romney faltered.

"My husband thinks Goldwater is the greatest thing since George Washington," volunteered Marsha.

Judy responded, "Wow, look at that!"

Spread out below them were the Rocky Mountains, their snow-covered peaks poking majestically through mantles of clouds. Again Marsha and Buzz crowded in close to take in the view. Which one of them, he wondered, is wearing that intoxicating perfume?

On the bus ride in from the airport, Buzz remembered colleague Jerry Finnerty's warning as he was packing up his gear the day before: "Watch out for those Republican women! Most of them lead pretty frustrated lives at home."

Reporter Happy Hooper had looked up from his typewriter. "Yeah, don't get your fingers burned."

"It wasn't his fingers I was worried about," responded Jerry.

Buzz had merely smiled. At the time, Republican women were the last thing he was thinking about.

Buzz was delighted to get out of town, to get a change of scenery. Coming home to an empty house was still as devastating as it was that first week he went back to work after Elaine's funeral. The house was just as lonely, even lonelier. No Elaine to greet him at the door. No Elaine to report cheerfully on how she had spent her day. No one to talk with about the things that had gone right at Baker Broadcasting. No one to listen sympathetically and to commiserate with him about things that hadn't gone so well. No one to sit with him on the living room sofa and hold hands as they watched the late news.

At work he could immerse himself in the hurly-burly of running a broadcast news operation. But that empty, lonely house still waited for him at the end of the day. He welcomed excuses to work late, to postpone the inevitable walk from the garage across the flagstones to the front door with nobody there to open it for him.

Covering Senator Edward Kennedy's plane crash just up the Valley in June had given him a shot of adrenaline. But it also had its downside: the unavoidable comparison in his own mind of the tragedies in the Kennedy family with the ill fortunes of the Buckleys, of which Elaine's death was the latest and saddest—and even sadder because it came only a few months after the deaths of his mother and father in an auto accident.

No, as he left the newsroom that Thursday, Republican women were the last thing on his mind. But now, riding into San Francisco on the bus after chatting with two attractive women on the plane and inhaling the intriguing perfume that one of them was wearing . . .

Massachusetts delegation headquarters were at the Chancellor Hotel on Union Square. It was one of San Francisco's older hotels but well kept up. It was also one of the smaller hotels. Buzz was sharing a room with delegate Max Feigenson. But Max wouldn't be here till Sunday.

Buzz emptied his bags and spread out his equipment on what he had determined would be Max's bed. There wasn't much of it. Just the tape recorder microphone, an alligator-clip patch cord for hooking into a telephone mouthpiece, some tapes and spare batteries, and the portable tape recorder itself. Portable? The damn thing must weigh ten pounds. He listed to the left every time he put the carrying strap over his shoulder.

Although theoretically he was representing both the radio station and the television station, Buzz knew most of his work would be for radio. He had no camera, no cameraman—and if he had, there was probably no way of getting film back to Massachusetts to get it on the

Durham Caldwell

air while it was still timely. Any reports he did for TV would have to be put together back at the station with video from the network or over still pictures from the United Press International picture wire. But as long as there was a phone handy, a radio report could be almost instantaneous. And every opinion, every activity of members of the Massachusetts delegation was a potential story—starting with the pieces he had accumulated on the airplane and written up on the bus ride from the airport.

At the orientation meeting for state delegation reporters the next day, ABC brass seemed disbelieving when Buzz said Senator Goldwater had the support of only five of the Massachusetts delegates. The Goldwater people were claiming substantially more.

2

Scouting for news Sunday morning, Buzz found Congressman Silvio Conte, the Massachusetts representative on the Resolutions Committee, eating breakfast. Conte was bristling after an all-night losing battle trying to give the moderates some say in shaping the party platform.

"These Goldwater people won't give an inch. They want to give field commanders more say over when to use nuclear weapons. They're even against the hot line with the Kremlin.

"Extremists?" This was a word once reserved for the ultraconservative John Birch Society and the Ku Klux Klan but now being applied by more and more moderates to the Goldwater forces. "These are the guys the term was invented for."

Max was unpacking his bags when Buzz got back to the Chancellor. "Don't you ever sleep? Every time I turned on the news, you were there with one of those damned reports. 'Buzz Buckley in San Francisco!'" he intoned in an exaggerated imitation of Buzz's standard signoff.

Buzz had known Max since he was a rookie radio newsman and Max was making his first run for the City Council. Max at the time was a political unknown, but Buzz thought he was talking a lot of sense and made sure his major points got time on the radio news. A firm friendship had grown between the two.

Max was about the same age and same height as Buzz but scrawny and with a fondness for tweed jackets and flannel trousers that made him look more academic than lawyer-like. In fact, some of his fellow attorneys called him "Professor."

A strong Scranton supporter, Max had picked up a rumble in the lobby that Goldwater people were claiming between fourteen and twenty of Massachusetts' thirty-four votes.

Durham Caldwell

"Wishful thinking," Buzz told Max. "Goldwater probably gets the same five votes he started with. But overall it looks like he's too strong to stop.

"John Volpe may be on the fence."

Buzz rewound his tape recorder so Max could listen to his interview with Volpe.

"I was elected as an uncommitted delegate," the former governor's crisp, almost staccato voice came out of the speaker, "and I'm still uncommitted. I don't think the national ticket has much effect on the state ticket in Massachusetts." Volpe could say that, having bucked the Kennedy-for-President tide in Jack Kennedy's home state to win the governorship in 1960. He'd lost it two years later when he'd gotten lazy about campaigning.

While Max was putting away his clothes, Buzz thumbed through the copy of the *New York Sunday Times* that Max had brought with him. CBS had a full-page ad in the television section: "Walter Cronkite extends his record as the only television reporter to cover every convention and election since 1952 . . . he's the man to watch at the Republican National Convention." Cronkite was going against NBC's team of Chet Huntley and David Brinkley, which had dominated network convention coverage since 1956, and the new ABC team of Howard K. Smith and Edward P. Morgan.

The local news, which Buzz and Max watched together before turning in, confirmed Buzz's conclusions about Goldwater's strengths. It also showed an estimated forty thousand demonstrators, most of them Negroes, staging an anti-Goldwater march through downtown San Francisco. Their favorite sign seemed to be: "GOLDWATER '64, BREAD & WATER '65, HOT WATER '66."

On the way to the bus Monday morning for the first convention session, Buzz ran into Tommy Goldman, an active Young Republican from back home. He was one of the handful of staff members who had come to San Francisco with former vice president Richard Nixon, the party's 1960 presidential nominee. "The Old Man," Tommy called him.

"What's Nixon gonna do here?" Buzz inquired.

"Off the record?"

Buzz nodded, then wished a moment later that he hadn't.

"He's gonna wait for a deadlock between Goldwater and the other guys. Then step in and accept the nomination."

Buzz looked skeptical.

"Mark my words, Buzz. The Old Man didn't come here to hibernate."

The convention was at the Cow Palace, a huge arena ten miles south of the San Francisco hotel district which billed itself as "the largest indoor stadium west of Chicago." It was built with public money during the Depression for livestock shows, among other things, and some wiseacre columnist, probably the San Francisco version of a Donald Dibble, derided it as "a palace for cows." The name stuck. Convention bigwigs traveled back and forth by limo, rank and file delegates and most news media representatives in a fleet of chartered buses, the idling wheezing engines of which filled the streets near the hotels and the Cow Palace parking lots with choking blue diesel fumes.

Boarding a bus for the convention's opening session, Buzz spotted an empty seat next to Elliot Richardson, the former U.S. attorney who was the Republican State Convention endorsee for lieutenant governor. Buzz had gotten to know this stiff, proper Yankee during his vigorous but losing campaign for attorney general against Ed Brooke in '62. He plopped down in the empty seat beside him.

He kicked himself moments later when Marsha Antonelli walked up the steps into the bus. She had left her tailored suits in her hotel room closet and was wearing a pretty flowered dress which further confirmed Buzz's conclusion that she had matured from a pretty teenager into a pretty woman with an elegant figure. She gave him a nod of recognition as she walked past him. He would have sprung up to sit with her except that Elliot had begun to lay out the inside story of the fight by Scranton people to challenge seating of some of the Goldwater delegates.

"Can you believe, Buzz, there are only about a dozen Negro delegates in the whole convention? The test case is a Lieutenant George

Durham Caldwell

Lee from Memphis. That's his first name—Lieutenant. He's been a delegate to every national convention since 1940. Gave a second for Bob Taft in '52. But the Goldwater people in Tennessee changed some rules and left him off their slate. We're going to move to amend the temporary rules of the convention. I will second the motion. We want to bar from the permanent roll any delegate where it's determined that discrimination played a part in the seating."

The convention was barely underway when Buzz phoned his first story from the Cow Palace back to the station: "Scranton forces lost their first floor battle in a thunderous chorus of noes which left no doubt that Goldwater backers are in full control of the convention. Delegates by voice vote turned down a motion by Newton Steers of Maryland, seconded by Elliot Richardson of Massachusetts . . . "

After that, the Goldwater people easily won vote after vote.

Despite Ex-President Eisenhower's pre-convention coolness toward Goldwater, delegates interrupted him repeatedly with applause when he addressed the convention Tuesday night. His biggest crowd-pleaser was an appeal not to be divided "by those outside our family, including sensation-seeking columnists and commentators . . . who couldn't care less about the good of our party!"

His listeners directed a chorus of boos and catcalls at the press section. Many jumped up and shook their fists at the glassed-in TV booths above the arena. Buzz heard one delegate yell, "Down with Walter Lippmann!" Lippmann's columns had not been favorable to Goldwater. A beaming Ike walked off the stage to a standing ovation as the band played, "I Love the Sunshine of Your Smile."

Governor Nelson Rockefeller of New York was booed unmercifully as he spoke in favor of a platform amendment to repudiate the John Birch Society and other "extremist" organizations. On one of Buzz's rare encounters with Judy Ferguson and Marsha Antonelli—in a Cow Palace corridor right after the Rockefeller heckling—Judy told him, "People where we were sitting were scared. Our alternate section is way up back, right in front of the galleries. The things they were shouting were appalling. They were acting like thugs. Some of us were afraid they'd start throwing things or climb over the railing."

Tumultuous Affairs

"A little old lady from the Middlesex delegation," Marsha added, "was so frightened that she broke down and cried."

Goldwater himself had the reputation of being a laid-back, relaxed, almost loosey-goosey character. But his minions running the convention were uptight. It was as if they had come this far, had the nomination all but locked up, but feared someone would sneak in at the last moment and steal it from them—the way Willkie and Ike had stolen it from Bob Taft in '40 and '52. On the second day, they exercised their firm control of the convention apparatus by temporarily closing the floor to the news media and other non-delegates without notice and without explanation. This was especially frustrating to Buzz who had just waited in line for forty minutes for a temporary floor pass good for only half an hour.

Taking a break in the ABC convention newsroom, where side-by-side overhead monitors showed all three network broadcasts, Buzz saw a sergeant-at-arms order NBC's John Chancellor to clear the aisle. When Chancellor, in the middle of a live interview with a former governor of Alaska, didn't move fast enough, the sergeant-at-arms called for reinforcement. Buzz saw Chancellor hustled off the floor by two burly security men, disappearing from camera view with the words, "John Chancellor reporting from somewhere in custody."

The Massachusetts delegation was a curious mix of the old and the new. Present-day leaders like U.S. Senator Leverett Saltonstall and Attorney General Ed Brooke, the first Negro to hold statewide office anywhere in the country since Reconstruction. Has-beens like former speaker Joe Martin, who had chaired the conventions that nominated Eisenhower; Chris Herter, governor during the fifties and John Foster Dulles's successor as secretary of state, now painfully crippled with arthritis; and Bob Bradford, one-term governor during the forties, now barely able to hobble to his seat.

John Volpe got off the fence and declared for Scranton. A young Texan named George Bush, who was running for the U.S. Senate, spoke for Goldwater at the Massachusetts luncheon hosted by Senator Saltonstall, the delegation chairman. He tried to dispel the notion that Goldwater somehow was a way-out right winger but didn't cut much ice with most of the delegates. Salty introduced him, almost apologetically, as "the son of my old colleague, Pres Bush." Prescott Bush had been a U.S. senator from Connecticut.

By the time the convention got to the Roll Call of the States on Wednesday night, the only suspense was which state in the alphabetical roll call would put Senator Goldwater over the top. Massachusetts cast 26 votes for Scranton. There were five for Goldwater, the same five he had come to San Francisco with—nobody had switched. But Goldwater was now five votes closer to nomination.

The South Carolina delegation was seated directly behind Massachusetts. As the roll call progressed, excitement grew among the South Carolinians. Those keeping a tally of the votes looked at each other with expressions of increasing anticipation. Pennsylvania voted. South Carolina pencils marked the new numbers down swiftly and added them on. Without waiting for Rhode Island, South Carolinians jumped on chairs, pounded each other on the back. "We gonna do it! We gonna do it!" they shouted to each other, to their Massachusetts neighbors, and to everyone else within hearing range.

And they did it.

"South Carolina!"

"Mistah Chaihman, we are humbly grateful that we can do this foh America. South Cah'lina casts all its sixteen votes foh Barry Goldwatuh!"

The Cow Palace erupted in cheers, whistles, and foot pounding. With 655 votes needed for nomination, South Carolina had brought Goldwater to 663. It seemed that almost the whole convention was standing on chairs screaming in delight and waving Goldwater signs and banners. But Buzz noted that in a handful of delegations, including Massachusetts, most of the delegates remained in their seats or stood solemnly in front of them as a new Goldwater demonstration surged up the aisles.

First ballot totals showed 883 for Goldwater, 214 for Scranton.

Delegation chairman Saltonstall had been on the winning side at every Republican convention since 1928—until tonight. But hiding his chagrin, he was on his feet, waving the Massachusetts standard seeking recognition to move for unanimous endorsement. Some of

Tumultuous Affairs

the state's delegates walked out rather than be a part of it. Others yelled across the seats, "No! No!" But Salty ignored them and made the announcement anyway, "Maz'chusetts wishes to change its vote ..."

It was midnight by the time Buzz stepped off the bus near the hotel. He walked briskly into the Chancellor lobby to keep a prearranged rendezvous with Max for dinner. The other district delegate, Vern Fletcher, along with Riverbridge newspaper reporter Roger Davis and Judy Ferguson, joined them.

They took a cab to a restaurant Vern had dined at earlier in the week. It was full. They hailed another cab and went to a succession of San Francisco's better restaurants. After the first disappointment, the others would wait in the cab while Vern went inside to check and then came back shaking his head. Waits for a table were at least an hour and a half. After the fifth stop, Max asked the cabby, "You know any restaurants we can get into?"

"You might try Chinatown."

Chinatown streets were almost deserted. The cabby stopped in front of a place called the Red Dragon. Roger, with the experience of many meals in Boston's Chinatown behind him, told the others, "Wait here," and went to peer in the restaurant's front window. He turned and waved to the others to come in. As they were paying off the cabby, Roger told them, "It must be okay. They've got some Chinamen in there eating."

There were indeed four Orientals finishing up their meals at a table near the front of the restaurant. The rest of the good-sized dining room was empty. They couldn't tell whether the deadpanned waiter was pleased or displeased to welcome a party of five at what must be pretty close to closing time.

The waiter set a steaming pot of tea down before them. At about the same time, a smartly-dressed Oriental woman appeared from somewhere in the back of the Red Dragon and sat down on a stool at the nearby bar, and the four Oriental customers pushed their chairs back and left the restaurant.

Durham Caldwell

Max picked up the teapot and invited the others to pass him their cups. Buzz had turned to talk with Judy when out of the corner of his eye he saw the usually steady and reliable Max pouring tea all over the table.

As Roger and Vern joined Max in sopping up the tea with napkins, Buzz looked to his right and saw why Max had been distracted. A tall dark-haired Caucasian woman—almost six feet tall, the showgirl type—had approached the bar and was standing there, talking animatedly to the Oriental woman. She was wearing one of those elegant black dresses which had become notorious in San Francisco that summer—dresses that were a tabloid photographer's dream with an opening in the front that plunged all the way from the neckline almost down to the navel. She was a generously endowed young woman, and as she stood there, gesticulating as she talked, her endowments would roll toward the opening in the front of the dress, stopping just short it seemed of complete exposure.

Judy, whose back was to the bar, must have wondered why the four men were trying so hard to stifle smirks. She took a quick look behind her, then turned back to her table companions with a big, knowing grin.

The two women at the bar were talking louder now. The tall woman had apparently been stood up by her date, and the Oriental woman was sympathizing with her. They appeared to look frequently at the table where four men sat with a pretty young woman.

Roger leaned over the table. With a wink at Buzz and in a conspiratorial whisper loud enough for his companions to hear, he said, "Hey, Max, those poor kids are all alone. Why don't we invite 'em over to join us?"

Max looked aghast. "Oh, no," he whispered, holding up a hand, "those kind of women are trouble, big trouble. We don't want to have anything to do with them."

Buzz lay awake for a long time, thinking about that tall dark-haired showgirl and those breasts that rolled to the right and then to the left. He had been purposely keeping himself very busy, working very hard, since Elaine died. But he was suddenly acutely aware it was a long time since he had been with a woman.

3

Max greeted with a shake of the head the news that Senator Goldwater had chosen William Miller, the congressman from New York and outgoing Republican national chairman, for the party's vice presidential nomination. "The only thing he brings to the ticket is that he makes Lyndon Johnson tear-ass."

The first speaker at the convention's closing session was Richard Nixon. The former vice president gave a speech so thoughtful and so dynamic that Max Feigenson told Buzz, "If he'd campaigned in 1960 like he spoke today, he'd be the president."

As he left the floor to turn in his pass, Buzz spotted Tommy Goldman, the Young Republican activist from back home who was on Nixon's San Francisco staff.

"That was supposed to be his acceptance speech." confided Tommy. "He's been working on it for weeks. The Old Man was sure almost right up to yesterday that this was gonna be a deadlocked convention—and they'd turn to him, waiting in the wings, to give him the nomination."

Max and the rest of the Massachusetts delegation were looking forward to Goldwater's acceptance speech. Max called it the senator's chance to reach out to the moderates to try to bring them into the fold and to allay their fears about the "extremism" they linked to his wing of the party.

In the speech, Goldwater called for regional compacts and balance between branches of government at every level, for keeping streets safe from bullies and marauders, and for enforcing law and order. He saluted the Eisenhower administration for "keeping the peace and passing along a great arsenal." He blasted communism, and—with a jibe at John F. Kennedy—he called "development of a great Atlantic civilization more inspiring than a moonshot."

Durham Caldwell

Then he got down to "unthinking and stupid labels."

"Extremism in the defense of liberty is no vice!" shouted Goldwater. "Moderation in the pursuit of justice is no virtue!"

Buzz, who was on the floor, detected an audible gasp from members of the Massachusetts delegation. But most of the conventioneers erupted in applause. Max Feigenson and Vern Fletcher exchanged glances and walked out of the hall.

When he got to the rendezvous point that Max had set up in the Chancellor lobby, Buzz was pleased to see Marsha Lockett—oops, Marsha Antonelli, he corrected himself—waiting with Judy Ferguson.

A good-looking pair of women, he thought, as he approached them. Handsome women. Beautiful hair. Makeup, if any at all, subtly applied. Tailored suits almost identical except for the shade of the pinstripes and the cut of the lapel. As his eyes took them in, he could feel his heart beat a little faster.

"Hi, good-looking! I brought reinforcements," greeted Judy. "We were having such a good time gabbing back there in the alternate section that I said, 'Why don't you come along?'

"When she found out you were gonna be here, she almost backed out," Judy laughed a lilting little laugh.

"Not so," Marsha protested, and smiling that special smile at Buzz. "you're the main reason I came."

Max and Vern appeared, cutting off the banter, with Roger Davis only a few steps behind.

Max doubted they could all fit in one cab.

"Don't worry, Max," Judy assured him. "You're a skinny guy. You can sit on my lap. And Marsha and Chet Huntley here were high school sweethearts—they won't mind squeezing together."

Marsha blushed a very tiny blush. They all laughed. The doorman blew on his deep-throated San Francisco whistle—something between a tugboat whistle and a foghorn—to summon a cab. They all squeezed into the taxi.

Max had reserved a table at Ernie's.

Tumultuous Affairs

"Remember 'Vertigo'?" he asked, referring to the Alfred Hitchcock movie. "This is the place Jimmy Stewart used to take Kim Novak for dinner. My informants assure me it's one of the best restaurants in town—at least one of the best we can afford."

It was apparent right away that Max had made a good choice. Despite their reservation, they were told there would be a twenty- or-thirty-minute wait for a table. Looking around the sumptuous waiting room, they spotted Walter Cronkite standing at the far side of the room with two women—probably his wife and daughter, Buzz thought—also waiting to be seated.

Buzz recognized Frank McGee, the NBC floor reporter, and introduced himself as "one of your bush-league competitors."

McGee responded with a friendly smile and launched into a brief discussion with Buzz on the convention. His conclusion: "We'll look back someday and see that this convention marked the start of a completely new direction for the Republican party. For better or worse, the Midwest, the West, and the South have taken over the party. The Northeast is on the outside looking in."

When they eventually got into the dining room and were seating themselves at one of the tables with Ernie's checkerboard tablecloths, Judy made Vern change seats "so Chet Huntley can sit next to his old girl friend."

Buzz wished Judy would stop calling him "Chet Huntley" just because he and the NBC anchorman were both in television. But he welcomed the opportunity to chat with Marsha without having to share the conversation with people sitting between them.

Marsha ordered a vodka collins.

Buzz asked, "What's that?"

"Like a Tom Collins—except vodka instead of gin. Very refreshing."

He told the waiter, "Make it a vodka collins for me, too."

"Smooth," he said when he took his first sip. After the third or fourth sip, the room began to tilt.

"Ooh, I'm woozy," he confessed in a low voice to Marsha. "Not used to booze."

Durham Caldwell

She laughed. "Get some of this into you." She passed him the bread plate and reached for the relish tray. "Sop up the alcohol. You'll feel better."

She was right. As the conversation about Goldwater's acceptance speech went on around him, he gradually began to pick up the drift. It centered almost exclusively on "extremism in the defense of liberty" and "moderation in the pursuit of justice."

"If he'd been shooting off his mouth, that'd be one thing," observed Judy. "But this was a prepared speech—something you assume he's given careful consideration to."

Vern summed up the feeling at the table in four words: "There went the ball game."

By the time the waiter brought their orders, Buzz at last was feeling clear-headed. Marsha chatted amiably with him throughout the meal, mostly about high school days. Judy was keeping up a running conversation about politics with Max and Vern and Roger.

When the waiter came by the table to ask if he could bring anybody anything else, Marsha fixed a mischievous smile on Buzz. "Another vodka collins?"

"Go to hell. One's my limit. I almost didn't make that one." He was smiling inwardly—he was enjoying so much being with her.

Max went up to the room as soon as they got back to the Chancellor. The others sat around the lobby for a while reliving the high moments and the low moments of Convention Week. As Roger and Vern went in search of one last drink, Buzz found himself on the elevator with Judy and Marsha.

"Floors, ladies?"

"Five."

"Seven."

He pushed both buttons, then pushed ten for his own floor.

Judy moved to the door at five.

"Should we walk you to your room?" Buzz asked.

"Not necessary. My room's right there."

He held the elevator door until they could see she was safely inside.

At seven, Marsha looked at him with that saucy smile. "My room's a long walk down a dark hallway. I'd feel safer with an escort."

Neither was the walk long, nor the hallway dark, but Buzz didn't mind. It gave him another minute to enjoy Marsha's company.

She turned to him at the door to her room. "Thanks for being such a gentleman." Then, she made it appear almost as an afterthought, "Why don't you come in for a little while? We've still got so much to talk about."

The invitation took him by surprise, but he was quick to accept. He had enjoyed chatting with her on the plane. He had found her a pleasant addition to tonight's dinner party and to the gab session in the lobby. To be truthful about it, he hadn't felt like this with a woman since losing Elaine. What a shame she's married, he said to himself.

He sat down in the wooden-armed padded chair that she indicated to him. She sat down near him on the straight-back desk chair.

They chatted gaily for a long time about old friends and old times. She remembered the counting game they used to play in sophomore French class—the game Miss Avery called "Buzz." Going up and down the rows, students would count in French, substituting "buzz!" for any number containing a seven or any multiple of seven.

"*Un, deux, trois, quatre, cinq, six*, buzz!" she recited. "And the girls who thought you were nice would look at you and put a romantic inflection on it: 'bu-u-zz!' You would blush. Everybody would giggle. And it took Miss Avery a long time to figure out why."

They reminisced about class picnics, the handful of movies they had seen together, school dances, the junior class sailing trip, and about the careers and whereabouts of classmates. They even talked about the stories they each had covered at the convention. Then, suddenly, as sometimes happens during even the most spirited conversations, both parties fell silent for apparent lack of something to say next.

Those old feelings Buzz had felt stirring inside him had gotten stronger and stronger as they talked.

Durham Caldwell

After what must have been a half minute of silence, Marsha asked softly, "A penny for your thoughts."

Christ! He couldn't give a truthful answer to that one. Then it came to him.

He laughed. "I was just thinking how different our lives might have been if you'd said 'yes' the night I wanted to kiss you good night." Good recovery, Buzz. Good recovery. "Do you remember that?"

"Yes, I remember. Guess I was playing hard to get. Or maybe because Dad was being transferred—and this wasn't a time to get serious. If you'd asked me again next time you took me out, I probably would've said 'yes.' But you never took me out again."

"I was too humiliated. I can laugh about it now. But for a seventeen-year-old kid who's taken a month to get up the courage, you get a girl you really like, and she tells you, 'Let's leave things the way they are'—that's a tragic moment in a young life."

"Is that what I told you?"

"That's what you told me. Sure, I should've tried again. Or I should've taken you in my arms and just done it. That's what I did when I got serious about Elaine. So you see, I did learn something."

Again, a moment of silence.

"You asked about my thoughts? I was thinking about that kiss I didn't get."

"I could make it up to you now."

She got up from the straight-back chair and leaned down to give him what he expected would be a light, perfunctory peck on the cheek. Instead, it was a warm, moist, lingering kiss full on the lips that demanded he kiss her back. Only their lips were touching, but it was a delightful kiss. And that close to her, he breathed in the subtle, intoxicating perfume he had first noticed on the airplane as he peered out over the shoulders of both Marsha and Judy Ferguson, wondering which woman was wearing it. Now he knew.

He fought off the urge to help steady her by cupping his hands around her breasts and rib cage. He didn't want to offend her.

Still bending over him and with her lips still pressed gently and invitingly against his, she moved to put her hands on his shoulders to steady herself. As she did so, one hand grazed his neck. The touch of the fingers on his skin—coupled with the kiss and the perfume—turned him into a wild man. He sprang up from the chair, picking her up bodily as he rose, dropped her on the bed, and threw himself on top of her.

She locked both arms around his shoulders and, with her right hand on the back of his head, pushed his face against hers, clamping their lips together. His right hand groped under her blouse. Then he had an awful realization. As she loosened her grip on his head and turned her face, breaking off the kiss to catch her breath, he moaned in anguish, "Oh, God! I want you so badly, but I didn't bring any protection."

"Shhh!" she whispered, putting a finger to his lips. "Nothing to worry about."

She pushed up on his shoulders and slid out from under him.

"Wait a minute—I'll be right back." She disappeared into the bathroom. When she emerged, she was wearing a blue quilted robe, which he knew instinctively had nothing under it but Marsha.

Afterwards, as they lay there holding hands, he said to her matter-of-factly, "That was a kiss worth waiting for." And after a pause, "I've never thrown a woman on a bed before. I hope I didn't frighten you."

"Well, you startled me." She raised herself up on an elbow, bent over his face, and kissed him. "But Buzz, I'd been wanting you all evening. When you dumped me on the bed and jumped on top of me, that was a dream come true."

She was silent for a moment, as if contemplating.

"Is that really the first time that you've thrown a woman on a bed?"

"The very first. I carried Elaine over the threshold on our wedding night, but I didn't throw her on the bed."

"Romantic! Did she like that?"

"She struggled and kicked and hit me with her fists till I put her down. But she didn't hit very hard."

Durham Caldwell

Buzz tried to sneak into his room without disturbing Max. But Max was wide awake.

"Where in hell have you been? I was about to ask the cops to put out an all-points bulletin."

"Well, I was talking with an old friend. The time got away from us. Then I had to finish my reports and make my feed to the station. I didn't want to wake you up at 3 a.m."

"Talking with an old friend? All night? What a crock of bullshit! Buzz, you disappoint me. Unless I miss my guess, your old friend is a married woman. You could be headed for a pile of trouble."

"And if I need a lawyer, will you represent me?"

"Screw you! If a jealous husband comes after you, you're on your own. You need a lawyer? I'll sit down and help you review your will."

4

Buzz and Marsha sat next to each other on the flight back to Boston. His tape recorder and her big black purse on the empty aisle seat effectively discouraged company from intruding. Judy walked by once and nodded to them but made no effort to join them. Max, thankfully, was on another flight.

He asked the question that had been gnawing at him.

"Did you come to San Francisco looking for adventure?"

He thought he detected the very slightest of blushes.

"Buzz, I have a lousy marriage. I'm not sure what I was looking for. When I saw your name on the state committee's passenger list, I figured it was probably you. Couldn't be two Buzz Buckleys. Then, when I saw you on the plane, I recognized you. I was genuinely sorry when you told me you'd lost Elaine. I have only fond memories of her. At some point, it occurred to me you might be as lonely as I was."

Then he asked the question he was almost afraid to ask.

"I realize it's none of my business. But don't you and your husband love each other?" Thinking of the warmth of the love that he and Elaine had shared for so many years, the mutual respect between them, and the lifelong affection between his mother and father and between Elaine's mother and father, he found it difficult to envision a different kind of married life.

"We did. At least I thought we did. We met in college. He was a couple of years ahead of me. You know: older, more sophisticated. A dashing, outdoorsy kind of guy. Mom used to say he swept me off my feet.

"He was pre-med, then changed to dentistry. He didn't have any GI Bill. Punctured ear drum kept him out of the draft. I worked like a son of a gun to keep food on the table and pay the rent while he went to dental school. And maybe that's when the resentment started. You know: he couldn't do it on his own; his wife had to help him.

Durham Caldwell

"His best friend is his stock broker. He's a gun nut—guns all over the house. He drives around town in a fancy sports car and puts on the dog at the country club—when he's not deer hunting or shooting at the revolver club. It's gotten to be a marriage pretty much in name only.

"I've stayed with him—put up a front—mostly because of our daughter. Jenny's a nice kid, a sensitive kid, and I didn't want to do anything to hurt her. And his parents—they're old school Catholic. Nicest people in the world. If Leo and I got involved in a divorce, it would just about tear them apart.

"I'll spare you the way things have degenerated over the years. I thought for a long time that he had a mistress. God knows, he didn't bother me very often. And maybe he does . . ."

She paused for a moment, then put her hand on his.

"Buzz, you gave me more pleasure last night, more real satisfaction, than I've had in years and years."

Buzz squeezed her hand. "You know," he said, "I want to see you again."

"I want to see you again."

The words bounced around inside his head. Only after he'd walked into the darkness of his own living room did the enormity of what he'd done in San Francisco hit him. He was an adulterer! No way of sugarcoating it—he had committed adultery. You don't do that in proper families like the Buckleys.

He sat down heavily on the sofa. As his eyes became accustomed to the dim glow from the street light shining in the front window, he picked out the reflection from the glass over the photograph of Elaine which sat in the center of the mantel over the fireplace. He felt for the lamp on the end table, turned the switch, and retrieved the photo. He kissed it. It was one of the few things in the house he had kept dusted since Elaine died.

He sat down again, his gaze transfixed by the photo. It had been her surprise birthday present to him on his fortieth birthday—the year before they discovered the tumor. There she was—smiling at him with that same radiant smile he had noticed for the first time that day early in their senior year when he sat down beside her on the high school front steps. It was in response to her invitation, "You're good at math. Help me with this trig problem." The way she had smiled at him, he couldn't refuse.

He helped her with trig—and later with solid geometry. She was editor of the school newspaper and recruited him as a reporter. She coached him on his writing. In fact, she was a better writing coach, he thought, than all three of their high school English teachers.

By spring, his goal was to be a newspaper reporter—he'd already lined up a summer job with the local weekly—and he and Elaine had begun dating. He was surprised and flattered that one of the school's most popular girls, and certainly its prettiest, seemed to like him as much as he liked her.

He still marveled even now at how he—good old dependable but plodding Buzz—had managed to snare the belle of the senior class away from half a dozen rivals.

They had gotten married when they were still twenty and he needed parental consent. It was partly to keep him out of the first peacetime draft. He remembered the idyllic early months of their marriage. And he remembered the rocky ones—the ones he wished he could forget. Getting patriotic and volunteering for the Army shortly after Pearl Harbor. Leaving Elaine with a one-year-old when he went overseas. Gone for three years—five months of it in a German POW camp.

She had been the strong one—the one who kept the marriage together. Always loving and understanding despite his many shortcomings, especially the ill temper that accompanied him home from Germany. Ill temper brought on by the staff officers who left his small unit in an inexcusably isolated position as the German advance through the Ardennes enveloped them, by the British Spitfire pilot who gunned down a dozen of his fellow POW's on a work detail after mistaking them for German soldiers, and the shock of learning after arriving back in the States about the death of his kid brother Buddy in the shelling of a theater in Belgium at the beginning of the Germans' December offensive. Why hadn't Buddy gone to the movies some other night? Why hadn't Intelligence briefed fighter pilots on the location of prison camps? Why hadn't the brass looked at the map before leaving units like his out there all alone?

It was Elaine's love, her patience, that had turned him around. Made him a decent human being. Well, he told himself as he sat there, at least halfway decent.

It was Elaine who had critiqued his reporting. Generous in her praise. And always soft and kind in her helpful suggestions on how he might make something better.

What a wonderful woman, and how he missed her! And now he had profaned Elaine's memory and all they had meant to each other by climbing into bed with Marsha Antonelli. It had been lust, pure and simple. But that didn't make it any more excusable.

He looked at the smiling face in the photograph.

"Oh, darling, I'm sorry." There were tears in his eyes as he said it. And yet—yet—he did want to see Marsha Antonelli again. He felt like a criminal. He kissed the photo another time, put it back on the mantel, and dragged himself to bed.

He tossed and turned with more self-recrimination. But it had been a long day, a long week. Finally he dropped off into a deep sleep—a sleep eventually interrupted by a dream. Elaine was sitting on the edge of the bed stroking his forehead to comfort him. She was smiling down at him with the same smile he had found so entrancing that day on the high school steps when she had asked for help with trigonometry. He took it as a sign that she wasn't upset with him, bad as his behavior might have been.

5

After the adventure of San Francisco, Buzz found the atmosphere in the newsroom at Baker Broadcasting something of a letdown. There were the same half-empty coffee cups leaving brown rings on the counters, the same stale cigarette smoke, the same coarse humor as at the convention. But while dozens of reporters, cameramen, and producers walked through the newsroom in the Cow Palace in the course of an hour, there were never more than half a dozen in the newsroom at any one time at Baker Broadcasting—and that was only in the afternoon when the television street reporters were back from their outside work getting their scripts ready for the six-thirty news, the cameramen came in to shoot the breeze or give a progress report on film going through the processor, and the director bent over a desk methodically marking switching cues on the completed script pages with a foul-smelling grease pencil—"blocking the script," they called it.

The only constant was the radio newsman down in the far corner of the room pecking away at an old Remington typewriter, making an occasional phone call to check on a news story, responding to calls on the two-way radio, stepping periodically into the alcove where the UPI teletype chattered away non-stop, ripping the wire copy from the machine in long strips, tearing it into individual stories on the sharp edge of his desk, assembling the ones he wanted with his local copy into a newscast, and rushing into the adjacent radio news booth seconds before his next broadcast.

The police and fire department radios blurted out occasional calls for working fires, traffic accidents, purse snatches, but most of their output was just routine noise—the trick was having an ear that would pick up potential news stories and ignore the garbage.

Yes, it was a letdown after the excitement of San Francisco. But getting caught up on paperwork after being away for more than a

Durham Caldwell

week, reining in anchorman Jerry Finnerty's tendencies to go overboard on most stories involving politicians, and planning legitimate local followups to the Goldwater nomination gave Buzz a busy first week back in the city.

    Friday evening, as he headed for dinner at the Heidelberg, Buzz kept the New York City all-news station on for a minute after parking the car at the curb. He wanted to hear the end of a story quoting President Johnson. Johnson had said final responsibility for use of nuclear weapons "must rest" with the president alone. So much for Senator Goldwater's position that he would allow generals to decide how to win in Vietnam, including whether to use nuclear bombs. Buzz nodded in silent agreement as he turned off the ignition and strode into the restaurant.

    Elaine, even as she lay dying, had attempted to patch over the estrangement between her husband and son. One of her last requests before she lost the power of coherent speech was that Johnny and Buzz meet for dinner on Friday nights at the Heidelberg. The quaint German place tucked away on a side street downtown had been Elaine and Buzz's favorite restaurant, and they had often brought Johnny with them as he was growing up. The two men had honored the request for two years now, missing only an occasional date when one of them was out of town or tied up on a major project. They honored it not because either got any real enjoyment out of the other's company but because they had made a promise to the woman they both loved.

    There had been a long history of friction between them—starting from Buzz's return from the war—a return to a young wife and a four-year-old son who had no memory of him. The boy appeared resentful of having to share his mother's time and affection with this stranger father—a stranger father who came home tired and tense and prone to snap at anything that irritated him after the grueling experiences of Normandy, the Bulge, and prison camp. And Buzz made a big mistake right off the bat.

    His own official name was John James Buckley Jr. But he had been Buzz as long as he could remember. John J. Buckley III, he decided, should be known as "Buddy"—the same nickname carried by his brother, who had been killed in the war. But Johnny would have none of it. "I'm Johnny," he insisted, sometimes tearfully, "not Buddy." Finally Elaine, who for the rest of her life scrupulously avoided taking Johnny's side against her husband, told him quietly, "Buzz, I think we better drop the nickname business."

Buzz also realized now that proud as he was of coming home to a bright, handsome four-year-old, he also had so looked forward to resumption of his and Elaine's affectionate home life that he developed some early resentment of his own when she cautioned him with words like "Not in front of Johnny" or "Be quieter, or you'll wake up your son."

Then there were the two years he was mostly away finishing up college on the GI Bill at a school with a highly-regarded journalism program. He and Elaine agreed later it had been the wrong thing to do, but because of the shortage of family living quarters on campus, Elaine and the boy stayed back home in the little apartment they had rented before he went into the service.

When he got the job with the newspaper, they all moved to Riverbridge together. But at the times of day other dads were reading their sons bedtime stories, tossing baseballs or footballs with them, or shooting basketballs at the hoop on the front of the garage, Buzz was off covering the City Council or the Planning Board or the police blotter for the next day's paper.

By the time Buzz moved to broadcasting and more normal hours, things did seem to be going better between him and Johnny—a lot better. But abruptly they changed. His last couple of years in high school, Johnny was not only a star athlete and a good scholar, he was also Mister Know-It-All. His dad's new employer, Baker Broadcasting, became a special target for derogatory comments.

Elaine's lingering death brought father and son closer together probably than they had ever been. Despite his son's arrogance—he had really become a stuffed shirt, Buzz thought, with a Phi Beta Kappa key and quick success in business—Buzz had to acknowledge that Johnny had a deep and abiding love for his mother. The young man's

Durham Caldwell

sadness at her passing seemed to match his own although both had known for months that it would be the eventual outcome.

But Johnny had come out of his funk. He was ribbing his dad again about the shortcomings of his news department. "That Laurence Olivier Finnerty had me weeping when he went on and on the other night about the tragedies in the Kennedy family." Or "Who named your reporter Happy Hooper? He hasn't cracked a smile since his first grade picture."

Johnny had scored a business coup right out of college. During his senior year, he was student manager of the campus bookstore. He spotted so many shortcomings in the way things were being done and saw so many possibilities for profitable change that he convinced college administrators to lease him the space for a privately operated store. He did so well that he doubled the size of the store and quickly expanded to two other campuses. He had dreams of taking over bookstores at campuses all over New England. Grandiose maybe, but Buzz knew that even after paying interest on his loans, his son was already earning more than he was. Things had always come so easy for Johnny while Buzz himself had to work hard for everything he got.

Tonight, after some opening digs at Baker Broadcasting, Johnny was twitting Buzz about how he was pricing sports cars, and how Buzz embarrassed him by driving around in a 1954 Plymouth. "Not only is it old and falling apart, that wasn't even a good year for Plymouth to begin with." As Buzz tried to frame a response, he looked across the Heidelberg dining room toward the door and his eyes fastened on the younger of two attractive women standing together waiting for a table. It was the Heidelberg's busiest hour, and the restaurant was more crowded than usual because of a downtown business convention.

"Excuse me, son. You don't mind sharing our table, do you?" Buzz asked as he pushed back his chair. Without waiting for an answer, he navigated his way through the closely-spaced tables to greet City Councilor Judy Ferguson and her employer, Myra Heywood, the *grande dame* of Main Street businesspeople. It was the first time he could remember Judy when she wasn't wearing a tailored suit. Tonight she had on a flowered skirt and a plain knit jersey which clung to her like a glove, accentuating the fullness and shapeliness of her figure.

"Why don't you join my son and me? We haven't ordered yet, and our table has two extra chairs."

The two women looked at each other and nodded assent.

As Buzz walked the women across the dining room to the table where a curious Johnny waited, he could sense the eyes of the male diners rivet on Judy just as his had.

"My son, John Buckley III," he told the women.

"Johnny, this is City Councilor Judy Ferguson. And Johnny, this is Myra Heywood."

Johnny jumped up and helped his father pull out the chairs for the newcomers. "Nice to meet you, Judy. And Mrs. Heywood I've met. We're both in the bookstore business."

"That's right," said Myra Heywood, who ran Heywood's Bookstore, the biggest such establishment in the state west of Worcester. "You're the one who's doing so well on the campuses."

Judy turned to Myra as she adjusted her chair to the right distance from the table. "I knew TV newsmen had to be handsome, but I didn't know they had such handsome sons!"

Johnny responded by turning on his own thousand-watt personality. But while his conversation at first included everyone, Johnny couldn't keep his eyes off Judy. Neither for that matter could Buzz. He dismissed his own attention as platonic—he was, after all, twice her age. But God, wasn't she ever just right for Johnny.

Well before they got to dessert, Johnny and Judy were focusing almost exclusively on each other. Myra flashed a knowing smile on Buzz and focused on him. Buzz was flattered by Myra's attention. He was also surprised to detect what he thought was a little glint in her eye as she invited him to stop in at the store and have a cup of coffee with her when he was downtown.

Before dinner was over, Johnny had made arrangements to phone Judy for another meeting. And Buzz had assured Myra he would try to stop by though he was rarely covering the news downtown any more.

Durham Caldwell

Johnny insisted on paying the whole check despite the two women's protests. After the women excused themselves and Johnny was waiting for change, he turned to his father. "Wow, Dad, you do know some good-looking women! I wish I'd gone to San Francisco with you." And then, "Dad, why don't you make a play for Myra Heywood? She's not bad looking for a woman her age. Money, too. We could double date."

"Thanks, but no thanks." Myra Heywood was widowed, wealthy, and indeed well preserved for a woman approaching fifty. But Buzz knew she was also probably the most conservative of all the city's conservative businesspeople. He knew, for example, that Heywood's had yet to hire its first Negro clerk despite the city's rapidly growing colored population and persistent prodding from Jim Foster of the Urban League. Foster was anxious for the big book, toy, and office supply store to set an example for other Main Street merchants. "She told me," Jim had recounted, "that she doesn't care to be first in anything but the profit column."

She was also—according to the scuttlebutt—in a long-term relationship with a lawyer named Erwin Edwards. Evem though Myra might have a roving eye, Buzz was not about to get in a competition with the man known in the YMCA locker room as Erwin the Elephant. Besides, despite his recurring feelings of guilt, his thoughts were on a gray-eyed, sandy-haired woman in Worcester County.

6

"This'll show the damned gooks they can't frig around with Uncle Sam!" That was Jerry Finnerty's reaction to President Johnson's decision to send naval aircraft to bomb "selected targets" in North Vietnam. The decision came after reports that North Vietnamese PT boats had fired on American destroyers patrolling international waters in the Gulf of Tonkin .

Jerry Finnerty was from the old school, probably ten years older than Buzz. He'd been Buzz's predecessor as Baker Broadcasting's television news director. Jerry would probably still have that job, Buzz well knew, and he himself would still be handling radio news only, if it hadn't been for Jerry's recurring fondness for the bottle. As anchorman for the six-thirty news, he was still the face of Baker Broadcasting for most of the general public.

Jerry's face was still handsome—in a careworn sort of way. His head of wavy once-coal-black hair had turned steel gray, but every strand was immaculately in place when he got the hand signal that he was on the air, and without a drop of hair spray. He had been a lady killer for sure in his bachelor days and—despite two divorces—still fancied himself as the deity's gift to women.

The name on his birth certificate was Fintrilakis. It became Finnerty after an early employer had pointed out that there were more Irish-American TV viewers in most Massachusetts cities than Greek-American viewers. Riverbridge was no exception.

Jerry had a self-deprecating sense of humor. A favorite was. "Goddammit, Buzz"—or H.B. or Al or whoever he felt was asking for uncalled-for effort—"my name is Jerry, not Jesus!" And he had a salty collection of phrases—"as welcome as a whore in church," "cold as a witch's underwear," "as unusual as a virgin Miss America"—which station management crossed its fingers would never get uttered on an open mike.

Durham Caldwell

Despite a general disdain for politicians, Jerry was the news operation's Mister Patriot. In his eyes, Uncle Sam and Uncle Sam's military could do no wrong.

"Let me do a man-on-the-street on this," said Jerry, one of whose favorite pastimes was sidewalk interviews on subjects ranging from affairs of state to the Beatles and topless bathing suits.

"No," replied Buzz, "I don't think people know enough about it at this point. Go after one of the foreign policy experts at the colleges. And see if Eddie Boland's around." Boland was the congressman from the district.

Two days later, Congress passed the Gulf of Tonkin Resolution supporting "the determination of the president" to repel armed attack against U.S. forces and "to prevent further aggression." The vote in the House was 416-0, in the Senate 88-2. Only Wayne Morse of Oregon and Ernest Gruening of Alaska voted against it. "Damned Copperheads!" Jerry Finnerty called the two dissenting Democrats.

That same day, Marsha called Buzz at his office. If she was disappointed he hadn't called her, she didn't show it. And hearing that throaty voice again relegated any lingering guilty feelings to a far distant corner of his mind.

She opened the conversation, "Are you going to Atlantic City?"

That was where the Democrats were having their national convention. And yes, he was going.

"Guess what? So am I. My paper liked those stories I did in San Francisco so much that they asked me to do the same thing with the Democrats. Won't pay much money, but they'll take care of expenses. And it'll be fun. I'm all set with credentials, just have to make my room reservation. Delegation's at the Lafayette Motor Inn, right?"

He shuffled through the papers in a wire basket on his desk and pulled out literature for the Lafayette and a copy of the reservation form he had mailed in. He thought he had seen something in the fine print. Yes, it was there.

"You're in luck." The fine print told him that the price per room was the same whether for single or double occupancy. "How would

Tumultuous Affairs

you like to be the Democratic National Convention guest of Baker Broadcasting?"

"You mean share your room?" She seemed startled. He was startled by his own boldness. She let it sink in for a moment. "Buzz, I'd like that."

He kicked himself afterwards for not pressing Marsha for an earlier meeting. The Democratic convention was still a couple of weeks away. Well, that made the last week in August certainly something to look forward to. And give him time to shop for a new car. He'd drive her to Atlantic City in something more elegant than a '54 Plymouth.

Buzz, driving his new Ford, picked up Marsha at the bus station the Friday before the Democratic convention. Her gray eyes were sparkling. The special smile crinkled her face just the way it had in San Francisco. She's as eager as I am, he told himself.

Once, as they approached a toll station on the Garden State Parkway, she picked up his hand and very emphatically removed it from her knee. After they were past the toll taker, she glanced at him and said softly, "You can put it back now."

They were half listening to some news on the car radio when one story caught their attention. Mayor Wagner of New York City had endorsed Attorney General Robert Kennedy for U.S. senator from New York. Kennedy was expected to make a formal announcement on Monday or Tuesday.

They both wondered how somebody who lived in Virginia and was a legal resident of Massachusetts could run for the Senate from New York.

The Lafayette Motor Inn was on North Carolina Avenue, a block from the Boardwalk and several blocks north of Convention Hall. Buzz asked for two keys for the room.

"Certainly, Mister Buckley." replied the clerk as he handed over both keys. "Nice to have you and Mrs. Buckley with us."

"Do you want to walk on the Boardwalk?" asked Buzz after they'd eaten dinner. It was still daylight.

Durham Caldwell

"We can do that tomorrow. Tonight let's get reacquainted."

They had been in each other's company all day after being apart for five weeks. Getting reacquainted was satisfying but swift. And when they were finished, she demanded more.

He was not certain he could perform again so quickly.

"Aren't you afraid you'll atrophy from disuse?"

Disuse or misuse? he thought. In that distant corner of his mind, a little voice was telling him it wasn't right to make love to another man's wife. But when she leaned over and kissed him entreatingly, he blanked out the little voice. He might not be able to perform again, but he could try.

Buzz and Marsha were at breakfast Saturday morning in the Lafayette dining room when Buzz spotted a courtly pink-faced man with an impeccably groomed mane of wavy white hair standing in the doorway looking for a table. The man grinned when he recognized Buzz and came forward, despite his robust frame, with the bouncing step of an old basketball player as Buzz beckoned for him to join them.

"Marsha, this is James A. Garfield McCann, the mayor of our fair city—and a lifelong Democrat despite his Republican name."

"There were eight of us." explained the mayor as he eased himself into a chair, being careful not to wrinkle the trousers of his expensive, well-tailored summerweight suit.

He spoke with the hint of a brogue. "My father and mother were so proud to be in America that they named every one of us after a president. And when they got down to me, Garfield was the only name left that they could think of. They didn't realize till years later that old Jimmy Garfield was in the wrong party."

"And this, Mister Mayor, is Marsha Antonelli, one of my competitors from Worcester County."

"I didn't know Worcester County had such fetching women, I'll have to get over there more often."

"This man," said Buzz to Marsha, "is a folk hero back home. He's the one who after half a century of other people trying became the first Irishman to wrest the mayor's office away from the Yankee Republicans."

"The Yankee and the French-Canadian Republicans. Remember, there were a couple of them, too." The mayor turned to Marsha. "Is that the way it is in your part of Worcester County? They came down from Canada to work in the mills and pretty soon they were just as Republican as the old Yankees. We Irish were never like that."

Before Marsha could answer, Buzz picked up again. He knew the mayor had a weakness for flattery. "Since that first time—what was it, Mayor, sixteen years ago?"

"Seventeen."

"Since that first time, all Big Jim has to do to get reelected is to put his name on the ballot." It might be flattery, but it wasn't far from the truth.

"If it were only that easy," sighed Big Jim.

"Don't be modest, Mister Mayor. You'll get reelected just as long as you want to keep running, and you know it."

The conversation turned to state politics. Senator Ted Kennedy would have a free ride in the Democratic primary even flat on his back in the hospital after his plane crash, they all agreed—not like his first run two years ago when he and then-Attorney General Eddie McCormack, the speaker's nephew, had waged a knockdown dragout fight.

"McCormack was a hypocrite," observed the mayor, "when he told Teddy that his candidacy would be a joke if his name were Edward Moore and not Edward Moore Kennedy. This from the man who was elected attorney general solely because his uncle was Congressman John McCormack.

"No, no excitement in the Senate race. But governor is something else again. That upstart crewcut little so-and-so got what he deserved at the state convention"—Buzz knew Big Jim was talking about Lieutenant Governor Francis X. Bellotti, who was challenging the reelection bid of his fellow Democrat, Governor Endicott Peabody—"but I fear he may give the governor a trimming in the primary."

"Why do you say that?" asked Buzz.

Durham Caldwell

"Chub Peabody's a decent man. But a lot of people have the impression that back in his football days"—he'd been an All-American at Harvard—"he made too many tackles without his helmet on. Plus he's Episcopalian in what a lot of narrower-minded Democrats think of as a Catholic party."

"Something else, Buzz." He leaned across the table so he could talk more softly. "This capital punishment thing will hurt him. At this point, there's nothing out in the open. But you get around law enforcement people—and remember, my brother Cleveland and my brother Andy are both cops—you get around law enforcement people, and there's an undercurrent. 'We're gonna turn out the governor because he wants to eliminate capital punishment.'"

Big Jim turned to Marsha with a sudden look of concern on his face. "I'd forgotten I was with reporters. What I've just said, my dear, is all off the record."

"Of course, Mister Mayor, I'll just attribute it to the handsome silver-haired mayor of a leading Western Massachusetts city . . ."

Big Jim started to sputter something, then realized from the flippant look on her face that she was putting him on. But before they could resume their discussion, a tall, slim Negro approached their table. He had on a tan tropical worsted suit, the fabric and tailoring of which seemed to match the mayor's dollar for dollar.

"Morning, Mayor. Morning, Buzz," he said in a deep mellow voice that seemed to have been fashioned for a pulpit. "Mind if I join you?"

He pulled out the remaining chair at the table for four and sat down without waiting for an answer.

"Marsha Antonelli, reporter," Buzz made the introductions, "this is the Reverend Doctor James Shoemaker."

Buzz knew Jimmie Shoemaker well. He was pastor of the city's biggest Negro church, president of the local NAACP, and a political activist. He had probably done more than any other community leader to swing Negro voters away from their traditional loyalty to the party of Lincoln and into the column of Big Jim McCann. And Buzz had interviewed him so often for television that Jerry Finnerty had begun calling the six-thirty news "the Jimmie Shoemaker Show."

Tumultuous Affairs

The Reverend Doctor Shoemaker got right to the point. "Mister Mayor, there's one whale of a fight brewing over seating of the Mississippi delegation. The Freedom Democrats make their case today in the Credentials Committee against that lily-white slate of so-called Regular Democrats.

"If Credentials goes the wrong way, Your Honor, you can be an immense help. You could buttonhole all the mayors from Massachusetts, and any that you know from outside the state, to whip up as much support as we can get for a floor fight.

"God knows," Jimmie Shoemaker added, directing his mellifluous bass voice at Marsha and Buzz as if he were hoping to enlist their support, "the Negro folk down in Mississippi were willing to work with those mossback rednecks to send a biracial delegation up here. But the state convention was rigged, just like it always has been. What could the black folk do besides hold their own convention?"

"Will you help him?" Marsha inquired as the clergyman left the dining room.

"You know, his boy's been down in Mississippi since last year," replied the mayor, "helping Negroes register to vote and helping those Freedom Democrats get organized. That takes guts to let your boy do that. Think of those three other kids who were murdered—Goodman, Schwerner, and whatever the other one's name was. Of course I'll help him. I owe it to him. Besides, he's right."

Big Jim paused for what appeared to be a moment of reflection, then turned back to Marsha. "And young lady, I don't know how this will play back home—do you, Buzz?—but that's on the record."

Buzz wondered afterwards why he hadn't turned on his recorder and gotten the Freedom Democrats story on tape from both the Reverend Doctor Shoemaker and the mayor. But he remembered enough of what they said to phone a voice report to the station. And he alerted John Madigan, the old-timer running the ABC convention news desk, to the move in the Massachusetts delegation to help the Freedom Democrats. Madigan told him there was a strong rumor going around that President Johnson didn't want a fight on credentials.

Durham Caldwell

Buzz found the mood in ABC's convention newsroom upbeat. ABC had pulled only fourteen percent of the convention audience at San Francisco, but that was a healthy improvement over the junior network's 1960 showing. NBC's team of Huntley-Brinkley pulled fifty-three percent of the viewers, increasing NBC's lead over CBS. Buzz had a wry smile as he looked at CBS's full-page ad in the *Sunday Times* and saw how the network had panicked.

Cronkite—billed in San Francisco as "the only television reporter to cover every convention and election since 1952"—was now a non-person. Co-anchoring the CBS convention coverage were the collegiate Roger Mudd, only two years with the network and a floor reporter at San Francisco, and Bob Trout, the debonair veteran of radio news whose credentials included being the only American broadcaster at the 1937 coronation of George VI. Trout had been behind a radio mike for fifteen consecutive hours at the 1952 Democratic convention. But this was his first stab at convention television.

CBS also bragged to its viewers about its "top political analyst, Eric Sevareid," and reporter Dan Rather, who "accompanies President Lyndon Johnson wherever he is during the convention." Rather, like Johnson, was from Texas. The network's *Times* ad showed fifteen faces—but not Cronkite's. His only convention duty was anchoring the CBS Evening News.

The Republicans bought the biggest billboard in Atlantic City to push for votes for Barry Goldwater. Its message to the thousands of Democrats strolling the Boardwalk: "In your heart you know he's right." Buzz and Marsha, finally strolling the Boardwalk together, got a charge out of the tiny sign some wiseacre Democrat had nailed up underneath it: "Yes, extreme right."

The Credentials Committee took testimony in the Mississippi dispute. Key witnesses were Fanny Lou Hamer, a sharecropper's wife, who told of being jailed and beaten for trying to register Negroes to vote, and the Reverend Edwin King, the white chaplain at Tougaloo University, who had a similar story.

In the Lafayette Lounge where members of the Massachusetts delegation were relaxing, drinking, and telling each other stories, there was talk about Bobby Kennedy's resignation as a delegate. "He

Tumultuous Affairs

couldn't very well sit with us and run for senator from New York at the same time," said one delegate.

There was speculation, too, about whom President Johnson would choose as his vice presidential running mate. Most Massachusetts delegates favored Senator Hubert Humphrey of Minnesota. But Johnson, seeing himself as a master political showman and certain of his own nomination, appeared not about to tip his hand. That bit of showmanship allowed the Mississippi credentials squabble to dominate the convention news.

Buzz saw Big Jim McCann moving around the Lafayette lobby and around the dining room quietly talking with other delegates, especially fellow mayors, about the Freedom Democrats. "If it comes to a floor fight," he predicted to Buzz, "Massachusetts will support the Freedom Party."

Maurice Donahue, Massachusetts Senate president, reported to the delegation caucus on the Credentials Committee's failure to resolve the Mississippi issue. "A subcommittee of five people will work on it tonight to try to bring in an effective compromise. A guy named Mondale from Minnesota—he's their attorney general—is chairman of the subcommittee."

Buzz ran into Governor Peabody Tuesday afternoon in front of the Lafayette. Peabody was waiting for a car to take him to the airport to pick up Joan Kennedy. Senator Kennedy's attractive blonde wife had spent most of the ten weeks since the senator's airplane crash at her husband's bedside. Now, with Ted Kennedy still in the hospital strapped to a board as his broken back mended, she was coming to Atlantic City to replace brother-in-law Bobby Kennedy as a Massachusetts at-large delegate. White House aide Kenny O'Donnell had already taken Teddy's convention slot.

The two appointments, by the Democratic State Committee, had come in for criticism in the press, criticism that party leaders brushed off. "It wouldn't do," observed Chub Peabody, "to have a Massachusetts delegation without a Kennedy on it."

Abruptly the governor issued an invitation. "Come on, Buzz, ride out to the airport with me to pick up Joan."

Durham Caldwell

Buzz figured Peabody was looking for a listener, other than his driver. He was right. On the way to the airport, the governor talked at length about the campaign—not about his primary campaign against the "traitor" lieutenant governor, Frank Bellotti—but about the national campaign and its potential impact on the November gubernatorial race against John Volpe.

"It's fun," said Peabody, "to run against Goldwater."

Buzz didn't say it out loud, but remembering the breakfast-table comments of Big Jim McCann, he thought to himself, first you've got to lick Frank Bellotti.

With Judy Ferguson far away in Massachusetts, Buzz decided Joan Kennedy might well be the most attractive blonde in Atlantic City. She was smiling and relaxed as the governor greeted her at the airport and chatted easily in the car on the ride back to town. Talking into the mike of Buzz's tape recorder, she gave an optimistic progress report on her husband's recovery from his plane crash injuries. She expected to enjoy being a convention delegate—she certainly enjoyed being a candidate's wife.

Buzz found her well-briefed on convention issues—quietly articulate as well as personable. But there was also a shyness, a modesty, about her. She was so different from the other Kennedys he'd met during Jack's and Teddy's campaigns—Jack the president, Rose the matriarch, the three sisters and their husbands, Bobby and Ethel and their bubbly brood of kids. He wondered how Joan fit into the competitive touch-football atmosphere of Hyannis Port.

That same day Bobby Kennedy officially declared himself a candidate for the U.S. Senate from New York, Watching the story on the TV news, Buzz and Marsha had to chuckle as the incumbent, Republican Kenneth Keating, responded by offering the newcomer to New York politics a guidebook and state road map.

7

Mossie Donahue was civil rights oriented, but he was also a believer in the practical politician's art of compromise. When he reported the Credentials Committee's solution to the Mississippi hassle—hammered out according to rumor in Hubert Humphrey's hotel room—he urged Massachusetts delegates to support it. They did—though for some it required swallowing hard to do it. The committee voted to seat the members of the Regular delegation who would take a loyalty oath to the Democratic ticket, seat the Freedom Democrats as convention guests, and make two of the most prominent Freedom Party members, druggist Aaron Henry and the Reverend Edwin King, convention delegates-at-large. The party would also take steps to assure no discrimination in the choice of delegates to future conventions.

Big Jim McCann seconded the motion in the Massachusetts caucus to support the compromise. He told Buzz later that there were not enough votes in the caucus for a stronger position. The Reverend Doctor James Shoemaker described himself as "disappointed but not disheartened."

But the Mississippi Regulars dashed any Lyndon Johnson hopes of unity when only three of them signed the loyalty oath and took their seats. After a commotion, which looked to Buzz from the other side of the auditorium like a scuffle, those three left the hall. Members of the Freedom Party, who had also rejected the compromise, moved into the delegation's seats.

The Democrats approved a platform which said, "We condemn extremism whether from the right or left."

And Buzz heard the story making the rounds that President Johnson, upset by the effect of the delegate fight, had called the president of one of the TV networks and told him, "Get your cameras off the goddam niggers out front and back on the speaker's stand inside!"

Durham Caldwell

Buzz and Marsha avoided raised eyebrows by coming down to breakfast separately, usually ending up eating together at a table with other reporters or with convention delegates. "Nice to see you again," one might say to the other.

After breakfast, they went their separate ways, she chasing delegates from Worcester County and he the Western Massachusetts contingent. But the ease of getting interviews around the Lafayette and the leisurely convention schedule—all the official activity was during the evening to take advantage of prime time on TV—left them generous opportunities to get to know each other better. They would slip off to meet at out-of-the-way restaurants or at the beach. And, yes, he decided, she filled out a bathing suit even better than she did as a teenager.

They were shooting for different audiences and different deadlines—but when they compared notes over lunch or swapped story ideas back in the room, he found her surprisingly well informed about the subtle undercurrents within the delegation and able to feed him as many tips as he fed her.

Buzz's friends in the Massachusetts delegation expressed a sense of relief when LBJ finally revealed Hubert Humphrey as his vice presidential choice on Wednesday evening. There was a last excruciating bit of suspense in which Johnson had Senator Thomas Dodd of Connecticut accompany Senator Humphrey on a flight from Atlantic City to Washington. Humphrey was left to guess right up till the minute he got off the plane whether the president was choosing him or Dodd. The country got the answer about eight-thirty p.m. when Johnson and Humphrey were boarding a plane for Atlantic City at Andrews Air Force Base and Johnson told reporters, "This is the next vice president."

"A good man." observed Big Jim McCann catching some fresh air outside Convention Hall.

"The very best," intoned his companion, the Reverend Doctor James Shoemaker.

Buzz noted that most of the seats in the Alabama delegation were empty. Alabama delegates, like the Mississippi Regulars, pulled out rather than sign the loyalty oath. It mattered little. The convention endorsed both Johnson and Humphrey by acclamation.

Johnson broke all precedent by appearing at Convention Hall on Wednesday evening, joining Lady Bird and their two daughters in the presidential box. Reporters from all three networks converged on Johnson for a joint live interview. Buzz happened into the ABC newsroom as the interview unfolded. A group of ABC staffers was gathered around John Madigan's desk, their eyes fastened on the three network monitors. Sander Vanocur of NBC was asking most of the questions, but ABC's Frank Reynolds clearly had the best camera angle—head on. Reynolds held his microphone with the ABC logo at an angle and distance from Johnson's face that made it difficult for NBC and almost impossible for CBS to crop it out of their camera shots.

"Atta boy, Frank!" yelled one member of the newsroom crew. "Hold it up there, Frankie baby!"

The only way CBS—the network that had Dan Rather "accompanying President Lyndon Johnson wherever he is during the convention"—could cut the ABC logo out of its shots was to tighten up to the point where Johnson's face had only mouth, nose, eyes, and forehead.

Bobby Kennedy got a sixteen-minute standing ovation Thursday evening when he appeared on the platform to deliver a moving eulogy to his dead brother and introduce a film about his presidency, "A Thousand Days." Then, with the sentiment out of the way, Johnson and Humphrey went after Barry Goldwater in their acceptance speeches.

Humphrey spoke first. "In the last three and a half years," he thundered, "most Democrats and Republicans have agreed on the great decisions our nation has made . . . but not Senator Goldwater!

"Most Democrats and most Republicans in the U.S. Senate voted, for example, for the nuclear test ban treaty . . . but not Senator Goldwater!

"Most Democrats and most Republicans in the Senate, in fact four-fifths of the members of his own party, voted for the Civil Rights Act, but not Senator Goldwater!"

Durham Caldwell

Now the delegates and the spectators were into it. As Humphrey reeled off the other things that most Democrats and most Republicans had voted for, his audience picked up the refrain at the end of each point, "But not Senator Goldwater!" The crowd loved it.

The president had his own invitation for the audience to join in:

"Most Americans want medical care for older citizens, and so do I!

"Most Americans want fair and stable prices and decent incomes for our farmers, and so do I!

"Most Americans want a decent home in a decent neighborhood for all, and so do I!"

It was a decent speech—and well received—but, Buzz thought, it didn't have the Humphrey ring to it. Hubert had upstaged the president. Buzz was amused to read in the *Times* the next day that a Johnson aide named Bill Moyers had helped out on the Humphrey speech. He wondered if LBJ might be having second thoughts about lending out a speechwriter.

Marsha was sitting at the hotel room desk writing postcards when Buzz got back to the room. He pulled open the curtains to show the dazzling display of fireworks in progress up by Convention Hall.

They watched together as a mass of aerial bombs exploded simultaneously, forming a huge multicolored portrait of LBJ himself which hung in the air over the Boardwalk.

"Want to go out and join the celebration?" he asked her.

She watched the likeness of LBJ dissolve and disappear, then pushed the drapes closed.

"Mister Buckley, this is our last night together in Atlantic City. Two nights in a row we've been too tired to do anything but sleep." She flashed her dimples at him. "The only fireworks I want to remember are not out on the Boardwalk."

8

A few weeks after the Democratic convention, Buzz got a phone call from Johnny.

"Dad, I've been dating Judy Ferguson. You don't mind if I bring her along to the Heidelberg tonight, do you?"

Mind? "Of course not. I'll be delighted to see her."

Buzz could tell by the way Judy and Johnny looked at each other as they sat down to join him that they had been getting along very well together.

There was a bit of small talk—including approval of LBJ's stance of "no wider war" and mild surprise at Frank Bellotti's defeat of Chub Peabody by twenty-seven thousand votes in the Democratic gubernatorial primary. Then Judy surprised Buzz by asking him, "Have you seen any more of your old high school sweetheart since San Francisco?"

Buzz blushed. Johnny's antennae went up.

"Marsha?"

"Marsha!"

"Gee, Dad, you didn't tell me about an old high school sweetheart."

"Not much to tell. She's a married woman. We met on the plane going out. Had dinner together—what were there, Judy, six of us?—the last night of the convention."

"I'd forgotten about the husband. A dentist, right?"

"A dentist. But matter of fact, I did see her in Atlantic City. She was doing stories for that little paper she works for. We had some breakfasts together."

The truth, the whole truth, and nothing but the truth? Well, hardly, thought Buzz. But he'd given Judy a truthful answer—as far as it went.

"You two just about monopolized each other on the plane home," Judy recalled.

"Well, when you go to school with each other for ten or eleven years, then don't see each other for twenty-seven years, you've got a lot to talk about. Nice girl, Johnny. I went with her for a little while before I started going with your mother."

"Was she as pretty as Mom?"

"Almost."

"She's still a pretty woman," declared Judy.

"Speaking of pretty women, did I tell you, Dad, that I'm going with the prettiest woman in Western Massachusetts?"

Buzz, glad to have the conversation turn away from Marsha, responded, "Western Mass.? I'd say the whole darned state."

The following Friday, Johnny brought Judy to the Heidelberg again. When Johnny excused himself to go to the men's room, Judy reached her hand across the table and put it on top of Buzz's.

"Mister Buckley, I think it's only right to warn you that your son and I are becoming increasingly serious about each other."

He turned his hand over and grasped hers.

"Miss Ferguson, we Buckleys are famous for our good taste."

Before the dinner party broke up, Judy reminded Buzz of his agreement on the plane to consider a series of TV programs on racial issues. They went in together a few days later to see station owner H.B. Baker.

The "H.B" stood for Hillerich Bradsby, the name which H.B.'s eccentric millionaire father had insisted on for his fourth son. When an outraged Mrs. Baker discovered months later that Hillerich Bradsby was not a Baker ancestor but the name of the company which manufactured Louisville Slugger baseball bats, her husband explained, "Hey, number four in the lineup—he's the cleanup hitter."

H.B. shed the childhood nickname Hilly, the pet name his mother imposed on him, by the time he was in high school. From that point on, he was simply "H.B." to his friends and later his business associates—some of whom kiddingly called him "Hard-Boiled"

Baker. But to his critics, including most of the staff at the radio and television stations his father's money had helped him build, he was "Half-Baked" Baker.

At fifty, H.B. had a small bay window and was tending toward jowliness. He was red-faced and balding with a temper that occasionally sent the redness in his face traveling all the way up to the shiny spot under his thinning hair. A reincarnation, Buzz thought, of his nineteenth-century mill owner ancestors—a curious mixture of tight-fistedness and paternalism. Most of his hourly employees worked six-day weeks—the first forty hours at straight time, the next eight at time-and-a-half as required by federal law. Some favored workers were on the books for sixty hours. Because of embarrassingly low hourly rates, they needed the extra time to make a decent take-home pay. But whether they ordinarily worked forty-eight hours or sixty or somewhere in between, the "paid" vacation for everybody was a straight-time forty hours, forcing some staff members to make tough choices. Stan Wlodyka, Buzz's number-one news photographer, who was trying to raise five kids, rarely took vacation time. "I can't afford the pay cut" was Stan's explanation. Still, when Gert Broadbent, the longtime traffic manager, was out of work more than a year before dying of lung cancer, H.B. kept her on the payroll with a check in the mail every week right up until she was buried. And when Elaine died, H.B. pulled Buzz away from the other mourners at the wake and told him quietly, "Take as much time as you need. Don't come back till you're sure you're ready."

H.B. was cautious, as Buzz had expected him to be, when Judy laid out the arguments for programs on racial problems. "I don't know. There's so much polarization already—we could just polarize things worse. And I have to worry about our advertisers and what they'd think."

They were clearly getting nowhere. And H.B. also kept glancing at the clock.

Eventually Judy stood up. "I really thank you for seeing me, Mister Baker. I understand where you're coming from. Buzz, thanks for arranging the appointment. I'm going to see Mister Cochran tomorrow. I'll let you know how I make out."

Durham Caldwell

Mickey Cochran was the manager of the other Riverbridge TV station—and, by reputation, not a whit more liberal than Half-Baked Baker. Buzz doubted that Judy had an appointment with him, but she had made H.B. prick up his ears. He also knew that H.B., a man of very regular habits, was glancing at the clock because he didn't want to be late for lunch with his Mattawampus Club cronies. He saw the time as ripe for proposing a compromise—or at least something that H.B. might accept as a compromise.

"H.B., I've got an idea. Instead of a program just on racial issues, why don't we do a series called 'Issues '64'? We can work in the racial stuff that Judy has been talking about but cover other things, too."

Whether the idea appealed to him, or whether it was just that he was anxious to head for lunch at the club, Buzz wasn't sure. "Okay, you're on! But Buzz, I want you to produce and moderate the program yourself. I don't want Mister Flamboyant or any of those half-baked kids doing it."

Buzz had to chuckle to himself at Half-Baked Baker's reference to half-baked kids in the newsroom.

"If Miss Ferguson's willing to help you, wonderful. Work out a time slot with Al. And Miss Ferguson, do me a favor. Stay the hell away from Mickey Cochran. Let him work out his own programs."

Judy nodded in agreement.

With H.B.'s door closed behind them, and no one else in sight in the corridor, Judy took Buzz by the arm and stretched up to kiss his cheek.

"You Buckleys are masterful men."

"Do you really have an appointment with Mickey Cochran?"

"No, but I would've tried to get one."

As he walked her down the corridor, Judy asked him, "Who's Mister Flamboyant?"

"Jerry Finnerty. H.B.'s afraid if he tangled with a guest, Jerry might tell him he had a brain as solid as Swiss cheese—or ask him which rack at the Salvation Army he picked his suit from. Except he'd call it 'the Starvation Army.' And he probably wouldn't be able to resist calling your friend Barbara Olsen the president of the 'League of Women Vultures.'"

Tumultuous Affairs

"That's what they call us anyway."
"Yes, but not on camera."

"Issues '64" premiered with a mini-documentary on racial problems in the city followed by a panel discussion involving the Reverend Doctor James Shoemaker of the NAACP, James Foster of the Urban League, Barbara Olsen of the League of Women Voters, and Frank Leatherbee, general manager of the Chamber of Commerce.

Buzz was surprised that the participants went through a discussion of police/minority relationships without once invoking the term "police brutality." But the Reverend Doctor Shoemaker made a strong appeal for "sensitivity training" for policemen. And Jim Foster, who had been pushing for many years for more minority representation in the Police Department, expressed a hope for "assignments of greater visibility" for the handful of Negroes who were on the force.

The panel also touched on housing and job discrimination and on *de facto* segregation, or racial imbalance, in the schools. Schools with predominantly Negro student bodies, Jimmie Shoemaker maintained, were not being given the same resources as predominantly white schools. And Jim Foster, a walking encyclopedia of statistical information, said elementary schools in the part of town known as the Central City ranged from eighty-five percent Negro to ninety-two percent.

Barbara Olsen agreed that predominantly minority schools were not getting a fair shake. It was a statewide problem, she said, in cities with large minority populations.

Leatherbee was new in town and unencumbered by past philosophies. Rather than being put on the defensive by the others, as Buzz feared might happen, he said the school situation certainly deserved looking into and struck out vigorously for business involvement in opening up more opportunities for minority workers. He even twitted the Reverend Doctor Shoemaker and Jim Foster, in good natured fashion, for the differences in approach between the NAACP and the Urban League. "We don't really know sometimes which voice speaks for the minority community."

Durham Caldwell

Jim Foster had a ready answer. "Look at the United States government. You have what they used to call the War Department, and you have a State Department. The NAACP, in a sense, is the minority community's War Department. And when you need the diplomats, the Urban League is there."

After the program, as the participants were shaking hands, Buzz heard Jim Foster say to Frank Leatherbee, "I just wish my diplomacy was bearing a little more fruit down on Main Street. Any help you can give me I'll certainly appreciate."

Frank Leatherbee had an idea. "Why don't we get you into Rotary? You'd get a chance to interact with a lot of the movers and shakers."

Jim Foster smiled a thin smile. "You're a newcomer. One of the preacher Rotarians put me up for membership a couple of years ago. I was—what's the word?—blackballed. The truest sense of the word."

Frank Leatherbee looked embarrassed. He clearly didn't know what to say.

After Leatherbee had left, Foster turned to Buzz. "I always thought it was Money Bags." Money Bags was the nickname of Malcolm Bruce Jardine III, the city's wealthiest industrialist. "But it could've been any one of a dozen of 'em. Or the whole dozen."

Hubert Humphrey—"the Happy Warrior," as Lyndon Johnson had dubbed him—brought his vice presidential campaign to Mount Holyoke College. As a Baker Broadcasting sound camera recorded it, he responded to the warm ovation in the college amphitheater and to a handful of front-row hecklers:

"Members of this fine, wonderful, enthusiastic, charming, enlightened student body. Yes, that includes you, my dear.

"You know, I'm so happy to see these young smiling ladies who carry the banner of the opposition . . . because whenever I see one smile . . . I know deep down in their hearts"—he dragged out the words from the Goldwater advertising campaign for maximum impact—"they want to vote for Lyndon Johnson!"

The crowd in the amphitheater roared. Buzz thought he saw Judy Ferguson among those on the film cheering. Well, he thought, why not? She's an alumna as well as a Republican—and she doesn't like Goldwater.

"Pretty much what we expected," said one of Buzz's Election Night guest experts, a political science professor from Mount Holyoke. Goldwater took only six states—his native Arizona, Louisiana, Georgia, and South Carolina—plus the two whose delegates had walked out at Atlantic City rather than sign the loyalty oath to the Democratic Party ticket, Mississippi and Alabama. The prof had a note of caution for the winners. She pointed to the Republican inroads in what since Reconstruction had been the Democrats' Solid South.

Buzz and the professor agreed that ticket-splitting was alive and well in Massachusetts. The state gave Johnson seventy-five percent of the vote but elected Republicans John Volpe governor and Elliot Richardson lieutenant governor and reelected Republican Ed Brooke attorney general. Ted Kennedy, still on his back in a hospital bed, won a full term to brother Jack's old Senate seat. His older brother Bobby was the new senator from New York. In Texas, Goldwater backer George Bush lost his Senate bid.

Three months after meeting each other, Johnny and Judy officially announced their engagement. A week or so later Buzz met Johnny for their usual father-son Friday evening dinner at the Heidelberg, this time without Judy who was working late.

When they ordered drinks, Johnny squinted at his father. "Dad, you're not becoming an alcoholic, are you? You order one of those damned vodka collinses nearly every week."

"You think I'll become an alcoholic on one drink a week?"

"Probably not the way you nurse it along. But you never used to drink anything."

"Well, not very much." He had come to like the sweet, sour coolness of the collins. And he tried to tell himself that the vodka relaxed him and helped dispel the lingering tenseness he still felt at meetings with his son. But he knew the real reason he ordered one on those Friday nights at the Heidelberg was that it reminded him of

Durham Caldwell

being with Marsha—and made just a little bit more bearable the wait until he could see her again.

    Buzz was managing to get to Worcester County to see Marsha every two or three weeks. He made the trips on weekdays during the daytime. He had saved up so much vacation time and compensating time for working holidays and weekends that getting away was not usually a problem. It would have been more romantic to meet after dark but also more apt to arouse the suspicions of a husband who kept professional office hours.

    On their first meeting, they drove to a little town on the New Hampshire border, lunched at a restaurant on the picture postcard town common, then checked into a motel on Route 2. They had an enjoyable encounter but agreed that the motel scene, complete with the indignity of checking in under false names, was too tawdry to repeat. She volunteered her own bedroom. Her husband, Marsha assured him, was a man of very fixed habits. He was in the office till five every weekday. If he had cancellations, she said, he would lock the office door, spread out the dental journals in the waiting room, and catch up on his professional reading.

    She laid down just one condition. "You can't come on Mondays. That's the day my cleaning lady comes. We've got to keep our priorities straight."

9

At City Hall, a vote was overdue on the centerpiece of Mayor McCann's current administration, urban renewal in South Park, a largely Negro neighborhood on the edge of the downtown business district. "Slum clearance" was one catch phrase. "Rebuilding Riverbridge" was another. And federal dollars were to make it possible.

The plan was grandiose. First, clear eight hundred acres of land, demolish hundreds of dilapidated three-decker tenements, abandoned warehouses, and boarded-up factories. Then, a combination of public and private redevelopment. Just a stone's throw from the landlocked business district, put up a fifteen-million-dollar office tower/shopping center/parking garage complex. Build the city's first new hotel since the 1920s. Loop an expressway through the edge of the project to serve the new complex and to ease downtown's traffic congestion. Use the rest of the land for an industrial park.

The magnitude of the project excited the whole city. Jardco Industries, the city's biggest employer, pledged to build a new plant in the industrial park and to relocate its corporate headquarters to the new office tower. Major regional department store chains were lining up for the retail complex. The local newspaper wrote glowing editorials about the project and expressed an interest in building a new plant of its own next to the expressway.

Early on, Jim Foster of the Urban League told Jerry Finnerty in a TV interview, "This humdinger of a project has just one drawback—they aren't thinking about the six hundred families who live in the project area."

"Buzz, a lot of those folk do live in crumbling old three deckers with the wooden porches and outside back stairs that make them four-alarm fires waiting to happen," the Reverend Doctor Shoemaker told Buzz in a follow-up interview, "but many of them live in substantial housing. Laurel Street, Mayfair Street, Oak Street. Not new homes by any means. But they're well kept up. Nice yards. Nice gardens. You've seen them, Buzz. To tear down those houses and put those folk out on the street—that would be criminal."

The Redevelopment Authority insisted that everything had to be cleared.

"They'll get fair market value for their property," the chairman of the Redevelopment Authority insisted during an "Issues '64" appearance.

"A lot of those folk rent those houses," Jimmie Shoemaker responded. "You think there are five or six hundred residential vacancies out there in the city waiting for people of color to come and rent them? And remember, those are old houses. For the folk who do own their own places, fair market value won't build new ones." But the Redevelopment Authority wouldn't budge. And the two Jimmies, Foster and Shoemaker, could see the handwriting on the wall—those houses in South Park were coming down, and they had better make sure South Park people had homes to move into. They convinced a third Jimmie—Mayor McCann—to incorporate public housing into the renewal plan, a series of half a dozen small-to-medium-sized developments spread around the city.

The newspaper editorialized against it on philosophical grounds: let the private market provide the housing. Columnist Dibble called it "socialism" and "the latest move by liberal elements to throw a monkey wrench into the wheels of progress." City councilors heard outraged cries from constituents because some of the proposed public housing locations would be in white neighborhoods.

The question before the City Council was whether to make approval of the urban renewal plan contingent on an application to the federal government for public housing units. The night of the vote, Happy Hooper, Buzz's regular City Council reporter, was sick. Buzz took on the job of covering the meeting. He saw Judy in the hallway outside the council chamber.

"You wouldn't believe the pressure I've been under to vote against public housing," she whispered to him. "Myra Heywood's been working me over all week."

"What're you gonna do?"

"Do what's right. Vote my conscience!"

It was clear very quickly where Judy's conscience lay. She seconded the motion to apply for public housing.

Champions of "urban renewal without strings" rose to attack the motion. Rowdy Hennessy, one of the old Regular Democrats from the Irish turf known as the Patch, was a contemporary of the mayor and usually his most loyal supporter on the council. They had played together in the Old Brickyard and in the parochial school basketball league where Rowdy's scrappiness earned him the nickname which he adopted as his legal name when he went into politics. He talked with the same hint of a brogue as the mayor. He was as good humored as the mayor. But whereas Big Jim was as smooth and polished as a finely crafted piece of furniture, Rowdy was rough hewn, like a stump of swamp oak that an unskilled woodman had hacked down and tried to square off using a dull ax. And on this one, Buzz knew that Rowdy was not in the mayor's corner.

"We can't afford the delay to South Park that all the rigamarole of public housin' applications will surely bring," his deep voice echoed off the walls of the chamber. "Right now the economy's right. Redevelopers are poised pen in hand to swoop in and sign on the dotted line for the more desirable parcels. Wait six months, wait a year, while we wait for approval on public housin', and we don't have a tinker's dam of an idea what the economy'll be like—or how many of the developers'll decide that a bird in the hand in some other city is better than piddlin' around waitin' for us. I say let us vote down this ill-advised housin' motion and then vote unanimously for South Park!"

Buzz knew that Rowdy had a personal stake in getting the project moving quickly. His nephews owned the biggest wrecking company in Riverbridge. They could see dollar signs flashing in front of their eyes whenever anyone mentioned "slum clearance." And Rowdy had admitted, off the record, to Jerry Finnerty in justifying his split with the mayor, "Blood is thicker than water. The mayor and I are just old friends."

To be sure, Rowdy was embarrassed to be on the same side of the issue as Domenico DiTotola and Silent Joe DeRosier. But, he also admitted to Jerry Finnerty, "Politics makes unusual bed partners."

Durham Caldwell

Domenico DiTotola—or "Domenic," as he usually called himself—was a political maverick, unpredictable, except he was against more things than he was for. The wonder was not that he was against the housing but that he favored urban renewal. He was originally from New York. Jerry Finnerty called him "that bulky, bald Bronx bastard."

Domenico was nasty, brutally nasty, in council debate. A councilor who disagreed with him might be "my ignorant and unloin-ed friend." The mayor was "dat superannuated hero in da mahogany office."

Big Jim, who over a long career had learned to let most criticism roll off his back, found Domenico DiTotola a special irritant. Making a projection at his desk one day on how the votes would split on a major upcoming issue, he noted that Domenico DiTotola's initials in mayoral shorthand were "DDT." He began referring to DiTotola as "Mister DDT." And in case anyone was slow to pick up on the insecticide reference, he would usually add, "He's real poison," or with close friends, "a real poisonous sonuvabitch."

Both Rowdy and Domenico were big men—with rugged builds from working outdoors most of their lives which had grown a little paunchy with age and with voices that boomed off the walls and spilled out into the far reaches of the City Hall corridors when they got warmed up.

Now it was Domenico's voice that was bouncing off the walls, translating some of columnist Dibble's most vitriolic attacks on the housing proposals into his Bronx vernacular. "Da may'r," he bellowed, "sends us dis oiban renool. He says it's da greatest t'ing since Barnum met Bailey. Den he hears a few noises from da lib'ruls and da minorities, and he's ready ta build t'ree, four, five hunderd units public housin' all over da city. Well, we don' need no more public housin' projects screwin' up good neighborhoods! We don' need people what made a slum makin' more slums!"

Joe DeRosier spoke next. His nickname was Silent Joe, he spoke so seldom. He worked for Malcolm Bruce Jardine III, who because of his initials and the fact that he headed the Fortune 500 company that was the city's biggest employer, was known by the nickname "Money

Tumultuous Affairs

Bags." M.B. Jardine III relished the nickname and the inference of power that went with it.

The company, started by the first Malcolm Bruce Jardine, a Scottish immigrant, and his bachelor brothers around the turn of the century, manufactured toys, games, bicycles, and school furniture. Money Bags had shortened the company name from Malcolm Jardine and Brothers Company to Jardco Industries and endowed it with a red shield trademark—with JARDCO in white letters running diagonally across it—that made company products instantly recognizable in stores from coast to coast. Silent Joe didn't display a trademark, but when he spoke on the council floor, his colleagues just assumed he was speaking for Money Bags.

"The fact of the matter," said Councilor DeRosier, "is that public housing is socialism. It also disrupts neighborhoods. It takes land that could be kept as open space or used for parks and playgrounds. And we know how long it would take to prepare the plans for six separate projects, put them out to bid, and get them built. It would put South Park urban renewal years behind schedule. Think what that means in terms of potential jobs and the delays in downtown revitalization and the easing of traffic congestion. Private builders on the other hand can move quickly. Look at all the subdivisions they've developed in the city since the war."

"I wonder who wrote Silent Joe's speech?" Judy whispered to Buzz during a short recess.

"And how many substandard subdivisions he'd like us to forget about?" asked Buzz.

When debate resumed, Max came down from the rostrum to speak in favor of the motion. "This is an important project for the future of the city," he told his colleagues, "but we can't forget the future of six hundred families who stand to be displaced."

Domenico DiTotola reclaimed the floor. "Our esteemed prez'dent who lives out on Balfour Av-noo don't stand ta have no public housin' across da street from his place."

Judy waited till all the other councilors had spoken before asking for recognition. After listening to Domenico's vituperation, Buzz was halfway expecting, maybe even hoping for, more sarcasm along the lines of her memorable "Dribble-I-mean-Dibble" address. Instead she was all peaches and cream.

"Our president has pointed out the human element in our deliberations this evening. Some of the families who live in South Park have been there two, even three generations. We're ready to uproot these families for what we hope is the greater good of the city as a whole. The least we can do in return is to see to it that suitable replacement housing is available.

"I understand the concern that tying housing to urban renewal will delay the South Park project, but there's no reason for that to happen. Housing occupies only a portion of the eight hundred acres of South Park. Work on clearance of the rest of the area can begin immediately, and building can begin on those portions of the area as soon as they are cleared.

"Mayor McCann, who can very well be called the Father of South Park, has endorsed the housing component of the program, and I feel we should, too."

There was applause from members of the clergy, South Park residents, and other representatives of the Negro community who were sitting together in the spectator section.

Max banged the gavel with a smile. "Please. No demonstrations from the audience."

Domenico was on his feet before the applause for Judy ended. "Da may'r don't give two hoots about no housin' component. He said he's for it ta t'row a bone ta Preacher Shoemaker an' dem udder guys what rounds up colored votes for him in da Central City. It's alla same ta him if we vote it down. An' Miss Beauty Queen here"—pointing to Judy—"she don't stand ta have no public housin' across from her place needer."

A claque of DiTotola supporters, seated across the aisle from the group which had applauded Judy, clapped and whistled.

Max banged the gavel again. This time he wasn't smiling. "Any more outbursts"—he indicated uniformed policeman Anthony Grimaldi at the rear of the chamber—"and I'll ask the officer to remove the offenders."

Tumultuous Affairs

Judy ignored the beauty queen remark. "I saw lights on in the mayor's office. Why don't we suspend the rules and invite the mayor in to tell us whether he's secretly hoping that we vote down the housing? We all know that what Councilor DiTotola has told us is absolutely ridiculous. In fact, I think it calls . . . "

But DDT, seated two chairs over, wasn't listening. He had turned his back on Judy to address a snide remark to Silent Joe and then swiveled his chair around to play to his friends in the gallery.

Judy momentarily lost her cool.

"We listened attentively to the councilor from the West End during his remarks—or I should say, his diatribe—earlier this evening. If he would shut his big mouth once in a while and listen to somebody else, he might learn something."

There was a smattering of applause from the same group which had applauded her earlier.

Max banged the gavel again.

"Councilors will please refrain from personal remarks. Councilors who do not have the floor will please remain quiet."

He banged the gavel again as Mister DDT whispered a loud aside to Silent Joe. "Mister DiTotola, that means you, too!"

Nobody took Judy up on her suggestion to bring in the mayor. The motion to make the urban renewal plan contingent on housing failed by a vote of six to three. Judy and Mister DDT both jumped to their feet shouting, "Mister President!"

"The chair recognizes Councilor Ferguson."

"I serve notice of reconsideration at the next regular meeting." The parliamentary maneuver closed the whole urban renewal question for the evening.

"Mister Prez'dent!" yelled Domenico DiTotola. "I challenge da chair's rec-uh-nition o' Councilor Foiguson! I was on my feet foist!"

Buzz knew Max had recognized Judy because Domenico would have moved for immediate reconsideration, assuming it would lose by the same six-to-three margin and allow an immediate up-or-down vote on South Park.

Max banged his gavel, hard this time.

"Councilor, you're out of order!"

63

Durham Caldwell

"Mister President!" Judy shouted. "I move we adjourn!"

"Mister Prez'dent!" yelled DDT.

"The councilor knows a motion to adjourn is not debatable! Councilor Fifield seconds the motion!" Barney Fifield, the councilor who had voted with Max and Judy, actually hadn't opened his mouth. "All in favor say aye! The ayes have it! The council is adjourned till next Monday at eight p.m.!"

Max strode briskly into the anteroom, leaving DDT sputtering and fuming.

"Christ," laughed Buzz when he caught up with Max in the men's room, "that was a faster gavel than they use at the State House! Who the hell said 'aye' besides Judy?"

"Hey, I didn't hear any nays, did you?"

"You didn't ask for any, you crooked bastard!"

"Democracy in action!" grinned Max.

Buzz didn't see what happened outside City Hall, but the stories he got independently from several eye witnesses seemed to confirm that it was this:

Domenico DiTotola, still sputtering about being gaveled out of order, was only a few steps behind Judy Ferguson as she walked down the stairs from the council chamber. He caught up with her as she was exiting the side door.

"Whaddaya doin', Blondie, sleepin' wid dis guy Max? Yer allus votin' wid 'im," he sneered. "Ya know, Blondie, yer very pretty when ya get mad and dem big bazooms bounce up 'n down."

Judy walked on, ignoring him. But Rowdy Hennessy was close enough behind Domenico to hear what he said. He grabbed his colleague forcefully by the collar.

"Domenic, I'm ashamed of you. I want you to apologize to that lady."

As Rowdy loosened his hold, Domenico instead of going after Judy spun around. "Go fuck ya'self!" He threw a sucker punch that caught Rowdy square on the chin, staggering him backward and knocking off his old cloth hat.

Rowdy was at least ten, maybe fifteen, years older than Domenico. But he lurched forward, blinking off the effect of the blow, grasped the younger man by his shirt front, and unleashed a roundhouse right to the nose that was so sharp that those close by could hear the nose bone snap. As Domenico flailed away impotently at Rowdy's huge body, the older, slightly bigger man struck him twice more, once on his left cheek, once on the left ear.

"He would've killed him right then and there," one of Buzz's informants told him, "except Tony the Cop came out the door and broke it up."

Judy heard the noise but kept walking. As she reached the curb where her car was parked, Rowdy came huffing and puffing up behind her.

"Miss, I want to apologize for what that dirty little man said to you. I want to apologize on behalf of all your colleagues. We can disagree in the council chamber without bein' disagreeable. Miss, if that little Eyetie bastard bothers you again, you tell Rowdy. I'll make those initials 'DDT' stand for 'damned dead turkey.'"

Judy started to thank him for his concern, but he held up a hand.

"Somethin' else, Miss. The things you said in there tonight, you and Max, you said very well. I went in there with my mind made up. I'm a pretty stubborn old coot, but I said to myself, you know, what that lady says makes a lotta sense. Why can't we start the demolition but spare the homes till new housin's built? I want to think some more about what you said."

Officer Grimaldi walked up and handed Rowdy the cloth hat that Domenico had knocked off his head. As he put it on and adjusted it, he told Judy, "We'll see what happens when we reconsider."

The lobbying over the next few days was furious. But Buzz and his reporters found Rowdy the only council member considering changing his vote. Big Jim McCann could also count votes. He called a private meeting with the Reverend Doctor Shoemaker, Jim Foster, and the three councilors who had voted in favor of housing. Judy told Buzz about it afterwards.

Durham Caldwell

"The mayor looked very sad. He told us the housing, the six sites in different parts of the city, wasn't going to fly. He had a compromise—a project for four hundred families at the Old Brickyard. A high-rise project. Call it Garden Towers or something else fancy like that. That's what we'll try for Monday night."

"We argued against it," Jimmie Shoemaker told Buzz. "We pointed out that it's an isolated area. No public transportation—and a lot of those folk in South Park don't own cars. And that's a horrendous number of families, a horrendous number of kids, to jam all together in one little area.

"But it has the advantage from His Honor's point of view that the land already belongs to the city. Any additional landtaking will be minimal. And with the city dealing with just one architect and one contractor, the buildings can go up pretty rapidly.

"And because it's isolated, it won't stir up the populace, the friends of Councilor DDT, who are so concerned that a bunch of dirty niggers will be moving into their pristine neighborhoods."

"In other words, you don't like it?"

"I don't like it, Buzz, but what Jim Foster calls 'the white power structure' is determined to move ahead and clear that land. And for those folk who are losing their homes, a roof over their heads in the Brickyard is better than no roof at all. And better than waiting for private builders to put up houses they can't afford."

At the next council meeting, Judy's motion for reconsideration failed, as she knew it would. Without any great enthusiasm, she then moved to couple approval of urban renewal with public housing at the Old Brickyard. That motion passed on a vote of seven to one with virtually no debate. Councilor DiTotola missed the meeting, nursing what friends said were a broken nose and assorted other injuries. Only Silent Joe DeRosier voted "no."

10

As Buzz drove east on the turnpike, his ears pricked up at a news story on the Albany public radio station. The New York Bar Association, studying revision of the state criminal code, had given its endorsement to removing adultery from the list of criminal offenses. I'll buy that, thought Buzz. He wondered what the law was in Massachusetts.

Buzz felt uncomfortable the first time he visited the Antonelli apartment—and even more uncomfortable when he saw the collection of firearms that Doctor Antonelli had on display throughout the foyer, the living room, and the den. He had resolved, on that first visit to the apartment, to do nothing more daring than sitting and talking. But when Marsha sat down on the sofa and kissed him, their appetites for each other militated otherwise. After that first time, it was easier for Buzz to forget the dentist and to forget the guns and to take it on faith that Leo never left the office before five.

Buzz would have been content, at least during some of his visits, just to walk or drive with Marsha through the countryside, or to sit and talk in the park. She liked politics almost as much as he did and fed him a Worcester County cast of characters nearly as colorful and nearly as devious as Big Jim, DDT, and the others from Western Massachusetts. He was a nominal Democrat and she was a nominal Republican—but they shared admiration for John F. Kennedy's style while disagreeing on his accomplishments; they shared admiration for Massachusetts Republicans like Saltonstall, Volpe, and Brooke; they shared almost a reverence for Martin Luther King.

They swapped accounts of the stories they were covering, compared stratagems for getting cooperation from reluctant subjects, and laughed together about the idiosyncrasies of their respective bosses and coworkers.

Durham Caldwell

They both kept up on world and national affairs. They approved LBJ's War on Poverty but looked with concern on the growing involvement in Vietnam. Many other things they debated fiercely but always in good sport. They were relaxed and easy with each other right from the beginning.

He found her sense of humor as saucy and delightful as her smile. She was quicker with *double entendres* than a burlesque comedian and just as bawdy, something that shocked him at first, but which he quickly got used to.

One rainy day when he was thinking about what driving conditions would be on the way home, she scolded him for giving her a rather mechanical kiss.

"Sorry," he apologized, "my thoughts were somewhere else."

She leaned over and gave him one of those Chancellor Hotel I-could-make-it-up-to-you kisses—long and lingering.

"So are mine," she said.

Another time, on one of their rare weekend trysts—Leo was at an out of-state shooting competition—they stopped to walk through a village fair on the green of a little rural town. They bought a bag of fresh roasted peanuts from a wrinkled vendor with a graying old-country mustache and a beaten-up straw skimmer. They sat on a park bench, shelled the still-warm peanuts for each other, and ate the whole bagful. They enjoyed them so much that Buzz went back for another bag, and they devoured those.

Later, as they enjoyed the privacy of her bedroom, Marsha turned philosophical—or at least that's the way Buzz thought of it. "Why is making love like eating peanuts?"

"Why?"

She tried to keep a straight face, but in the dim light of the bedroom he could see the dimpled smile spread over it.

"Because once you get started, it's very hard to stop."

A puzzled look replaced the smile.

"Maybe I've got it backwards. Maybe it should be, why is eating peanuts like making love?"

Tumultuous Affairs

If Marsha were a cloistered nun and he could talk with her only through an iron grate, he would still call on her, Buzz told himself, because she was so much fun to be with. He would have taken her to dinner at fashionable restaurants, to the theater and to concerts, but they agreed that would be risky—a friend or somebody who recognized her as Doctor Antonelli's wife was bound to see them sooner or later. So they kept to out-of-the-way places—and to the apartment.

Despite—or perhaps because of—the many other joys they shared, they usually wound up in bed. Sometimes it happened without a word. There would be an unexpected lull in the conversation, like the one that first night in San Francisco. She would look at him. He would look at her. Their faces would break simultaneously into broad grins, and they would walk hand in hand into the bedroom.

But more often, she would determine the moment. "I can't let you drive all this distance without a reward," she might say as she got up from the sofa and took his hand.

Sometimes her invitations were coy: "Is there anything else you'd like to do before you go home?" or "You've got a long drive ahead of you. Want to lie down for a little while?"

Occasionally they were as blunt and demanding as, "You've filled me with a good lunch. Now fill me with something else."

Double entendres were her stock in trade.

"I can't let you go home without easing your anxieties."

"You've been here quite a while. Why don't we visit now?"

Or, the one that amused him the most: "You've gotten me all feverish. I think you'd better take my temperature." A pause. "You did bring your thermometer?"

Once in the bedroom, the usual ritual was to undress each other, for her to excuse herself "just for a minute to get ready," and, on her return, a warm embrace and what she liked to call "letting nature take its course."

Occasionally he was the initiator. "It's been such a long time," he might say. "I don't want to forget how to do it." To which she might respond, "Don't worry—I have a long memory," or "I've been keeping good notes."

69

Durham Caldwell

But usually he left it up to her—and after a while, he began to look forward to what he thought of as *"l'approche du jour."*

Her bawdiness reminded him of the Rabelais he had read in college. He even called her "Mrs. Rabelais" during one especially jocular lovemaking session.

"*Madame Rabelais!*" she corrected him. And then, "*Un, deux, trois, quatre, cinq, six,* BUZZ!"

He was sure Miss Avery had never thought of her substitution-for-sevens counting game in that context during high school French class.

He responded, "*Huit, neuf, dix, onze, douze, treize,* BUZZ!"

"*Quinze, seize,* BUZZ!"

By the time they got to "*vingt-six,* BUZZ! BUZZ!!!" they were both laughing so hard they could barely continue.

God, she was fun to be with!

On the drive home that day, he wondered to himself how he had been so lucky as to win the companionship of this exciting woman.

In the newsroom, staff members talked among themselves about "the new Buzz." The new Buzz smiled frequently, something the old Buzz hadn't done since the death of his wife. He still wanted perfection in terms of performance, but he was less of a driver and more tolerant, more understanding of mistakes.

The mellowing, the noticeably buoyant effect of occasional phone calls from a throaty-voiced woman who identified herself as Marsha, the frequent days off all pointed in the same direction. "He's got a girl friend," Happy Hooper speculated one day as Buzz walked out of the newsroom whistling.

"Be happy for him," responded Jerry Finnerty.

"He wanted to walk Bobby down the aisle at the Senate next month for their swearing in," Buzz told Marsha. "Looks like he may be able to do it after all."

They were talking about Senator Edward Kennedy and how, just two weeks after taking his first steps since breaking his back, he had walked out of the hospital under his own power.

"We Republicans well know," Marsha responded, "never sell a Kennedy short."

With the coming of the new year, Baker Broadcasting's "Issues '64" became "Issues '65," Max Feigenson was reelected president of the City Council, and troubling new racial tensions joined the old ones that had never been resolved. "Racial imbalance" replaced "police brutality," "housing discrimination," and "job discrimination" at the top of the Reverend Doctor James Shoemaker's list of grievances to be addressed.

Predominantly Negro schools in the Central City, Jimmie Shoemaker and other Negro leaders reiterated, were inferior to the schools in the city's white sections. Buildings were inferior, they said; teachers were inferior; test scores were lower; white parents had clout with the school system, Negro parents didn't. Achieving racial balance in the schools was the only way, they claimed, to insure equal educational opportunities for all students. They pressed the School Committee to "end *de facto* segregation"—though they were short on specifics of how to do it.

School Committee members reacted defensively. They agreed the "racial concentration" that existed in some schools was "not desirable." But schools in Negro neighborhoods were on a par, they insisted, with schools throughout the city although they had no explanation why teacher turnover was so much higher. Lower test scores must be a reflection of the home environment. And they put a new scare word into the popular lexicon: "busing." Busing, a two-way exchange of students between white neighborhoods and Negro neighborhoods, they said, would be the only way to relieve an imbalance caused by housing patterns.

The NAACP filed suit in U.S. District Court. Buzz, covering the hearing, heard this exchange between plaintiff's attorney and the superintendent of schools:

Q: What is the School Committee doing about racial imbalance?

A: I don't know that there is racial imbalance.

Durham Caldwell

Q: Do you know the sections of the city that are predominantly Negro?

A: I never took a head count.

Q: When you visited schools in the Central City, wasn't racial imbalance visible to the naked eye?

A: I saw the children as students, not as members of any race.

The District Court judge found the situation in Central City schools "tantamount to segregation." He gave the School Committee three months to come up with a corrective plan. But the Circuit Court of Appeals set aside the order with the words, "There is no constitutional right to the complete elimination of racial imbalance."

Judy brightened Buzz's days at the station by coming in every Tuesday afternoon for conferences on "Issues '65." She bubbled with ideas for program topics, for guests, and for approaches to the subject matter. Keeping Buzz's bargain with H.B., they explored a variety of subjects outside the area of race relations, but they saw to it that racial issues, especially racial imbalance, were dealt with candidly and in depth as they developed.

One Thursday night, two old friends, Jimmie Shoemaker and Big Jim McCann, tangled in front of the cameras. Big Jim, as mayor, was *ex officio* chairman of the School Committee. Jim Foster of the Urban League opened the discussion with a suggestion that the School Committee consider "pairing" of schools. "Team up a school from the Central City," he explained, "with the nearest predominantly white school. Have them exchange students."

"But Jim, that would require forced busing. That's something that I oppose."

"But Your Honor," responded the Reverend Doctor Shoemaker, "the School Committee had no compunctions about the forced busing of forty Negro students out of the Miller Street school district a year ago."

"James, that was different. We had to move those children because Miller Street was overcrowded. We found room for them at another school. It had nothing to do with racial imbalance."

Tumultuous Affairs

"Your Honor, it was still forced busing," said Jimmie Shoemaker in his deep preacher voice.

The only concession the School Committee would be willing to make, the mayor predicted, would be to allow parents voluntarily to transfer their children to schools which had empty seats if the transfers would improve racial balance. "Limited open enrollment," the mayor called it.

"If we vote on that, it won't be unanimous," promised School Committeewoman Lucille Cournoyer, who was also a member of the "Issues" panel. "There is no real advantage to deliberately mixing the races."

Judy appeared on only occasional "Issues" programs herself, but she used her contacts, especially in the minority community and with church groups, to help Buzz develop angles and pull in guests he would not have thought of on his own.

He found her a pleasure to work with and a challenge to keep up with. He would give his right arm to have somebody on his news staff with half her brain power.

And looks? She turned the heads of every male in the newsroom when Buzz escorted her into his little office. She repaid the compliment by flirting with each of them. Buzz overheard Jerry Finnerty muttering to Happy one day, "Just one time, Lord, just one time," as their eyes followed her across the newsroom to the water fountain.

Thursday nights, after taping of the program, Judy would link her arm in his as Buzz walked her to her car. He knew she did it because he was her fiance's father—but for him, it was an exciting experience. As their respect for each other grew through their professional contact, he could feel their mutual affection for each other growing too.

"Buzz, look at this." Jerry Finnerty handed him a piece of UPI wire copy. Lyndon Johnson was responding to Vietcong guerrilla attacks on American air bases by dispatching U.S. ground forces to Vietnam. Thirty-five hundred Marines were to lead the way, followed shortly by soldiers. "Those gooks will really get it now," predicted Jerry.

Durham Caldwell

With troops committed, the country seemed to unite behind the president. Dave Vigneault, probably the most liberal member of the Western Massachusetts legislative delegation, walked through Baker Broadcasting one morning handing out stamped metal red, white, and blue American flag lapel pins. Buzz pinned one on his sports coat. He hadn't liked that Tonkin Gulf business last summer, but when the chips are down, you support your president and the men in uniform.

Buzz thought he had put the guilt thing about his relations with Marsha well behind him, but it hit him again one afternoon on the drive home from Worcester County. Not guilt about cuckolding Doctor Antonelli. It was that he was sullying his long and mutually devoted relationship with Elaine, that he was being untrue to her memory.

It bothered him for more than a week. Then, one night, he had another dream. This time he dreamed he was in bed with Marsha when Elaine suddenly appeared at their bedside. It was the earlier Elaine, before the illness had ravished her features. Maybe even the Elaine of their honeymoon. And it was her bed, Elaine's bed, that he and Marsha were making love in. But there was no anger in Elaine's face, only peace, and then a broad smile—as if she was happy that he had found love again and as if she was not only condoning what they were doing but actually cheering them on.

He could almost feel Elaine's hand resting gently on his shoulder. He awoke with a start. The hair on the back of his neck was standing up straight.

Usually Buzz couldn't remember his dreams. They popped like soap bubbles the instant he woke up. But this time he seemed to remember everything: what he and Marsha were saying to each other, the dress that Elaine was wearing when she appeared to them, how young she looked and how at peace, and how the big glowing smile he remembered so fondly had spread over her face just the way it did before she got sick.

He took it as a sign. She seemed to be saying, he thought, enjoy life; it's not wrong to love someone; it's very right. And he suddenly remembered one of the last things she had told him as she lay dying, "You live for today, not yesterday."

He never told Marsha about the dream, but he thought of it sometimes when they made love to each other—Elaine was there in the room, cheering them on.

One rainy day, when it seemed just too miserable to drive anywhere, Marsha sat Buzz down in the living room with a scrapbook of newspaper clippings while she went into the kitchen to fix some sandwiches.

The clippings, from the local paper, all had the byline "By Marsha Antonelli." He thumbed through the pages quickly. The ones in the front of the scrapbook were feature stories, and there were often gaps of several weeks between the dates which had been carefully noted in ink. But as the pages went on, the gaps shortened, and hard-news issues stories began to supplant the features.

He turned back and read a couple of the early ones. Good description, he thought. And she really knows how to capture emotion. Then he flipped to the most recent stories. She had a knack for getting to the nub of the issues and of explaining them in clear, direct terms.

She appeared in the door with a tray of sandwiches and coffee.

"Say, these are good! I knew you were writing, but I didn't realize how good you were."

"Any suggestions?"

"Not really. You've got good material. You handle it beautifully, judging by the ones I read. Just one small thing maybe."

"What's that?"

"Spend a little more time thinking about your leads. Not that the ones I saw were bad. But some of them could've been a little stronger. I tell my people to use their lead sentences to draw the audience into the story, to lock 'em in before their attention can stray.

"Print's a little different. The headlines and the layout help to pull the readers in, but the more solid the lead paragraph the better your chance of getting 'em to read the whole piece."

"Thanks," she said. "I'll remember that. And I'll have quick chances to practice. The editor's asked me to go on full time."

"That's great! Congratulations."

"Of course, the hometown paper is just a beginning. Maybe some day I'll get to the Worcester paper or to Boston.

"I start Monday. I made just one proviso: a day off once or twice a month. Health reasons, I told him."

"Health reasons?"

"If I couldn't see you on a regular basis, my mental health would deteriorate very quickly." A smile crept over what to now had been a serious face.

He put a hand on her breast, as he often did when he kissed her.

"I'm glad to see your physical health is still holding up."

"That's suggestive." She glanced down at his hand. Her dimples had never looked more provocative.

"Suggestive of what?"

She began unbuttoning his shirt.

"The sandwiches can wait."

II

Buzz might be a professional newsman, but his reaction to the events in Selma, Alabama, on March 7, 1965, was the same as that of television viewers across the country: indignation. State troopers and sheriff's deputies had used clubs, tear gas, and bull whips to turn back six-hundred-and-fifty civil rights marchers bound for the state capitol at Montgomery with a voting rights petition. The indignation grew when, a few days later, a Boston clergyman, James Reeb, was fatally beaten while taking part in a sympathy march. The two incidents together outraged the country. Two weeks later—under protection of a federal court and close to three thousand soldiers, federalized National Guardsmen, and United States marshals—thousands of marchers, black and white, set off down the highway. They were led by two Nobel Peace Prize winners, the Reverend Doctor Martin Luther King Jr. and Doctor Ralph Bunche, undersecretary of the United Nations.

In the ranks of those who completed the five-day trek from Selma to Montgomery—and who listened to King tell a huge crowd in front of the Alabama capitol, "We ain't goin' let nobody turn us around"—were Bobby and Lenora Clark, two of the younger and more activist members of the Reverend Doctor James Shoemaker's NAACP branch.

The Clarks came home after the march determined to speed up the process of equal opportunity, equal education, and equal protection under the law by every possible nonviolent means: marches, sit-ins, picketing—whatever it took.

And for whatever reason, Jimmie Shoemaker, never a shrinking violet, became more militant than ever. Buzz and Judy, when they talked about it together, wondered whether it was the preacher's personal reaction to Selma—or a feeling that he had to keep up with

Bobby and Lenora to maintain his place of leadership in the community.

The Clarks were an enigma to Buzz and his fellow reporters. Bobby was a firebrand soapbox speaker, unlettered but with a natural-born ability to arouse a crowd and hold it in the palm of his hand. But there was an undercurrent of belief that Lenora was more radical than Bobby and that it was she who was setting their agenda. In fact, a much discussed question in both white and black communities was who wears the pants in the Clark family? Bobby, when Jerry Finnerty put the question to him point blank, smiled a gap-toothed smile. "We're a team," he said.

But whoever was doing the leading, the Reverend Doctor Shoemaker's pronouncements were straining the clergyman's long and close relationship with Mayor McCann. "We are prepared to lie down in the streets," he told interviewer Happy Hooper. "We are prepared to stage sit-ins in the school superintendent's office. We are prepared to organize boycotts. These things will happen—I assure you they will—if this city doesn't take steps right away to end *de facto* segregation in the schools."

Big Jim McCann was outraged when Buzz phoned him at home to see if he wanted to make a response.

"Buzz," he said, "how can you give air time to a rabble rouser like that?"

The newspaper coupled its report on Jimmie Shoemaker's new remarks with a reflection on the sporadic burning, looting, and other racial violence across the country the previous year. It editorially predicted "a long, hot summer here in our own city."

Ten days after the Reverend Doctor Shoemaker's on-camera warning, Bobby and Lenora Clark, seven other Negroes, and three whites staged a midmorning sit-down in the office of the school superintendent. Most of them went limp when police came to arrest them.

Police handled the matter casually, seeing to it that they had at least three officers, and usually four, to carry each of the protesters as gently as possible down the stairs from the second-floor office and into the waiting patrol wagon. In fact, they did it so casually after the first word came over the police radio that Buzz had time to drive from the station with Stan Wlodyka and interview the last of the group on camera as they were being picked up and lugged to the stairs.

As the patrol wagon headed to the police lockup with its passengers, a cruiser headed in the other direction—toward the hospital. Buzz reported that one of the officers had strained his back helping to carry a protester down the stairs and out of the building. The protester was Lenora Clark—a detail that Buzz did not mention. Lenora weighed close to two hundred pounds.

Judy's parents wanted the wedding to be in Ohio, back among the home folks. But Judy insisted that home for her was now in Massachusetts, and the home folks could travel east. It was to be a church wedding with the reception afterward in the Glen Meadow Restaurant on the edge of town.

On one of Buzz's visits to Worcester County, Marsha pulled an invitation from the drawer of her writing desk and began to read: "Dr. and Mrs. Luther Ferguson request the pleasure of the company of Dr. and Mrs. Leo Antonelli at the wedding of their daughter, Judy Louise..."

Marsha held up a small piece of note paper. "She put a note in: 'I thought you might like to see your old boy friend's son get married.'"

"Are you coming?"

"I'll try. Judy and I really hit it off well in San Francisco. She's a good kid. But I don't think Leo will come. That's one of his big firearms competition weekends—some place in New Hampshire."

It'll be nice to have Marsha at the wedding, Buzz told himself as he drove home. But then he had another thought. If Max was at the wedding, he and Marsha would have to be very circumspect in the way they behaved toward one another, or he could expect another sermon. Small matter maybe, but he was relieved when Judy told him Max had sent his regrets. He had to be in Baltimore for a nephew's *bar mitzvah*.

Mayor James A. Garfield McCann headed the list of political invitees at the wedding, looking more elegant with his wavy white hair and his tailored double-breasted suit than the male members of the wedding party in their fancy tuxedos.

It was warm at the reception. Most of the men took off their coats, but not Big Jim. He recognized Marsha immediately as she chatted with Buzz. "Ah, Buzz," he said, "this is the young beauty you monopolized at breakfast every morning in Atlantic City."

Myra Heywood was there—with her longtime companion, Erwin Edwards. She was wearing a dark blue designer dress that Buzz figured must have cost her at least five hundred dollars, maybe a thousand. She filled it out pretty well, he thought. Not a bad looking woman for someone well into middle age—despite her politics. While Erwin was at the punch bowl, she cast a come-hither eye on Buzz and remonstrated with him for not stopping in to accept her invitation for coffee.

Judy wore one of those wedding gowns cut square in front, showing off the upper halves of her shapely breasts in all their delicate whiteness. She was unbelievably beautiful. Buzz had difficulty taking his eyes off her, even to pay attention to Marsha. He could just imagine how eager Johnny must be to get the hell out of there and get the honeymoon started.

The Fergusons were a gregarious clan. Buzz especially liked Judy's mother, Louise. She was sixty, a little smaller than Judy, with beautifully brushed blonde hair which showed not a strand of gray. She had almost the same face as Judy and the same stunning figure.

"Buzz, you have a wonderful son," Louise told him. "When Judy brought him home to meet us, I told Doctor it was no wonder she fell in love at first sight."

"That's the way it was with us too, Mother," reminded her husband. "I was a young doctor just out of med school, Buzz. I was interning at a big hospital in Cleveland. That first morning, on grand rounds, I spotted this beautiful young nurse in the maternity ward. I couldn't help myself. I winked at her. And when she winked back, I knew she was the girl I was going to marry."

"I knew it, too," said Louise. "It must run in the family."

"I only hope," said her husband, "that Judy makes Johnny half as happy as Mother has made me."

Judy interrupted the conversation to introduce Buzz to her father's brother.

"Uncle Harvey, Mom, Dad,"—she took Buzz by the arm and pulled herself close to him—"one of the bonuses of marrying Johnny is that I get this wonderful man for a father-in-law."

Through the thin sleeve of his shirt, Buzz could feel the warmth and softness of her breast against his arm as she told Uncle Harvey and Mom and Dad that Buzz was the best news director in Massachusetts "and a very wonderful, very sensitive man."

He would have been embarrassed by her words. But with that warm breast against his arm, he was only half listening. God! he was thinking, Johnny, you are one lucky bastard!

Later Louise confided to Buzz, "We'd almost given up on having a baby when Judy came along. I think Doctor got me pregnant the night before he left for the war. I always thought it was God's way of leaving a little bit of him with me in case he didn't come back."

The reception broke up at mid-afternoon. Myra Heywood and Erwin Edwards had left early. Buzz wasn't sure whether it was a political argument, one or the other of them paying too much attention to guests of the opposite sex, too many trips to the punch bowl, or a combination of all three. But he was close enough to tell that harsh words were passing between them and to see Erwin grasp Myra firmly by the elbow and guide her out of the banquet room and out of the restaurant.

As Buzz escorted Marsha to her car, she asked him, "What have you been telling your son about me? He said you were right."

Buzz looked mystified. The only time he'd had any discussion with Johnny about Marsha was that night at the Heidelberg. Something clicked. That was it!

"Judy mentioned you one night as my old girl friend. He asked me if you were as pretty as Elaine."

"What did you tell him?"

"I told him almost."

"That's a fair answer. Actually very flattering. Thanks."

As they reached her car, he asked her how soon she had to get home.

"Not till tomorrow night. That competition up in the North Woods is due to last the who-o-ole weekend."

"You want to stop by the house?"

"I was going to be very disappointed if you didn't ask."

That evening, Buzz interrupted their lovemaking to glance at the bedside clock. "I guess by now the honeymoon is really underway. But the son couldn't possibly be having a more delightful time than his old man is."

They were awakened by the rays of the rising sun shining through the maple tree outside the window and dappling the ceiling with a slowly changing panorama of light and shadow. She squeezed his hand and gently kissed the lobe of his ear.

"Oh, Buzz, what a fool I was twenty-eight years ago not to let you kiss me goodnight."

"That's right, you were." That's all he said. She would have made a wonderful lifetime companion, of that he was sure. Still, he thought, if he and Marsha had stuck together back in high school, he would have missed out on Elaine. As much as he loved Marsha, and he loved her deeply—as much as she had eased his anguish over Elaine's loss, had helped him get his life back on track—he wouldn't trade those years with Elaine, not even the difficult ones, for anything.

12

After nothing else seemed to be succeeding against the Vietcong, President Johnson and the Pentagon elected to try B-52 heavy bombers. Eventually it came the turn for crews from nearby Westover Air Force Base to go to the Western Pacific to take over the bombing of Vietcong and North Vietnamese targets. Jerry Finnerty covered the sendoff of the first contingent, complete with wives and children bidding their men farewell and a military band accompanying the loading of the transport planes and the take offs with the rousing strains of "Off we go into the wild blue yonder, off we go into the sun." Jerry's story conveyed the feeling of excitement and high spirits that permeated the base.

Buzz got caught up in the enthusiasm as he watched Jerry's piece. But he wondered: even refitted to drop conventional bombs, could B-52's, built as high-altitude nuclear bombers, be effective in a jungle war?

Judy started work as executive vice president of Buckley College Bookstores the day she and Johnny returned—all smiles and just slightly tanned—from a Caribbean honeymoon.

"I promised I'd take her back sometime to see the scenery," Johnny quipped with a knowing glance toward Judy.

Judy's parting with Myra Heywood had been amicable. "She was probably as glad to get rid of me as I was to go. The 'Issues' TV programs really bothered her."

Judy also made the announcement to Buzz at their first Friday evening dinner after the honeymoon that she would be Mrs. Buckley at work but continue as Judy Ferguson on the City Council.

"I'll be a Lucy Stoner."

"A who?"

Durham Caldwell

"A Lucy Stoner. Lucy Stone was one of the first graduates of Mount Holyoke College—back in the 1840s. She got married but scandalized polite society by keeping her maiden name."

"And did you scandalize Johnny?"

"Maybe at first, but he's getting used to it."

"She didn't tell me, Dad, till we were on the airplane. She knew I wouldn't blow the honeymoon arguing over a name."

Buzz was pleased to see Johnny take Judy's hand and squeeze it as he spoke and to watch the warm smile envelop her pretty face. Nice to see two kids so much in love with each other.

"Actually, Dad, she has an ulterior motive. She's afraid she'll lose male votes all over the city if they realize I've married her and taken her out of circulation."

Judy playfully slapped his hand.

"That's not it at all. It's a matter of principle, a matter of pride in being a woman."

Her voice softened, and she took Johnny's arm. "And it doesn't mean for a second that I'm not pleased and proud to be Johnny Buckley's wife."

Ted Kennedy's next appointment with the voters—1970—was still more than five years away. But the senator was keeping a close eye on his relations with the press. When he and Joan issued an invitation to media representatives from across the state to join them for an outing at the family compound in Hyannis Port, Buzz was quick to accept. He asked the staffer in Teddy's Boston office who took his phone call, "You don't mind if a bring a Republican newspaperwoman with me, do you?"

"No, the more the merrier. Maybe we'll convert her."

By fortunate happenstance, it was one of Leo Antonelli's out-of-state competitive shooting weekends. Buzz picked up Marsha at her apartment, and they drove to Cape Cod under a warm sun.

They followed their directions to the Kennedy compound and parked on the grass beside the narrow road as directed by a uniformed officer. Three or four dozen other cars had gotten there ahead of them.

Tumultuous Affairs

"Neighbors must love the Kennedys," mused Buzz, wondering if any driveways had been blocked.

"Everybody in Massachusetts loves the Kennedys," said Marsha, "even we Republicans."

There was a cool breeze coming off Nantucket Sound. Marsha tied on a kerchief. Buzz was glad he'd brought his windbreaker. He hung Elaine's old Brownie Hawkeye around his neck. Should be a good place to get some pictures. They pasted on the name tags that a Kennedy staffer handed them as they checked onto the grounds.

"Hello, Buzz, good to see you again. Nice to see you, Miss Antonelli. I have a lot of friends in youah paht of Woos-tah County. Glad you could come."

Teddy and Joan were at their affable best. The senator relished playing host and being in the spotlight. Joan was a little more laid back but seemed to be enjoying herself. Teddy was still walking with a cane. He looked almost boyish with his trim frame and his dark brown hair blown down over his forehead. He had on a sleeveless sweater over his open-collar shirt and a brown corduroy blazer over that. Joan wore dark glasses and a floppy, wide brimmed pink hat to protect her eyes from the sun and a pink cable-knit sweater to ward off the onshore breeze.

Teddy and Joan had commandeered the entire family compound. Food and drink were plentiful. Kennedy retainers like Joe O'Reilly from back home manned the grills, which turned out a steady if sometimes overcooked supply of hot dogs and hamburgers. Others, like Joe's wife Mary Lou, led tours through the houses. The *grande dame* herself, the frail but smiling Rose Kennedy, made a brief afternoon appearance on her veranda to wave at the guests. Buzz got her in one of his snapshots.

Buzz and Marsha were in the small group which followed Teddy's slow steps down to the family pier for a ride in his sailboat. A little boy in bathing trunks was playing in the sand near the pier.

"Hello, John-John, how ya doin'?" asked Uncle Ted. John-John barely looked up. He was too busy with his sand toys. Buzz snapped a picture.

Durham Caldwell

A couple of women in the group let out a gasp as they recognized the swimsuit-clad woman coming out of the water as Jackie Kennedy, John-John's mother.

Lewis Bay was smooth as glass. The senator, carefully stowing his cane in beside him, took a boatful of media people on a short cruise, then went back for a second boatload. John F. Kennedy Jr. was still playing in the sand as Buzz and Marsha walked back to the compound.

After Teddy hobbled up from the pier, he became a vociferous cheerleader for first one side, then the other, in a game of touch football in progress on one of the spacious lawns. He acted as if he would like nothing better than to be playing in the game.

Too soon, Buzz thought, it was time to leave if Marsha was to get home before Leo returned from his shooting competition. Because of the number of people clustering around Teddy and Joan, they decided to leave as unobtrusively as they could, but Teddy saw them going. He came over to shake hands and to accept their thanks for a wonderful day. Spotting the Brownie camera hanging from Buzz's neck, he hailed Joan and Mary Lou O'Reilly and had Mary Lou snap some pictures of him and Joan with Buzz and Marsha.

A nice day, Buzz and Marsha agreed, as he headed the car into Sunday afternoon Cape Cod traffic. Nice couple, Ted and Joan.

13

Bobby and Lenora Clark started a local chapter of CORE—the Congress for Racial Equality. Despite the support their post-Selma agenda was getting from the Reverend Doctor Shoemaker, they sensed some hesitancy among old line rank-and-file NAACP members and other Negro pastors to move as fast as they wanted to move.

Early in the summer, the Clarks shifted their emphasis away from the schools following a Saturday night incident at the Golden Lounge, a Central City nightclub. Police, getting a complaint of noise and brawling outside the club, sent two squad cars. The lounge had just closed, and several hundred people filled the streets *en route* to their homes or their cars. Alarmed by the size of the crowd, the first police on the scene called for extra officers. What happened after that was a matter of contention.

Those who left the club first agreed there were a couple of brawlers on the sidewalk but said that they were pulled apart by friends and sent on their separate ways. Police claimed they broke up a brawl in progress and arrested two men. Sergeant Michael Davitt Murray, ranking officer at the scene, said the whole crowd was unruly and uncooperative. "We couldn't get 'em to move along." There was some pushing and shoving—and disagreement on who started it.

The nightclubbers claimed the police were unnecessarily rough and unnecessarily rude and that most of the arrests were unjustified, that the only reason for them was failure to move fast enough to satisfy the officers. Some officers swung night sticks. At least three of the nightclubbers were banged up bad enough to require emergency room attention.

As luck would have it, Bobby and Lenora Clark were in the nightclub crowd, but on the far edge, away from the spot where police swung their sticks.

Durham Caldwell

The Reverend Doctor Shoemaker called a Monday evening community meeting in his church sanctuary. Emotions were running high. Buzz was glad he hadn't brought along a cameraman. In fact, Bobby Clark protested to Jimmie Shoemaker about "that white reporter sittin' down in the front row."

A murmur went through the packed church. Buzz estimated the crowd was ninety-nine percent Negro. Jimmie Shoemaker held up a hand for quiet. "I've known Buzz Buckley for a long time." It was his most reassuring pulpit voice. "If all the reporters were like him, we wouldn't have any problems with the media."

At Jimmie Shoemaker's invitation, Bobby Clark mounted the steps to the pulpit "to fill us in on what really happened outside the Golden Lounge." The clergyman emphasized the "really." In other words, Buzz interpreted, don't believe what the media have been telling you.

The way Bobby Clark told it, the nightclubbers were peacefully leaving the lounge. "Suddenly po-lice cars is comin' in from every di-rection. Po-lice is jumpin' outta the cars wavin' their billy clubs, smashin' heads, and yellin' for everybody to git on outta there and go home."

This was an even more dramatic account of the episode, Buzz realized, than the ones the eye witnesses who were up close had given the TV news reporters. More dramatic, he wondered, but how accurate?

Bobby Clark concluded his account with a question. "And do you know who the po-liceman was who was leadin' the charge? The one who musta give the order to crack those black skulls? None other than Sergeant Murray, who just happens to be the brother of the chief of po-lice!"

The Reverend Doctor Shoemaker stood up. "We kno-o-ow Sergeant Murray beats people!" He drew out the "know" to twice its normal length.

Buzz had been reporting police news in Riverbridge for fifteen years. He knew there were some bad apples in the department. But this was the first time he had heard a bad word about Mike Murray.

Did Jimmie Shoemaker know what he was talking about? Or was he talking through his hat?

The meeting agreed to the naming of the Reverend Doctor Shoemaker, the Clarks, and a couple of other activists to draw up a list of "demands" to serve on the mayor and the Police Commission.

The "demands" got a cold reception at City Hall. "The Reverend Doctor Shoemaker knows I've always been willing to talk with anybody," Mayor McCann told the news media, "but you don't start a responsible conversation by making 'demands.'"

On a Tuesday morning, Bobby and Lenora Clark led about two dozen demonstrators down the hill from the Central City to the steps of City Hall. Some of the group carried hand-lettered signs: "STOP POLICE BRUTALITY"; "ENOUGH IS ENOUGH"; "WE GOT OUR OWN SELMA"; "END RACIAL IMBALANCE"; "CITY HALL AINT LISTENIN." Jimmie Shoemaker had objected to the last one on grounds the marchers should set an example by using correct grammar, but Bobby Clark insisted that this way it would attract more attention.

There had been civil rights marches in the past, but Bobby Clark told the TV cameras and the newspaper reporter that this one was different. "We gonna stay here on these steps till the city ad-dresses the problems of po-lice brutality and *de facto* school segregation. This what you call a vigil. It goin' on day and night, night and day, till the city resolve these problems."

"You're damned lucky it's a warm, sunny day," observed Jerry Finnerty, never reticent about trying to get a rise out of an inter-viewee.

But Bobby Clark knew Jerry Finnerty's style and was ready for him.

"Yes, Mister Finnerty, the good Lawd be smilin' on us. But if he send rain or hail or sleet, we still be here—like the postman makin' his rounds. And you know somethin' else, Mister Finnerty? You be here too cuz you don't wanta miss the news. And I gonna save my biggest announcement for the middle o' that first sleet storm. And I gonna give it to you ex-clusive—because you so damned sympathetic to our little vigil."

The little vigil grew to fifty strong at the end of the work day and swelled to as many as seventy during the evening when Bobby Clark made a speech and Lenora led the group in singing freedom songs. The Reverend Doctor Shoemaker showed up briefly during the early evening, made a short talk complimenting those who had turned out, shook some hands, and went home. The Police Department sent two uniformed officers to keep a watchful eye on the vigil—one white officer, one Negro officer.

At sunrise Wednesday, twenty protesters were still on the steps. Numbers fluctuated throughout the day and evening and again on Thursday. Those keeping the vigil most faithfully began to look tired but showed no signs of breaking it off. Nor was there any sign that the city was about to take steps to meet their demands. But they were getting media coverage: interviews, stories in the paper and on TV and radio every day.

Police kept the same ratio of officers observing the vigil—one white and, despite the department's limited number of minority officers, one Negro. Buzz wondered if the chief was consciously responding to Jim Foster's call for "more visible assignments" for Negro policemen.

Adding to the tensions as the vigil went into its third day was news from the other side of the country, where protests fueled by racial grievances had also been taking place. Shooting had broken out in Watts, a predominantly Negro section of Los Angeles. Comedian Dick Gregory, who had been appealing to a crowd to go home, was hit by a bullet in the leg. He was among one hundred people injured.

Locally, Buzz was beginning to wonder if the station should continue to cover the vigil on every newscast. The stories were starting to sound the same. Even Bobby Clark's rhetoric had begun to have a sameness to it. But Thursday night, as Buzz watched the eleven o'clock news at home, the vigil led off the newscast. Happy Hooper and photographer Benny Goodreau had been johnny-on-the-spot for a new development. As the protesters swung into their mid-evening round of freedom songs, jeers and hoots greeted them from across

Tumultuous Affairs

the street from the edge of City Hall Park. Benny's camera picked up City Councilor Domenico DiTotola and a gaggle of tough-looking young white men on the sidewalk, with DDT grinning broadly as the young men shouted such remarks as "Go back to Africa!" and "Abe Lincoln made a mistake!"

Buzz watched in taut suspense, as TV viewers all over the city must have been doing, as the camera showed one of the two officers on duty calling for reinforcements from a nearby public phone—and Bobby Clark sending a dozen sign-carrying young people, male and female, across the street to parade with their signs right in the faces of the young toughs.

"Worried police officers," Happy's narration came over the TV set, "herded the sign carriers back across the street to the City Hall steps after nothing more than an exchange of words with the group on the sidewalk. But it was easily the tensest few minutes since this vigil began on Tuesday."

Buzz was at his desk the next morning, catching up on accumulated paperwork. His phone rang. Linda, H.B.'s shapely secretary—the woman Jerry Finnerty had nicknamed "the Employee Benefits"—was summoning Buzz to H.B.'s office.

Buzz had found over the years that one of the pluses of working for H.B. was there was very little second guessing. Very little praise, but very little second guessing either. Buzz, with the people working under him, chose the stories to cover, chose the way to cover them, chose where to place them in the newscast. H.B. was station manager for both the radio and TV stations, as well as president and general manager for the whole operation, and busy enough with all those duties that he didn't have much time to think about news—except for occasional moneysaving gambits like "no more trips to Boston."

But as Buzz plunged his news department even deeper into the city's growing racial tensions, H.B. had begun to get restless. He had begun to say things like "Did we really need Jimmie Shoemaker on again last night?" "Don't you think people are tired of hearing this Bobby Clark blast the cops and the School Committee?" "Aren't we really whipping things up when we keep covering this racial bullshit?"

Durham Caldwell

And the topper: "This 'Issues '65' program I let you and that blonde daughter-in-law of yours talk me into is bad enough. Do we have to cover those things on the news, too?" Buzz had a premonition that on this Friday morning H.B. wanted to talk about coverage of the City Hall vigil.

H.B. was sitting behind his ornate mahogany desk, the only wooden desk in the building. Seated to his right was the yes-man program director, Al Maroney. To his left was sales manager Hy Golden. Golden was usually a pretty good guy, his only major faults being a fondness for cheap cigars and the football Giants. But seated beside the other two, he struck Buzz on this particular morning as one of a panel of three hanging judges.

Buzz took the chair placed for him in front of the desk. The defendant's seat, he thought to himself.

Buzz found out immediately that his premonition was correct. H.B. was leadoff man for the prosecution. "Buzz, you know I've had some questions about how we're covering civil rights and these damned militants. I was worried we were going overboard. Let me just cite a little chapter and verse.

"These jigaboos sit in at the School Department. What—a dozen of 'em? You're down there with your goddam camera and microphone interviewing 'em while the cops are hauling 'em out of the building. You're interviewing goddam criminal trespassers on our TV station!"

"H.B., they weren't jigaboos. They were nine Negroes and three whites."

"Nine niggers and three nigger lovers—what's the difference?"

Buzz knew there was no way he could win this confrontation. He sat in grim silence as H.B. moved on to the second count of the indictment. "This frigging march downtown this week. This time, what—two dozen of 'em? And you make it the number-one story on the news.

"They've been on the City Hall steps ever since. A goddam vigil against racial injustice they call it. Nothing's happened since Tuesday. But they're on the goddam early news every night—then you come back with a new story for eleven.

Tumultuous Affairs

"And Buzz, that's no high and mighty moral crusade they're running down there. They've been fornicating in the shrubbery at night—fornicating right there in front of City Hall—after your goddam news camera goes home. How do I know? Because the city solicitor told me so last night at the club. The evidence is there in the goddam grass in the morning. They don't even clean up their rubbers after themselves.

"And this is on top of all the bullshit that's gone on before. Jim Foster's push to get Negroes behind store counters. Do you realize how many customers that would drive away? The bullshit about schools in the colored neighborhoods being inferior and all this other commie crap!

"A little is okay, but we're overdoing it."

Buzz's face, ears, and neck were burning, but he kept his mouth shut.

"Al," H.B. said to the program director, "read him those figures."

"Sure, H.B. I've gone back through the scripts for the past three weeks—both newscasts. And I've counted up the total number of stories you've done, Buzz, on civil rights, race relations, the sit-ins, and so forth—and compared those with the total number of stories on the air.

"Now, Buzz, as you well know, Negroes make up about fifteen percent of the population here in Riverbridge. But the city is just one part of our coverage area. I've checked the census figures very carefully against the contours on our coverage map." He pointed to the map with its elongated, irregular coverage area extending from Northern Connecticut up into Vermont which hung on the wall behind H.B.'s desk.

"We have two hundred and twenty-five thousand households in the coverage area. Now given an average of two-point-two family members per household, that means approximately half a million people."

What the hell is he getting at? wondered Buzz.

"And in our overall coverage area, the Negro population is only four percent. Not the fifteen percent that it is here in the city. And yet in those three weeks that I counted stories, seventeen percent—almost one in five—were Negro stories. Given the makeup of our overall audience, that's four times as many—almost five times as many—as we should've run."

Buzz was seething. How he kept his famous temper under control was a mystery even to him. He wanted to call Al Maroney "a frigging idiot," or worse, but he didn't.

"H.B.," he said in a voice as even as he could keep it, though he knew it had an edge on it, "race relations is the biggest news story in the country right now. Los Angeles is exploding. The whole damned country is a tinderbox."

"All the more reason not to give it so much air time."

"All the more reason to let people know what the local angles are to the big national story. We're very careful not to use inflammatory language on the air."

"But you are using inflammatory stuff! The school superintendent pointed out to me last night at the club—our stories on schools in the Central City have been grossly inaccurate!"

So that was it—what Jim Foster called "the white power structure" was trying to put a lid on the news.

"H.B., the superintendent and your other fat-cat friends at the Mattawampus Club"—and again Buzz kept his voice as even as he could, even as he saw H.B. begin to redden all the way up to the shiny spot under the thinning hair at the top of his head—"they had better get their heads out of the sand. This is 1965, not 1865. I've been in those schools. Everything Jimmie Shoemaker and Bobby Clark are saying about them is true! They're a dumping ground for lousy teachers. The roofs leak. The floors and stairs are a mess. Some of the books go back before the war. The superintendent ought to be working on the problems, not bitching about us."

Before H.B. could bluster out a response, Hy Golden pulled the cigar out of his mouth and spoke for the first time.

"Buzz, it's not just the fat cats at the Mattawampus Club. You know what they're calling us all up and down Main Street? 'The Nigger Station!' First that 'Issues '65' program—and now this racial business all over the news, day in, day out. We lost three accounts this week"—he punctuated his remarks by jabbing forward with his cigar—"including Old Lady Heywood at the bookstore. Why? Because they say we're giving too much time to Jimmie Shoemaker and the City Hall vigil and all that other race relations/racial tension stuff. I had one guy tell me right to my face that when he wants to get news for white people, he switches to the competition.

"Buzz, I know you want to do the right thing covering the news, but you're hitting me and my salesmen right in the pocketbook."

Before H.B. could follow up, Linda the secretary stuck her head into the office. "Buzz, the newsroom says you have a very urgent phone call."

Buzz looked at H.B.

"Go ahead, take it. This has already gone on longer than I wanted it to. I gotta go to lunch. Buzz, you do some hard thinking over the weekend. We'll talk some more Monday morning."

The phone caller was Rowdy. He was speaking in a low voice as if to make sure nobody nearby could hear what he was saying.

"Buzz, Big Jim wanted me to give you a tip. Strictly off the record." The way Rowdy twirled the "r's" in his hint of a brogue heightened Buzz's anticipation for what must be a good story if the mayor was taking this way of passing on the tip.

He restrained himself from mimicking Rowdy's brogue. "Okay, Rowdy, off the record."

"They're gonna move those demonstrators off the City Hall steps at five o'clock. The Law Department's drawin' up a paper. They'll have to vacate or be arrested for trespassin'. That bit with DDT and his ilk last night was the final straw. His Honor's afraid that if Bobby Clark and his bunch stay there another night, real trouble could break out.

"And Buzz, the mayor's not tellin' any other reporters, just you."

Buzz put the Monday showdown with H.B. temporarily out of his head. Five o'clock was nearly two hours beyond the normal deadline for getting newsfilm into the processor for the six-thirty news. There would have to be some major adjustments in their regular way of doing business. And they would have to have other material on standby, ready to use on the newscast, in case the City Hall story proved to be a fizzle. Buzz wondered what H.B.'s friend, the city solicitor, was coming up with to justify ending the vigil. Didn't the First Amendment give Bobby Clark and everybody else freedom of speech and assembly? Trespassing? On the steps of a public building?

14

The newspaper must have gotten wind of the impending breakup of the vigil from another source, maybe the Police Department. Two reporters and a photographer from the paper were in front of City Hall when Buzz pulled into the adjacent alleyway around four-thirty with two TV news cameramen. But Buzz was pleased to see that Big Jim had kept the news from reaching the other broadcast outlets. The earliest that newspaper readers could get the story would be tomorrow morning.

Meanwhile, the teletype in the newsroom had been chattering with news of racial violence in Chicago as well as Los Angeles.

The twenty-five or so protesters at the top of the City Hall steps looked down with curiosity as Benny Goodreau went about the business of setting up a sound camera. They knew this wasn't the time the TV people had been coming by for interviews. Stan Wlodyka, the other cameraman, stood ready with his hand-held Bolex silent camera. Police were in the same strength they had been in since the vigil started—two uniformed officers, one Negro and one white, keeping an eye on things from sidewalk level.

There were sounds of surprise from some of the female demonstrators as a small police convoy pulled up at the curb: two cruisers and two patrol wagons. Experienced local reporters didn't call them "paddy wagons" because they knew the term infuriated the Irish-American police chief as well as the mayor.

Four uniformed officers got out of the first cruiser. Six more alighted from the two patrol wagons. The driver and front seat passenger of the second cruiser sprang out and opened the rear doors for the chief and the captain of the four-to-midnight shift. Buzz glanced at his watch. It was four-forty-five. He took the tape recorder microphone out of its case and plugged it in.

Durham Caldwell

Chief Robert Emmet Murray was in full uniform—resplendent in gold braid, the four stars of a full general on each shoulder—the uniform he normally wore only at mayoral inaugurations, the Policeman's Ball, and departmental funerals. Captain Arthur Griffith Murray Jr., the chief's nephew with a little gold braid of his own, carried a bullhorn. There were five other Murrays in the department—a lieutenant, Sergeant Mike Murray, and three patrolmen. All except the lieutenant were close relatives of the chief.

Chief Murray strode halfway up the steps, stopping—Buzz noted—gratifyingly close to Benny's sound camera. His nephew switched on the bullhorn, tested it with a low cough, and handed it to the chief. Benny adjusted his camera's zoom lens. Buzz got as close as he could to the chief without blocking Benny's camera shot, holding in his same hand the sound camera microphone and the mike from his tape recorder.

"You people on the steps, give me your attention!" the chief commanded as his amplified voice echoed off the steps, the statues, and the marble columns of City Hall Plaza. "You have the right to assemble peacefully on these premises during the normal office hours of eight-fifteen a.m. to four-forty-five p.m., Monday through Friday. Persons found loitering on these premises at other times will be subject to arrest for trespassing. In the interests of public safety and law and order, I direct each and everyone of you to remove yourselves from these premises by five p.m. Any persons remaining will be arrested for trespassing!"

Bobby Clark moved to the front edge of the little plaza at the top of the steps. He had no bullhorn, but he had no trouble making himself heard. Buzz again held up both his microphones. "There be a number of in'ividuals congregatin' on the other side of the street from us all week. But I don't hear the chief of po-lice directin' no orders at those in'ividuals who still be congregated there. They not been asked to move. The chief di-rect his remarks only at the civil rights group. We gonna ask these folk up here if they wanna move. Some will. And I assure you, some ain't gonna move."

Two of the older women and a couple with a young child left the steps.

Tumultuous Affairs

Exactly at the hour of five, the fourteen uniformed policemen on the sidewalk moved in a skirmish line up the long flight of pink granite steps toward the remaining demonstrators. The protesters shot glances of encouragement at each other and prepared to go limp. At that instant, the huge bronze front door of City Hall swung open and out marched another two dozen uniformed officers—this group wearing white plastic helmets and carrying riot sticks two feet long. Their appearance took demonstrators as well as onlookers by complete surprise. Commanded by Sergeant Michael Davitt Murray, the chief's brother, this was the newly-formed Special Squad, which nobody outside the department even knew was in existence.

Officers hustled two young women down the steps, one officer on each arm. Lenora Clark went limp. Three officers struggled under her considerable weight and called for help from a fourth. They half carried her, half dragged her down the steps. Helmeted officers picked up and carried two more.

Benny was swinging his sound camera around on its tripod to follow the progress of police carrying or dragging demonstrators down the steps to the patrol wagons, then swinging back to pick up the next bunch. Buzz held out the camera mike to pick up the natural sound. Stan Wlodyka raced up and down the steps grinding away with his Bolex.

Chief Murray and Captain Murray stood at the side of the steps, watching carefully and quietly encouraging their men. Buzz heard the chief tell his brother, the sergeant, "Do it right. I don't want any more wrenched backs!" The officers responded in some cases by waiting until they had one policeman for each limb, in other cases by dragging rather than carrying a protester down the granite steps.

Suddenly, from the midst of those left at the top of the steps, Buzz could hear what he knew was Bobby Clark's powerful baritone voice sing out the first line of "We Shall Overcome." The others still on the steps joined in, hesitantly at first—"We shall overcome . . ." And then from the two patrol wagons at the curb, Bobby was answered by a full-throated chorus—women's voices from one patrol wagon, Lenora's voice unmistakably among them, men's voices from the other—"We shall overcome some da-a-a-y."

Durham Caldwell

Four officers half-carried, half-dragged Bobby Clark's limp body down the steps, his hindquarters going thump-thump-thump against the granite, but he still sang with the others, "Deep in my heart, I do believe, we shall overcome some day."

As the loaded patrol wagons rolled off toward police headquarters, the voices poured out of them, "We are not afraid, we are not afraid, we are not afraid toda-a-a-y . . ."

Saturday night, Buzz got wind of another march. He nominated Stan Wlodyka to help him cover it. Stan might grump a lot, but with five kids he rarely turned down overtime.

They caught up with Bobby Clark leading a group of about one hundred and fifty Negroes and whites from the Central City to City Hall Park. Bolstering bailed-out veterans of the arrests on the City Hall steps were recruits from both inside and outside the city, some from as far away as Hartford and Providence. Because they had no parade permit, they kept carefully to the sidewalks. Marshals wearing white armbands torn from an old pillowcase at NAACP headquarters just prior to the march enforced Bobby Clark's edict to cross busy intersections only with the light. "We ain't gonna give 'em no excuse to turn us around," explained Bobby.

They sang freedom songs as they marched. Two cruisers shadowed them from a discreet distance. When the marchers reached the park, two foot patrolmen replaced the cruisers. There was more singing at the park. Bobby Clark and some of the others made speeches. The Reverend Doctor Shoemaker appeared briefly, shook a lot of hands, but left without speaking. The number of policemen keeping a wary eye on the proceedings from outside the park's ornamental fence grew to half a dozen.

Midway through the evening, a squad car pulled up outside the park. Two helmeted officers jumped out the front doors to open the rear doors for the chief and for Captain Griffith Murray. This time the chief was in his usual rumpled business suit. Accompanied by his uniformed nephew, he made his way to the center of the crowd to speak with Bobby Clark. Buzz and a newspaper reporter tried to follow the chief into the park, but the white-helmeted Sergeant Mike

Tumultuous Affairs

Murray barred their path. They were too far away to hear what appeared to be an animated conversation between the chief and Bobby Clark. The chief and the captain climbed back into the cruiser without comment and pulled away.

Buzz directed Stan to take the evening's film back to the station to get it processed for the eleven o'clock news. "Leave your Bolex here, and show me how to use it, just in case something happens before you get back."

Stan put in a new hundred-foot reel, refreshed Buzz on how to sight the camera and pull the trigger—something he hadn't done since his early days in television news—and how to wind it when the spring ran down.

Buzz was getting bored and wondering if he should pack it in and go home. The competition had departed long since. It appeared some of the demonstrators were getting ready to bed down for the night.

Then, almost as if on cue, two cruisers and two patrol wagons pulled up alongside the park and disgorged a dozen uniformed officers. Sergeant Murray's white helmets, who had marched out the front door of City Hall the afternoon before, marched out of a side street on the other side of the park.

Buzz hoisted the strap of the cumbersome light pack onto his left shoulder as the two groups of officers converged silently on the demonstrators. He turned on the light, squinted through the eyepiece of the Bolex, and pulled the trigger as the first group of officers moved toward him and the patrol wagons—grasping some demonstrators by the arms, carrying some like limp sacks of flour, dragging others along the asphalt crosswalk. As they moved by him, Buzz heard one of the officers say something to another about "trespassing in the park."

Buzz frantically rewound the camera. It was happening so fast that he didn't know whether he was getting anything or not. He felt a tap on his shoulder. His first impulse: it's the cops—they're arresting me for trespassing. But it was Stan Wlodyka, returning from the station and reclaiming his camera to continue the filming.

Durham Caldwell

Captain Murray appeared at curbside to give Buzz and the newspaper reporter an explanation. "If they didn't try to sleep in the park, it woulda been okay. The chief chased down the city solicitor and got a rulin' campin' in a public park violates city ordinances."

Just as the last demonstrators were being hauled away, the officer in the nearest cruiser ran up to Griffith Murray. "Cap, all hell's set ta break loose in the Central City! Big mob in Triangle Park!"

"If you guys come," the captain shouted over his shoulder to Buzz and the other reporter, "keep the hell out of the way."

As Buzz and Stan drove toward the Central City, police traffic and fire alarms vied for space on their scanner.

"Car Four reports about a hundred people there in the Triangle, Cap!"

"All Fire Department cars! Telephone alarm for the Central City A&P!"

"Fire, this is police. Civilian tells us somebody just threw a fire bomb through the window at Henry's Variety!"

"Deputy Chief to Fire! This A&P is goin' like hell! Send me two more water companies!"

Stan, who was driving, looked at Buzz for directions.

"Stop here!" Buzz commanded. "Now swap seats! I'll drive. You be ready to shoot!"

The A&P was indeed going like hell, the whole interior a mass of flames. Two engine companies and a hose company were pouring water into it. Two more companies which had just arrived were trying to locate hydrants to hook up to. Another stream of water poured down from an aerial ladder as flames ate through the roof and leaped into the night sky.

Stan shot up the rest of his roll of film, maybe a minute's worth, and reloaded as Buzz led the way over a side street to the Triangle. From a distance they could see a crowd milling in the triangular park which formed the center of the neighborhood business district. Approaching on foot, they saw that cruisers ringed the park. The crowd appeared to be mostly young people and solidly black. They carried hand-lettered signs that illustrated how fast news can travel: "FREEDOM OF SPEECH!" "LET MY BROTHERS GO!" Captain Murray, bullhorn in hand, was striding into the crowd with his white-helmeted uncle and several other officers right on his heels.

"Now listen, everybody," the captain was saying over the bullhorn. Buzz was surprised at how calm he sounded. "We had some problems downtown tonight. A few folks—a lot of 'em outta town agitators—tried to camp in the park, and that's a violation of city ordinances."

He spoke slowly to let his listeners absorb the impact of his words as they reverberated around the Triangle and off the nearby storefronts. "Now this is a city park right here. Normally you could stay out here all night so long as you aren't campin'. But we've had two fires up here tonight. At least one of 'em's a real bad one. Now I know you're all peace-lovin' folks. Nonviolent, right?"

A small chorus went up, "That's right!"

"I don't want you to get messed up with any troublemakers out there startin' fires. So I'm gonna urge everybody to go home. It's midnight. Nobody out here to watch you demonstrate anyway. You wanta carry signs, come back tomorra in the daylight."

As the crowd melted away, Buzz put a question to Captain Murray. "What would you have done, Griff, if they wouldn't go home?"

"Call in every on-duty cop in the city, and pray like hell."

The Molotov cocktail hurled through the window of Henry's Variety, a small white-owned store on a side street, burned itself out with no damage beyond the smashed window and a charred circle in the middle of the floor.

By the time Buzz and Stan got back to the A&P, firefighters were at last getting the upper hand. But the grizzled and sooty-faced deputy fire chief was calling the big food store a total loss. "And I don't mind tellin' you," he volunteered, "it pisses me off no end that my guys hafta miss their sleep—let alone risk their lives—because some good-for-nothin' nigger bastard has a hair across his ass because they arrested some of his good-for-nothin' buddies! And you can quote me on that if you want to!"

Buzz felt they had plenty of news without the fire chief's salty comments. Three major stories in two days—no, four, counting dispersal of the crowd at the Triangle—and the other TV station nowhere in sight for any of them. That would help even the score, Buzz thought, for the times they've creamed us. This time, the competition's news anchor could read wire copy just like Baker Broadcasting's people were doing for the new violence in L.A. and Chicago—or rewrite from the newspaper.

But then he wondered: will H.B. climb all over me again Monday morning for all these new "Negro stories" from over the weekend? Hell, you can't ignore stories like this unless you're as stupid, or as unlucky, as the competition. But as he thought about it, he wondered for the first time if there might be some truth in what H.B. and Hy Golden were telling him. Was he putting Jimmie Shoemaker and Bobby Clark on camera more often than good judgment dictated? Did he overplay the sit-in at the School Department and that tiny City Hall vigil? Was the newsroom taking sides with Jim Foster and the Urban League against Main Street businesspeople?

He wrestled with the question most of Sunday except when he was viewing the previous night's film and writing script for it. Should he stick to his guns right down the line? And if he did, would he be out on his ear? Would he think more of himself for standing up for principle and being heaved out of the job—or for finding some way to compromise which would not strip him of his ability to influence news coverage? Even after sleeping on it Sunday night, he wasn't sure. As he had done at many other critical junctures in his life, he resolved to wait for H.B.'s Monday morning summons and to play it by ear.

The summons never came. Buzz wondered if the boss's friends at the Mattawampus Club had enjoyed the station's weekend coverage—with all those niggers and nigger-loving whites hauled off to the police lockup—and urged him to keep it up. Had the fire at the A&P convinced him at last that the city really did have to look closely at race relations? Or was the new talk of a massive protest march the following weekend persuading him to keep the old news director on the job at least till then?

Hy Golden didn't say anything either. Buzz noted from the daily logs that Hy and his salesmen seemed to find other accounts to replace any that had really canceled.

Tumultuous Affairs

As for that massive march, the preliminaries alone set Riverbridge on edge probably as it had never been since the final raid in the last of the French and Indian wars. CORE—the Congress for Racial Equality—was recruiting marchers from all over the Northeast to protest the arrests on the City Hall steps and in the park. There were predictions of as many as five thousand marchers. Mayor McCann issued a formal statement which took note of the tensions in the city and urged demonstrators to stay home—but which also begrudgingly acknowledged "the right of CORE or anybody else" to practice freedom of speech and assembly.

But then Chief Robert Emmet Murray weighed in with a public appeal to the mayor not to grant a parade permit. The proposed parade would not be freedom of speech, he charged, but "incitement to riot." He told the television cameras: "With the tensions that exist in this city right now, our police force is stretched to its very limit. There's no way we could protect the safety of marchers or spectators in the numbers that Mister Clark and his associates are predicting."

The mayor backpedaled. "I certainly have to consider the advice of the chief."

Privately Big Jim told Buzz one morning in his office, "The sad thing is that Robert Emmet Murray and every one of his brothers—Arthur Griffith, Michael Davitt, John Redmond, Daniel O'Connell—bear the names of great Irish patriots. These were men who worked long years and were willing to risk their lives for the freedom and the civil rights of their countrymen. But the chief has no sympathy for black people trying to do the same here in America.

"Partly my fault, Buzz. I've named some weak sisters to the Police Commission, and they've let the chief run the show the way he wants to. Sure he has a few Negro cops. Damn few. And remember the struggle we had trying to line him up for some simple sensitivity training? He wasn't about to let Jimmie Shoemaker tell him how to train police officers. If they'd had that training, we might have avoided that bad scene at the Golden Lounge."

Both Bobby Clark and the New England director of CORE insisted their march would be a one hundred percent peaceful protest.

Durham Caldwell

The Reverend Doctor Shoemaker chided "my old friend, the mayor" for footdragging on the parade permit. CORE threatened to take the city to court for violating citizens' constitutional rights. Chief Murray reiterated that a march would be a provocation and that he could not guarantee the protection of participants.

Jimmie Shoemaker told the TV camera that a phone caller had given him ten days to get out of town. "My wife said we can't leave now—we just got our new rug laid." It was the first bit of humor that Buzz had detected all week.

The mayor called the governor's office. Governor Volpe agreed to send in a thousand National Guardsmen to patrol the parade route and to police the site of the speaking program which would follow the march. The mayor officially proclaimed "a state of great public excitement" and ordered bars and package stores to close for the weekend.

That led to the week's second bit of humor. Domenico DiTotola, who had announced his intention to run against Mayor McCann, had to make a choice between postponing a fundraising party or holding it without liquor. He postponed, accusing the mayor and "dem civil rights people" of conspiring against him.

After the week of pre-parade tension, the march itself was an anticlimax. About a thousand participants, approximately one for every Guardsman, marched twelve abreast from the Central City to City Hall Park. They wore their Sunday best and chanted freedom songs as they marched.

Two thousand supporters awaited the marchers at the park. There were more freedom songs, some fiery speeches, and when it was all over, participants shook hands with each other, with the national guardsmen, with the local police officers, even with some of the reporters, and went home in peace. The state troopers, which the commissioner of public safety had smuggled into the local armory as reserves in case the National Guard couldn't handle things, never left the armory.

15

Thank God, we've got something else to put on the news, thought Buzz, besides rioting and looting and fighting in Vietnam. Americans were cheering the eight-day flight of astronauts Gordon Cooper and Charles Conrad in Gemini-5. Cooper, a veteran of Project Mercury, set a new individual record for time in space, eclipsing a Soviet cosmonaut's one-hundred-nineteen hours. A boost to morale in the country at a time it was needed.

Cameraman Stan Wlodyka, who was somewhat of a space buff, sat in the mobile unit listening to the latest on Gemini-5 from the all-news station in New York while Buzz stopped in at the mayor's office.

Buzz found Rowdy Hennessy in Big Jim's mahogany-paneled inner sanctum with the mayor when secretary Ginny Bruce gave him the go-ahead to go in. The two old friends were chatting amiably about old days in the Patch and the early days that both of them had shared on the City Council.

The mayor waved Buzz into one of the big red leather upholstered chairs. Buzz was reluctant to interrupt, both men were having such a good time gabbing. Eventually, at the end of a jolly story about Cowboys and Indians in the Old Brickyard, in which Robert Emmet Murray, the future chief of police, was left tied to a tree when the others went home for supper, Big Jim silenced Rowdy by holding up a hand.

"Let's find out what brings the pleasure of a call by our favorite news director."

"I just stopped in to say hello, Mister Mayor—see if you had any news. Maybe I could do a story someday with both of you on the Old Brickyard. Be a lot of fun for you as well as me. You gents keep talking. I'll be on my way."

Durham Caldwell

Big Jim held up another hand. "Hang on for a few minutes, bucko. Another old friend of yours may stop by. You might get a story out of it."

The old friend was Max Feigenson, who despite his status as president of the City Council rarely got a summons to the mayor's office except on meeting day.

Big Jim looked at Buzz. "Buzz, I know I can't hold you to it, but I'd like you to keep this off the news till tomorrow night and don't mention about our little meeting here with Mister Feigenson. Maybe you can accommodate me."

Buzz was a guest in the office. "Just as long as I don't read it in the morning paper."

"I wouldn't give those character assassins the time of day. I don't even think I'll invite them to my press conference. What do you think about that, Rowdy?"

"Serve the bastards right. Let 'em see it on television."

"I think I'll do that."

Max was getting fidgety as the byplay continued between the two old war horses.

Buzz was wondering, What's he doing—putting an urban renewal project in Max's backyard?

But Big Jim was enjoying the suspense.

"You know, Buzz, when it was that the paper turned against me? It was when the Liquor Board turned down a license for Mister Dribble-I-Mean-Dibble's brother-in-law. He had a location for a bar down by the railroad station. The Liquor Board figured they had enough licenses down there already. So they gave the license to one of Rowdy's cousins up in the Patch. Dribble never forgave me for it. Even, Max, though I assured him I never meddled with the Liquor Board. There's people on that board if I meddled with them, they'd have a resignation on my desk in the morning. Just think of the poor publicity from that.

"Now, Max, when you become mayor, you can run the Liquor Board any way you want to. But my advice is: keep your fingers out of it. If they're intelligent people, they'll know who your friends are. You won't have to tell 'em. Right, Rowdy?"

Tumultuous Affairs

"Absolutely, Jim. You never said a truer word."

Max finally got a word in. "I'll remember that when I get elected, Mister Mayor. But I've got a better chance of getting elected president. You look healthy enough to keep the office for another ten or twenty years."

The mayor smiled in gratitude at the compliment.

"Ah, flattery. It's not just we Irish, Rowdy, who have kissed the Blarney Stone. Mr. President here is also pretty good at it. But in truth, Max, what I invited you in for was to hear from my own lips that I'm not running."

Max's jaw dropped almost as precipitously as Buzz's did. Rowdy, clearly in on the secret, looked with great delight on the show of utter astonishment on the faces of the two men, who were supposed to be among the most politically astute in the city.

"No, Max, I've had it long enough. I might win again, Max, and I might not. That little itch of a Dribble doesn't bother me. Nor that bag of superheated air at the other TV station who makes his nasty remarks in front of a camera every Tuesday. A pox on both of them.

"A mayor is at the top of his strength at the end of his first term. He's made some people happy by finding them jobs. He's filled the worst holes in the streets. And there hasn't been time for people to get angry with him.

"But after that first reelection, a slo-o-o-w erosion sets in. Mister Dribble isn't the only one who thinks his brother-in-law deserves a liquor license. You miss a few holes in the streets. And how come you didn't appoint me a police commissioner? Yes, Max, a slo-o-o-w erosion.

"Sure, I think I could win another term. I'd plaster that flabby bugger DDT—wouldn't I, Rowdy? He's the only one circulating papers so far."

"Plaster him? You'd bury the baldheaded guinea bastard."

Buzz saw Max stir uncomfortably. Max didn't like ethnic epithets.

"Can you imagine him," Big Jim went on, "the mayor of a city of one hundred and forty thousand souls?"

Durham Caldwell

"Jim, he couldn't line up the vehicles for a one-car funeral," asserted Rowdy.

"The real problem, Max, is I've run out of gas. We got through this recent bit with the civil rights people. But that was probably the straw that broke the camel's back. Jimmie Shoemaker—I worked with him so closely for so many years. You were there last year, Buzz, at Atlantic City. No other mayor from Massachusetts worked as hard as I did for the civil rights plank and the Mississippi Freedom Democrats.

"This year these young Turks come back from Selma. And what Jimmie and I and Jim Foster from the Urban League have been working on for years—Dribble even called us 'the three Jimmies' because we were working so closely on one project—these young Turks are going to fix things overnight, even if they have to turn Riverbridge upside down to do it. And Jimmie Shoemaker, he goes to bat for the young Turks. The 'militants,' they call 'em. That caught me flat-footed.

"My dear wife called it 'ingratitude.' In politics we have another word for it, 'double cross.' Right, Rowdy?"

"Right as rain."

"Understand me, Max. I can't put the whole onus for giving up this lovely office"—he waved his hand around the room at the mahogany paneling, the ornate hand-carved fixtures, the oil paintings of previous mayors—"on my old friend, the Reverend Doctor Shoemaker. He was just the last straw. The fact is, Max, that for me it's no fun any more to be the mayor. Come the first week of January—what's that Japanese word, Buzz?—oh, I remember: *sayonara*. The first week of January, Max, I will say a very grateful *sayonara* to City Hall.

"And Max, if there's any doubt in your mind why I asked you to stop in twenty-four hours before my official announcement, it's because I hope you will be the next man to sit in this chair."

Buzz by now had suspected that Big Jim was about to urge Max to run for mayor. But Max seemed to have been caught off guard again despite Big Jim's gradual buildup to this new surprise.

"Max, I'll give you as much support, or as little support, as you want me to give you. I'll come out in the open—although endorsements these days don't seem to be worth any more than—what was

Tumultuous Affairs

it, Rowdy, that Vice President Garner said about the vice presidency: not worth a bucket of warm spit?"

"That's the way they printed it in the paper, Jim, but you and I know he didn't say 'spit.'"

"I'll come out in the open if you want me to," continued Big Jim. "If you think that would hurt more than it would help, I will just give you all the support I can *sub rosa*." His brogue made "*sub rosa*" sound like a Gaelic phrase.

Max finally got out a few incredulous words. "You'd support me, Mayor, a Republican?" Max went far enough back to remember that it was Big Jim McCann who broke the Republican monopoly on the mayor's office in that bitter partisan campaign right after the war.

"Max, your Grand Old Party, as some of the older Republicans like to call it, had a stranglehold on this city for eighty years. But Rowdy and I, and some buckos who learned in the Army and the Navy how to fight, changed all that nearly twenty years ago."

"The Yankees didn't realize it," interjected Rowdy, "but all durin' the Depression, when they were havin' one or two kids or none at all, the Irish were still breedin' like rabbits. The Depression started here, remember, back in the early twenties. We ate a lotta stew. We all had patches on our pants—that's how the Patch really got its name: from the patches on our clothes. But when the servicemen came back from the war, a lotta these little Irish bunnies were votin' age."

"And don't forget our allies from the Polish parish and the Italian parish," said the mayor. "Together we turned the Republicans out of City Hall."

"Amen!" said Rowdy

"Now the way you Republicans started to sneak back in, Max, as you well know, was to change the ballot to nonpartisan. But I didn't oppose the referendum because I knew by then there's no Republican way to patch a hole in the street. You patch 'em the same way the Democrats do. At the city level, the only difference between parties was who controlled the jobs. I figured I could do that just as well nonpartisan as I could do it as a Democrat. Give me a bigger field to choose from.

Durham Caldwell

"People know I'm a Democrat, Max. They know you're a Republican. But the city's officially nonpartisan now. You never voted against the things I sent up to the council because I was a Democrat. I am grateful for the way you've supported most of my programs. And though it hurts me to concede it—probably hurts Rowdy, too—you're the best man on the council, barring of course himself. And he refuses to run for mayor—I asked him already. You're the one to take over.

"Max," said the pink-faced, white-maned mayor, "they don't call me Big Jim because I'm six foot. They call me Big Jim because I have a big heart. And right now, in talking with you, I have the good of the city at heart.

"Max, the filing deadline is just a week away. Mister DDT is a lightweight. Just ask Rowdy here. Rowdy was the heavyweight boxing champ in the Old Brickyard. And DDT knows he still packs a wallop. You'll have no problem with DDT. But Max, the big business folk, Money Bags Jardine and his rich friends from the Mattawampus Club—where you would be about as welcome as Rowdy and me—they'll run a candidate. And they'll finance him. They've been itching to run a candidate ever since I beat that banker for my first term—I don't do their bidding like some of the old Republican mayors—but they feared they couldn't beat me. Now they'll try it. They may not do it in the open, but they'll have a man in there, mark my words. And big bucks to back him.

"It won't be easy. The paper will be against you because you're a good man. There are more anuses on that newspaper than a busy proctologist sees in six months."

"Ah, Your Honor, if Sister James Mary could hear you now," interjected Rowdy. He explained to Max and Buzz, "She was our eighth grade teacher."

"No, Max, it won't be easy," the mayor continued. "But you have a good organization even if it is overly heavy with Republicans. With a twenty-four-hour head start, you have a good shot at beating whoever Money Bags and his crowd put up. Will you do it?"

Max was wary.

"What would you expect in return?"

Tumultuous Affairs

"Good government, Max, good government."

Linda, "the Employee Benefits," summoned Buzz to H.B.'s office. This time he was alone. He looked very pleased.

"Buzz, I know you're a hard-ass newsman. But I want to talk to you off the record."

Buzz nodded. He's the boss—what the hell else can I do?

"I'm going to run for mayor!"

Buzz could hardly believe what his ears had just heard. H.B.—mayor? Why not governor?

"God, H.B., if you want to be mayor, shouldn't you have a couple of terms on the City Council first?"

"Well, I thought of that—but we figure now's the time to go for it. Big Jim's out of it. You know, get the mayor's office back in the right hands."

"We?"

"Yeah, we got together and set up a political committee last night at the club."

So, Big Jim was right on the money, thought Buzz.

"We talked for a long time about the right candidate. You know, hashed over the pluses and minuses of this guy and that one. Finally Money Bags says, 'H.B., you're the guy. People love you for those commentaries you do on television. And we can't think of a single negative thing.'

"Well, of course, I was flattered. I told them I wanted to think about it overnight, talk it over with the wife, and so forth. Well, Miriam thought the idea was great. So I just called Money Bags and told him I'm in.

"Now, Buzz, I don't expect any special treatment from the newsroom. In fact, I told 'em last night that our news department would play it straight, same as it would with any candidate. But Buzz, I want one favor. Filing deadline's Tuesday. We're gonna file at the very last minute, five minutes of five, because we don't want to tip our hand. You know, I might scare people away. Our best shot against that Jewish lawyer, Max What's-His-Name, is to let a few more candidates get in the race to split the vote.

Durham Caldwell

"So we get our papers in right at the deadline. And we have a big press conference Wednesday morning, eleven o'clock, to make the official announcement. If you could cover that yourself, Buzz—you always do a great job on political stuff—if you could cover that yourself, I'd appreciate it."

"H.B., are you sure you're ready to run for mayor? Do you have time to run? It's a big job." He was being protective of his friend Max. But he also had a certain fondness for H.B., despite H.B.'s moral myopia, and all he could see down the road in a run for mayor was embarrassment, God forbid that he might win.

"Buzz, the time's right!"

"Financing? Organization? You know, it's late."

"That's what makes it so great. I'll have the best financed campaign in the city's history. Money Bags himself has promised me five thousand bucks. And the other guys on the committee will all pitch in.

"Organization? This is a real professional group. They've already lined up a brass band for the press conference Wednesday morning. Money Bags says he'll get Volpe and Elliot to come in for rallies, get his Boston ad agency to do the ads and the TV spots. All I gotta do is make speeches, go to coffee hours, and kiss babies. They're even circulating my nomination papers."

Christ, Buzz thought, Half-Baked Baker will be putty in the hands of M.B. Jardine and those other Mattawampus Club bastards if by some fluke he should get elected. Volpe and Richardson coming in to endorse this clown? Does Money Bags' money talk that loud?

Tuesday morning a genuine surprise candidate entered the mayoral race, the Reverend Doctor James Shoemaker.

"Christ," observed Jerry Finnerty, "there aren't enough nigger voters in Riverbridge to elect Martin Luther King, let alone Jimmie Shoemaker."

"He must have something else in mind," speculated Buzz.

"Like what?"

"Like whipping up some political enthusiasm in the Central City. Like unifying the Negro community." Buzz paused to reflect,

Tumultuous Affairs

then went on. "Maybe sending a message to City Hall. Getting a discussion on the issues he wants to discuss."

"You know, you're probably right."

H.B. suffered two major disappointments. When he turned in his nomination papers just before the five o'clock Tuesday deadline, he learned that Max Feigenson and Domenico DiTotola, along with Jimmie Shoemaker, were still the only other candidates. Nobody else to split the vote in the white precincts.

The following morning, just as Buzz was about to leave for H.B.'s command press conference downtown, his phone rang. It was Linda, H.B.'s secretary.

"The announcement's off. The boss says to tell you he's pulling out of the race."

Will surprises never cease?

"Pulling out? How come?"

"His campaign committee screwed up. The city clerk just called up. Said the nomination papers were short by ten signatures. Can you beat that—ten signatures!"

"How's he taking it?"

"Pretty bad. He's wondering how he's gonna break the news to Money Bags and the other big shots at the club. Of course, it's their fault—they're the jerks that were circulating the papers."

As much as H.B. might have wanted to sit on the story of his aborted campaign, too many people knew about it. The fact of his filing papers had already made the news. And Buzz knew the competition would be using the story on the signatures. So he gave the order for both radio and television news departments to include it in their newscasts. Jerry Finnerty came into Buzz's office at mid-afternoon with a sheet of script paper.

"How do you like my lead?" he asked Buzz and proceeded to read:

"Hillerich Bradsby Baker, the rookie mayoral candidate who bats right and throws right, far right, and who envisions himself the Louisville Slugger of local politics, struck out today before the game

Durham Caldwell

even started. In an act of omission matched only by the storied Fred Merkle's failure to touch second base, candidate Baker's campaign workers failed to file enough legal signatures to qualify Mister Baker for the ballot. Mister Baker briefly considered a write-in campaign, but chief fundraiser Money Bags Jardine advised against it. 'If our people can't count,' said Mister Jardine, 'how in the friggin' hell can we expect them to write in a name?'"

Buzz laughed. "Make sure that script never gets near the studio!"

16

Buzz and Marsha debated the continued U.S. buildup in Vietnam one Wednesday as they drove over back roads around Mount Wachusett. The 1st Cavalry Division was joining U.S. ground forces in the war zone.

"If you're gonna fight a war," Buzz maintained, "you've gotta fight it to win."

"But Buzz, how do you beat them when you can't find them?"

They stopped for a pizza, drove to a state park, and gingerly carried the still piping hot pizza box to a picnic table overlooking a lake. Buzz had a momentary fright when a smiling woman with a little boy in tow walked up to them and inquired of Marsha, "Aren't you Doctor Antonelli's wife?"

But Marsha had seen her coming and answered without missing a beat, "'Fraid not. You must have me confused with somebody else."

The woman made an embarrassed apology and tugged the little boy, who was admiring the pizza, away from the table. "Come on, let's go see the ducks."

"You're a cool one," Buzz complimented as the woman moved out of earshot.

After finishing the pizza, they drove around a little more, then returned to the Antonelli apartment. She led him directly to the bedroom.

"You didn't know, did you, that pizza is a famous old-world aphrodisiac? Why do you think Italians have so many children?"

They had just finished undressing each other when they heard a door open and a male voice from the entryway, "Marsha, you home?"

"My God, Leo's home! In the closet, quick!"

She pushed him toward her bedroom closet, scooped up his clothes and dumped them into the closet on top of him, grabbed a robe from the hook on the closet door, silently closed the door, kicked his shoes under the bed, and struggled into the robe—all in one fluid, continuous motion—as her husband's footsteps came down the hall.

"You're home early."

"Lost power at the office. Some jerk in a backhoe broke the underground cable." Then getting a good look at her, "Hey, what're you doing in a robe this time of day? Oversleep that much?"

"No, I was doing some housework, got all sweaty. I was just getting ready to take a shower," she lied.

Crammed into Marsha's closet, Buzz could hear everything including the pounding of his heart. It was pounding so loud he was sure Leo Antonelli must be able to hear it. But he couldn't see anything. He could only imagine what was happening in the bedroom.

He heard Leo tell his wife, "I'd forgotten how beautiful you are underneath that expensive wardrobe you usually wear."

He must have opened her robe—if indeed she had been fast enough to get it on and belt it.

"Forgotten? Yes, it's been a long time." Buzz didn't detect even a modicum of warmth in her voice.

"You're right. Let's start making up for lost time right now."

He must be touching her, Buzz thought.

"Leo, in the daytime?"

"If the daylight bothers you, just close your eyes. Or I'll blindfold you. C'mon, slip out of that robe. My, you are a beautiful woman!"

Buzz's impulse was to burst out of the closet and physically restrain Leo Antonelli. But even without considering the arsenal the doctor had scattered around the apartment, he realized he would hardly be in a position to defend a lady's honor—jumping out of her bedroom closet stark naked.

"Give me a minute to get ready," he heard her say. The bed creaked. Leo must be sitting down on it, taking off his shoes.

Buzz was forced to crouch there in silence in the closet, his own shirt and underwear hanging over his left ear, Marsha's dresses and skirts enveloping his head and shoulders, the aches in his knees and calves becoming progressively more painful as he dared not change his position. Besides his physical agony, there was the mental anguish—

listening to Leo's low whistle as Marsha came back to the bedroom, to the squeaking bedsprings and the other sounds of the Antonellis' lovemaking. It was stomach churning to have to endure the sounds of pleasure from another man enjoying the body of the woman you loved—and the woman who you knew loved you.

And there was dust in the closet. Buzz felt a tiny tickle in his nose which grew progressively more insistent. He fought with all his will power to stifle what otherwise would have been a powerful sneeze. It was still ungodly loud, but it came at the exact moment Leo was accompanying the final pleasures of lovemaking with such loud un-doctorlike shouts that he probably wouldn't have heard a locomotive. And Marsha followed by emitting what Buzz took to be shrieks of delight. It made him feel like vomiting. He had never been so uncomfortable in his life, mentally as well as physically.

Leo and Marsha lay there afterward for what seemed to Buzz an eternity. He moved the shirt and underwear away from the side of his face and tried as quietly as he could to stand up among the dresses to relieve the cramps that were cutting into his bent legs. But he couldn't unbend them. He wondered if he would ever be able to straighten them. He also wondered if the oxygen supply in the closet would run out—and what Leo Antonelli would say if he found a naked male corpse in his wife's closet.

He heard someone stirring in the bedroom. It sounded like Leo was kissing his wife. Then it sounded as if he might be putting his clothes on. "I'll go down to Joe's for a pizza," he heard Leo say. "Be right back. You were very nice! We shouldn't wait so long between times." Buzz heard Leo walk down the hallway. As the front door clicked closed, Marsha rushed to the closet without taking time to pull on her robe.

"Oh, you poor darling!"

She helped him stagger out, actually crawl out, of the closet, leaned over him to kiss him on the cheek, and began to massage his calves to relieve the cramps.

"And you had to listen to that!"

"Sounded like you enjoyed it," he said in a voice that was cooler than he intended.

Durham Caldwell

"I should get an Academy Award for best actress." She put a hand under his chin and tilted his face up to kiss it. "Buzz, I was screaming because I was afraid you'd sneeze again, and I was hoping desperately to keep Leo from hearing it."

"You heard me sneeze?" There was some humor in the situation after all.

"I heard it. I don't know how Leo missed it. I guess he was just too busy. Buzz, I wasn't screaming because I enjoyed it. I was in agony. You're the one I want. I want you desperately right now. But I'll try to control myself till Saturday. If you'll be home, I'll drive out Saturday morning when he goes up to New Hampshire to shoot his damned revolvers.

"Now get dressed and get out of here before he comes back. Your shoes are under the bed—unless Leo put them on by mistake."

As she walked him down the hall, clinging close to him in the robe she had hurriedly pulled on, she groaned. "I just thought of something. You know the worst part? I'm going to have to eat pizza twice in the same day!"

When she arrived on Saturday, Marsha brought with her a bouquet of cut flowers, searched the cupboards for a vase, and plunked the vase down on the living room coffee table.

"Just to brighten things up a little bit."

"You're all the brightening I need," he said, drinking in her smile. "The flowers are superfluous."

She brought flowers almost every time she came—sometimes for the living room, sometimes for the dining room table, sometimes for the dresser in the bedroom. He came to love them. Not only did they brighten the empty house when she wasn't there with him, they also served as a reminder of the loving woman who had brought them and provided him the assurance that she would soon be there again.

If any of Buzz's neighbors noticed the blue Pontiac that was sometimes parked in his driveway, or the casually dressed woman who got out of it, they didn't mention it. Their first thoughts might have been that she was the cleaning woman. They surmised Buzz had not been an especially meticulous housekeeper since Elaine died. But

Tumultuous Affairs

if they made note of the flowers—and the frequency with which she and Buzz took her car or his for a drive—they more likely would have concluded that the visitor was a lady friend. But heck, there was nothing wrong with a widower as young as Buzz having a lady friend. Besides, she was usually gone well before dark.

Actually, Marsha was both lady friend and cleaning lady. Buzz had made token attempts to clean the house, but on her first visit—not counting the night of Judy and Johnny's wedding—Marsha pulled out the vacuum and gave it the best cleaning it had received since Elaine got sick. And she would touch up the rooms that needed it most on her subsequent visits.

"We're becoming quite a domestic couple," Buzz remarked one morning as he emptied the vacuum cleaner bag. "Why don't you get a divorce from that tooth doctor and move in here and be my full-time cleaning lady?"

"I'd like that, but getting a divorce in Massachusetts isn't that easy. And I don't want to hurt Leo's parents."

Besides the forays into housecleaning, Marsha's visits took on an increasingly professional character. She would bring with her a manila folder of her latest stories from the hometown paper and ask him to critique them. A strange turn of events, he thought, me coaching Marsha on her writing, the way Elaine used to coach me in high school.

He began calling her "Mar." Marsha sounded too formal after seeing it so many times in her byline. She wrote well. She researched well. He was often reduced to what he knew was nitpicking just to convince her that he was reading the material carefully and putting thought into his remarks.

"This is a nice piece, Mar," he might say. "You could've made it just a little bit clearer if you'd put in the man's last name here in the fourth graf instead of just calling him 'he' or 'him.' But there's nothing else in there that I would change a word of."

Or, "This long piece here on the zoning, you mention Building Inspector Alcide Fournier up near the top. Then he doesn't reappear till way down at the bottom. Here, instead of just 'Fournier,' you could say 'Fournier, the building inspector' so the reader who doesn't remember wouldn't have to go back to the top to hunt up who he is."

She took the criticism well, even on those very rare occasions when he detected what he felt was a genuine shortcoming. She was determined to become a first-class reporter, and she was well on her way to doing it. And she made it no secret that when the time was right, she hoped to move on to a bigger paper.

The Reverend Doctor James Shoemaker accomplished two things in the city mayoral campaign. He excited and united the Negro community, which turned out at the polls in much greater numbers than ever before. And he kept before the entire city the issues of racial imbalance in the schools and training of police officers to cope with the problems of a multiracial society. Max Feigenson was an easy winner with about sixty-five percent of the vote. But the Reverend Doctor Shoemaker, with some citywide support from white liberals, did almost as well as the runner-up, Domenico DiTotola.

Judy won easy reelection to the council. Johnny played an active role in the campaign, doing everything from stuffing envelopes to accompanying the candidate on her rounds of coffee hours and forums. To those who didn't recognize him as Judy's husband, he took great delight in identifying himself as "just one of the councilor's admiring campaign workers." Max, with his landslide victory, brought enough "good guys" along with him to have working control of the council on most issues. Judy was excited about the prospects of working with the new mayor.

She was also excited about her business partnership with Johnny. "Your son is such a sweet guy to work with," she told Buzz one Friday evening as they waited at the Heidelberg for the late-arriving Johnny. "We're doing very well. We've got two campuses we're actively gunning for—and some more in preliminary contact status. And Buzz, it's been kind of a long haul, but we're getting some minority clerks behind the counters! We hired a black bookkeeper at State who's an absolute gem! And I think I have Johnny sold on a management training program!"

"You're moving fast!"

Tumultuous Affairs

"Buzz, you can't imagine how it feels to be able to do things on your own. Heywood's was a great place to learn the business. But working for Myra—she might have been one of the great minds of the Gilded Age—was a frustrating experience."

Mar was always eager for news about her old convention friend Judy and her new husband. She had reduced them to shorthand. Her usual question was, "How are J and J?"

Buzz always had good things to report. There had been such a change in Johnny that he had actually begun to like the kid. He had always loved his son—but liking him was something else again. Buzz assumed it was Judy who had made the difference in him. Gone were the smart-ass remarks. Gone was the stuffed-shirt know-it-all attitude. Things still came disgustingly easy for him, Buzz thought, but no longer did he lord it over his father—something he had once taken so much relish in doing. Instead of bragging about legitimate accomplishments with the bookstores, he would laugh them off as luck or being in the right place at the right time—or give the lion's share of the credit "to my brilliant executive vice president," kissing Judy on the cheek or putting his hand on hers, just to make it clear she was the executive vice president.

Buzz reported to Mar with fatherly pride about Johnny and how well he was doing and what a great guy he had become. But when he talked about Judy—about her accomplishments at City Hall, about her contributions to the "Issues" series, about her role in the bookstores—he fairly glowed, something not lost on Mar.

"If I were your son." she told him one day as they sat on the sofa together, "I wouldn't turn my back. My old man might be beating my time with my wife."

Buzz put his hand on the outside of Mar's knee and ran it up her flank.

"As long as you keep me happy, Johnny's got nothing to worry about."

She made him very happy that afternoon before he reluctantly saw her to the door for her trip home. Later he remembered her remark about Judy and laughed. Judy, a very desirable young woman to

123

be sure—but young enough to be my daughter. Besides, Mar, I'm in love with you.

One of Big Jim McCann's final acts as mayor was to turn the first shovelful of earth in a ceremonial groundbreaking for the Garden Towers Apartments. The ground was frozen solid. It took a jackhammer to loosen it up enough to dig in, but the Housing Authority wanted to give Big Jim the honor of turning the earth before he went out of office. The real construction work would begin in early spring. The architect had hurried things along by borrowing liberally from the other red-brick high-rise low-income projects which had sprung up around the country.

Judy and Mayor-Elect Max were among the councilors and other city officials who lined up alongside the mayor to play to the cameras and take stabs with gold-painted shovels at frozen chunks of earth. A stupid practice, official groundbreakings, thought Buzz as he and cameraman Benny Goodreau shivered in the cold. And he wondered, why the hell do we keep covering them?

Big Jim—his pink face even pinker in the cold—fortuitously kept his remarks very brief. He noted, with teeth chattering, that he and Councilor Hennessy used to play football and Cowboys and Indians here—and now the Old Brickyard would be home to a new generation of kids.

After the ceremony, Buzz went up to say hello to Judy. "Well, Miss America, I was glad to see you put on your best smile for the cameras."

Instead of the bantering reply he expected, she told him very matter-of-factly, "I wasn't smiling on the inside. This place will be just too big."

"And too far away from everything," added Max, who had turned to join the conversation. He shook his head. "And the new mayor will have to deal with it."

17

Buzz jumped party lines to vote for all the top Republicans in the 1966 midterm elections. Governor Volpe clearly deserved another term. And Buzz took pleasure in helping elect the personable attorney general, Ed Brooke, to the United States Senate. Brooke became the first Negro senator since Reconstruction, winning the seat held for more than two decades by Leverett Saltonstall.

Buzz hadn't paid much attention to California where former movie actor and television host Ronald Reagan was elected governor—he'd been too busy covering Massachusetts. He remembered Reagan as second banana in a couple of Errol Flynn movies, for playing "the Gipper" in "Knute Rockne, All-American," and for his folksy television appearance for Barry Goldwater on the eve of the '64 election.

"That speech was what got his bandwagon rolling," Judy commented as she and Buzz and Johnny reviewed the massive Republican victories nationwide over dinner at the Heidelberg. She was not enthused by California's governor-elect.

"He's not my kind of Republican. I think he's further right than Goldwater. And so good on TV he could sell people snake oil."

"Well, you can be happy about Brooke and Volpe," observed Johnny. "Of course," he teased, "they're both too liberal for me."

"Oh, and Buzz, did you notice?" asked Judy. "That fellow George Bush—the one who spoke to us about Goldwater at San Francisco—he got elected to Congress. First Republican ever elected to represent Houston in the House."

"Bush?" The name was drawing a blank. Then a light went on. "Oh, yeah, Prescott Bush's son. He spoke at Salty's luncheon." She must be reading the inside pages of the *Times* pretty closely.

"So what lessons do you draw from the election, Buzz?" Judy wanted to know.

Durham Caldwell

Buzz thought a moment. "People are unhappy with Johnson. They couldn't get him this time, so they knocked off some Democratic congressmen and governors. And George Bush is just one example of how the Solid South isn't so solid any more after Goldwater and after the Civil Rights Bills.

"Number two: making a political comeback isn't easy. Volpe did it in '64 when the Democrats were split. But Peabody tries it this year"—the former governor had battled Attorney General Brooke for Saltonstall's Senate seat—"and Brooke clobbers him. Eddie McCormack goes for governor—first time out since he lost to Teddy in '62—and Volpe clobbers him. And Bellotti, the guy who split the party in '64, tries to redeem himself by running for attorney general, and Richardson beats him—by what?—ninety thousand votes?"

"Give Elliot a lot of credit for giving up lieutenant governor to run for A.G.," said Judy. "That took some courage."

"It did," agreed Buzz. "But was his motivation keeping the job Republican or keeping Bellotti out?"

"He did a good job," Johnny said, "trying to tie Bellotti to the mob. Raised doubts in a lot of minds. Personally, I thought it was kinda dirty. Elliot, of course, comes across as Mister Clean."

"Anyway," concluded Buzz, "this was not a year for comebacks. I wonder if Richard Nixon took note."

Democrat Buzz got some needling from good old Republican Max about the election results. But Buzz figured he'd find something to razz Max about before too long. Max's administration at City Hall so far had proved to be a curious mixture of courageous steps forward and political hesitation.

During his first months in office, when Max concluded that his own appointees on the Police Commission were dragging their feet on key issues, he summoned commission members to a closed-door meeting. As in most closed-door meetings, the substance leaked out. Max didn't pussyfoot. He told commissioners, for example, that he wanted an affirmative vote on the long-pending matter of sensitivity training for police, told them that if he didn't get it that he would replace them with new commissioners.

Tumultuous Affairs

Max got the affirmative vote. He also got the resignations of two commission members who rebelled at "being dictated to, when we were appointed to the commission to exercise our independent judgment." Columnist Dibble got in his usual digs: "the Emperor Maximilian I," "the little dictator in the mayor's office," and "what decent citizen would accept an appointment from this guy?"

But Max found no shortage of potential appointees. And the vote on sensitivity training was so clearly overdue that even H.B. Baker patted the mayor on the back in one of his commentaries.

On *de facto* segregation in the schools, on the other hand, Negro leaders accused Max of foot-dragging. Even Judy expressed disappointment. The state's Racial Balance Act, signed into law by Governor Volpe in 1965, defined any school with more than fifty percent minority enrollment as racially imbalanced. There were six such schools in the city, all elementary schools. The law contained a carrot and a stick. The carrot was an increase from forty percent state reimbursement for new school construction to sixty-five percent where construction alleviated imbalance. The stick was the threat to withhold state aid from any community not submitting a satisfactory plan to eliminate the imbalance problem.

The School Committee, with Mayor Feigenson as *ex officio* chairman, nibbled around the edges. The plan submitted to the state closed one of the imbalanced schools and redistributed its student body. It redrew some district lines. It talked vaguely about building new schools outside the Central City. And, despite the opposition of Committeewoman Lucille Cournoyer, it put into effect the limited open enrollment program, inviting parents, both Negro and white, to enroll their children in schools outside their districts if so doing would reduce imbalance.

More than four hundred black parents—and just over a dozen white parents—signed up their youngsters for the new program even though the NAACP and other community groups campaigned against it. The Reverend Doctor Shoemaker protested, "It puts all the burden for movement outside their neighborhoods on our children." He emphasized "our." "The burden should be shared."

Durham Caldwell

School Committeeman Henry Doane accused the NAACP of "trying to block everything we try to do to help them."

The state Board of Education withheld approval of the city's plan pending more specifics on construction and a firm timetable for eliminating the imbalance that still existed. Five Riverbridge schools still had student bodies ranging from sixty-three to ninety-one percent Negro. The School Committee wrote a letter of protest and tried to drum up support among area legislators to change the state law.

Max told legislators at a meeting in the mayor's office, "The bottom line is this: the only way we can get the balance the state wants is to force white kids to enroll in ghetto schools."

The legislators clucked sympathetically, but the Racial Balance Law affected only a handful of cities, and—except for Boston, which was also facing integration pressure—there was no movement among their colleagues to change it.

As the bodies started coming home from Vietnam, the bodies of young soldiers and young Marines, Buzz was determined—much as he was now questioning the war—that Baker Broadcasting would give full coverage to these young men's burials. Because so many of the services were in the early afternoon, after the day crews were normally back at the newsroom preparing their stories and before the night crew reported for work, Buzz took many of the assignments himself.

At the first one, he almost came apart. He knew he should have been ready for it, but he wasn't. The grieving family at graveside, the clergyman praying and offering words of comfort—suddenly he was back in France twenty-odd years earlier, part of a platoon of grimy GI's gathered around the freshly-dug temporary grave of one of his best friends as a chaplain prayed and talked about courage and sacrifice.

The volley of rifle shots—"Squad! Ready! Aim! Fire!" BLAM!!! "Fire!" BLAM!!! "Fire!" BLAM!!! They were firing blanks. But they were as real to Buzz as the gunfire in the Ardennes that bleak day in December when the Germans surrounded and decimated his outfit before the handful of survivors surrendered. As real to Buzz as the machine guns of the RAF fighter pilot who swooped down to wipe out a dozen of his POW comrades.

Buzz fought the urge to turn and run. He blotted the tears from his eyes and his cheeks with his handkerchief and mopped hard under his nose, which was running profusely.

The notes of "Taps" echoing through the cemetery were almost unbearable. Buzz dug his fingernails into the palms of his hands. He was glad he was standing at the rear of the small group of people around the gravesite and that his photographer was on the other side of them. His eyes cleared a little bit as the honor guard sergeant boxed the flag that had covered the casket, presented it to the dead soldier's mother, and saluted smartly. He was relieved to notice many other handkerchiefs mopping away tears.

After that first one, he was better prepared. He made sure he had an extra handkerchief. He would keep his eyes straight ahead as the mourners gathered at the grave, avoid looking at their faces. He would take notes as the clergyman prayed. He would grit his teeth and clench his fists as the rifle squad fired its agonizingly long volley. But no matter how many burials he went to—no matter how many times he endured the ritual—he could never hear "Taps" without having tears fill his eyes and spill on his note pad.

Most of the families took their loss with dignity. One proud mother confided to Buzz when he offered condolences after the service, "I wouldn't have done it this way. But Bill told me before he went overseas that a military funeral is the greatest honor a soldier can receive." She paused. "I'm glad we did it."

Buzz wondered if soldier Bill had a premonition that this was the way he would be coming home.

Most families tolerated the presence of Buzz and the TV photographer with an unobtrusive hand-held camera at the graveside services. Many seemed to welcome it as a sign of community respect for a fallen son. Only once, when because of the time factor they tried to catch the funeral party leaving the church instead of at the cemetery, did a grieving family react with hostility.

It had been an emotional service, inside a Negro church. A warm summer day. Windows open. The sounds of grieving—loud and an-

Durham Caldwell

guished wails of grief—spilled out onto the sidewalk where Buzz and Stan waited as inconspicuously as they could.

There was no military honor guard at this funeral, no flag on the casket. The family had chosen to eliminate every vestige of military trapping.

One of the first mourners out of the church spotted the two white faces across the street, one of them putting a Bolex camera up to his eye, and came running at them, shouting, "Get outta here! Don't you have no respect?"

Buzz and Stan beat a quick retreat to the news car.

It puzzled Buzz that the other TV station never covered a serviceman's graveside service and that the newspaper only rarely sent a photographer. This, thought Buzz as he watched the boxing of the flag from still another casket, is what the Vietnam War is all about.

It puzzled Buzz, too, that none of the public officials, except occasionally the commissioner of veterans' services, appeared at servicemen's burials in the city—and only rarely were representatives of veterans' groups in evidence. But in the small towns on the outskirts, selectmen and other town officials were almost always on hand—and usually the caps of the American Legion, VFW, and Disabled American Veterans were sprinkled through the graveside group. Buzz wondered why his old buddy Max, a World War II Marine, never left City Hall for a serviceman's funeral. Too busy? Or fear of being overcome by emotion that a middle-aged mayor wasn't supposed to show?

Buzz at first was determined to ignore what General Westmoreland, the U.S. commander in Vietnam, called "unpatriotic acts here at home." But the demonstrations against the war got too big to ignore. To be sure, you could overlook the handful of old-time crusaders who gathered once a week for a peace vigil in City Hall Park. But when a couple of hundred students from the colleges marched through the streets, a newsman couldn't turn his back on that. Unless, of course, you were Jerry Finnerty. "Damn Copperheads," complained Jerry. "Oughta snatch up their draft deferments and put 'em on the first boat to Vietnam. Don't send me to cover any of their goddam demonstrations." You, thought Buzz, are the last person I'd send.

Tumultuous Affairs

Buzz was there himself for the antiwar parade in Northampton. Local police were out in force. So were students from little Northampton Commercial College. These were blue collar kids, not the elite from Amherst, Smith, and UMass. And they were patriots. They went after the marchers verbally. And a few went after them physically, grabbing an American flag out of the hands of one of them and landing enough punches to give the cops a workout to keep the confrontation from degenerating into a full-fledged melee.

Despite the increasing amount of newspaper space and broadcast time occupied by the war and the war protests, the fight over balancing the schools continued to dominate the local news.

One Friday evening at the Heidelberg, Buzz asked Judy, "Why doesn't Max see the handwriting on the wall and realize that sooner or later we'll have to go to two-way busing?"

"I hate to say it," responded Judy, "but it looks like he's trying to put off a decision until after the election. He knows that integration is the right way to go."

Johnny rarely interrupted political discussions between his wife and father—the people he sometimes referred to as "the two experts." But this time he broke in.

"Could it be that Max is smarter than both of you? Could it be that Max figures that a white parent whose kid faces a bus ride to Miller Street or one of those other Central City schools is gonna start looking for a house in the suburbs? You get enough white families moving out, more black families from the South moving in—pretty soon, maybe Max figures—ten, fifteen, twenty years from now—you've got more black kids in the city than white kids. Then you can bus 'em anywhere you want to, and the damn school—all the damn schools—have more than fifty percent black kids.

"And remember, they're already out-reproducing us. And that's not even taking into account the Puerto Ricans. You drive through the West End, the Puerto Ricans are getting quite a foothold. Where do they fit in this racial balance formula business?

"Maybe Max is more far-sighted than you give him credit for."

Durham Caldwell

Buzz and Judy admitted that Johnny had made a good point. But Johnny didn't have the state Board of Education among his listeners. After months of dickering and failing to get what it wanted, the board voted to put a freeze on state aid to the city. That hit Max where he was most vulnerable: in the budget. This time, with the help of a new superintendent who told the School Committee very candidly, "The neighborhood school concept is dead as a dodo," the mayor prodded the committee to put some more specifics into the plan.

The new plan would build a new school in the South Park urban renewal area, put additions on two existing elementaries in white neighborhoods, close the two oldest Central City schools, and balance races at the remaining three through a combination of open enrollment and additional changes to boundary lines.

Jimmie Shoemaker called the plan "wishful thinking." The balance, he said, "is only on paper." But the Board of Education, possibly as weary of the hassle as Max was, approved it. With an election on the horizon, Max and his School Committee colleagues had staved off two-way busing.

Judy had toyed with the idea of passing up a bid for reelection to the council to run for the School Committee. Max talked her out of it. "I need you on the council. Besides, voters might not take to a woman on the School Committee who doesn't have any kids." Lucille Cournoyer, the only current female member, was the mother of seven.

Buzz had begun to wonder if Johnny and Judy were ever going to have children. Mar once in a while would ask, "Isn't Judy pregnant yet?" Much as he would like to have a grandchild, he realized that how Judy and Johnny felt about the subject was none of his business. And Judy might well be one of those women for whom career takes priority.

There was more excitement about the 1967 Red Sox—who were winning Boston's first American League pennant in twenty-one years—than there was about the local election. Max was easily reelected to a second term as mayor, Judy to her third term on the council. Almost as satisfying to both of them, Domenico DiTotola was beaten decisively in his bid to regain his old council seat.

18

Republican Max, winding up the first month of his second term in the mayor's office, couldn't resist the opportunity for a gentle dig at the new troubles of the Democratic administration. North Vietnamese forces had observed Tet, the Vietnamese lunar new year, with an offensive of unprecedented proportions. Vietcong troops attacked thirty South Vietnamese provincial capitals and laid siege to the city of Hue. Enemy soldiers occupied the American embassy in Saigon for six hours before being dislodged by U.S. paratroopers. All this on the heels of Pentagon and Johnson administration claims that North Vietnamese forces were exhausted and on the verge of defeat.

"What's your buddy LBJ gonna do now?" Max demanded the morning after the offensive got underway.

Buzz was tempted to zing back at Max with something about his troubles with the state board over racial imbalance. But he knew that was a sore subject with the mayor and held his tongue. He contented himself with answering the LBJ question.

"Damned if I know. Maybe it's not as bad as the first reports make it out." And indeed that was the spin the Pentagon and the White House tried to put on it in the days that followed.

Besides their Friday evening get-togethers at the Heidelberg, Johnny and Judy frequently invited Buzz to their place for Sunday dinner.

"It's the only time during the week I can get her to cook anything," joshed Johnny.

"You keep her so busy at the company, it's a wonder she cooks for you on Sunday." She was a good cook, something Buzz acknowledged by adding, "If you ate this well all week, you'd have to buy your suits in the fat boys' shop."

Durham Caldwell

Buzz enjoyed these visits. It gave him the opportunity to see a different Judy—the domestic Judy. The tailored suits, the smart but severe career-woman dresses were hung away in a closet. The domestic Judy wore a T-shirt and shorts in warm weather, a sweater and slacks when it was cooler. A few of them were oversized and baggy, but most of the T-shirts and sweaters reminded him of the jersey she was wearing that first night at the Heidelberg—they fit her form like a glove. Johnny had difficulty keeping his hands off her, and Buzz could understand why. God, she was a beautiful woman! Yes, Mar was an attractive woman, too—and he was deeply in love with Mar. But when you visited your son and daughter-in-law, it wasn't wrong, was it, to admire the scenery?

Occasionally Judy and Johnny would invite Buzz to stay and watch television with them. Usually he would decline. But the night in March 1968 that Judy said, "C'mon, watch LBJ with us," he replied, "Well, why not?"

As she turned on the big color set—Johnny would have nothing but the best—she told the two men, "I've got a hunch about this speech. My intuition tells me Johnson's going to pull out of the election."

"Your intuition?" Johnny laughed. "Has it ever been right before?"

"Well, there was that first night at the Heidelberg, the night your dad introduced me to you. My intuition told me this is the man I'm going to marry."

He pulled her down beside him on the sofa, hugged her, and kissed her as she struggled to free herself.

"Of course," she giggled, pushing herself away from him, "it had already told me the same thing about six other guys, so I didn't know whether to believe it."

"You bitch," he said, pulling her toward him again and kissing her some more.

Judy freed herself again and turned to Buzz flushed with embarrassment. "Buzz, you'll have to excuse us. I married a wild man."

"You made me wild. I never looked at a woman till I met you. Right, Dad?"

Tumultuous Affairs

Judy snuggled next to him as LBJ came on the screen from the White House.

Buzz was delighted to see "the two kids," as he often described them to Mar, so happily in love with each other. Delighted—but at the same time, if he had looked deep within himself and been utterly honest about it, just the slightest bit jealous of John J. Buckley III.

This was President Johnson's first television appearance since his near defeat in the New Hampshire primary by Senator Eugene McCarthy, who was campaigning on an antiwar platform. And it was coming just two days before the Wisconsin primary, where polls had McCarthy well ahead of the president. The advance publicity had it that Johnson was to speak about the war in Vietnam.

Judy's intuition has deserted her, Buzz thought, as Lyndon Johnson read from the teleprompter that he would take the first steps to de-escalate the war and "substantially" reduce "the present level of hostilities." He had ordered aircraft and naval vessels "to make no attacks on North Vietnam." He had appointed veteran diplomat Averell Harriman to begin peace negotiations.

"Doesn't sound like a guy who's gonna quit," Johnny observed.

"Shhh! It's not over."

But it appeared to be over, Buzz thought. Johnson had made his points. It looked as if he was no longer staring at the teleprompter but directly at the viewer. About to say goodnight, Buzz thought.

Instead Lyndon Johnson made all three of them sit bolt upright. He spoke of "divisiveness among us," of not permitting victory to be "lost in suspicion, distrust, selfishness, and politics . . . I shall not seek, and I will not accept, the nomination of my party for another term as your president."

"Good for you, Lyndon! Good for you!" Judy clapped her hands in applause. Buzz and Johnny joined in.

Said Johnny, "I will never mistrust your intuition again."

Four days later, Buzz was cleaning his desk to go home for the day when he heard an imperious ten bells from the UPI teletype.

Durham Caldwell

"FLASH. MEMPHIS—THE REVEREND MARTIN LUTHER KING JR. HAS BEEN SHOT AS HE STOOD ON THE BALCONY OUTSIDE HIS MEMPHIS MOTEL ROOM."

My God! Buzz tore the copy from the teletype, raced into the radio news booth, signaled the disc jockey on the intercom that he had a bulletin, and read the flash on the air. ABC broke in almost simultaneously on television.

King was badly wounded. That was clear from the beginning. He was taken to a hospital but clung to life only briefly before word came over the teletype that he was dead. The newsroom, often a boisterous place during the early evening, became quiet as a tomb.

King had been in Memphis to give backing to a strike by city sanitation workers. And it was almost as if he'd had a foreboding, telling supporters the day before, "I don't care what happens to me now because I've been to the mountaintop . . . And I've looked over and I've seen the promised land. I may not get there with you, but I want you to know that we as a people will get to the promised land . . . I'm not worried about anything. I'm not fearing any man. Mine eyes have seen the glory of the coming of the Lord!"

As Buzz drove home, he strained his ears to pick up the all-news station in New York for more details on the shooting. Dr. King had been leaning over the second floor railing outside his motel room chatting with two friends, Jesse Jackson and Ben Branch, when he was hit by a bullet from a high-powered rifle. The assassin was still at large. King had just asked Branch, a musician, to perform the old spiritual, "Precious Lord, Take My Hand," at a rally for the striking sanitation men.

And there were other reports coming in. Sporadic violence in Negro sections of New York. Looting and/or rioting and/or burning to varying degrees in Washington, Newark, Memphis, Nashville, even as close by as Hartford. On a whim, Buzz turned around and headed for the Central City.

For the most part, Central City sidewalks were deserted. Most of the stores were closed. Buzz noted a few men walking in pairs at a businesslike pace. Didn't look like trouble makers. Automobile traffic was light. He noticed a police cruiser on patrol, another one parked

Tumultuous Affairs

just off the main drag. Then, up ahead, two men stopped in front of a food market and walked toward the door. He recognized the taller of the two as the Reverend Doctor James Shoemaker. As he pulled up to the curb, he could see Jimmie Shoemaker and his companion talking quietly with three youths who apparently had been standing in the darkened doorway. After a minute or so of conversation, the three youths walked out onto the sidewalk and headed off down the street talking animatedly to each other.

Buzz got out of his car and approached the two men.

Jimmie Shoemaker chuckled. "Bu-u-u-z-z," he said, drawing out the greeting to almost three syllables. "Checking up on us, huh?"

"Just driving home. When I spotted you, I thought I'd better say hello."

"You're going out of your way," Jimmie Shoemaker chuckled again, "unless you moved to South Park."

No putting anything over on the Reverend Doctor Shoemaker. "You're right. When I heard what was happening in Washington and New York..."

"Buzz, we didn't have to hear. You can't imagine the sadness and the frustration in this community over losing Martin. But the leadership here knows that rioting and burning are not an appropriate response to anything. The Pastors Conference has talked about it many times. Every black minister has been out on the street all evening along with some of the lay leaders." A year earlier, he would have said "every Negro minister," but language, noted Buzz to himself, is always evolving. "Brother Leroy here is president of the Men's Club at church and—what is it, Leroy, worshipful master?—worshipful master of the Elks Lodge."

Buzz shook hands with Leroy.

"We've been patrolling," Jimmie Shoemaker went on, "talking with the few people we run into, like those kids—just to make sure they're not planning trouble. Even went into the bars. Imagine me, Buzz, going into a bar? Shoot, most of those bar patrons actually recognized me. Maybe I've been on television too many times. Worse, I recognized some of them. Some pretty angry people in some of those bars. But I think we calmed them down. Told them there were bet-

Durham Caldwell

ter ways to honor Martin's memory than by tearing down their own neighborhood."

"I think we reached most of 'em," volunteered Leroy. "But shoot, Brother Shoemaker could talk the stripes off a zebra!"

19

When Buzz relayed the story of Judy's intuition to Mar on her visit a few days later, Mar suddenly said, "Gee, I'd like to see Judy again. I haven't seen her since the wedding. That's been three years!"

"Well, why don't I call her up at the office, tell her my mistress is in town and would like to see her."

"You are a bastard."

"Nothing wrong with calling her up yourself. Tell her you thought of her while you were driving through town and wanted to know if she had time for lunch."

"I think I will. But my intuition tells me to make a bet with you. If she's in, and does have time for lunch, I bet she asks you to join us."

"You're on. What are the stakes?"

She thought a minute. "If I win, next time we do it my way."

"You phony, we always do it your way."

Judy was in. She invited Mar to stop in and gave her directions to the office. Half an hour later, Buzz's phone rang.

"Hi, good-looking. This is Judy. I'm glad I got you. The newsroom said you had the day off and they didn't know where you were."

"Just loafing for a change."

"Good. Join Johnny and me for lunch. We've got a surprise for you. Heidelberg. Twelve-thirty."

"What kind of surprise?"

"Never mind. Just be there."

This would be fun, but could they pull it off? As far as "the kids" knew, Buzz and Mar hadn't seen each other since their wedding day. In point of fact, they had been seeing each other almost every other Wednesday.

Durham Caldwell

Buzz got there a few minutes late on purpose. On the way to the restaurant, he practiced what he would say. By the time he walked in and saw Mar sitting opposite "J and J" in a booth, he had it down perfect.

"Marsha! This is a surprise!" He put the accent on the "is."

She had been rehearsing, too. She extended a hand for him to shake.

"Buzz! Nice to see you again!"

He slid into the booth beside her.

In response to her question, Buzz gave a brief fill-in on his television work and how valuable Judy was in helping on "Issues '68." Judy and Johnny gave a thumbnail description of how their business was expanding to still more campuses. Then Mar related some of the stories she had been covering for the hometown paper.

Buzz, who had seen the clippings of every one of the stories, observed, "Golly, Mar, sounds like you've been doing some interesting stuff."

Judy gave him a quizzical look, but she said nothing.

"So, Mar," Buzz asked a little later, "are you still married to that dentist?" Another quizzical look.

"Yes," she said in a resigned tone, "I can't get rid of him."

"Shucks," he replied with mock sadness. "If you do decide to get rid of him, I'm still available." They all laughed.

After the waiter brought their orders, they talked for a while about the upcoming presidential primary. Governor Volpe was on the Republican ballot as a favorite son candidate, but it was no secret he was there as a Nixon stalking horse—and quite likely hoping for the number-two spot on a Nixon ticket. Neither of the two Republican women expressed any great enthusiasm for Richard Nixon. Mar even told Judy, "I hope you won't hold it against me, but my favorite candidate is Bobby Kennedy. He strikes me as having the kind of courage and vision we need in the White House." Kennedy, the New York senator, had gotten into the Democratic race after McCarthy's strong run against Johnson in New Hampshire.

Tumultuous Affairs

"Are you going to the conventions, Mar?" Buzz asked. "My boss says he can't afford to send me this year. ABC won't kick in the twenty-five bucks a day they did in '64."

Judy was silent no longer. "What's this 'Mar' business? You were calling her 'Marsha' at San Francisco."

Oh-oh, Buzz said to himself, the cat's out of the bag. He could feel himself blushing.

But Mar was quick to the rescue. "Oh, that's what they used to call me in high school."

Under cover of the tablecloth, Buzz put his hand on her knee and gave her a squeeze of gratitude for bailing him out. He detected a small smile of acknowledgment. He left his hand on her knee until he saw the waiter coming back with the check.

Johnny looked at his watch. "Judy, we've got to get back to the office. That contractor's gonna be there in twenty minutes." He looked apologetically at Mar. "New store we're opening in Vermont."

"You want to come back? The meeting shouldn't take long," Judy explained to Mar.

"No, I've got to be getting along. It was great to see all three of you."

When Buzz let Mar into the house, they collapsed into each other's arms laughing.

"'Nice to see you again, Buzz!'" he mimicked. "You sounded just like Ted Kennedy." Kennedy was notorious among the city's newsmen for consulting with an aide as he entered a room, then greeting the individuals whose names the aide had just given him, "Nice to see you again, Buzz"—or "Jerry" or "Happy" or whoever.

"'Marsha, this is a surprise!'" she mimicked him. "And what did I tell you about my intuition?"

"Oh, God, you won the bet!"

"Come along," she said, flashing her sauciest smile, "I've thought of something very special."

It was a few weeks later, early June. Buzz heard Mar's footsteps on the stairs. She'd been puttering in the kitchen while he shaved. He wondered if she'd found anything more interesting than his usual dry cereal. Her rare overnight visits were certainly a treat. How wonderful to hold her in his arms all night. As he screwed the cap back on his after-shave and went into the hallway to meet her, he was wishing that Leo would take more out-of-state trips to conventions. He was expecting Mar's face to reflect the happiness in his, but as she reached the top step, he saw one of the saddest, most anguished faces he had ever seen.

"Oh, Buzz!" she sobbed as she threw herself into his arms, "somebody shot Bobby Kennedy!"

He held her close, trying to convince himself that she really didn't say it and he really didn't hear it. But he knew from the huge sobs that wracked her body that he had heard her only too well.

"The radio," she choked out between sobs, "makes it sound like he won't live. Oh, Buzz, what's happening to our country? We're killing our leaders—the president, Doctor King, and now Bobby!"

And Medgar Evers, and Malcolm X, and Viola Liuzzo, he silently added to the list. Schwerner, Goodman, Chaney. Reverend Reeb in Selma. Oh, God—how much more hate can the country stand?

He held her there against him for a long time before the sobs quieted. She pulled a tissue from the pocket of her robe, his robe actually—she traveled light when she came to visit. She wiped away the tears and with some difficulty smiled at him.

"Sorry," she said. And then, as if it was a relief to find something else to think about, "Come on, we've both got to get to work."

He always felt lonely when he said goodbye to her. This morning he felt lonelier than usual—he felt empty—as she backed down the driveway and headed for Worcester County and he drove to the station to supervise what turned out to be a day-long death watch. It wasn't until early the next morning that Bobby Kennedy died. He'd scored a decisive victory over Gene McCarthy in the important California presidential primary and had only a few minutes of consciousness to savor it before Sirhan Sirhan shot him.

Jerry Finnerty came up with the local angle. Larry O'Brien—Western Mass. native, political organizer *par excellence,* legislative aide to Presidents Kennedy and Johnson, postmaster general, and then

Tumultuous Affairs

campaign aide to Bobby Kennedy. Larry O'Brien was the only member of the Washington establishment to have been with both JFK in Dallas—and now RFK in Los Angeles. But no one in the newsroom, not even Jerry, had the *chutzpah* to try to reach him.

Tommy Goldman stopped by the station for an interview before leaving for the Republican National Convention in Miami Beach. He had been working with the Nixon organization during the primaries and again was on the Nixon convention staff.

"It's pretty much in the bag—1968 is our year!" Tommy told Buzz with the camera rolling. "The Old Man—I mean R.N.—has done so many favors for so many Republicans across the country that it'll be closer to a coronation than a convention. Watch when the TV cameras start showing you the scenery in Miami Beach. See how many of our signs you see: 'Nixon's the one!' You better believe it!

"And I'll make you another prediction. John Volpe will be the pick for vice president. He almost blew it when he fell asleep during the presidential primary and let Rocky beat him. But that was only the beauty contest—the presidential preference vote. Volpe controls most of the delegates. More important, R.N. likes him. It would put a Catholic on the ticket. And he knows Volpe will help him with moderate Republicans here in the Northeast."

Tommy was half right. Nixon won on the first ballot. But Senator Strom Thurmond among others convinced him that the way to Republican victory included expanding on Barry Goldwater's inroads in the once-Democratic Solid South—and that Maryland's Governor Spiro Agnew would play better in Dixie than John Volpe.

Buzz watched most of the convention on CBS, now that Cronkite was back as the network's convention anchorman. Cronkite's CBS Evening News had been doing increasingly well against NBC's Huntley-Brinkley Report, and the network was hoping "Uncle Walter," as more and more media columnists were calling him, would also cut into NBC's convention audience. Buzz's own network, ABC, streamlined its coverage, carrying regular programming until nine-thirty, and only then joining the convention. Buzz liked ABC anchorman Howard K. Smith, but he couldn't warm up to the network's "guest political observers," columnist William H. Buckley Jr. and novelist Gore Vidal. On top of that, he had to keep defending himself against Jerry Finnerty's continuing jibes that Bill Buckley and Buzz Buckley were third cousins.

Mar didn't get to the convention. Her editor, like H.B., had pleaded poverty. But Judy was there, this time as a delegate. By prearrangement with Buzz, she phoned the newsroom at least once a day with a fill-in on Massachusetts delegation news, most notably the disappointment over Nixon's choice of Agnew over Volpe. "Governor Volpe was waiting for the phone call," she said, "but the call never came."

Judy put Max on the phone to predict that Volpe would wind up in the Nixon cabinet. "Of course, we've got to elect Nixon first, but with the disarray among the Democrats, I think we will."

Then Judy reclaimed the phone and giggled a final comment: "The most memorable thing all week was a big colored lady about eight and a half months pregnant, standing outside Convention Hall. She was holding one of those signs, 'Nixon's the one.'"

Democrats nominated Vice President Hubert Humphrey for president in a tumultuous Chicago convention. But the nomination was overshadowed by the bitterness of supporters of antiwar candidate Eugene McCarthy and by street clashes between police and antiwar protesters.

Buzz, looking for local reaction to the Humphrey nomination, figured the Friendly Ice Cream shop in the Patch would be a good place to get it. Big Jim McCann had made coffee at Friendly's a morning ritual since leaving the mayor's office. Councilor Rowdy Hennessy and a few other aging Brickyard athletes usually joined him to rehash old times and to chew over the news of the day. So regular were they that each had his own special stool at the counter, and woe be to any newcomer who inadvertently occupied one of them.

"Cripes, Buzz, I'm a has-been. You sure you want to interview me?" asked the former mayor.

"Positive!"

Stan set up the sound camera right next to the counter. "Just be sure to get the Friendly Ice Cream sign in the background," advised the manager.

"Buzz," said Big Jim as the film rolled, "this is the first Democratic National Convention I've missed since before the war. And it was also the sorriest. I'm glad I was not a part of it. If I had been there, I would have told Mayor Daley a thing or two. Letting his cops beat up on those antiwar people like that. Not that the antiwar people were any angels. Far from it. But those cops going in there bashing heads, firing tear gas—disgraceful! It makes the antiwar people look like heroes—it makes the Democrats look like bums. If Daley thought Senator Ribicoff told him off, he should hear what I would have told him." Good start, thought Buzz. Connecticut's Abe Ribicoff had blasted Daley's police from the podium while the mayor mouthed obscenities at him.

"Now tell me, Mister Mayor"—Buzz still called him "Mister Mayor" even though Big Jim had been out of office for three years; he couldn't bring himself to call him anything else—"what do you think of Hubert Humphrey's chances of winning the election?"

"Buzz, the convention in the end did the right thing—it nominated the best man for the job. But he starts off with two strikes against him. First, there's the public perception that the Democratic Party is somehow responsible for that debacle caused by Daley's cops. Second, there are the soreheads that backed the good Senator McCarthy who forget that in a democracy the majority rules. If those soreheads sit on their hands, and keep spouting their claptrap, Richard Nixon will be our next president—and that will be a sad day for all of us."

As Stan was packing up the gear, Big Jim told Buzz, "I didn't want to say this on camera—but Hubert has to find himself a position on the war that he's comfortable with and the public is comfortable with. He's been so loyal to Johnson, we really don't know where he stands. And Johnson"—there was bitterness in his voice as he spoke—"he could have been one of our greatest presidents. Civil rights, Medicare, the War on Poverty—the stuff of greatness, Buzz,

Durham Caldwell

greatness! But he squandered it, squandered everything, on this asinine war in Vietnam."

Rowdy, who had been listening in silence, now put in his two cents' worth.

"Buzz, my street's the shortest in the Patch. Only six houses. Kids Jim and I grew up with livin' in all of 'em. I'm the only one doesn't have a son or a son-in-law over there with the Army or the Marines. Three years ago, Johnson woulda got a hero's welcome. My neighbors'd be fightin' over who could have 'im for a beer or for their backyard cookout. Today, on my street, he wouldn't dare ta get out of his car. They'd plaster him with tomatoes and maybe somethin' harder. That's part o' what Hubert's gotta overcome."

20

To Buzz's amusement, Mar had sort of backed around into Nixon's corner after the death of Bobby Kennedy—she thought Democrat Humphrey too garrulous to switch parties for. But there was no mention of the Nixon victory over Humphrey in their first meeting after the 1968 election. She had something more important to talk about. "Buzz, I've changed my mind about getting a divorce." She said it very matter-of-factly.

"That's the best news I've heard in a long time." He wondered why she didn't seem more excited about it. "What changed your mind?"

"The miserable sonuvabitch of a husband of mine did have a mistress after all. Probably a whole series of them. And I thought he was just hung up on revolvers."

She was mad at him for cheating on her? Buzz was about to ask a question but thought better of it. *Just let her tell me at her own speed.*

"One of them came to me and told me. His office manager, can you believe that? And the only reason she came is that he's dumped her for a new one, his cute little red-haired hygienist. I bet he's been banging most of the women who worked for him—none of them hung around there very long. This one, she's so peed off she's just itching to go into court and testify against him."

"Is that what's going to happen?"

"My lawyer says we'll get a deposition. She bets that Leo will let me have the divorce uncontested to save his reputation. Small town like ours, she says, he'd lose a lot of female patients if the story got out. Men wouldn't let their wives and daughters go to him."

"That's one way to do it, I guess. But you'll miss your chance to get on the stand and testify how you yourself have been a model of fidelity."

Durham Caldwell

"You bastard!" she laughed.

"You could give another one of those Academy Award performances."

She threw a pillow at him. He rolled off the sofa onto the floor to avoid it. She pounced on top of him laughing, and they nearly tore the clothes off each other.

"Can you imagine?" she asked with a touch of indignation in her voice as they lay there afterwards. "Most of those revolver meets he told me he was going to must've been one-on-one peter parties with one of those floozies from the office.

"And when he locked himself in the office when his appointments canceled, what do you bet he wasn't locked in there by himself?"

"Disgusting, anybody who would transgress on the sanctity of marriage."

"You are a bastard," she giggled as she grabbed a pillow and hit him in the face.

"Mar, you want to see Nixon?" Buzz was on the phone to Mar at her desk at the paper. It was January 9, and the president-elect was coming to Massachusetts to celebrate his fifty-sixth birthday in the company of daughter and son-in-law Julie and David Eisenhower. Julie was a junior at Smith College in Northampton, David a junior at nearby Amherst. They had been married in New York during Christmas vacation.

The divorce papers had been served, but Buzz and Mar were still treading cautiously to avoid tipping off Leo to possible grounds for a countersuit. When they met in front of Julie and David's apartment near the Smith campus, it was, "Oh, Buzz, what a surprise to see you here," and "Benny, this is an old friend of mine, Marsha—what's your last name now, Antonelli?—Marsha Antonelli."

The president-elect, Mrs. Nixon, and daughter Tricia got a warm greeting from a waiting crowd that Northampton police estimated at around two thousand, many of them young people from Smith and the other colleges in the area. The president-elect pushed past his security men to wade into the crowd and shake hands.

Tumultuous Affairs

Most of the crowd was still there when Nixon, looking amiable and relaxed, came out of the house with his wife and daughter about two hours later. Amid the cheers, the crowd spontaneously burst into several choruses of "Happy Birthday." Nixon shook more hands and then stood in the doorway of his car, looking over its roof to wave at those on the other side and seemingly reluctant to tear himself away from this friendly welcome.

Buzz whispered to Mar, "Gonna take me a while to get this written up. You want to wait for me at the house?"

"Sure. Leo's away. I'll use your typewriter and get started on my own piece."

He got home just in time for them to watch his story leading off the eleven o'clock news. Benny's camera following Nixon's stroll up the sidewalk to the front steps had a clear shot of Mar standing next to Buzz in the coterie of reporters lining the walk.

"I better volunteer to Judy and Johnny that I bumped into you tonight before they ask me about it," he laughed. He switched off the set without waiting for the rest of the news.

They went upstairs and helped each other undress. As she helped him out of his trousers, she burst out laughing.

"What are those?" she asked, pointing, as she tried to control her laughter.

He had forgotten the bright plaid flannel pajama pants he was wearing under his trousers.

"Oh, Christ!" he moaned when he realized what she was pointing at. "I was worried it might be cold up there. I don't own any long johns. These were the best substitute I could come up with on short notice."

"Well, I guess I know what to give you next Christmas."

"Long johns?"

"Among other things," she replied with the dimpled smile. And then, "Buzz, I'm terribly cold . . ."

"President Richard Cathouse Nixon will take the oath of office tomorrow as the nation's thirty-seventh president."

Durham Caldwell

Jerry Finnerty was going through a mock rehearsal for the lead story on the news. Jerry, despite his superpatriotism, had no reverence for any public official, not even presidents—or maybe especially presidents. In his lexicon, LBJ was "Lyndon Bulb-Brain Johnson," Harry S Truman was "Hairy Ass Truman," and Ike was "Dwight D. Eisenhoover." Buzz, along with H.B., kept his fingers crossed that irreverences like these would not get on the air.

Buzz and Mar, both of whom had declared Inauguration Day a holiday for themselves, watched the inauguration together on his living room TV. They heard the new president call for "goodness, decency, love, kindness" and challenge a nation "rich in goods but ragged in spirit" to close ranks and work together to make peace welcome, strong, and permanent.

"Good speech," Mar concluded.

"Yeah, but can we trust him?"

"Buzz, I don't know. But remember Truman. Remember how he grew in the presidency?"

"I remember how when he left office, his administration was pretty much in disgrace. He was so low in the public's estimation that Estes Kefauver beat him, or just about beat him, in the New Hampshire primary. No wonder he wouldn't run again. Just like Johnson this time.

"More immediately, what's Nixon done to your Republican Party here in Massachusetts, grabbing off Volpe and Elliot?" Nixon had picked Governor John Volpe to be his transportation secretary, Attorney General Elliot Richardson to be undersecretary of state.

"Sarge is going to be a good governor," Mar assured him. Francis Sargent, the lieutenant governor, would serve as acting governor for the next two years.

Mar did indeed get the divorce uncontested—and even with the blessings of Leo's Catholic parents when they learned the circumstances. She also got a generous amount of alimony and the furnishings of the apartment, except for the firearms and Leo's professional library.

Tumultuous Affairs

Buzz thought that he and Mar had a tacit understanding that they would be married after a suitable interval. On his first visit to the newly weapon-free apartment, he asked her to set a date. His timing was unfortunate.

"Oh, Buzz, I didn't tell you this because I didn't want to get my hopes up too high, but I applied to the *Globe*—months ago—and they've hired me! I just found out yesterday. The *Boston Globe*! It'll be such a big change from this little paper here—I don't think I can handle thinking about marriage right now. Let's leave things the way they are."

"Leave things the way are"—almost the exact words she had used as a teenager in denying him his first kiss. But this time the impact was so much sharper, so much deeper. They weren't teenagers. This wasn't puppy love. For more than four years he and this wonderful woman had been seeing each other, loving each other—and he had just assumed that she would be as anxious as he to transform a loving affair into a loving marriage.

The shock and the pain must have shown in his face.

"Buzz, I don't want to hurt you. I do love you, love you dearly. But this is my chance to shine. You've been shining for a long time. News director. Television. Awards. Everybody in Riverbridge looks up to you. I've been a housewife, a clubwoman, small-town reporter, nobody. You helped give me the skills to be somebody. And I want to do it.

"We'll still see each other. We'll just have to drive a little farther—or meet in the middle. And with the divorce over, we can eat out in public, go to the concerts and plays you always wanted to take me to, not have to hide things any more from J and J, even stroll by Leo's office holding hands."

She accompanied her attempt at humor with as much of the saucy smile as she could manage. She could probably tell that he was fighting to hold back tears.

"Buzz, we've had four wonderful years without being married to each other. We can still have a wonderful time. But not marriage, at least not right now. We can wait a little longer."

Before he left, she handed him a gaily wrapped package. "Don't open it," she said, "till you get home."

He thought afterwards that it was a wonder he got home without driving off the edge of the turnpike. His eyes were clouded with tears for the whole trip. For four years they indeed had blended a love affair with careers and done it successfully despite the distance between them, the long days apart, the secrecy, the risks of exposure, and even the husband who came home too early. But he had always felt a touch of sadness when she kissed him goodbye and they separated. Now she was free. She could stay with him every night, her body pressed against his. He could look across the table at her every morning, put his arms around her at the sink seven days a week, sit beside her on the sofa holding her hand as they read the paper or watched the TV. They could plant a garden together—just as he and Elaine used to do.

He had a saving thought. Maybe she was just playing hard to get, the way she might have been as a teenager turning down that request for a goodnight kiss. But the saving thought vanished as quickly as it had come. He knew she really did want to "leave things the way they are."

When he got home and got into the house, he remembered the package Mar had given him. He went back to the car to get it and took it back inside to open. It was a pair of long johns. Another time, opening such a gift would have left him laughing. This night it brought not even a smile.

The next evening, when she came to the station for the weekly taping of "Issues '69," Judy sensed that something was amiss. Buzz seemed not to be paying attention to the flow of the discussion. He let the guests wander at will, not bringing them sharply into focus on the subject matter as he usually did. As he went through the post-taping ritual of straightening up his desk, she asked him, "Buzz, what's wrong?"

"Wrong?"

"You're not yourself tonight."

Was he that transparent? He certainly was to Judy. He was tempted for a moment to sit her down in the chair in the corner of his little office and tell her the whole story. She'd understand. But, no, that's not something he should burden her with.

"Just feeling a little down. It'll pass."

On the way through the parking lot, her hand resting gently on his arm, she made another attempt. "Want to talk about it? We could stop over at Friendly's for coffee."

He patted her hand. "Thanks," he said, "I'll be okay." He said it without conviction, but she didn't press further.

As she stretched up to kiss his cheek, she squeezed his hand. "Good night, you beautiful man. I don't like to see you sad. Call me if I can help."

He came as close to smiling as he could and gave her hand a return squeeze. "Thanks. I will."

Despite his assurance to Judy, he was far from okay. He was mature enough, he told himself, not to break it off with Mar, the way he did as a teenager, without at least attempting to keep it going. But when he visited in her new apartment in the Boston suburbs, he felt more was coming between them than the extra miles. Even the lovemaking wasn't the same. She seemed preoccupied—as if she were trying to put together a solid lead sentence or composing questions for an interview.

One Sunday evening, as he said goodbye, he told her he probably wouldn't be seeing her for a while, that he had an especially busy period coming up at the station. It looked as if she was starting to say something, maybe register an objection, and then thought better of it. She gave him a perfunctory goodbye kiss. He walked to the elevator feeling even more lost and disappointed.

It was a Saturday afternoon. Buzz was driving alone and aimlessly through the countryside, still blue over the loss of Mar. Without realizing he was doing it, he had automatically turned off the highway and onto back roads that he and she had driven together so often. He flipped on the radio to catch the news, maybe get his mind on something else.

Durham Caldwell

The lead story was from Edgartown on Martha's Vineyard. A car driven by Senator Edward Kennedy had plunged off a narrow wooden bridge on Chappaquiddick Island during the night, killing a pretty blonde secretary riding with the senator. The body of Mary Jo Kopechne had been found in the rear seat of the submerged automobile. Kennedy was being charged with leaving the scene of an accident after failing to report the mishap until nine a.m.

God, Buzz thought, the Kennedys have worse luck than the Buckleys—can't something good ever happen to either of us?

Driving through a small town, he pulled up in front of a drugstore where he knew the soda fountain was the town's social center as well as the purveyor of an excellent coffee frappe.

"Haven't seen you for a while," said the plumpish middle-aged woman behind the counter. "Where's your lady friend?"

"She couldn't come today."

As he sipped his frappe, he listened to the conversation at the other end of the counter. The news had barely come over the radio, but already they were talking about Teddy Kennedy and the girl in the car and that island—Chappa-what-was-it?

"I'll tell you one thing," said an older man wearing a visored John Deere cap and a wrinkled blue Cape Cod T-shirt, "Teddy's chances of making president died with that girl."

Buzz didn't want to admit it—he had come to like Ted Kennedy, like him a lot, since voting against him in '62—but his first thought on hearing the news story had been the same as the man in the John Deere cap: another Kennedy, like Bobby and Joe Jr., who'll never make president.

Buzz stood in the crowded control room at the station a few days later watching Teddy, on TV from Boston, make his *mea culpa* speech. He called his conduct after the accident "indefensible" and described himself at the time as "overcome by a jumble of emotions—grief, fear, exhaustion, panic, confusion, and shock."

Buzz was inclined to accept the senator's "confession" at face value. From his Army days, he remembered enough reactions of people under stress, including his own, to conclude that shock could in-

Tumultuous Affairs

deed have kept Teddy from reacting rationally to the accident. But he heard muttering from some of the other staff members who had been standing behind him. "What a crock!" said one as they filed out of the control room, a remark to which several others assented.

Buzz watched the TV screen intently as the space-suited figure stepped onto the surface of the moon. The day campers watching with him erupted in cheers.

"One small step for a man, one giant leap for mankind!" That was Apollo 11 command pilot Neil Armstrong's message to earth as NASA made good on President Kennedy's resolve to land a man on the moon before the end of the 1960s.

Despite the blanket network coverage, Buzz had assigned his own staffers to the local angle. Buzz and Benny were set up at the YMCA, which had suspended outdoor activities so that kids in the day camp program could follow the landing on TV sets in the gym. Kids usually make good television, and there were lots of excited kids, including some very knowledgeable ones.

Next morning, after the news had been digested, Jerry Finnerty did one of his patented man-on-the-street interview sessions in front of Heywood's Bookstore. He came back with some colorful reactions, including one from "an unpatriotic sourpuss," as Jerry called him, who thought the space program was a waste of money. And Jerry came back with something extra—news that Myra Heywood had eloped!

Myra had met Gage Packard, a top executive in one of the big Connecticut insurance companies, on a Caribbean cruise. She was on the rebound from the breakup with her longtime lawyer friend, Erwin Edwards. Erwin kept his silence, but rumor at the Y had it that he finally couldn't take any more of Myra's conservative politics, especially when she kept inserting them in her conversation during what were supposed to be intimate moments.

Gage was probably ten years older than Myra, but he was every bit as wealthy, was a widower, and had been high up in the Goldwater and the Nixon campaigns in Connecticut.

Durham Caldwell

"This," Judy told Buzz and Johnny over a table at the Heidelberg, "was not a case of opposites attracting."

The newlyweds built themselves an elegant new home just below the Massachusetts-Connecticut state line, within easy driving distance of their respective business establishments.

Only difference detected by her employees from Myra's new status was her formal signature—now Myra Heywood-Packard—and the informal one she used for bulletin board memos, "Myra H-P" instead of "Myra H."

21

Judy brought an "Issues '69" program suggestion from the mayor's office: the Garden Towers Apartments. And she added her own suggestion: instead of part film, part talk, make it a full-fledged documentary. "Plenty of material," she said. Buzz knew she was right.

This byproduct of South Park urban renewal, like so many 1960s high-rise low-income public housing projects across the country, had become, in the words of Jimmie Shoemaker, "an instant slum the day it opened." Buzz jumped at the suggestion for the documentary, motivated partly by a compulsion to tell the story, partly by the hope that an undertaking this big would help get his mind off his broken love affair.

Other parts of the huge South Park redevelopment effort had made good progress. The expressway and the retail complex both opened on schedule, the parking garage almost on schedule. Initial occupancy of the retail complex was a satisfying seventy-five percent. Rentals in the office tower came a little more slowly, but Money Bags Jardine gave the tower a big shot in the arm by taking over five floors for Jardco's corporate headquarters. The Redevelopment Authority claimed to be in the final stages of negotiations with a major hotel chain to build next to the office tower.

Most of the firms already in the industrial park were small local ones classified as light industry, but Jardco and the newspaper company, two major tenants, had both broken ground and were putting up steel. The Chamber of Commerce was continuing efforts to attract new companies from out of town. The Chamber's Frank Leatherbee told the "Issues '69" audience, "The best salesman the city has is Mayor Feigenson."

The continuing series of groundbreakings, ribbon cuttings, and speculative stories about possible new development brought civic morale to what former Mayor James A. Garfield McCann insisted was its "highest level since V-J Day." Big Jim, whose administration conceived the project, was a regular participant in the groundbreakings and ribbon cuttings.

Max—and close associates like Judy—tempered their enthusiasm for the urban renewal plan's business successes with their knowledge of what Max freely admitted was "the Garden Towers disaster." Buildings were overcrowded. Maintenance was almost nonexistent. Illegal liquor sales, even drug dealing, went on practically out in the open. Break-ins and muggings were frequent. Vacant ground-floor apartments were boarded up to keep intruders out. The combination of boarded windows and vandalism left the almost new project looking like a war zone. Social programs were slow to get started and never adequate to meet the needs of so many families with so many children.

As black families who had owned their own homes in South Park gradually found ways to move out of the Towers, Hispanic families moved in. The child population soared even higher—Jerry Finnerty recommended "birth control pills in the drinking water." Friction between blacks and Hispanics contributed to an atmosphere of fear that made some parents reluctant even to let their children leave their apartments.

"I could have said, 'We told you so,'" the mayor told a Chamber of Commerce breakfast. "Instead I'll ask you to watch Buzz Buckley's TV special and then give us your best advice, individually and collectively, on what we can do to turn Garden Towers around and make it a decent place for people to live."

The problems at Garden Towers had been coming to the attention of the news media in dribs and drabs, but the "Issues '69" special brought the full scope of the situation into the public eye for the first time. Doing the interviews and doing the filming had been a sobering experience both for Buzz and for Stan Wlodyka, who had done most of the camera and editing work. Infrequent drinker Buzz found a vodka collins an especially welcome companion when he dined with Johnny and Judy after a Friday at Garden Towers.

Tumultuous Affairs

Buzz watched the broadcast of the program at Johnny and Judy's house. Even though Buzz had screened the finished product at the station as well as individual segments, some many times over, as Stan worked on the editing—and even though Judy had seen some of the segments—all three of them sat in silence as the program unfolded.

The documentary opened with scenes of drab high-rise red brick buildings, their windows filled with mostly black and Hispanic faces trying to catch some air on a humid summer evening, spaces between the buildings bare of grass and teeming with children, close-ups on doors with broken glass and missing doorknobs, elevators with crayoned signs reading "OUT OF ORDER," darkened stairwells where all the light bulbs had been smashed or stolen and where wind and rain swept onto the landings through broken windows, apartment ceilings stained by leaky drain pipes a floor above, a basketball court littered with broken bottles.

A young black mother comes on screen surrounded by half a dozen children. "They told us it would be paradise," she said. "On Oak Street, we had porches and trees and flower gardens. And it was cool. Here we got nothin'. So hot in the summer, you cain't stay in your apartment. So dirty and dusty out here, you cain't keep clean."

A second young mother, this one in curlers: "They's fifteen hunderd kids in these buildin's, most of 'em in the five high rise. You send the kids out to play. Where they gonna play? They got ten swings for fifteen hunderd kids."

Back to the first young mother: "No bathrooms out here. Sometimes the kids wait a little too long. They gotta go back up to the sixth, seventh, eighth floor to go to the bathroom. Half the time the elevator don't work. Or it gits stuck between floors. The kids, they cain't wait—they go the closest place. They do their numbers in the hallway or on the elevator and hope nobody sees 'em."

Stan's camera focuses on youngsters playing in some of the two dozen abandoned cars scattered through Garden Towers parking lots. "A favorite playground for the kids," Buzz narrates, "despite their smashed windows, vandalized upholstery, and the beer cans littering the floor, a souvenir of their use for drinking parties. A fascinating place for kids to play because it's just about the only place they have.

Durham Caldwell

Tenants are outraged that it takes the Housing Authority as long as a month to get an abandoned car towed away."

The face of an older woman fills the screen. "Garden Towers is an eighteen-million-dollar mistake. I'm not used to livin' this way. I'd move out if I could. But I can't afford a-hundred-twenty-five, hundred-fifty dollars a month for an apartment."

A teenage boy: "Some o' the buildin's, they got rats and roaches, and they don't do nothin' about 'em. Yeah, they sprayed last spring. Spray draws more roaches, makes 'em grow fatter."

The camera goes into the attractively-decorated, immaculate apartment of a Puerto Rican woman. She, along with her husband and five children and all the other tenants of the building, Buzz narrates, "have been living with the unbelievably foul stench of a sewer backup in the building's basement." The camera shows a tenant with a yardstick measuring overflow in the basement at thirty inches deep.

The mother, in halting English, tells Buzz that they have been living with the stench for a whole month. Raymond Barksdale, the black manager for Garden Towers, tells the camera that tenants blocked the sewer pipe by trying to flush objects like drapes down the toilets. But he adds, "Downtown," meaning Housing Authority headquarters, "puts us at the bottom of the priority list for maintenance. The elderly projects come first. Then the others. Then us, maybe. Even on an emergency call, we wait and wait and wait. That sewer backup is a big job, but I'm ashamed it's taken this long. They claim they couldn't find a contractor to do it. But they found one yesterday when they heard you people were in there taking pictures."

"The blockage was cleared on a Thursday," Buzz reports, "but five days later, water-soaked trash and garbage still clutter the basement hallway and the elevator shaft." The camera shows the heaps of soggy refuse. "No work done over the weekend, no work done Friday or Monday beyond the maintenance crew's normal four p.m. quitting time, and today the maintenance people are involved in the more pleasant task of mowing grass."

Raymond Barksdale appears on camera to point out that despite being project manager he has no authority over the maintenance staff. "Priorities," he says, "are goofed up."

Tumultuous Affairs

The Housing Authority executive director from "Downtown" blames "poor communication" for the delay in cleaning up the mess.

Buzz: "Tragedy while we were filming this report. A three-year-old boy falls to his death from a third-floor window. The buildings have no security screens."

Architect: "Federal Housing Administration regulations wouldn't let us include showers or washers in the design. We had to use materials that I wouldn't use in a private building."

Housing Authority Chairman: "The federal government is giving us some modernization money, but it's taking a long time to get here. It's taken us two years to put in the first deadbolt lock—they're the first line of defense against break-ins. Our priority need is for a security force, but we can't use that modernization money for anything except bricks and mortar."

U.S. Senator Edward Brooke: "I was appalled by my visit to Garden Towers. These have to be among the worst housing conditions in Massachusetts." Brooke promises to work to make federal housing assistance more flexible.

The final segment of the program spotlighted recommendations of a local task force appointed by the mayor. These recommendations included such elementary proposals as giving the Garden Towers manager authority over the maintenance crews, getting somebody on the office staff who can speak Spanish, filling a spartan meeting room with ping-pong and pool tables and other recreational equipment, and engaging the Boys and Girls Club to manage a recreation program. The major task force recommendation was to relocate most of Garden Towers' large families into existing or new homes scattered around the city and to convert most of the space at Garden Towers into housing for the elderly—a goal it estimated would take three years to accomplish. "Drastic conditions," explained the task force chairman, "require drastic changes."

The mayor appeared on camera to say he would ask the City Council and the U.S. Department of Housing and Urban Development to help him and the Housing Authority put task force recommendations into effect.

Durham Caldwell

Station Manager H.B. Baker concluded the program with an editorial calling for support for the task force proposals "including a citywide housing construction program." He called for "an end to federal red tape and lower echelon buck passing which have helped make a mess of Garden Towers and most of the low income housing projects in the country." The federal role in the future, he said, "should be limited to financing, preferably in the form of block grants, and to technical assistance when requested." And tenants, he said, "should have a piece of the action, a role in policy decisions."

H.B. had been reluctant to take an editorial position on something as "radical" as public housing, but after seeing the first completed segments of the program, he had joined in enthusiastically.

When the program ended, Judy kissed Buzz on the cheek. "Great job!" she said softly. Johnny walked over and shook his father's hand. "Dad, I take back all those nasty things I've said about your news department. That was a first-class piece of work!"

Buzz was pleased. Probably the best piece of work he had ever done. A moving piece. He was enthused. He couldn't wait to tell Mar about it, and how much J and J had liked it. Then he remembered—Mar, with whom he had shared so many smaller triumphs—Mar was no longer part of his life.

For months after Buzz said goodbye to Mar for the last time, he lay awake at night, sometimes asking aloud plaintively, "Why, Mar? Why?" Had she grown tired of him? Was it the old business, he wondered, about forbidden fruit being the sweetest? Had she reveled in their love because it was secret and soured on it when the opportunity came at last to bring it into the open and sanctify it with marriage?

The house had been so empty and lonely after Elaine died. Mar had brightened it with her visits and brightened it with the bouquets of flowers she brought with her and placed in vases around the house and which served as reminders that she would soon be coming again. Now the vases were empty, the house was emptier than ever.

"Why, Mar? Why?" he asked, sometimes in a voice so anguished he felt she must surely hear him way off there in the Boston suburbs. But no answer ever came.

Tumultuous Affairs

He responded to the breakup with Mar the same way he had handled the death of Elaine. He buried himself in work. He came to the newsroom early and left late. It was almost as if he wanted to avoid going home to the empty house where again the dust was beginning to accumulate unchallenged by Mar's periodic assaults with the vacuum cleaner.

He stopped taking days off. He was again his old irascible self. He snapped out orders, demanded perfection, and took on for himself many of the most challenging assignments. Colleagues who had once talked among themselves about "how Buzz has mellowed" now assured each other, "That's the real Buzz."

Buzz tried extra hard to put on a smiling face when he met with Judy or with Judy and Johnny. He wanted to allay the concern Judy had expressed for him that Thursday evening at the station. He had wrestled again with telling her the whole story but again had decided against it. Really, what could she do besides feel sorry for him—or maybe scold him for carrying on an illicit romance?

Even after he got his emotions more or less under control, Buzz missed Mar dreadfully. Determined as he was to forget her, he couldn't. He would be in the van with Stan or Benny riding to a news assignment and finding himself wondering what the *Globe* had Mar doing that morning or that afternoon. He would be walking past a newsstand, determined to keep going, but finding himself being pulled back to buy the *Globe* and search for Mar's byline.

The work she was doing for the *Globe* gave him a feeling of pride—even though he blamed the paper for coming between them. From the initial routine assignments, the editors were giving her increasingly difficult, increasingly important stories to cover. She had the knack of asking good questions, of explaining complex issues in simple language. And he marveled at the style and the sensitivity with which she wrote.

As time passed, he found it increasingly difficult to believe this accomplished woman had allowed him to be her lover for so many years. How had he been so stupid as to let her get away from him? How he longed to hold her in his arms again, to feel her soft hair against his cheek, to bask in that mischievous smile.

Durham Caldwell

Many evenings, in the loneliness of his living room, he toyed with picking up the phone and dialing her number. It would just be a friendly conversation between two old acquaintances. How wonderful it would be to hear that throaty voice again. But pride kept him from phoning—or was it fear, fear of being hurt yet again by this woman who had hurt him so badly?

22

In the 1969 local elections, Mayor Feigenson was an easy winner for reelection. Mister DDT lost another bid to get back on the council. Judy won a fourth term, and Johnny gave pride in Judy's vote as the reason for whisking her off to the Caribbean for a second honeymoon.

Judy and Johnny were still away when, as Jerry Finnerty daintily put it, "the fecal matter hit the fan" at the city's high schools. Racial violence. There had been sporadic incidents previously. White youths had ambushed black youths at a school bus stop to teach them a lesson about flirting with white girls. A white youth and a black youth had come to fisticuffs in a lunchroom over some unknown grievance, and supporters of the two combatants had filled the air with milk cartons, fruit, and even a few trays. And there were one-on-one fights which principals usually denied were racially motivated. "Isolated incidents" was the School Committee's party line. Stepped up vigilance by administrators had always kept things from getting out of hand—up till now.

This time another lunchroom brawl spread to two dozen or more youths from each race. It spilled out onto the sidewalk in front of Lincoln High. Police called to the scene were just getting it under control when another brawl erupted in back of the school. Every cruiser in the city responded. The seriousness of the situation was apparent in the voice of the police radio dispatcher. Buzz and Stan sped to the scene with Buzz directing the newsroom to locate Happy and Benny and get them on the way. He figured he might need the extra help.

Buzz and Stan pulled up behind the school. Stan jumped out of the car, assumed a crouched position, and put the viewfinder of his Bolex to his eye to catch a vicious brawl between two whites and two blacks that police had not yet gotten to. He had filmed for about ten seconds when Buzz saw one of the white youths, a tall beefy kid with a shaved head, turn and head toward Stan. Before Buzz could get close enough to intervene, the youth had slammed the palm of his hand over the lens of the camera and pushed it back into Stan's face, bowling him over on his back. The rubber eye piece protected his face, but Stan lost control of the camera, and it clattered to the pavement, bouncing a few feet away.

The white youth and his companion ran off in one direction, the black youths in the other, as club-carrying police converged on them.

"You all right?" Buzz asked Stan in a worried voice as he helped him up.

"Yeah, I'm okay. The sonuvabitch caught me by surprise! I shoulda been watchin' out."

"How's the camera?"

Stan was looking it over. He wound it and shot a few feet of film.

"Seems okay. These Bolexes are tough cameras."

Without waiting for instructions, Stan took a cover shot showing the whole wild scene, then ran toward another spot where the brawling was continuing. Punches were raining in all directions, supplemented by a few kicks and slaps.

Police finally cleared the area. Buzz and Stan ran around to the front of the building to look for the principal. They found him already doing an on-camera interview with Happy. Stan aimed his camera at two cruisers pulling away from the curb, handcuffed black youths in the back seat of one, handcuffed white youths in the other, including the kid with the shaved head who had bashed Stan's camera. It did Buzz's heart good to see the news car from the other TV station just pulling up to the curb.

Just then, on the radio of the nearest parked cruiser, Buzz heard a call from a clearly agitated dispatcher. "Trouble at Washington High! All cars that can be spared from Lincoln, get over there right away!"

Buzz and Stan got to Washington just after the first cruisers. The principal was standing on the front steps telling the officers that

Tumultuous Affairs

half a dozen black teens, probably from Lincoln, had smashed the glass on a side door, raced through the corridors knocking over any white kid who got in their way, and then run out the rear door onto a side street.

Stan ground away with his Bolex at the angry principal, then followed Buzz around to the side to get a picture of the broken glass. They saw a commotion on the side street behind the school, ran over there and saw a policeman and some passersby attending to a middle-aged white man, an unsuspecting pedestrian, who had been assaulted by the black youths as they fled the school. His face was bleeding profusely.

The police radio broadcast reports of a fight between white and black teens at a downtown bus stop. A gang of whites jumped the younger son of Jimmie Shoemaker as he walked up the hill toward the Central City. Parties unknown threw a paving brick through a classroom window at the city's third high school narrowly missing the teacher. Buzz and Stan in one news car, Happy and Benny in the other, raced back and forth across the city trying to keep up with things.

Eventually the police radio was silent. Buzz sent Stan's film back to the station with Happy and Benny so Benny could get it into the processor. He and Stan drove to the School Department's central office. They met a grim-looking Mayor Feigenson on the walk leading into the building. Max's only words before he disappeared behind the closed door of the superintendent's office were, "Thank God we've got Rod Berry."

Rodney P. Berry, Ed. D., was the new Riverbridge school superintendent. He came from a long line of educators. His great-great-grandfather, Nathan Berry, had worked with education pioneer Horace Mann back in the 1830s, and at least one Berry from each generation—more often two or three—had served Massachusetts public schools ever since. The School Committee had hired him from out of town over the objection of member Lucille Cournoyer, who called him "too liberal."

Durham Caldwell

Since his arrival in the city, Rod Berry had gently prodded the committee to do something meaningful about racial imbalance, so far without notable result. "The race riot at Lincoln," as the daily paper termed it, and its spillover into the other schools and onto the streets would be Rod Berry's first big test.

The superintendent and the mayor moved fast. While Buzz and Jerry were still preparing the early news, a phone call came from Max himself.

"Buzz, we're closing all the high schools till further notice. Hope to reopen Washington and Jefferson day after tomorrow. Lincoln'll probably take longer.

"We've called the Council of Churches and the Pastors Conference—the black ministers—for help. Jimmie Shoemaker's going to open his church tomorrow morning for a mass meeting of all black teenagers. The church council's going to let us know shortly which church it'll be for the white kids.

"When the schools do reopen, we'll have plenty of cops. We'll give special attention to bus stops, to the junior highs, so the trouble doesn't spread there, and to anywhere else the chief or the superintendent say we need it."

"You mean you're actually going to approve police overtime?" Budget conscious Max had threatened the chief that he wouldn't get new cruisers if he didn't drastically cut overtime spending.

"Don't be a wise guy!" Max didn't see any humor. "This is a crisis situation. We've got reports about kids raiding trash piles to get bricks and clubs. Cops stopped a couple lugging baseball bats. We don't want a goddam war!"

"Max, forget my little joke. You want to come on the news live and tell us just what you're doing?"

"I'll send you Superintendent Berry. I've got to be on the other station."

"How come?"

"We drew straws."

"Who won?"

Tumultuous Affairs

"No comment," laughed Max, who hadn't lost his sense of humor completely.

Buzz attended the emergency meeting of the School Committee that night. Max asked the committee to ratify the steps he and the superintendent had already taken.

Lucille Cournoyer objected. "Mister Mayor, we should have been consulted in the beginning."

"Mrs. Cournoyer," said Max impatiently, "you want to be out there on the sidewalk with a riot helmet on, next time we'll call you. Mister Berry, make a note of that. Now, on the motion . . ." It passed with only Lucille in opposition.

The two churches hosting the morning meetings of teens barred the doors to reporters. "We want these young people to speak their minds freely," Jimmie Shoemaker told the disgruntled newspeople gathered on his church's front steps. "If you desire it, we'll let the participants choose a spokesperson to converse with you afterwards. But I just hope you'll all recognize, these young folk are not necessarily sophisticated in the ways of the media"—he smiled at Buzz—"like some of us. And remember, too, we have a very sensitive situation here. We're trying to defuse it, not exacerbate it. We hope you gentlemen can appreciate that."

"What a vocabulary!" Connie Hogan of the other TV station commented as the Reverend Doctor Shoemaker went back into the church.

There was a good attendance of teenagers at both churches. And according to the students selected as spokespersons at the two locations, a very similar list of grievances. From the meeting of the white students: there's favoritism—the teachers favor the black kids; black kids are too aggressive, always shoving white kids around; they're always making fresh remarks about girls; they call us "honkies." From the black students: teachers play favorites—the white kids are the favorites; too many white kids have chips on their shoulders and push us around; the boys don't have any respect for black girls; they call us "niggers" or "boogies."

Durham Caldwell

"You'd think the same kid wrote both lists," Buzz commented to Jimmie Shoemaker.

"It demonstrates the deep gulf in understanding between the two groups. But it also shows the groups are remarkably similar. We'll try to build on that."

"But Buzz, these were pretty much the good kids that were here today. They can put policemen in the schools and on the sidewalks from now till Easter—and there could be an eruption on Easter Monday—unless somehow the good kids can convince the troublemakers to talk out their problems and their frustrations, not try to settle them with mayhem."

Superintendent Berry worked quietly with the clergy, with the mayor, and with the police to get things back as close as possible to normal in the high schools and as quickly as possible. He himself seemed to be everywhere.

He directed principals to select a cross section of black students and a cross section of white students to meet together in a continuing series of interracial dialogues. He scheduled faculty meetings to discuss the perceptions about favoritism and other grievances stemming from the church meetings. He directed the deputy superintendent to work full time at Lincoln High alongside the principal till further notice, plucked half a dozen experienced counselors from other assignments to work at the same school, and spent a major amount of his own time visiting the three high schools, talking with both faculty and students one-on-one or in small groups and encouraging them to treat those of the other race the same way they wanted to be treated.

But not all parents were convinced by the assurances of the mayor and the superintendent that the reopened schools were safe. "The buildings are too big for the police to be everywhere," one parent told the paper as justification for keeping her high schooler at home. Absenteeism, both white and black, ran high at all the schools, especially at Lincoln, for several days after they reopened. In a new incident, two black girls threw a cup of water in the face of a white girl in a Lincoln upstairs corridor. The white girl was frightened and

Tumultuous Affairs

got her blouse wet but was not really hurt. Her parents railed at failure of the School Department to make the schools safe.

The next night, Buzz covered a quickly-called meeting of outraged white parents. He went alone. No cameraman. A good place, he thought, to keep a low profile. But halfway into what was turning into a meeting of "us against them" invective, one man stood up and pointed a finger at Buzz.

"I see Mister Buckley here from the TV station. Maybe Mister Buckley will tell us why the news media never tells the true stories about these incidents."

Buzz sat silently, but others—men and women—yelled, "Come on, Buckley, tell us!"; "Yeah Buckley, how come you never tell our kids' side?"; "Hey, Buckley, do you know what really happened?"

When the man chairing the meeting pointed at him and said, "How 'bout it, Buckley?" he reluctantly got to his feet.

He thought it was like making a speech at your own lynching. He felt like calling them all a bunch of racist bastards. But, speaking as calmly as he could, he said, "Look, I can't speak for the other media, but where I work, we try to get the facts. Sometimes it's tough to do, but we try. We work hard at it. We try to be factual, not inflammatory. What you want, and what the black parents want, is the same thing." Moans of disbelief from the crowd. "You both want the bad apples taken care of, whatever color they are. You both want a place where your kids can go to school where it's safe and where they can learn. I've lived in this city a long time. I know a lot of black parents, and I know a lot of white parents. And it bothers me to hear some of this talk here tonight where you make it sound like black parents are encouraging their kids to beat up your kids . . . "

The audience wouldn't take any more.

"Ah, sit down, Buckley!"

"That's all you know about it!"

The man chairing the meeting banged for order with the carpenter's mallet he was using for a gavel. He recognized a man in a flannel work shirt a few rows behind Buzz. A tall, husky man that Buzz didn't recognize.

Durham Caldwell

"I just want to put in a word for Mister Buckley. He didn't have to come here tonight. But he's here listenin' to what we have to say. We oughta be workin' on how to solve this problem of kids beatin' up kids, not takin' potshots at the other kids' parents, and certainly not takin' potshots at a newsman who tries to do his job."

There was enough grumbling to cause the chairman to take another whack at the table with his mallet. The remarks of Buzz and of the man in the flannel shirt did not change the direction of the meeting, but it proceeded, Buzz thought, with a little less vitriol. He was glad to leave without any more barbs thrown at him, but he was disappointed that the man in the flannel shirt disappeared before he was able to express his gratitude to the man for sticking up for him.

23

For the second time since his election as president, Richard Nixon was coming to Massachusetts to celebrate his birthday as the guest of his daughter and son-in law, Julie and David Eisenhower. This time the birthday coincided with the coldest night of the 1969-1970 winter. As Buzz stood shivering on a snowbank outside the Eisenhowers' apartment, he had a sudden regret that he hadn't assigned the story this year to somebody else—not because of the cold, but because it came to him that a year ago Mar had been standing next to him along this same sidewalk. He would almost push her out of his mind—then a memory like this would suddenly pop up and begin haunting him all over again.

He'd been lonely. So lonely he'd asked Linda, "the Employee Benefits," who he knew was a divorcee, to go to dinner with him.

She'd looked disappointed. "Oh, Buzz, if you'd only asked me a month ago. But the guy I've been dating—last week we got engaged. He'd shoot me if I went out with anybody else, even one of the bosses from the station."

He had even toyed for a moment with checking out Myra Heywood. She had often flashed a come-hither look. But no, she was married—it wouldn't be right, would it, to hit on a married woman?—and, without stopping to consider that this was something he'd done already with a certain Mrs. Antonelli, he recognized right away that Myra would not be a direction he wanted to go in, married or single or however lonely he might be.

The crowd waiting at Julie and David's apartment for the presidential party was smaller than the previous year. Blame that on the cold, Buzz thought—it couldn't be much more than ten degrees. It was a generally friendly crowd that greeted the small Nixon motorcade, but sprinkled in with the "HAPPY BIRTHDAY" signs were a few others with such legends as "WAR ISN'T THE ONLY WAY" and "NO BIRTHDAY FOR 40,000 MEN."

Christ, thought Buzz, has the damned war killed off that many?

While the Nixons celebrated inside the apartment, the press and some of the security people warmed up inside the nearby St. Michael's School where the sisters provided steaming pots of hot coffee.

When he and Benny went back outside and walked up the hill to Julie and David's apartment, Buzz could sense a change in the composition of the crowd. Some of the older well-wishers, probably numbed by the cold, had disappeared. In their places were more young people of college age. Some carried lighted candles and crosses made of white cardboard. The antiwar signs had multiplied.

As the president, Mrs. Nixon, and Tricia emerged from the apartment, anti-war chants like "One, two, three, four! Tricky Dicky, stop the war!" vied with the cheers of supporters for the president's attention. This time, Nixon didn't linger.

As the engine of the news car wheezed to life and the tires crunched on the snow in the St. Michael's parking lot, Buzz ordered Benny, "Turn up the heater all the way!" As the two commiserated with each other about the cold, Buzz noted, "Thank God, I was wearing my long johns!" And then it occurred to him for the first time—these were the long johns Mar had given him, given him gaily wrapped that same night she had told him she wasn't ready for marriage. Push her out of his mind? God, it was hard to do. He rode the rest of the way back to the station in silence.

Mar's disappearance from his life had given Buzz new cause to envy his son. Johnny, for whom everything had always come easy, had a woman, a beautiful loving woman. Buzz, for whom everything had been difficult, had nobody. He had always enjoyed Judy's visits to the station, the Friday evening dinners at the Heidelberg, and the other occasions when they got together. But now she was filling a huge void. The Tuesday afternoons and the Thursday evenings when they worked together on "Issues" became the central points of his life. On those very rare occasions when she couldn't get to the station, or when Johnny came alone on Friday evenings, he felt stood up, empty. He kept denying it to himself—just as he had once denied an early symptom to Mar—but he was slowly, surely falling in love with his son's wife.

What had started as "Issues '64" was now, almost six years later, such a fixture on the TV station's Sunday morning schedule that community leaders vied to get the program to cover their pet projects and to appear as guests.

H.B. had never paid Judy a nickel, and she had never asked for one, but she still met faithfully with Buzz almost every week to plan future programs. She still greeted him in the lobby with the same flirtatious smile, the same flirtatious remarks, the same lilting little laugh that used to be her trademarks at City Hall and around town before she and Johnny were married. Marion, the receptionist, got a big kick out of their byplay, which she assumed was just for her benefit.

"You're so good looking I don't know why H.B. doesn't have you on TV all day," Judy might say.

"He wanted to put you on," Buzz might reply, "but I warned him your smile would melt the lens on the camera." But once in his office, she was right down to business as they talked about issues that needed bringing up, new ways to treat them, and the guests who would be the most informative and the most provocative.

Since Buzz's breakup with Mar, these planning sessions with Judy were like a tonic. Once, when he knew Judy was stretched out between the bookstores and an especially heavy run of council business, he suggested reluctantly that she might want to take a brief hiatus from the planning meetings. She reached across his desk and touched his arm.

"No," she said, "I don't see nearly as much of you as I'd like to. These Tuesday afternoons are a special time for me. I'll cut corners somewhere else if I have to, but not here." Those few words buoyed him up like nothing had since the false hopes that were born the day Mar told him she was getting a divorce.

Despite the other demands on her time, Judy was also usually at the station for the Thursday evening taping of the program. The post-program pattern was always the same. They would say goodnight to the guests, he would give his desk a final straightening and turn out the lights in his office. She would clasp his arm as he walked her through the parking lot to her car. She would always find something about the show to compliment him on. He would usually say quite truthfully that it was one of her ideas that had really made the show a good one.

At her car door, she would always stretch up on tiptoes and kiss him on the cheek.

Buzz now admitted to himself that his affection for Judy, strong right from the beginning, had grown far beyond the affection a normal father-in-law should feel for his son's wife. But he found it impossible to pull back from the precipice he felt himself speeding toward. When he got that kiss on the cheek in the parking lot, it was all he could do to restrain himself from enfolding her in his arms and telling her, "Oh, Judy, I love you so much!"

One Friday evening, as Buzz waited for his son and daughter-in-law at the Heidelberg, Judy walked in alone.

"Hello, Bombshell. Where's Johnny?"

"He had a business appointment. He should be along in a little while." The way she said it made him decide not to push for more information.

As Buzz nursed his usual vodka collins and Judy a grasshopper, they talked about the American "incursion" into Cambodia and how it was intensifying antiwar protests across the country.

"Nixon just can't get it through his head," Judy said, "that we've lost the damn war."

"I wonder what he thought when he came up to Northampton this time to visit Julie on his birthday," Buzz added, "and all those protesters gave him the business? Quite a change from last year when he was the guy who was going to bring us back together."

Just then Johnny came into the restaurant and walked toward them, smiling broadly. As he slid into the booth next to his wife, he told her exuberantly, "I got the job!"

Tumultuous Affairs

She put her hand on his arm. "Oh, Johnny, I guess I'm happy for you. But I'm sad, too. I've been having so much fun working side by side with you."

"Well, I'll still be your consultant."

"What's going on?" demanded a mystified Buzz.

"Dad, I'm going to work for Jardco. Buckley Bookstores made a couple of business deals with Money Bags Jardine. He liked my style, and he's been bugging me to join Jardco ever since.

"I didn't want to leave the business. It's got a great future. But Judy has come in and learned it up, down, and sideways. And Money Bags finally made me an offer I just couldn't refuse.

"Get this, Judy. I start off as Northeastern sales representative. And when old Milton Bradbury retires this summer, I move into his job as national sales manager!

"Think of it, Dad. National sales manager for a Fortune 500 company! And meantime Johnny's own little company steams full speed ahead from college campus to college campus with the smartest, most beautiful businesswoman in New England running the show!"

"It's all settled then?" asked Buzz.

"All settled!" said Johnny with a look at Judy.

She responded with what Buzz took to be an attempt at a brave smile.

A girl from one of the suburbs was a student at Kent State University in Ohio. She had witnessed the fatal shootings by National Guardsmen of four students who had been protesting the U.S. invasion of Cambodia. Her grandmother, who once worked in Baker Broadcasting's traffic department, brought the girl to the station for an interview the day after she got home from school. The young lady was well dressed and well spoken. But she embarrassed her grandmother and even left interviewer Jerry Finnerty momentarily speechless when she referred on camera to the trigger-happy Guardsmen as "those fucking pigs." Luckily it was a filmed interview and not a live one. And there was still enough invective left to let the young lady make her point even after Stan's judicious editing.

Durham Caldwell

Too bad I'm not still seeing Mar, Buzz thought. It was something she would have gotten a laugh out of.

Something else Mar would've enjoyed, Buzz was sure, was the raucous 1970 Democratic State Convention at UMass in Amherst. The new Democratic state chairman, fearful of protests like those in Chicago in '68, had installed a series of tough security measures including mandatory photo id's for officials, delegates, and the media. The protests never developed. The convention was a wild one but wide open. By the afternoon of the second day, Buzz counted dozens of people in the hall wearing other people's id's—unchallenged by anybody. But Mar wasn't there. The *Globe* had her covering a variety of stories, but not politics.

Senate President Maurice Donahue, he of the 1964 Democratic National Convention's Credentials Committee, was rewarded for his patience. Known as "Mossie" to his friends, he had gracefully accepted defeat in his bid for the 1966 state convention endorsement for governor. According to some accounts, he had even worked harder for convention nominee and eventual election loser Eddie McCormack than McCormack had worked for himself.

At this convention, Mossie won the gubernatorial endorsement. But it proved to be for nothing. Buzz shook his head as the returns came into the newsroom on Primary Night. Boston Mayor Kevin White, after losing to Mossie at the convention, was beating him in the primary.

Some of Mossie's people were so upset that they sat out the general election or even openly supported the Republican, Acting Governor Frank Sargent, for a term of his own. Coasting on the Democratic disunity and his own slogan, "Keep Sarge in charge," Sargent won in November by more than two hundred thousand votes out of just over two million cast.

Ronald Reagan was elected to a second term as governor of California. Judy, showing again how closely she was following the Republican Party nationally, remarked to Buzz when she came to the Thursday night taping session at the station, "Did you notice our Texas friend George Bush got beat again trying for the Senate? He should've stayed in the House."

Tumultuous Affairs

Buzz's observations were closer to home: "Keep your eye on Mike Dukakis. This is a guy with a lot of energy and a real talent for organization." Dukakis was the young state representative from Brookline who had battled his way to the Democratic endorsement for lieutenant governor in both the convention and the primary only to go down to defeat bracketed with Kevin White in the general election. "He'll be back," predicted Buzz. "He's excited a lot of people."

Frank Sargent, now governor in his own right, was a Massachusetts original. He was a tall, angular man—as loose and easy-going as his cousin, Elliot Richardson, was stiff and proper. He had a laconic, if sometimes coarse, sense of humor. He was an astute politician—and made a point of keeping himself well-informed.

H.B. Baker was earning himself a reputation among Baker Broadcasting employees as only a part-time executive during the summer months. It was getting to the point that four-day "weekends" were the rule rather than the exception. He spent more time at the helm of his sailboat, an elegant thirty-five-footer, plying the waters of Long Island Sound than he did behind his mahogany desk steering the company.

But H.B. was there when Governor Sargent came to Baker Broadcasting on a summer Monday for the ceremonial launching of the company's new and more powerful television transmitter. The transmitter had actually been on the air for a week, but this was the first opportunity to get the governor into the act. Sarge was to push a button on the TV console, with the cameras rolling, to "officially" inaugurate this new era in local television broadcasting. As Al Maroney led him into the control room to shake hands with Max and a few other assembled dignitaries, his eyes fell on Half-Baked Baker.

"H.B.!" Sarge exclaimed in mock surprise. And then in his Yankee drawl, "Youah not down on th' boat t'day!" H.B blushed right up to the bare spot under the wispy strands of hair at the top of his head.

After that, on those rare summertime Mondays and Fridays when H.B. showed up at the station, Jerry Finnerty would stop in at Hy Golden's office—or Hy would stop by the newsroom—and the

Durham Caldwell

visitor, with a hand cupped over the side of the mouth, would do his best imitation of the governor's drawl: "H.B.! Youah not down on th' boat t'day!"

And the other would come back with as witty a response as he could think of: "We ran outta booze," or "Money Bags needed a loan," or "Myra Heywood's husband was away, and she got lonely."

24

Just as Judy had sensed something was wrong with Buzz right after his breakup with Mar, Buzz now sensed that something was wrong between Johnny and Judy. He wasn't sure when it was that he first noticed it except that it was around the time Johnny went to work for Jardco. Probably it was no one thing, just a cumulative series of little things.

Johnny, who had seemed to turn over a new leaf when Judy came into his life, was sliding back more and more into the old Johnny. From small comments about his sales successes during their Friday evenings at the Heidelberg, he graduated to the point where he was talking almost incessantly about the orders he was taking for Jardco.

He talked about how he and Money Bags were planning strategy for the new products the company was bringing on the market. "Money Bags really likes my ideas. Of course, we don't call him 'Money Bags' to his face. It's always 'M.B.,' or the junior guys call him 'Mister Jardine.'"

Along with his bragging came a resumption of the gratuitous knocking. "Half-Baked Baker and his half-baked TV station. Dad, how long you gonna work for that cheap hicktown outfit? Judy and I'll give you a good job in the bookstores." And as in the old days, his father's news department was a particularly frequent target. "How many cans of hair spray does Jerry Finnerty go through in the course of a broadcast?" "Can't Hooper pronounce anything with more than three syllables?" "Another film break last night. Don't those yahoos know how to splice film?"

Judy looked embarrassed during Johnny's sallies. Buzz noted that when they were sitting in a booth and she was joining them late or returning from the ladies' room, she no longer moved in close to Johnny the way she used to. Nor did they hold hands and look at the same menu together. Rarely did they turn to each other with those spontaneous shows of affection that they used to shower on each other. Little things, but they worried him.

At the end of one of their "Issues '70" planning meetings, Buzz asked Judy, "What's wrong between you and Johnny?"

She looked as if she was about to cry. She bit her lip, looked away, then turned back to look him in the eye as tears glistened in the corners of hers. She put her hand on his.

"You don't miss anything, do you?" She tried to force a smile.

"Buzz," she continued, her hand still on his, "we're trying to work it out."

She leaned over, kissed him on the cheek, then walked out of the newsroom without waiting for him to get up and see her to the door.

Judy and Johnny seemed more cordial to each other the next few Friday evenings and on those less frequent Sundays when Buzz was invited to dinner. Johnny talked less, listened more, asked questions about the week at the bookstores and the week in the news business. Judy held his hand again and sometimes leaned her head on his shoulder. But to Buzz, it looked like play acting—as if Judy had told Johnny, "Let's at least try to put on a show for your dad." Just the way, he thought, that he had tried to put on a show for Judy after the breakup with Mar. And when he walked with them to the parking lot on Friday evenings, he noted that they had usually come in separate cars and that Judy always made the turn toward home but Johnny often drove off in another direction.

Though the play acting continued, there was an occasional barbed comment followed by a barbed response and then an embarrassed silence from both parties. They again gave up hand holding. Nor did Judy lean her head any more on Johnny's shoulder. Once Buzz got to the Heidelberg late and from across the dining room saw what looked like a bitter full-fledged argument in progress, an argument they broke off to greet Buzz with smiles and pleasantries as he approached the table.

Judy began missing many of the Friday get-togethers. Johnny usually offered the excuse that she'd had a busy week and was tired

Tumultuous Affairs

out. There were no more Sunday dinner invitations. Judy herself offered no explanations when she visited Buzz at the station. On these occasions, it appeared she was trying to be her usual personable self. She came close but didn't quite make it. Buzz knew something was wrong.

Another marriage was also in trouble. Several months after Mister and Mrs. Gage Packard moved into their new home just below the state line, Gage moved out. No one knew why, but there were rumors he had taken up with an attractive fortyish divorcee from New Haven. Myra never publicly acknowledged the split. She continued to commute to Connecticut. And she continued to sign her letters and contracts "Myra Heywood-Packard" and her memos "Myra H-P."

Jerry Finnerty got a laugh out of his newsroom colleagues by telling them "Myra H-P" stood for "Myra Hot-Pants." Most of them took it as just another Jerry Finnerty-ism. But Buzz wasn't so sure. He had seen Myra and Jerry engaged in very earnest conversation at the Chamber of Commerce outing one weekend—one of the very few outings he could remember that Jerry left early. Maybe Jerry had some personal knowledge.

Celebrity watchers in the United States as well as in Canada were titillated by the news that Pierre Trudeau, the fifty-one-year-old Canadian prime minister, had taken a twenty-two-year-old bride. Buzz's reaction: some guys do make out with younger women. Now, if only Judy weren't attached . . .

As he told himself this, looking in the mirror as he shaved, he shook his head—who's kidding whom? But he couldn't keep his mind off her. Her beautiful face. Her stunning figure. Her intelligence and her delightful personality. God, she was some kind of woman! A couple of times, he even found himself repeating Jerry Finnerty's little prayer: "Just one time, Lord, just one time." And though Buzz knew it was wrong even to imagine sleeping with a daughter-in-law even just one time, he couldn't stop doing it.

Despite whatever problems had developed between Johnny and Judy, the Friday night that she and Buzz drove Johnny to Bradley Air-

Durham Caldwell

port to catch a business flight to Florida, the couple maintained at least an outward show of cordiality. After he and Judy said goodbye to Johnny at the gate—Buzz thought the goodbye kiss rather automatic—he put his arm protectively around her to guide her through a crowd of departing passengers. She seemed to snuggle into his shoulder.

On the drive back to town, she was quieter, more subdued than usual. She even seemed to be a little bit on edge. As he pulled up the driveway to her front door, she said matter of factly, "You'll come in for a while, won't you?"

He probably would have accepted the invitation under any circumstances. But thinking there might be something she wanted to talk with him about, he felt he had no choice. She sat him on the brocaded living room sofa and went into the kitchen to mix him a vodka collins. "Easy on the vodka," he advised. "Remember, I've had one already." Watching through the kitchen door, he thought her hand shook just a little bit as she poured it from the bottle. He wondered why.

"I'll be right back," she said as she handed him the drink. "I want to get into something more comfortable."

She appeared to force a smile—it certainly wasn't the natural beaming smile that she could light up a room with. He assumed "something more comfortable" meant getting out of that pinstriped business suit and into maybe a pair of slacks and a sweatshirt. Instead she came down the stairs a few minutes later in a smartly cut blue-and-white-striped seersucker robe.

"You men," she sighed, "will never know what a relief it is at the end of the day to get out of a bra and panty hose. Like getting out of a straitjacket."

He thought she was trying to sound casual, trying to put on more of a smile than she actually felt. But then her tone changed as she knelt beside him on the sofa.

"Buzz, why do you always flirt with me?" Her voice was mischievous. "Do you think that's proper for a father-in-law?"

My God, he thought, is she scolding me just for being friendly?

"Me flirt with you? You flirt with me so shamelessly I didn't want you to feel that you were unappreciated.

"Actually," he said after a pause, "I like you very much." He was surprised at his audacity

At that she smiled what he knew was a genuine smile. He looked up into her amused face and smiled back.

"Buzz," she said, still smiling but with her voice slightly tense, "you're a very sweet guy. I've come to like you very much." She emphasized the "you." She leaned forward to buss him on the forehead. "In fact, I like you so much I'm going to seduce you."

His eyes drank in her flawless face and tried to imagine her body from what he could see of its outline under that seersucker robe. He put his drink down on the coffee table.

"You couldn't possibly seduce me," he responded, keeping his voice as level as he could at a time he wanted to shout from the treetops.

He saw a look of disappointment, almost panic, cross her beautiful face. He realized that what she had just said to him must have come only after a long inner struggle. He grasped her hand to reassure her. "You couldn't possibly seduce me," he repeated. And now there was a nervous edge to his voice. "Judy, I've hungered and thirsted for you for so long. By definition it's not seduction when the other party is a willing and eager partner right from the beginning."

The look of near panic disappeared. A smile enveloped her face. The real beaming Judy smile that lit up the room, the hallway, the kitchen, and probably the whole front yard. She leaned forward to kiss him on the lips. His hand found its way inside her robe. He cradled in the palm and the fingers of his hand one of those warm, soft breasts he had admired and coveted for so long.

He put his other hand on her knee. Her bare knee. She put her hand firmly on top of his.

"Not here," she said, the natural buoyancy coming back into her voice. "That's why they invented bedrooms."

There was a spring in her step as she took him by the hand and led him across the living room toward the stairs. He followed like an obedient puppy, marveling at the turn of his fortunes. He had never been a ladies' man. Elaine had been his only real love. And now what had happened to his lifetime of moral rectitude? In San Francisco,

Durham Caldwell

one of the prettiest girls from his high school class had thrown herself at him, and they had enjoyed a long and exciting affair. And now one of the most beautiful young women he had ever seen, a woman little more than half his age, was literally tugging him into her bed.

Twice blessed, he thought, as he followed her over the bedroom threshold.

Despite the confidence with which she had led him up the stairs, Judy was tense at first. Buzz diagnosed it as first-time jitters. Under the persuasion of his gentle kisses and caresses, she relaxed and was wide open to him.

As they lay there afterwards, his arm around her, she told him, "Buzz, I'm not the kind of girl who sleeps around. But I've wanted to do this with you for so long. I've just come to love you so much. I've fantasized about it so many times. But I was always too chicken to follow through. I'd wonder, would it really be a proper thing to do? Then tonight, when you put your arm around me in the airport, I knew it was right."

Such a little thing, he thought, putting an arm around her to guide her through the crowd. Little thing? A stroke of sheer genius.

"I was still nervous. You could probably tell. I knew you liked me. But you're such a moral guy. I didn't know how you might react to an aggressive young chick."

"And?"

"You made it so easy. I'm kicking myself for waiting so long when I wanted you so much."

"You wanted me? God, how much I wanted you!"

His thoughts drifted from the unalloyed pleasure he had just experienced to the man who was this bedroom's rightful occupant and this beautiful woman's rightful partner. It was the second time that he had turned his back on the Ten Commandments. Except this time the cuckold was not a faceless dentist but his own son.

As he thought about it, that made him feel better. What a joyous way to help even the score with his high and mighty offspring. But he wanted to reassure himself.

"You don't feel guilty, do you?" he asked her softly.

"Guilty about what?"

"Cheating on Johnny?"

She pushed herself up on a forearm, put the other arm around him, and kissed him. "Buzz, I know he's your son. But I've been living with him for six years. The first ones were wonderful. The last ones have been hell. Do you know why he flew to Miami tonight for a trade show that begins Monday?"

"To get things ready, maybe play golf?"

"Baloney! He's going to spend the weekend with the head buyer of South Florida's biggest chain of department stores. The female head buyer. And I don't think they're going to be talking product—though he'll probably get a big sale out of it.

"And he'll be seeing some managers and some other buyers later in the week. Servicing the accounts is what I think Jardco calls it.

"And do you know what else?" she asked as he lay there in stunned silence. "He has an affair going on right here in town with Myra Heywood."

Johnny and Myra Hot-Pants? "You're joking."

"Not a bit. Why do you think Heywood's has Jardco merchandise blossoming all through the store? It's not because Myra has any admiration for Money Bags. As far as she's concerned, Money Bags is a dangerous radical. He was for Eisenhower."

"Who told you all this?"

"Nobody told me. At least they didn't know they were telling me. I studied psychology in college. I possess pretty good instincts. And when I'm around other people from the company, other people from the bookstore business, other people from the Chamber, I listen a lot. I hear things. Sometimes I overhear things."

He was silent for a minute. "And you're using me to get even with Johnny?"

"Buzz, it may look like that. When I first started thinking about it, maybe it did figure in. But the more I thought about it, the more I realized I had really fallen in love with you. Those Tuesdays and those Thursday nights at the station, the Fridays at the Heidelberg, the times you came over for Sunday dinner—when you stop to think about it, we've spent a lot of time together. And you've grown on me. I've just come to have such a deep affection for you. You're everything Johnny isn't. You're kind, you're patient, you're thoughtful, you're a square shooter. Even DDT," she giggled, "thinks you're a square shooter."

He was embarrassed. That couldn't be him she was describing.

"Then tonight, at the airport, you put your arm around me. I knew it was right. I was so relieved, so happy, when you said you liked me and wanted to do it, too.

"Feel guilty?" She laughed her lilting little laugh. "Heck no. Do you?"

"Not in the least."

She kissed him again and lay back down in the crook of his arm. "Buzz," she said after a while and squeezed his hand, "I don't want this to be a one-night stand."

"If you did, you'd have to fight me off."

It was the gentle touch of Judy's hand that woke him.

The first feeble signs of daylight were peeking in around the window shades. This time she took full command. And the unbridled pleasure he took from her every movement was enhanced tenfold by the sight above him of her exquisite body bathed in the rays of the rising sun.

25

It was another local election year, and the names of potential candidates were beginning to surface. Max figured to be a shoo-in for a fourth term. With more and more pressure from the black community to correct racial imbalance in the schools, would-be challengers were shying away. Bobby Clark, the black militant, was collecting signatures. He would get a lot of space in the paper and on TV, but not many votes, Buzz predicted.

Bobby was promoting a new approach to *de facto* segregation. On one of the "Issues '71" programs, he floated the idea of "decentralizing" control of the school system. "Seems like local politics won't permit the power structure to balance the schools. Us black folks should switch our focus to quality education—quality education in schools controlled by the community."

Max, on the same program, said he sensed a change in the public mood, "agreement that quality education is more important than numerical balance." Perhaps the first step, instead of busing, should be lowering the pupil/teacher ratio.

Lucille Cournoyer and others on the School Committee found the idea of community control just as heretical as two-way busing. And there really wasn't enough space in the schools to give immediate attention to Max's suggestion of reducing class size.

Judy was planning to run for another term on the council. Depending on who else got elected, she would have a good shot in the coming year to be council president. She had a growing reputation for intelligence and steadiness to go with her seniority. But Johnny this time wanted no part of the campaign. He was too busy selling and traveling. And to one of their Friday evening dinners he brought the suggestion that Judy get out of the race.

They had been talking at the company, it turned out. Money Bags was thinking Johnny might be a good candidate for mayor a couple of years down the road, but of course he couldn't run if his wife was a member of the council. Besides they were putting some good candidates in the council race this year to give Silent Joe some help in speaking up for the business community—"You know, Dad, the people who provide the jobs." And if Judy stayed in, she could be embarrassed by getting beaten—this business ticket was going to put on a *gung ho*, well-financed campaign. They weren't going after Max, but with their five guys on the new City Council, they could block anything they didn't like that Max sent up to them.

Buzz took a big sip of his vodka collins and counted to ten. He didn't know whether to be more outraged at Money Bags Jardine's new attempt to control city government or Johnny's willingness to play messenger boy.

Judy gave a soft answer. There was a twinkle in her blue eyes as she gave it. "You tell Mister Jardine I'll think about his suggestion."

When Judy came into the station Tuesday afternoon, Buzz asked her if she had really thought about Money Bags' attempt to get her out of the race.

"Of course," she said, "I gave it all of about two seconds' worth of thought. My papers are in, my signatures are certified. But Buzz, this is going to be a rough campaign. You saw the names of the people they're putting in. Well known people. A little more forward-looking than Myra. Probably soulmates of Calvin Coolidge. They'll plaster those five names all over town—and they'll have plenty of cash to do it with."

The 1971 campaign was an advertising bonanza for the broadcast stations and the newspaper. True to Johnny's word, Money Bags and the Mattawampus Club crowd spent big money on their City Council ticket. Television spots produced by Jardco's Boston ad agency. Saturation coverage on drive-time radio. Full page ads in the paper.

But the big money ticket had a secret army working against it. Max, figuring Bobby Clark would not be hard to beat, put his organization to work for Judy and the other "good guy" councilors plus some attractive newcomers—a slate of six against "the big money five." Big Jim McCann, content to be on the sidelines during the two previous

Tumultuous Affairs

elections, reenergized the old McCann Machine "for one last push." And each of the "good guy" candidates threw his or her own friends and relatives into the united campaign effort.

At Judy's invitation and sworn by her to secrecy, Buzz sat in on a meeting with Max, Big Jim, Rowdy, and The Ad Man. The Ad Man's real name was Argirios Vaselacopoulos, but because that was such a mouthful, clients like Max and most of his friends called him by the catchy name of his one-man agency. The meeting was in the back room of the bar run by Rowdy's cousin.

They looked over the layout for a flyer they planned to plaster the city with the Sunday before the election. The front was a near duplicate of the Boston ad agency's flyer highlighting the names and pictures of the five candidates of the big money boys—except this one identified the five in big letters as "The Big Money Ticket—the names to avoid when you go to vote." And there was a big red "X" through each face.

"Where'd you get the photos?" Buzz wanted to know.

"Ah," said Big Jim with a chuckle. "Don't you know there are McCanns—and cousins of the McCanns and in-laws of the Mc-Canns—in every printing plant in the city?"

"They smuggled out the photos?"

"No, Buzz, nothing crooked like that. They just made us some extra halftones."

Inside the flyer, in big print, was a question, "Do you want Money Bags Jardine and the other big shots at the Mattawampus Club calling the shots for City Hall? If not, pull the levers next to these names." A list of the six "good guys" followed with a photo of each.

"So whaddaya think, Buzz?" Max asked with a laugh, enjoying the presence of a supposedly neutral newsman at a flagrantly partisan backroom political gathering.

"You got an artist? Why don't you put white hats on the good guys?"

"Go to hell!" said Max. He turned with a grin to The Ad Man. "Remember not to buy any time on his station."

The secret army not only delivered the flyer to nearly every home in the city, it rang nearly every doorbell to make a personal

Durham Caldwell

pitch to the householder to back up the flyer. The group had also raised enough money for its own full-page ad the day before the election, repeating the message of the flyer and listing phone numbers for transportation to the polls.

On Election Day, a fleet of automobiles ferried voters, especially senior citizens, to the polls and home again. Other volunteers held signs outside the polling places: "Beat the Big Money Boys!"

The last-minute blitz caught the big money boys by surprise. There wasn't time to react to the flyers—except for some nasty words in Donald Dibble's column on the morning of Election Day: "This cowardly last-minute attack..." And the big money boys had neglected an Election Day operation of their own. No cars. No signholders. No telephone canvassers. Buzz wondered if it was smugness—or ignorance—like the time their failure to gather enough signatures kept H.B. Baker off the ballot.

On Election Night, Buzz and Jerry Finnerty broadcast the returns with great glee. Of the five members of the big money ticket, only the veteran Silent Joe weathered the blitz, and he finished eighth. Voters turned back still another attempt by Domenico DiTotola to get back on the council. The six members of the good guys slate finished one through six. Judy was the top vote-getter among the council candidates—Johnny, after sitting out the campaign, begrudgingly offered congratulations. The other council winners were Slick Simpson, the only black member, and Billy Maguire, whose reputation for lack of productivity on the council rivaled Silent Joe's. Despite, or perhaps because of, his problems with the state Board of Education, Max rolled to reelection with his biggest majority yet. Bobby Clark polled strongly in the Central City but got few votes anywhere else.

Buzz's romance with Judy was not a one-night stand. Johnny was making frequent out-of-town trips. Since Judy was his daughter-in-law, Buzz could take her out to dinner without causing tongues to wag. After dinner, they would go for long drives in the country during the summer evenings, get out of the car at some secluded rest area, and walk hand-in-hand in search of gurgling brooks and hidden waterfalls.

Tumultuous Affairs

Occasionally they would go to the theater together or to the cinema—a thoughtful father-in-law looking after his son's wife while the son was away. Or he would take her home, she would invite him in, and they would spend hours together sitting in the living room and talking. They found so much to talk about. City politics, state politics, the big local issues, the big national issues. TV programs they had done together, new programs they would like to do. Their respective childhoods, colorful relatives, school experiences, places they had been, places they would like to go.

The day of the Memorial Day parade, Buzz talked with Judy about the war in Europe, memories he had repressed for more than a quarter century, things he hadn't even told Elaine about. She put her arms around him and hugged him close as he suddenly broke down in tears thinking about the friends he had left behind in Normandy and the Ardennes—and finding out when he got home about the loss of his brother Buddy. She held him and gently rocked him, not saying a word, until he was ready to talk about more mundane things.

He felt so close to her.

On the way home one night, Buzz found himself thinking the same thoughts he had once had about Mar: this woman could be a cloistered nun, separated from me by an iron grate, and I would sit outside that barred window for hours on end, she is such a delight to be with.

But Judy, like Mar, was no cloistered nun. And despite the fun they had together doing so many other things, Buzz and Judy frequently expressed their deep affection for each other in the big double bed "where," Judy sometimes reminded him with her glorious smile, "I first seduced you." Occasionally she would add, "And you had to spoil all my big plans—you claimed it wasn't seduction."

For Judy, as it had been for Mar, the act of sex—at least after what may have been the initial thrill of adventure had worn off—became an expression of the deepest love. She made allowances for the difference in their ages without in any way embarrassing her partner. She would make known her willingness in a dozen different ways, especially her smile and sometimes with a wink that would have done her parents proud. But—except for that first time—she was never insistent. She left it to Buzz to take the lead and invariably was a gracious and exuberant follower.

Like Mar, Judy derived great physical satisfaction from these acts of love. There was usually just enough light in the bedroom for Buzz to see and enjoy the radiant smile that wreathed her face. But in contrast with Mar, for whom the approach to lovemaking was invariably laced with humor, usually ribald humor, Judy approached it gently and often with great seriousness. The way she once described her feelings to Buzz, their union was a work of art as majestic as the music of Mozart or the poetry of Shelley. He found it difficult to believe how beautiful a love affair could be.

Johnny was out of town often enough and usually long enough to give them full freedom to enjoy each other's company. On those rare occasions when Johnny's schedule kept him in town for long periods, Buzz and Judy would sometimes set up a breakfast-time rendezvous at his house and get to work a little late—or leave work a little early and part by dinner time. It wasn't the way they liked to do it. But sometimes, they agreed, you made sacrifices to avoid being consumed by longing and to get on with the other parts of your lives.

A neighbor, spotting Judy's car in Buzz's driveway one morning, wondered if Buzz had a new cleaning lady. "No," another neighbor assured her, "that's just his daughter-in-law."

In the newsroom, Buzz was smiling again. He was encouraging coworkers instead of snapping at them. He was taking extra pains with the new people to help them develop their skills. He was more understanding of personal problems. But this time, Buzz wasn't taking a lot of unexplained days off. There were no calls from mysterious throaty-voiced females. In fact the only personal calls Buzz ever got were from his daughter-in-law.

The newspeople were glad of the change in Buzz's personality, even if they couldn't explain it.

Max's new term was marked by a tug of war on racial imbalance. Superintendent Berry would offer what to Buzz and Judy seemed like sensible solutions. Max and the School Committee would water them down, removing most or all of the two-way busing the superintendent had included. Lucille Cournoyer would vote consistently against even the watered-down versions. The Board of Education would hem and haw to cut off the state's allocation of local aid to the city.

In Washington, President Nixon called for a moratorium on court-ordered busing by federal judges. The same day in Boston, the Republican governor, Francis Sargent, promised to veto any attempt to repeal Massachusetts' Racial Balance Law.

Then the state board really got tough with Riverbridge, refusing to release state money on grounds the city had provided no firm timetable for addressing most of its racial imbalance problems. It was rumbled that this was in part a message to the Boston School Committee, which was also dragging its feet on balancing its schools.

The Riverbridge School Committee reacted by voting to go to court, charging the Board of Education with misreading its authority and with "massive and capricious enforcement of the law."

Rod Berry told Buzz and Judy "off the record" prior to an "Issues '72" taping, "The lawsuit means this thing will drag on for at least another year."

The superintendent was right. It took the Supreme Judicial Court of Massachusetts till the first of September to issue its ruling: Riverbridge must obey the state board's edict to balance all grades in all its elementary schools and do it "for the opening of school in September 1973."

Happy Hooper was covering an antiwar demonstration at the gates of Westover Air Force Base. In a live report for the top-of-the-hour radio news, he said excitedly, "They're blocking traffic into and out of the base." He set the number of demonstrators at more than seven hundred. He quoted one of them, President John William Ward of Amherst College, as saying, "We're here in response to the war. This is the country's most pressing problem." A few minutes later, Happy radioed the newsroom, "The cops are moving in! I could use some help at headquarters!"

Buzz gritted his teeth. Besides himself—and he was backed up with paperwork—Jerry Finnerty was the only reporter in the newsroom. Did he dare send him out on the story? If he did, would Jerry

Durham Caldwell

spend his time encouraging his buddies on the police force to use their billy clubs?

"Jerry, Happy says they're loading 'em up on buses. Get down to the police station with Benny. Get the buses unloading. See what they're doing with 'em. They can't get 'em all in the lockup."

Jerry went off grumbling about "the goddam draft dodgers."

Buzz called after him, "Jerry, be professional!"

Jerry surprised him. He came back with a short interview with the police chief.

"Utter chaos," the chief said. He complimented the demonstrators for their cooperation with his officers after their arrests. But he added, "There are just too many of them."

The court clerk had been too busy to talk. He waved Jerry off with the advice, "Come back next week—if they're not still waiting in line."

But what apparently registered most with Jerry was the speech-making and singing that continued inside and outside the police and court building as those under arrest awaited their turns to be booked and arraigned. Jerry wrote a script to go with Benny's natural sound film that played up the demonstrators' combination of seriousness and good humor. The script made it appear that if they hadn't won Jerry Finnerty over to the antiwar side, they had at least temporarily neutralized him.

26

The Reverend Doctor Shoemaker and Jim Foster of the Urban League were among the guests for the taping of one of the periodic "Issues" programs on minority employment and the new catchword, "affirmative action." Jim Foster said he was pleased there were now blacks behind the counters of more Main Street stores—and even in the teller windows of some of the banks. But he emphasized that the city still had a long way to go in the area of equal opportunity.

As Buzz and Judy walked the "two Jimmies" to the outside door after the taping, Jimmie Shoemaker suddenly stopped, pointed a finger at Buzz, and asked gently in his mellifluous preacher's voice, "Buzz, how many people of color work here at Baker Broadcasting?"

Buzz blushed. The clergyman had taken him by surprise. But he'd known the question was bound to come up sometime. And he knew the answer—just one, Booker Jones the custodian.

"Brother Foster," advised Jimmie Shoemaker, "maybe the Urban League should start calling on the broadcast community. There are more black faces in one little bank downtown than on both our local television channels. Good night, Buzz."

The two Jimmies went out into the dark. Buzz turned to Judy.

"We don't get black applicants, at least not for news. I figure any black kid coming out of college with any qualifications at all can write his own ticket in a market bigger than ours."

"Or her own ticket?"

"Or hers. Hey, at least we're starting to hire women. Three or four years ago, the only women we had were the office help. Now we've got two gals in the newsroom, a couple more in production."

Buzz didn't tell Judy about the time many years before that he'd suggested to H.B. and to Al Maroney that they look for a "colored" reporter to fill a news opening. He was not being altruistic. He was thinking mainly of the publicity it would generate for the station.

Maroney had responded, "There isn't an ounce of prejudice in my body—but we have to think what our advertisers would say."

H.B. had been more blunt. "I don't want those people on the air on my station. Most of 'em don't have the brains to do news. Damn few good niggers. Booker's one of 'em, but he knows his place."

The dearth of black applicants had made it easy—too easy, he realized now—for Buzz to avoid revisiting the question.

H.B. had okayed the hiring of the two women for the newsroom only with great trepidation. Al Maroney had expressed misgivings about how the audience would react to a woman performing a traditional male role. But their reporting—and even their occasional anchoring—had been accepted by the community without a murmur.

Now that Jimmie Shoemaker had broached the subject, the absence of "people of color" on Buzz's news staff gnawed at him. Here they were covering civil rights to the point they'd been called "the nigger station," here they were doing program after program on racial problems on "Issues," and they were as lily-white as Mickey Cochrdan's station acrxosss town, as lily-white as Heywood's Bookstore. As near lily-white, he corrected himself. Myra also had a black custodian.

One voice told him, leave it alone. You're doing a conscientious job reporting on the minority community. A valuable job with "Issues." Don't get H.B. riled up and jeopardize everything.

Another smaller voice was telling him, you've got a crew now that works pretty well together. Why screw it up by bringing in a black guy—or a black gal? That would be all you need to touch off Jerry Finnerty. And how would Stan or Benny or the other photographers react to taking directions from a black reporter?

He talked it over with Judy. She told him about her mostly good experiences with minority hires at Buckley Bookstores and how some had moved up into junior management.

"You don't have any openings right now," she said. "When you have one, do what's right."

The problem: what was right?

He talked with Jim Foster. Could the Urban League come up with a decent black applicant who would work in their size market? And how could they sell him—or her—to H.B.?

"One of the problems, Buzz," Jim Foster told him, "is that young people don't see any black faces—or any Latino faces—on television. They don't have any role models. There's no signal that the doors are open. So when they go to college—the ones that go—they don't even think of a career in broadcasting.

"Buzz, we'll be on the lookout for people with some promise. But you may have to provide OJT—on the job training—maybe a lot of OJT. You won't get another Jerry Finnerty overnight."

"Oh, God, that's the last thing I want."

"As for Mister Hard-Boiled Baker—as we friends from the Mattawampus Club call him—we can put a little State Department diplomatic pressure on Mister Baker when the time comes."

Buzz wondered out loud how Jim Foster knew what they called H.B. Baker at the Mattawampus Club.

"Buzz, I waited tables there. It was the only job I could get when I got out of college."

"You don't have any openings right now. When you have one, do what's right."

Judy's words echoed in Buzz's mind for many weeks. Then one day, he picked up the phone and dialed Jim Foster.

"Have you found anybody for me yet? We've got an opening for a street reporter."

"Buzz, I was just gonna call you. A young man came in yesterday. Never thought of television. Never thought of news. But he's got some smarts. He might be able to handle it."

Whitney Garland came to the station that afternoon. A young, light-skinned man—about the hue of Ed Brooke. Certainly not something most white people would see as a threatening hue. A bit on the pudgy side—not the matinee idol type. A couple of years of college. Good sense of humor. Courteous without being obsequious. Absolutely no experience. Hadn't even written for a school paper.

Buzz gave him a writing test and was pleasantly surprised at the results. Grammar was correct. Words were spelled right. Some awkward sentences—but that was something they could work on.

Durham Caldwell

Like most applicants, he was a little on the nervous side when Buzz gave him a script and put him in front of a studio camera. But when he made a bad fluff early on, he covered it with a smile and a clever remark and seemed to gain confidence after that.

At the start of the impromptu interview that Buzz customarily conducted with applicants with the camera still on and tape still rolling, Whitney laughed, "I guess I booted that one."

"No, you recovered very nicely. Do you think you'd really like to work in television news?"

"You know, Mr. Buckley, I hadn't even thought of it till yesterday when Mr. Foster said it might be a possibility. I watched the news last night—both stations. Saw what the reporters were doing. Saw a little bit of what was going on in the newsroom when I came to meet you. Hey, I think I'd like it!

"It would certainly be a challenge. It's not like anything I've ever done. Holy smokes, I'd have a lot to learn! But I like to meet people, like to talk to people. And you've probably heard this before—but I mean it—I'll work my tail off to learn to do it right!"

Good attitude, thought Buzz, as he shook hands with Whitney and told him he'd get back to him. Now the big job: selling H.B. and program director Al Maroney on a black reporter.

The next day, Buzz had the control room play Whitney's audition tape for H.B. and Al. They sat and watched in silence. Buzz braced for a negative response. He got it from Maroney.

"Is that all—only one? Buzz, you know we can't put a black guy out on the street representing the station. Me, I don't have an ounce of prejudice in my body, but we gotta think about the reaction from the public, reaction from the people who advertise with us."

H.B. held up a hand. Here it comes, thought Buzz as he braced again and tried in his mind to formulate a comeback.

To Buzz's surprise, the boss aimed his remarks not at him but at Al Maroney.

"Hold on a second, Al. I spent an hour on the phone this morning with Warren, our Washington lawyer, talking about license renewal. And Warren says we've got a problem."

Tumultuous Affairs

The problem was FCC rules requiring broadcast licensees to follow nondiscriminatory employment practices. There were no quotas, but broadcasters were supposed to make good faith efforts to bring minority employment up to levels reflecting the racial composition of their broadcast areas. And since last year, the FCC required broadcasters to file annual employment reports.

"We've done okay hiring women. But Warren says we gotta get some minorities on the payroll or we're gonna have big trouble. Buzz, can this black kid do the job?"

"H.B., he's on a par with some of the white kids we've hired. No experience. He'll take a lot of grooming. But his attitude's good. And he's a local guy. He'll be able to find City Hall without a road map."

"Then hire him. Considering all the viewers we have in the Central City, I got to admit it's probably time we got a black face in the news department. And Al, I want to see some black faces—and some Latino faces—on the floor crew and in the control room. And damned quick!"

Will miracles never cease? thought Buzz as he walked back to the newsroom.

"Whitney, can you start tomorrow?" Buzz asked into the telephone mouthpiece.

"You mean I got the job? I can't believe it!" Whitney sounded genuinely surprised and overwhelmed. "Mister Buckley, I can start this afternoon if you want me to."

Most new hires called Buzz "Mister Buckley" for their first two or three days on the job before adopting the "Buzz" that was standard for the rest of the newsroom. The shyer ones might maintain the "Mister Buckley" for a week. It was always a relief to Buzz when they dropped it. He read it as a small but important sign that they were settling in, were getting to feel at home.

Whitney seemed to be settling in. He had some rough edges, like most new people. But he took direction well—and rarely had to be reminded of something a second time. He seemed to be getting along well with the rest of the crew, even Jerry Finnerty. Stan and

Durham Caldwell

Benny came in separately to tell Buzz how they enjoyed working with him. But after a month on the job, it was still "Mister Buckley."

Buzz took him aside. "Whitney, there's only one 'mister' in the building. That's Mister H.B. Baker. My name is 'Buzz.'"

Whitney looked embarrassed. "Sorry," he said, "that's the way I was brought up—to be respectful of my elders."

"Okay, but no more 'misters' in the newsroom. Understand?"

"Not even Mister Finnerty?"

"Especially no Mister Finnerty."

Buzz wondered what ripples, if any, the first black reporter in the market might be stirring up with the public—or with that equally important commodity, Baker Broadcasting's advertisers. He got his answer straight from the cigar-chewing sales manager, Hy Golden.

"Buzz, First National Bank's opening a branch in the Central City. They're gonna make a big pitch for business in the black community. They want to know if they can use Whitney Garland for some on-camera commercials."

"Hy, you know we don't let newsmen do commercials. Destroy the news department's credibility."

Hy looked disappointed.

"But I'll tell you what—when they have the groundbreaking or the ribbon cutting or whatever, I'll do my darndest to get Whitney there to cover the story."

Buzz was guest speaker at the Kiwanis Club the day after the 1972 presidential election. Only Massachusetts and the District of Columbia had voted for Democrat George McGovern. Buzz got a big laugh when he told Kiwanians that President Nixon was proposing a new U.S. flag with forty-nine stars. He didn't tell them he had stolen the line from Jerry Finnerty. Nor could he have conceived that the largely-ignored break into the office of Democratic National Chairman Larry O'Brien in Washington's Watergate complex the previous summer would lead to Nixon's eventual downfall and to the blossoming of bumper stickers reading, "DON'T BLAME ME—I'M FROM MASSACHUSETTS."

Tumultuous Affairs

In mid-November, an old friend from his early days in journalism, now a producer at CBS News, was in town for a wedding. He and Buzz got together for lunch. Buzz complimented the friend on his network's Watergate coverage. Though lagging behind the *Washington Post*, CBS—with correspondent Dan Schorr doing most of the legwork—had easily outdistanced ABC and NBC.

The friend leaned across the table.

"Buzz, you wouldn't believe what happened with that Watergate two-parter on the Cronkite program just before the election. Part Two damn near didn't get on the air. After Part One, Chuck Colson from the White House called Paley"—William Paley was the CBS chairman of the board—"and put the screws to him. Told him the FCC was gonna be on our tail, *et cetera, et cetera*. Paley wanted to yank Part Two. Instead it got on—watered down and cut in half. Those bastards at the White House play tough."

In December, Nixon bombed the hell out of North Vietnam. It was local news because for the first time a B-52 crew from Westover Air Force Base was shot down. It also brought serious discussion to the peace talks in Paris. A peace treaty was initialed in January. Westover became an Air Force processing center for returning prisoners-of-war.

Buzz got plenty of wear out of his one pair of long johns as he and overtime-hungry Stan Wlodyka made many middle-of-the-night trips to the wind-chilled flight line to film the POW arrivals from the West Coast. It no longer bothered him, deep in his affair with Judy, that the long johns had been a gift from Mar. He was pleased that a couple of times Whitney Garland turned up at the studio unbidden to take the wee-small-hours ride to the flight line with him and Stan—and to probe Buzz on the way back to the station on how he planned to write up that night's story.

The biggest welcome of all was for the last airmen shot down and the last ones to come home—Westover's own B-52 crew. Buzz assigned the story to Happy Hooper and Benny Goodreau. He also sent Whitney and Stan along to look for sidebar material.

Durham Caldwell

The two reporters and their cameramen found a thousand or so excited well wishers jamming the designated welcoming area well in advance of the scheduled early evening touchdown of the returnees' plane. This was in contrast to the dozen or two who had been showing up for the previous post-midnight arrivals.

Announced over the public address system one at a time, the former POW's came down the steps from the plane, walked or ran across the tarmac to huge ovations and the hugs and kisses of loved ones. Only the senior officer, Major Fernando Alexander, took the opportunity to say a few words into a waiting microphone. But it was not the major's words so much as the action, and the emotion, that made Happy and Benny's film so compelling. Alighting from the plane, the major strode briskly across the pavement to where his wife and teenaged son and daughter were waiting. He draped a *lei* over his daughter's neck—the plane had touched down in Hawaii *en route* from Hanoi—embraced each of them in turn, then all of them together. A long, lingering embrace punctuated by kisses. Then the major picked up two other *leis*, which had fallen to the tarmac, and draped them over the heads of Mrs. Alexander and his son before turning to the microphone. A full minute of solid joy and emotion, and Happy and Benny ran the entire segment without a word of narration, the band playing "The Stars and Stripes Forever" in the background over the murmur of the crowd and a couple of happy shouts of "Hey, Alex!"

As he watched the film on the eleven o'clock news, Buzz thought back to the sendoff of the first Westover B-52 crews to the Pacific so many years before—and how Jerry Finnerty had made that event seem like a college pep rally. The enthusiasm of that earlier day was repeated, and then some, in Happy and Benny's homecoming story.

But it was not all happy ending. Whitney and Stan found the pathos—a handful of lonely signholders on the edge of the crowd—the signs inquiring about other loved ones. Two crewmates of the men just welcomed so joyously were still missing in action.

27

Rod Berry presented the School Committee with a plan to divide Riverbridge into five pie-shaped districts with the Central City as the center of the pie. Each district had within it one of the imbalanced schools and four predominantly white schools. Enough black kids would be bused out of the Central City and enough white kids bused in to balance all the schools. Columnist Dibble, seizing on the district's pie shapes, ridiculed it as "the Berry Pie plan—it deserves a big razzberry."

A public meeting pitted white parents against black parents. "A majority of people don't want busing. Whatever happened to government of the people, by the people, for the people?" demanded a young white mother.

"Segregated schools were wrong in Topeka in 1954. They're wrong in Massachusetts in 1972!" shouted Lenora Clark, wife of the black militant who had run for mayor the year before.

School Committeewoman Lucille Cournoyer dismissed racial balance as "something concocted by white do-gooders who know the answers to everybody else's problems."

Max called one of his rare formal news conferences to observe, "Parents don't appear ready emotionally for busing. I don't think the School Committee will endorse any plan till we find one acceptable to a majority of parents, black and white."

"Max is getting testy," Buzz told Judy. "He's been living with this racial imbalance thing too long."

School Committee members voted down the Berry Pie plan on grounds it involved too much busing, then directed Superintendent Berry to formulate "a new plan with a minimum amount of busing."

The stalemate dragged into the summer of 1973. The state board ended it by adopting the recommendation of a special task force and ordering the School Committee to implement the Berry Pie plan.

Durham Caldwell

But the board heeded the superintendent's claim that it would take six months to work out the plan's logistics and his adamant opposition to making changes midway through the school year. The board set September of 1974 as the implementation date.

"They've stalled it another year," observed the Reverend Doctor Shoemaker when Whitney Garland interviewed him for a reaction.

Buzz expressed disappointment when Jerry Finnerty came back from City Hall without an interview with the mayor. "His Holiness would only talk off the record," Jerry reported. "Predicts the School Committee will keep stalling. But he says they'll do it without him. Buzz, he's not running for reelection! Says this racial balance thing has worn him out. Formal announcement next week. Insists we keep it off the record till then."

Buzz called Judy.

"Judy, did you know Max isn't running?"

"You're kidding. He hasn't said a thing to me. Are you sure?"

Strange, thought Buzz. Judy was the heir apparent, something Max used to joke with her about. Why hadn't he confided in her?

"Jerry got it from Max himself off the record. He's telling the world next week."

"I just took it for granted he'd run again."

"We all did. Next question: are you ready to run for mayor?"

"God, Buzz, I didn't think I'd have to face that for at least another two years."

"Face it quick. Filing deadline's coming up before you know it."

"You're taking me to dinner tonight. We'll talk about it then."

Buzz had mixed feelings about it himself. Their time together now was so precious and so limited that he begrudged thinking about anything else cutting into it. Still, he had just assumed for a long time that she would be the city's next mayor if she wanted to be. It was her decision. He resolved not to push in either direction.

They talked about it at the restaurant. Yes, she agreed, this would be a good opportunity to move up the political ladder. After five terms on the council, it was probably time to move up or out. But mayor—that was a full-time commitment.

Tumultuous Affairs

They talked about it some more in Judy's living room.

"I really enjoy running the bookstore business. And there's nobody there right now who's ready to take over the top spot. We didn't need a strong number-two when Johnny was there. And I've been so straight out since he left that I haven't really groomed anybody."

They talked about other possible candidates from the City Council and from the community at large. None of the names they brought up enthused either of them. He could see her leaning toward running.

"Judy, there's one other thing you don't want to forget. The next mayor will inherit the thankless job of putting a racial balance plan into effect. Do you want to get stuck with that?"

He thought this question might encourage her to lean the other way. He was wrong.

"Buzz, I've been thinking about that. And frankly, I'm ambivalent on whether busing kids all over the city to come up with a magic number is a good idea. But the right person in the mayor's office may be able to keep the city from being ripped apart. Buzz, I've got to run. If I don't, and the city goes up in flames, literally or figuratively, I'd never forgive myself."

He took her in his arms and hugged her close to him.

"Just save some time for me," he whispered. "You can put me on the schedule as 'rest and recreation.'"

"A fat lot of rest you'd give me."

"How about the recreation part?"

Instead of answering, she asked him a question, a puzzled look on her face, "Buzz, why do you suppose Max didn't tip me off about his plans?"

"I don't know. I was wondering myself."

Suddenly she stood up, and her face took on a mischievous look that reminded him of Mar. She held out her hands to him, and as she pulled him up from the sofa with her lilting little laugh, she giggled, "I bet you've never gone to bed with a candidate for mayor!"

Buzz went with her to City Hall when Judy called on Max the next morning.

Durham Caldwell

"Max," she began after he confirmed he was stepping down, "isn't there anything we can do to make you change your mind? The city needs your kind of leadership now more than ever."

"Judy, I'm burned out. You can take the hammering only so long. And racial balance—there's no compromise, no solution. It's the same as it was with Big Jim eight years ago, Buzz. It's not fun being mayor any more.

"Besides I've got four kids. Sometimes when I come home, they say, 'Who are you?' Pretty soon they'll all be going to college. I've got to get back to my law practice and pull in some dough."

Judy swallowed hard. It was pretty much the answer she and Buzz had expected. "Well, Max, if you won't run yourself, will you support me? Will you encourage your organization people to work for me?"

Max's eyes narrowed. Buzz's heart sank. Max must be going to say how much he owed to Judy, how much he had appreciated her support, but it wouldn't really be right for an outgoing mayor to try to name a successor.

Instead Max looked directly at Judy. "Judy, there's more between you and this alleged broadcast journalist than a daughter-in-law father-in-law relationship, isn't there?"

Judy reddened—reddened right to the roots of her pretty blonde hair.

Buzz thought to himself, Oh my God, he knows.

Judy stammered, "Why would you say that? Is somebody who's out to get me telling stories?"

"Nobody told me anything. But twenty-five years in law practice and politics, I've developed a pretty keen sense of observation. And the looks that pass between you two from time to time, not to say anything about the amount of time you seem to spend together—they impress me as being well beyond the usual father-in-law daughter-in-law respect and affection. They impress me as what my dear departed grandfather used to call 'carnal attraction.'"

The room was dead silent.

Tumultuous Affairs

"Judy, how did a smart, sweet young girl like you—a girl with an unlimited future—get mixed up romantically with an old bastard like him? How did you let him drag you down to his level?"

"He didn't drag me. I went after him. Maybe it was a sense of adventure at first. I had a pretty sheltered background. Maybe even a little of getting back at a roving husband. But it deepened into something more than that. I love him deeply—and I think he loves me the same way." She gave Buzz a quick glance, then turned back to Max.

"And Max, he's not an old bastard. He's younger at heart right now than he's been in a long, long time. I'm glad that's at least partly my fault."

"If it gets public attention, they'll murder you both. Can you imagine DDT with an issue like that? Can you imagine what Dribble-I-Mean-Dibble would do with it? Your political career would die a sudden death. The people in this town might vote for a crook once in a while, but an adulterer—nasty word, but that's the technically correct one—is something else. Especially an adulterous woman. Rockefeller might get away with it, but if it had been Mrs. Rockefeller—no way. And besides, he wasn't her father-in-law."

"And Buzz," he addressed Buzz for the first time, "your credibility as a TV journalist would go down the pipe like a double dose of Drano. People would snicker at you when your face came on the screen. 'There's the guy that sleeps with his daughter-in-law.' And when people laugh at you—politician or media—you're dead."

Buzz was about to make his first entry into the discussion, to say something about how Max was right and how they appreciated his candor, but Max held up a hand to silence him. He turned back to Judy. His voice softened.

"Judy, I deplore the situation that you and my old friend here, and your respective hormones, have gotten yourselves into. It goes against the grain of everything I've learned since I was a kid. That's why I didn't talk with you ahead of time about what I was going to do.

"But just seeing you here reminds me what a great person you are—and what you can do for the city. I'll be very proud to support you for mayor."

Durham Caldwell

Judy and Buzz shot surprised glances at each other as Max continued.

"Judy, you've been the one consistent bright light on the City Council. I'm indebted to you more than I can say—not only for the way you've backed me with your votes but also for the skills you've built coalitions with.

"Can't you break off with this guy who's old enough to be your grandfather?"

She shook her head. "I don't want to."

"Well, at least for God's sake, can you use the utmost discretion? Can you get the electricity out of your eyes when you look at each other when other people are around?"

"We can try," she said.

Buzz nodded.

"If it comes out during the campaign, I won't have any choice. I'll have to tell 'em how shocked and dismayed I am and how of course I'll have to withdraw my support. But I want to beat DDT and Silent Joe—they've both got papers out—as bad as you do. I'll get my workers together, tell 'em I hope they'll work for you, and invite you up to give 'em one of your knockout speeches. How about Tuesday night?"

Max escorted his visitors to the door. Judy stood on tiptoes and kissed him on the cheek.

"Tuesday night," she said.

"And leave lover boy home. My people don't like reporters."

He put his arm in front of Buzz, barring the door. "Judy, wait outside for Grampa. I'll send him out in a minute."

He closed the door and looked straight into Buzz's face. "Buzz, you know I don't approve of this—any more than I approved your spending the night with that old classmate in San Francisco. Your morality stinks!"

Max paused, put a hand on Buzz's shoulder, and as he propelled him toward the door said in a low tone, "But I've got to hand it to you—when you pick a married woman to fool around with, your taste is excellent."

28

Buzz abided by the mayor's wishes and stayed home the night Judy met with Max's campaign organization. He paced the floor nervously. He knew that in this day and age political loyalties were mostly personal and not necessarily transferable from one individual to another. The phone rang. He glanced at his watch. Too early for Judy to be calling. He answered automatically, the way he did in the newsroom, "Buzz Buckley."

There was a moment of silence, then from a male voice with just a hint of the Patch in it, "Oh, sorry, Buzz, I was callin' your daughter-in-law. Too many John J. Buckleys in the phone book. I thought 'Junior' would be your son."

"He's John J. the Third."

"I didn't realize you TV guys had listed phones."

"Some of us do." Buzz couldn't recognize the friendly voice on the other end of the line, but it intrigued him.

"Buzz, you won't remember me. I'm Timmy McCann, Big Jim's nephew. I was one of my uncle's precinct captains in your old ward."

"Oh, sure, Timmy—you're the one they used to call Red, and I could never figure out why."

"I really did have red hair when I was a kid—before the worries of the world caught up with me and I lost it all.

"Buzz, it was nice talkin' to you, but now that I know what number to call, I'll dial Mrs. John J. the Third."

"She's not home, Timmy. Out at a meeting. You can try her in the morning. Or I could have Judy call you—she should be checking in with me after the meeting."

"Ah, what the hell, Buzz. I can tell you, and you can pass it on. You know, Uncle Jim talks to the mayor on the phone now and then. Can't get City Hall out of his system, I guess. This mornin', the mayor told him he was steppin' down and Judy was gonna run.

Durham Caldwell

"Well, Uncle Jim called all the captains and all the ward leaders—the ones of us that are left—called us over to the house tonight for a meetin'. Told us what a wonderful woman Judy was, what a fine councilor, and how she'll make a great mayor.

"Buzz, the old McCann Machine doesn't have the clout it used to. We keep lettin' that Frenchy bastard, Silent Joe, get reelected to the council—and that proves it. But Uncle Jim is askin' us to crank it up one more time. We've got a few friends still. And all the boys are spoilin' to turn out the vote for Judy. We sure as hell aren't gonna let Money Bags put Joe DeRosier in the mayor's office.

"One of the wise guys wanted to know if his precinct turns out the highest percent, would he get a private candlelight dinner with the new mayor?"

"If we win, we'll give the whole organization a candlelight dinner."

"That'd spoil it, havin' everybody there. But anyway, Uncle Jim put him in his place, reminded him that the councilor is a happily married woman."

"That's right," agreed Buzz, nearly choking as he said it.

"Uncle Jim's feelin' a little poorly himself, Buzz."

"I'm sorry to hear that."

"Well, Buzz, the old goat's gettin' up there in the years. But anyway, he wants me to be the contact between Judy and the organization. Let me give you my phone number. It's an easy one to remember. 567-1234."

"How'd you get a snazzy number like that?"

"Hey, Buzz, there are more than a few McCanns that work for the phone company."

Although she had made no formal announcement, speculation was running high among the city's political *cognoscenti* that Judy would be a candidate. She was next in line for those who had supported the Big Jim McCann-Max Feigenson approach to city government. But some Riverbridge movers and shakers didn't want another mayor of Max Feigenson's independence and especially an independent mayor of Judy Ferguson's energy and candor. That's what Buzz and Judy found out shortly after Johnny joined them for one of their Friday night dinners at the Heidelberg.

"Judy, I've been talking with Money Bags and some of the other top people at the company. We don't think this is the year you should be running for mayor."

"We?" said Judy quizzically. Johnny, after trying unsuccessfully to get her out of city politics, had pretty much ignored her last two years of council work.

"Well, especially Money Bags. Joe DeRosier's done him a lot of favors over the years, done favors for the whole business community. Joe's calling in his chips, and Money Bags figures they owe it to him to back him.

"The way they see it—the way we see it, I mean—is that if you're in there, it'll split the vote and Mister DDT could slip in. And no sane person wants that."

"Son, DDT's been out of office for eight years. The people wouldn't put him back on the council—why the hell would they elect him mayor? If Judy's in there, she's the favorite right off the bat. It'll be Joe DeRosier who's splitting the vote."

"Why's she the favorite?"

"Because she's been in there fighting and working. Joe's been sitting on his can, ducking most of the big issues—why do you think they call him 'Silent Joe'?—and voting the wrong way on most of the ones he votes on."

"Dad, this town has never had a woman mayor. Judy's only what—the second woman on the council? I can see it now: she's a carpetbagger; she went to one of those fancy colleges; why doesn't she stay home and keep house? This isn't the year, Judy. The city's not ready for it. Maybe ten years down the road, but not now."

"Is that what you think, son? Or is that what Money Bags and his flunkies have filled your ears with?"

"We talked about it, Dad. They made some points. I made some points. I reminded them what a good speaker she is and how well she gets along with people. But we came to a consensus just like I said."

Judy now spoke for the first time.

Durham Caldwell

"I'd like to do it with your blessing, Johnny, but unless a so-far-unknown first-class candidate comes out of the woodwork before the deadline for papers, I'm in. And you can tell Money Bags Jardine that I'm a better candidate than Joe DeRosier and I expect to get more votes than Joe DeRosier and Domenico Whosy-Whatsy put together."

H.B. Baker called Buzz into his office a couple of days later.

"Buzz, I won't mince any words. With Max Feigenson not gonna run, there's a lotta talk about your daughter-in-law running for mayor. If she does, you're either gonna quit and work in her campaign—or I'm gonna put you on an unpaid leave of absence. Otherwise you've got a real conflict of interest. I'm not gonna jeopardize our hard-won reputation for impartiality by having a news director whose daughter-in-law's running for mayor."

He wondered if H.B. was part of Money Bags' scheme to keep Judy out of the race. But Buzz had nursed some doubts himself about carrying on as head of the news department while working for Judy, even behind the scenes. He's making it easy for me, Buzz thought.

"Well, H.B, why don't we do two out of the three?"

"Two out of the three?" H.B. looked puzzled.

"I'll take an unpaid leave of absence. I'll work in Judy's campaign—if she wants me to. But I won't quit. If she loses the election, I'll still have a job here to come back to."

H.B. seemed flustered for a moment, then responded, "Yeah, okay. Isn't that what I just said?"

Buzz's only real regret about leaving the newsroom was that he hadn't had more time to spend with Whitney Garland. But with a year of news work under his belt, Whitney had become a reliable, if not completely polished, member of the Baker Broadcasting news team. Buzz hoped that Jerry Finnerty, or whoever took over the news operation, would have the time and the patience to continue with the young reporter's journalistic education.

With all the advance speculation, Judy's official announcement—with newly named campaign manager Buzz Buckley discreetly in the background—was no surprise to anyone. The surprise came the next day. Domenico DiTotola—possibly seeing himself as a distant third-place finisher—pulled out of the mayor's race.

"I don' wanna take no votes from my good friend Joe. Joe's gonna need all da votes he kin get ta teach dis beauty queen a lesson. If he beats 'er good, mebbe dis dizzy blonde'll give up on politics and go back ta keepin' house."

But pulling out of the mayor's race didn't mean giving up on politics.

"I'm gonna run fer da School C'mittee," he told the handful of reporters who had come to his news conference.

"Dat's where de action's gonna be. I'm gonna be da good right arm o' da new mayor. If I get elected, dere won't be no busin' 'less it's over my dead body."

"Does that mean you'd violate a court order, Domenic?" Happy Hooper asked him.

"Dat's a hypocritical question, Mister Hooper. I refuse ta answer on grounds o' possible self-discrimination."

Buzz, spending his last day in the newsroom, called Judy's office to tell her about the DDT development.

"He and Lucille Cournoyer will demagogue it together," Judy analyzed the situation. "They'll make the School Committee race a referendum on racial balance. Joe may try to do the same thing against me in the mayor's race. What's your advice, Mister Legendary Political Pundit?"

"Be statesmanlike and don't get rattled."

"You mean stateswomanlike."

"Stateswomanlike. Show 'em you're aware of the problem . . . the city is making progress . . . you hope to build on that progress . . . you hope to negotiate in good faith with the state board . . . that it's been dragging on for too long . . . and you hope to wind it up to everybody's satisfaction. How does that sound?"

"It sounds just like Max."

"Don't knock Max—he got elected four times. And Judy, we both know that except for some ministers, some Unitarians, and your friends in the League of Women Voters, there aren't many white votes in plugging for two-way busing."

Durham Caldwell

"You're right, Buzz. And we both also know that it's coming, like it or not, and the challenge is going to be doing it without tearing the city apart."

"But before you can deal with the challenge, you have to get elected."

They usually started the day with a meeting at campaign headquarters, a vacant store on Main Street which the owner, a good friend of Max's, let them have at a nominal rent. One day early in the campaign, Judy's car was in the shop overnight, and Buzz stopped by after breakfast to pick her up. He parked the car in the driveway, let himself into the living room, and called for her.

She startled him by coming in from the kitchen in her robe. She was walking with a limp, and as she came into the light, he could see that one cheek was bruised and puffy.

He bolted toward her and gripped her by the shoulders. "What happened? Did my son do that to you?" He fairly shouted at her as he felt a rush of adrenaline into his temples.

"No, lover, Johnny didn't do it. I did it myself. I fell on the stairs." She said it easily with a smile creeping over her puffy face.

"Judy, don't put me on!" His hands tightened on her shoulders. "If my son did that!"

She interrupted. "Buzz, relax. We've had our arguments, but Johnny has never laid a finger on me. He wasn't even in town last night. I fell down the cellar steps. Or at least halfway down. I was taking the laundry down to the washer. The heel of my slipper got snagged on a loose tread.

"I feel like such a fool. A grown woman tumbling down the cellar steps. Thank God, it wasn't all the way down.

"I don't think anything's broken, but I ache like hell. I'm going to see Doctor Connors at 9:30."

Nothing was broken. They rescheduled some appearances, and Judy stayed out of sight for a couple of days. Then, with some deftly-applied makeup on her bruised cheek and a scarcely detectible limp, she was back on the circuit.

Tumultuous Affairs

Max's little sermon weighed on Buzz's mind despite the hectic pace of his new campaign manager lifestyle, despite the new everyday closeness to the love of his life, and despite the firmness with which Judy had defended their relationship. It might be a step removed from incest, but from its beginning Buzz had known deep down that the relationship was an improper one. This time, there had been no dream of Elaine looking on approvingly to relieve his guilt. How could there have been?

How could he have let his lust draw Judy into such a relationship? That's what it was—lust. The lust of a lonely man for a beautiful young woman whose defenses were down because of trouble at home. A man who would be old and probably crippled with arthritis—like some of the Republicans at the '64 convention—when she would just be reaching the peak of her sexuality. Of course he loved her, and he was sure she loved him, but it was lust that got it started.

Max was right—Judy had an unlimited political future. She could be governor someday, a United States senator. But if Don Dibble, if Mister DDT, if any politically aware person in Massachusetts other than Max discovered what Max already knew, Judy's career would be over. Finished. How could he have been so selfish? How could he continue to be?

One morning they both arrived early at the little storefront headquarters to go over plans for the day. No one else was there.

"Judy, this is the toughest decision I've ever made in my life..."

"You're defecting to Silent Joe?" She must have anticipated what he was going to say and was trying to head it off with a joke.

"Judy, Max is right. We've got to break it off. You are the most delightful, the most desirable woman in the world. But your horizon's unlimited. It's not just what you can do here in the city the next two years, the next four years.

"You can't saddle your future by tying it to an old man who'll wear out while you're still in your prime—and who'll bring you tumbling down in a flick of the eye if tongues ever start wagging about 'she sleeps with her father-in-law.'"

She looked away from him when she realized the direction his discourse was taking and stared out the plate glass window at pedestrians hurrying by on their way to work. But now she turned and looked him square in the face.

"Buzz, number one, you're not an old man. Number two, you're the most precious thing in the world to me, more precious than being mayor, more precious than being on the City Council, and a lot more precious than any cockamamie talk about the future.

"I need you emotionally, I need you physically. I couldn't go on with this campaign without knowing that my lover was there beside me and without knowing that we could still get off once in a while and just be lovers.

"You were talking to me, Buzz, like a good campaign manager, giving me your best advice. But a principle of politics, the way I've always been taught, is that the candidate, after weighing the advice, makes the final decision.

"You can resign as campaign manager if you want to. I won't hold it against you." She put her hand on top of his. "But if you resign as my sweetheart, the campaign's over. I'm on the first plane to Alaska."

There was nothing he could think of to say, she had spoken with such finality.

They looked soberly at each other for a few moments.

Then she smiled and broke the silence. "But Max is right—we'll have to practice real hard to stop looking at each other with so much electricity in our eyes."

She pointed to the day's schedule lying before them on the table.

"Johnny's away again. Come over tonight after this last coffee hour. We can practice." Her eyes sparkled, almost crackled, as she said just what Mar might have. "Maybe I can think of a way to draw down your battery."

29

The Reverend Doctor James Shoemaker and Bobby Clark stopped in together at Ferguson for Mayor headquarters.

"Judy," began Jimmie Shoemaker in his deep, sonorous voice, "we thought we'd brighten your day. Mister Silent Joe DeRosier called on me this morning first thing, told me he'd appreciate my help in getting votes for him in the black community. I restrained myself from laughing in the poor man's face. With great difficulty, I might add.

"I asked him what he felt he might do as mayor to help our community. Well, he sat there—it must have been a full minute—like he was trying to think of something that he could do for us. And then he dug into his hip pocket and fished out his billfold. He slipped out of that billfold five crisp, new one-hundred-dollar bills. So crisp and new he must have gotten a direct shipment from the Bureau of Printing and Engraving."

Judy and Buzz were listening in fascination, Bobby Clark was grinning his gap-toothed grin, as Jimmie Shoemaker spun out his story.

"'Well,' he said, 'there's a lot that a friendly mayor can do for you. Like, for instance,' he went on, 'I'd like to make a contribution to the church building fund—or the pastor's discretionary fund.'"

"Did you take it?" asked Buzz.

"My church doesn't want that man's money," replied the minister, his voice rising. "We're a Christian church." He emphasized the word "Christian."

"But I was a diplomat. After all, he might get elected. The Lord does move sometimes in mysterious ways. I just told him we have a rule about not getting involved in politics unless one of our own people is running. And I told him to put those nice crisp Benjamin Franklins back in his billfold—and that if he really wanted to help the building fund, he could send something after the election. Then there'd be no reason for folk to have any suspicion about his motive."

Buzz chortled as he tried to picture Silent Joe's discomfiture. Judy laughed too, but she was more restrained.

"I wish I could've been there to see him," she said, "but I'm disappointed to hear the church has a rule against getting involved in politics. I was hoping you and some of your members might give me a hand."

"Judy, honey, you didn't hear me! I told that cracker that we don't get involved unless one of our own people is running. Judy," he said reprovingly and with rising inflection, "you're one of our people! We could always count on you to vote the right way without even asking you. Buzz, this is a smart lady. But better than that, she's a lady with a big heart. And she votes with her heart as well as her brain.

"Judy, you're going to make a fine mayor." Again the rising inflection: "Give you a hand? Judy, we've been talking you up ever since you made your announcement. Bobby and I, we've both had some experience running for mayor, organizing. Our folk are going to ring doorbells on every street in the Central City. You got some flyers you want us to pass out, we'll pass out flyers. If you don't have any, we'll print some ourselves. There might even be a few words from the pulpit the Sunday before the election—wouldn't you think so, Bobby?"

"Quite a few pulpits, Rev, I'd say."

When the two visitors left, Judy remarked to Buzz, "They didn't say a word about racial imbalance."

"Yes, they did. They said they could always count on you to vote the right way without even asking you. They don't know the right way to go on racial imbalance right now any more than we do."

Columnist Dibble took the predictable view of the Judy Ferguson campaign. If anything, he was more vicious than usual. He complained that women's place was in the home. One day he called her "the carpetbagger from Ohio by way of Mount Holy-Holy College." Another day she was "a shapely blonde more suited for the city recreation department than the mayor's office." She was "the hoity toity bookstore baroness who doesn't even deign to use her married

Tumultuous Affairs

name," "the blonde bombshell who would be more at home in the Miss America Pageant," "the candidate who got a head start on nepotism by hiring her father-in-law as her campaign manager—everybody knows TV newspeople work cheap."

Judy ignored Dibble's sallies, but they were getting under Buzz's skin—until the day he met Big Jim McCann at the prescription counter of a downtown drugstore.

"Every time Dribble takes one of his nasty pokes at that little lady," asserted the former mayor, "it gains her five hundred votes. Just pray that the little turd keeps writing."

Although candidate and manager were together almost continuously at headquarters and at forums, coffee hours, and other appearances all over the city, the campaign schedule began cutting deeply into their private time together. And then, something unexpected happened. Johnny blew his top at what must have been continuous pressure from Money Bags Jardine to get Judy out of the race. He walked out on Money Bags and his six-figure salary and joined the campaign.

From a husband who for more than two years had appeared completely indifferent or even opposed to Judy's political career, he was transformed into her most eager cheerleader, proudly accompanying her to speaking engagements, enthusiastically hitting up his friends in the business community for campaign contributions, and using his own considerable personal charm to woo voters one on one at coffee hour after coffee hour.

He did all these things while resuming an active role in the management of the bookstore business, something Judy admitted she had been letting slide since the campaign began. He also brought with him confirmation of the rumor that there were other reasons for DDT's departure from the mayor's race beyond fear of defeat and friendship for Silent Joe. "Money Bags greased his palm with five thousand bucks," said Johnny. "Called it 'a little contribution to help finance your School Committee campaign.'"

Buzz could only speculate—he made no inquiries, and Judy never volunteered—that Johnny was also becoming more assiduous at

Durham Caldwell

home in asserting his privileges and performing his responsibilities as the candidate's husband. Maybe the breakup of their love affair that Buzz had so reluctantly advocated and which Judy had so adamantly rejected was happening anyway.

He had even more reason to think so the Tuesday night that Johnny was out of town on a buying trip for the bookstores. Judy sat close to him as he drove her home from a radio panel program and gave him a warm goodnight kiss, but did not invite him in. A deep sense of relief blended with a feeling of genuine sadness as he drove home.

Buzz couldn't refrain from zinging Judy a little bit about "corruption in the Republican Party" the day that Vice President Agnew resigned from office and pleaded *nolo contendere* to evading $29,500 in 1967 income taxes. Attorney General Richardson said "critical national interest" justified the plea bargain agreement that kept the vice president out of jail even though evidence showed that Agnew asked for and received more than $100,000 in contract kickbacks.

That "critical national interest," Buzz and Judy agreed, was getting Agnew out of the line of succession for the presidency.

In the city election, Joe DeRosier, as well as Lucille Cournoyer and Domenico DiTotola, was indeed demagogueing the racial balance busing issue. Silent Joe didn't go quite so far as DDT's "over my dead body," but he came close. Lucille hammered away at "busin' " at every coffee hour, every panel, every forum. For someone who had never been to college, she was a reasonably well-spoken woman. She had no trouble with other "-ing" words. But she was never able to get the "g" on busing. It was always "busin' "—something like the way Joe McCarthy and other right-wing '50s Republicans had talked about "the Democrat Party," rather than the Democratic Party. She made "busin' " sound as sinister as syphilis or gonorrhea.

"Do you realize the strain and the stress that busin' will put on little children?" she asked at a League of Women Voters forum.

The Unitarian minister who was in the audience rose to his feet ostensibly to ask a question. "Just a few years ago," he recalled, "parents in the outlying parts of the city were screaming for buses so their kids wouldn't have to walk to school. They didn't seem to be worried about stress. And today parochial school children are bused from one end of Riverbridge to the other. From what I've observed, they don't seem to suffer from undue stress or strain."

There were some mutterings and even some hisses from the back of the auditorium. The minister's remarks sparked a smattering of applause from up front.

"The Unitarian section," Buzz whispered to Judy and Johnny.

"Do you want to put that in the form of a question?" moderator Barbara Olsen asked.

"Just an observation," replied the minister.

"Anudder lib'ral do-gooder," DDT stage whispered to Lucille, loud enough to be heard at least eight rows back and sparking a couple of hisses from the group who had applauded the minister.

Buzz had often wondered if any truly uncommitted voters attended these forums. The candidates seemed to bring their own claques of supporters. He doubted that what anybody said on the platform changed the votes of anybody in the audience. But candidates felt the forums obligatory to attend because of the media coverage. The paper always ran a report the next day, and frequently the TV stations would set up their cameras and broadcast a story with sound bites on the late news.

After the School Committee and City Council candidates had spoken, moderator Olsen called a ten-minute recess to allow audience members to catch a smoke outside or go to the restroom, refresh themselves with a cup of coffee from the table staffed by League members at the back of the hall, and, probably most crucial, give weary bottoms a brief respite from the hard wooden Depression Era high school auditorium seats.

People were slow coming back to sit down. The forum was already running late because of the number of School Committee and council candidates who had spoken and because the League could never get its forums started on time. Rowdy often applied his metaphor about organizing for a one-car funeral to the League as well as to DDT.

Durham Caldwell

The audience was a little thinner when Barbara finally got everybody in their seats. Some people had drifted out, along with their candidates, during the intermission. Whitney Garland and the other station's TV crew, cognizant of film processing deadlines, had already broken down their cameras and left. Just as Barbara was about to introduce the mayoral contenders, the double doors at the back of the auditorium swung open. In marched eighteen members of the Saint Aloysius Drum and Bugle Corps in plumed black shakos and shiny brass-buttoned blue and white uniforms. The brass instruments were silent. But the two bass drummers were pounding their instruments so hard that Buzz feared the plaster would fall from the ceiling of the old auditorium.

The faces of the bass drums had been painted with bold black letters "JOE D." Saint Aloysius was Silent Joe's home parish.

The drum major raised his baton, blew his whistle twice, the snare drums rolled, and the brass instruments struck up "The March from the River Kwai"—known as "Colonel Bogey" before the Alec Guinness-William Holden movie, "The Bridge on the River Kwai," spread its popularity. On cue, the Silent Joe cheering section in the audience leaped to its feet and began chanting along with the music, "Forward, with Joe De-ro-zee-ay!" They were giving DeRosier the French pronunciation to make it fit the music. "Forward, until Election Day! Forward, we go forward, with Joseph, with Joseph, today!"

The drum corps marched down the center aisle, circled up the side aisle, and then down the center again. St. Aloysius had always had a championship corps. Joe, seated on stage with Judy, stood up and waved triumphantly to the crowd. Judy shot a look of dismay down at Buzz and Johnny in the first row. The audience, after the tedium of listening to nearly two dozen School Committee and City Council speakers, welcomed this unexpected diversion. Many in the crowd were standing up and clapping in time to the four-four rhythm, some uncommitteds even joining Joe's cheering section in chanting the simple lyrics.

Buzz looked back glumly at Judy and shrugged. Silent Joe had clearly scored a noisy triumph with those in the auditorium. Buzz was glad the TV cameras had left. But the newspaper reporter had stayed.

Tumultuous Affairs

There were enough people still there to spread the word. And Buzz knew that Joe's musical coup would be talked about all over town.

Eventually moderator Olsen banged her gavel in an attempt to get the forum back on track. Most of the non-DeRosier people in the audience were now seated again. But the drum and bugle corps kept marching around the auditorium blasting out "The March from the River Kwai," the grinning Joe kept waving, and the DeRosier cheering section kept chanting, "Forward, with Joe De-ro-zee-ay!"

Barbara banged her gavel again and again. Shouts of "knock it off!" and "go home!" and "enough!" rose from the audience.

Barbara finally put her hand on Silent Joe's shoulder. Buzz thought he could almost read her lips from down in the first row. Johnny confirmed it. "She's telling Joe to get those clowns out of here," he whispered.

Joe was shrugging as if he didn't know how to stop them. Barbara pointed to her watch. Was she telling him she was calling off the forum—or that he would lose a minute of speaking time for every additional minute of "The March from the River Kwai"?

In any event, Joe held up his hands. The cheering section stopped chanting. But the drum corps, which had its back to the stage, got to the rear of the auditorium, wheeled, and was marching down the aisle again before the drum major got the message. He blew his whistle three times. The corps did an about face and marched back through the double doors, "The March from the River Kwai" gradually fading in the distance as the corpsmen went out into the night.

The mayoral part of the forum was anticlimactic. Barbara told the audience that because of the lateness of the hour she would limit it to twenty minutes, a decision greeted by rousing applause. Silent Joe basically repeated the Lucille Cournoyer-DDT arguments against two-way busing. Judy said she was sure the city and the state board could work out a fair solution and that it wasn't right for politicians to scare people just to gain votes.

"Very stateswomanly," Buzz complimented her on the way out of the auditorium.

"How did you like the drum corps?" she asked him.

Durham Caldwell

"I didn't like it at all the first couple of minutes. The next two hours were absolutely great."

"They weren't out there that long."

"It seemed like it. Remember, Councilor, as you climb the ladder, in politics timing is everything."

30

Buzz instinctively reached for the phone to give directions to the people in the newsroom on how to cover the local angle. It was a Saturday evening—October 20, 1973. The bulletin came over the radio as Buzz sat in his living room catching up on the week's newspapers. President Nixon had ordered the firing of special Watergate prosecutor Archibald Cox. Cox had refused to back off in his quest for White House tapes. Attorney General Richardson and Deputy Attorney General William D. Ruckelshaus resigned rather than carry out the order. Richardson cited his earlier pledge to give Cox "unimpeded authority." Solicitor General Robert Bork, as acting attorney general, did the firing.

Only after dialing the first two digits did Buzz remember that he was no longer H.B. Baker's news director. Jerry Finnerty and Happy Hooper would have to make their own decisions on local follow-up.

Monday morning at Judy's headquarters, there was as much comment on what was already being called the Saturday Night Massacre as there was on the local campaign. Elliot and Archie Cox were the good guys. Another black mark for Nixon. Impeachment, most of the headquarters people agreed, now looked like a real possibility.

Just before noon, the headquarters telephone rang. It was a call for Buzz that ended his involvement in any conversation about what might happen next in Washington.

"Hiya, buddy! Hy Golden here."

"Hey, Hy! How are things at Baker Broadcasting?"

"Could be better. News has gone to hell in a handbasket since you cut out. In fact, that's the name of one of the new people, Helena Handbasket."

"You're kidding."

Durham Caldwell

"Real name's Sanborn, Helena Sanborn. But Finnerty calls her Helena Handbasket. Very apropos. H.B.'s tryna save a buck—he won't give 'em any more help—at least any good help.

"But I didn't call about that. Listen, Buzz, you're an old buddy— and I thought you oughta know.

"The big shots backin' Joe DeRosier have produced a terrific one-minute spot. I think Money Bags Jardine's Boston agency put it together. They use the Saint Aloysius Drum and Bugle Corps. They got this catchy tune, 'Forward with Joe De-Roz-ee-air,' or however they say it in French. And they use one of the old Yankee Network guys from Boston to do the voice over. Do a little hatchet job on Judy at the same time. You know, woman's place is in the home. It's a honey of a spot. Real professional. They're gonna saturate with it at the very end of the campaign. They've already booked the time. But the spot's s'posed to be top secret till then."

"Well, how—"

"Money Bags and Silent Joe and a coupla the other Mattawampus Club big shots came up to the station to audition the video tape. H.B. invited 'em up. Musta been either audition it in town or drive to Boston. They cleared the control room, everybody but Turcotte— he's a cousin of Silent Joe's." Rene Turcotte was one of the television directors. "But Turcotte forgot to pull the patch that sends the audition channel down to the set in my office—that's so I can keep an eye on commercial production.

"Well, I see Money Bags and these other big shots troopin' inta the control room. So I turn on my set. They musta loved the spot because they kept playin' it so many times I wrote down the copy word for word. Then I see 'em shake hands with H.B. and walk outta the station with big grins on their faces. They must think they're gonna get some mileage outta that spot. They will, too—it's a good one.

"Buzz, I'll drop off the copy in your mailbox when I go to lunch. But mum's the word where you found out about the spot. I just think Judy's a pretty sweet broad—and you're an old buddy—so I thought you oughta know in case you wanta plan a counterattack."

"We gotta move fast. Only two weeks to go. You got some availabilities left for next week?"

Tumultuous Affairs

"Buzz, for you and Judy, I'll find availabilities even if I hafta double spot—or even if I hafta lose some o' the regular accounts for a day or two, if you know what I mean."

"And if we want to produce a spot of our own, can we do it at the station without Turcotte and H.B. finding out about it?"

"Buzz, you can do it at night or on the weekend when Turcotte and H.B. aren't here. Won't be able to keep it a secret maybe. But we can get the tape outta the station so they can't look at it till you bring it back in to go on the air."

What to do? Buzz and Judy knew that "Forward with Joe De-ro-zee-ay" was a catchy bit. And within the confines of a one-minute TV spot, it would avoid the tedious repetition that had spoiled its debut at the League of Women Voters forum. They sat down with Timmy McCann—who had become increasingly active in the campaign—and with The Ad Man, who had handled media so astutely for Max and who was performing the same function for Judy.

"Let's analyze the situation," suggested The Ad Man. Since the last election, he had let his thick sideburns grow stylishly long and added a walrus mustache. He twisted one end of the mustache. "Forward with Joe De-ro-zee-ay? What's forward about Silent Joe?"

"Not a darned thing," said Judy, his longtime City Council colleague. "The word 'backward' would suit him better."

"Backward with Joe De-ro-zee-ay," sang The Ad Man almost to the tune of "The March from the River Kwai."

"Whaddaya think? Possibilities there?" He twisted the other end of his long mustache. Maybe he should wax it, Buzz thought.

"Who could we get to do it?" asked Judy.

"We have a drum corps at Blessed Sacrament," volunteered Timmy McCann. "They're deadly rivals of the corps at Saint Al's. In fact, two of my kids are in the corps. They practice on Wednesdays. And the corps's always lookin' for ways to raise a little money—I assume we'd pay 'em. Lemme speak to the director. If he needs any backbone, we'll get Uncle Jim to call Father McGonigle. And if absolutely necessary, there are a few McCanns on the parish council."

"Wednesday," said Buzz, "day after tomorrow."

Durham Caldwell

It was a longstanding practice at Baker Broadcasting that the news cameramen could use station equipment for private jobs when they were off duty to supplement their meager wages—just as long as they paid for the film and a nominal charge for running it through the processor. Buzz lined up Stan Wlodyka for Wednesday afternoon to shoot the Blessed Sacrament Drum and Bugle Corps performing "Backward with Joe De-ro-zee-ay." Timmy recruited volunteers from the Blessed Sacrament choir to sing the new lyrics.

The Ad Man, with help from Judy and Buzz, put together some compelling lines for the announcer's voice over. They reminded Buzz of Hubert Humphrey at Atlantic City. "Yes, backward with Joe DeRosier! Joe DeRosier, the only member of the council to vote no on public housing! The only member to vote no on funds for the new West Side playground! The only member to vote no on new police cruisers!"

The music meanwhile would continue in the background.

"And why do they call him 'Silent Joe'? Because in a dozen years as a city councilor, he has rarely raised his voice on the critical issues of the day."

They decided not to dignify "a woman's place is in the home" with a direct answer. But included in the copy was "Meanwhile Judy Ferguson has been a leader in the City Council since her first election ten years ago, speaking out on every major issue and never shying away from a vote!"

The copy concluded, "Yes, if you want the city to move backward, vote for Silent Joe DeRosier. But there is a way to move the city ahead . . . " At which point the choir members and the horns and drums of the Blessed Sacrament Drum and Bugle Corps would blast in at full volume with "Forward with Judy Fer-gu-son!"

"Who's doing the voice over?" Buzz asked The Ad Man, assuming he had picked one of the mellow-voiced disc jockeys who did most of the local TV spots.

"Buzz, we're gonna use you! I talked to Judy about it, and she agrees."

Buzz started to protest.

Tumultuous Affairs

"Buzz, everybody in town knows your voice. You'll add more credibility to the spot than all those Yankee Network guys put together. And besides, Don Dribble says you work cheap."

That may be true, thought Buzz, but my voice on a Judy commercial could also be burning my last bridge with H.B. Baker.

For good measure, The Ad Man came up with a second spot. It was along the same lines as the first one—except this one devoted less time to knocking down Silent Joe and more time to Judy's accomplishments: "A highly successful businesswoman who will bring her business savvy to the mayor's office"; "an adviser since its inception to the highly popular 'Issues' television program"; and borrowing a line from Jimmie Shoemaker, "a brainy woman who has voted not only with her head but with her heart as a member of the council."

The spots were tricky to produce with the technology available at a TV station the size of Baker Broadcasting. But between Stan's film editing, Tom Santos in the audio booth, and Danny Cataldo on the control board, they came up with a finished product that had Buzz and The Ad Man and Timmy McCann hugging each other and hugging Stan, Tom, and Danny. And they did it in time to get both spots on the air on both TV stations a full eight days before the election.

Judy had stayed away from the taping, claiming she would be too nervous to endure it. When Buzz phoned her to pronounce success, he added, "I think Timmy McCann has earned a candlelight dinner with the new mayor. But he's an Irishman—he'll insist you bring along a chaperone."

That final week before the election, it seemed that all people were talking about when they drank their coffee at lunch counters around the city, when they gathered by the water cooler at work, when they greeted each other at the post office, church meetings, and a hundred other venues, was the competing TV spots of the two mayoral contenders. But it was hard to arrive at consensus on which spot was the better, or which one—if either—would pull more votes.

On Election Night, there was standing room only at Judy's storefront headquarters. Blackboards hung along the wall behind the bank of telephones which volunteers had kept busy almost right up till poll-closing time. Judy drafted Buzz to announce the results as they came in by phone from workers in the precincts. "After all," she reminded him, "you and Jerry were the Election Night voices of Baker Broadcasting ever since Warren G. Harding."

Not since Harding, thought Buzz, but it had been a lot of elections. He wondered how Jerry would do tonight with the spotlight all to himself. But then the calls started coming in one after the other. At times there were calls on all five phones simultaneously. Jerry vanished from his mind.

Judy by now had disappeared from the storefront, honoring the tradition that it's bad luck for the candidate to be at headquarters before the results are certain. She had accepted Max's invitation to watch the coverage on television in his law office upstairs in the same block.

The lead seesawed as the first precincts came in. Joe had a four-to-one margin in his home precinct, which voted in the Saint Aloysius Social Center. But Judy did well enough in the others to run even as two of the campaign workers hustled to cope with the arithmetic and to chalk in the newest running totals on the blackboards. There were loud cheers each time Buzz announced a precinct that had gone for Judy. Then the room quieted. Joe had moved out in front and was slowly adding to his lead.

During a lull in the phone calls, Buzz whispered to Johnny, who was standing next to him, "Looks like there are still people in the city who think a woman's place is in the home."

"Or they're worried what she may do about busing," responded Johnny quietly.

The next precinct was for Judy. Cheers.

The next one for Joe. Groans.

Buzz, the old hand at election nights, tried to encourage the crowd. "It's not just the number of votes, it's where they're coming from." He didn't see any precincts up on the board from Ward Five, which included most of the Central City, or from Ward Eight, which included the Patch.

Timmy McCann bustled in breathless, he had to park so far from headquarters.

Tumultuous Affairs

"They were still standing in line at Blessed Sacrament when the polls closed," he panted.

That was good news, Buzz thought. At least he hoped it was. Maybe they were standing in line, too, in the Central City. If they were, that could mean more votes for Judy. Silent Joe had what looked like a commanding lead by the time the first Ward Five precinct reported in. Johnny, who had wandered out to the back room where people were watching television, came back up front with a gloomy look on his face. He whispered to Buzz, "Your old co-star Jerry Finnerty says DeRosier has it locked up. Hogan on the other station is saying the same thing."

"Keep your spirits up, son—5-B just went for Judy, three to one."

By the time the rest of the Central City precincts called in, Judy was within striking distance. Headquarters reverberated with cheers as Buzz announced each new total. Johnny phoned the news up to Max's office. "Tell her to hang in there, Max."

A stray precinct from Ward Six and the first precinct from Ward Eight went to Joe, not by much, but by enough to turn the room silent again.

Then the Patch came in. "8-C! Ferguson, 497! DeRosier, 215!" The room erupted.

"8-D—as in dog!" This was the big one, Timmy's home precinct. "Ferguson, 672! DeRosier, 240!" It erupted again.

"8-B—as in baker! Ferguson, 511! De-ro-zee-ay!" Buzz paused for the laughter from the campaign workers. "De-ro-zee-ay, 213!"

When it was over, the Patch had swelled Judy's vote to fifty-two percent of the citywide total. Johnny jumped to the platform in front of the blackboards, elbowed his father aside, and began waving his arms choir leader fashion and belting out, "Forward with Judy Fergu-son!" The campaign workers joined in. Johnny stopped the choir directing after a second chorus. A spontaneous chant went up from the crowd: "Judy! Judy! Judy!"

They must have heard the shouts in Max's office all the way up on the fourth floor. The two TV stations, getting their results from the city clerk's office, not directly from the precincts, still didn't have the vote from the Patch. Buzz watched with amusement in the back

Durham Caldwell

room as his old partner Jerry Finnerty admitted with embarrassment, "It's getting closer than we thought."

The shouts of "Judy! Judy! Judy!" from out front gave way to a sustained building-rattling roar. Buzz squeezed his way out of the back room just in time to see a beaming Judy make her way to the platform through an aisle in the crowd that had miraculously cleared for her. Max was right behind her, beaming almost as broadly.

Her victory speech was a short one. It was interrupted so frequently by deafening cheers that she gave up with a wave and another room-brightening smile and waded into the crowd to accept congratulatory handshakes, hugs, and kisses. Buzz spotted a weary but happy-looking Timmy McCann standing at the side of the room out of the crowd and walked over to shake his hand.

"I guess we showed 'em the McCann Machine still has a little life in it," Timmy grinned.

The Ad Man came over to join them, grinning as broadly as Timmy. He rubbed Timmy's bald head. Timmy tweaked both ends of The Ad Man's walrus mustache. Judy spotted the three of them standing there together and gave each in turn the warmest and smilingest of hugs. Then her face turned serious.

"It's a great night," she said, almost shouting to be heard over the crowd, "but all four of us know that without those great last-minute commercials, we wouldn't have made it."

She hugged each of them again, then turned back to the merrymakers crowding in behind her.

Johnny returned from the back room, where he had been watching the wrap-up of television's election coverage. "It's not all good news," he told Buzz. "Lucille Cournoyer and DDT are both elected to the School Committee."

31

Buzz and Judy had never talked about what he would do after the election. If she lost, he had assumed he would go back to the newsroom. But now that she was mayor-elect, Buzz speculated that H.B. wouldn't want him back for fear he'd compromise the station's City Hall objectivity. And the other Riverbridge news media would be skittish about hiring him for the same reason.

But Judy had her own ideas. She wanted Buzz for the position of executive assistant to the mayor. He tried to talk her out of it. "Think of what Dribble-I-Mean-Dibble will write about it. Instead of nepotism, he'll call it 'father-in-lawism,' or something equally distasteful."

"Buzz, President Kennedy took us off the hook when he hired Bobby as attorney general. This job is executive assistant. It's a personal position. There's no reason, ethical or otherwise, that a mayor can't hire a family member for this kind of job."

As usual, Judy prevailed. Donald Dibble did write about "reverse generation nepotism" and about "Ferguson-Buckley-ism," but nobody paid much attention.

Max insisted that Judy set up a transition office in a seldom-used meeting room adjacent to his own City Hall quarters. One of the first visitors was Rod Berry, the superintendent of schools. Judy and Buzz were old friends from Rod's many appearances on "Issues."

The superintendent opened the conversation, "After Inauguration Day, I'll be calling you 'Madam Chairman' or 'Madam Mayor.' You don't mind if I call you 'Judy' today, do you? 'Madam Mayor-Elect' sounds too darned formal."

Judy laughed. "It does, doesn't it? Rod, you can call me Judy after Inauguration Day, too."

"Not at School Committee meetings. I called Mrs. Cournoyer 'Lucille' at one meeting. She practically handed me my head."

"What do I call you, Mister Superintendent?"

Durham Caldwell

"Mister Berry will be fine."

"Doctor Berry," Judy corrected.

"Skip the 'doctor.' 'Mister' is fine. I've met too many pompous 'doctors' in the superintendents' association." He changed the tone of his voice, signaling that the small talk was over.

"Judy, I want to talk to you off the record."

"Would you like me to leave?" volunteered Buzz.

"No, no, Buzz. Nothing you can't hear—long as you haven't gone back to being a reporter.

"Judy—racial imbalance. We're still ducking it, but it's coming to a head. The state commissioner is a good friend of mine. He tells me the state board isn't going to pussyfoot around with us any longer. As you know, they've ordered us to put what Mister Dribble calls 'the Berry Pie Plan' into effect next September."

"That's your plan to divide the city into pie-shaped slices . . ." noted Judy.

"Not my plan. Though it seems to have my name on it. 'Berry Pie' was just too good for Dribble and the others to resist. The Research Department came up with it. I put it before the School Committee as a way to balance the schools with the least amount of pain. The committee wouldn't even take a vote on it, and now they're asking the court to overrule the state board.

"The state board, they're looking for an official timetable on the planning. You know, determine how many children have to be bused where to get the Central City schools down below fifty percent black, what the bus routes will be, which teachers will we move, and the other logistics—and when will we have each part of it worked out? It's six months' worth of work. Staff's been doing a little of it on the QT, but the committee won't authorize us to submit anything."

"What happens," Judy asked, "if the committee still won't budge?"

"The attorney general, as the state board's lawyer, will go for an order of the court. He'll probably get it.

"The timing's the crucial thing. The court could throw everything out the window and order us back to square one. Otherwise, the best case scenario is that the court upholds the state board and tells us to implement the plan with the opening of school next September. Worst case scenario is that another appeal could push us into the middle of the next school year. We've dragged our feet for so long that neither the board nor the court is likely to have much sympathy for us. If we have to implement a plan partway through the year—move all those kids, rearrange the bus schedule—the school year is shot to hell.

"Judy, I don't know that I've told you anything you didn't know already. Too bad it's being dumped on you. Max wouldn't move on it. Or couldn't." He stood up to leave. "And I don't have to tell people as astute as you and Buzz that the makeup of the new School Committee won't make it any easier for you."

Herb Mason, the city solicitor, also came to call and also brushed aside Buzz's offer to leave so the lawyer and the mayor could talk privately.

"Judy, I won't beat around the bush. The solicitor, as the city's lawyer, serves at the pleasure of the mayor. Most mayors bring in their own solicitor, somebody they have confidence in. If you have somebody all lined up, that's great. I'll be happy to work with him during the transition."

"Or her?"

"Or her." If Herb was embarrassed by the oversight, he didn't show it. "If you don't have somebody lined up, I'll give you a small sales pitch."

Johnny walked in to take Judy to lunch. She waved him to a chair, then turned back to Herb.

"You know my husband." The two men exchanged waves of recognition. "Herb, I really haven't had much time to think about solicitor. Give me the sales pitch."

"Judy, there are probably fifty lawyers in this town who know as much about municipal law as I do, maybe more. But one thing I probably know more about than those fifty put together is the Racial Balance Act. I don't know where you stand on the issue. I don't even know where I stand. I've helped Max and the School Committee steer through the law and skate around it for half a dozen years. I helped them stall not necessarily because I wanted to, but because I was their lawyer and that's what they asked me to do.

"Basically, I guess what I'm saying is that if you want a solicitor who won't have to start from scratch on racial imbalance, I'm available."

"Can you come to lunch with us?" Judy asked. "We can talk some more."

In a back booth at the Heidelberg, Judy plied Herb Mason with questions. His analysis: the School Committee with Max gone but DiTotola added would continue to reject any plan involving two-way busing; the state board would insist that the city balance its schools by September using the Berry Pie formula unless someone comes up with a better one; and the court would back the state board "regardless of the eloquence" of the lawyer defending the School Committee's position.

"I just wish," he said as he stirred the sugar and cream into his coffee at the end of the meal, "that Rod's plan was a little fairer."

"He claims it's the fairest he could come up with," said Judy. "An equal number of white kids and black kids ride the buses."

"True," observed Herb, "but take my daughter. She's a kindergartner. Where we live, she could be put on the bus all the way to Miller Street for the next six years—never set foot again in the neighborhood school right down the block. Is that fair to her—fair to us if we want to take part in the PTO and so forth? And the same for the black families whose kids get bused out to our neighborhood."

Johnny, who had been doodling on a napkin sketching caricatures of his father and the moon-faced Herb Mason with a red ballpoint, put down the pen.

"Hell, I can solve that problem. Your daughter goes to your neighborhood school for three years—what school is that, Harkins?—then goes to Miller Street for three years, or vice versa. The black kid that she's changing seats with goes to Miller Street for three years, then to Harkins for three years. That's what you lawyers call 'equal inconvenience,' isn't it?"

"What do you think of Mister Mason," Judy asked Buzz and Johnny as the three of them walked back to City Hall.

"He seems honest," replied Buzz, "not dogmatic on either side. He's a good lawyer."

"Lot of good lawyers in this burg," commented Johnny. "Not sure how many honest ones."

"Maybe the most important thing, Judy," Buzz resumed, "is that he seems to have the confidence of the School Committee. If he has to tell 'em they're gonna lose the court case, he doesn't come in as some wild-eyed radical trying to stuff something down their throats."

"Good point," said Judy. "Let's keep him."

Rod Berry liked Johnny's modification to the five-district busing plan. "Why didn't I think of that myself?" he wondered. "Or even more to the point, why didn't the people with the fancy degrees in the Research Department think of it?"

He also told Judy, "You better warn your husband that Dribble will probably start calling it 'the Johnny Cake plan' instead of the Berry Pie plan."

"No, he won't, because nobody except us knows that it wasn't your idea."

"Maybe I'll tell him. Anything to get rid of that Berry Pie bit."

A couple of days later Judy and Buzz worked late, until after all the other City Hall offices closed. As he walked her to her car in the almost deserted City Hall parking lot, his hands thrust deep into his trench coat pockets to protect them from the cold, she put a hand gently on his forearm and kept it there as they walked across the bare cement. At the door to her car, Judy turned to him. "Buzz," she said in a clear, soft voice, "three months ago, I expected to be with you the rest of my life. I'd even begun fantasizing about marrying you and moving to Colorado or Oregon after I was finished being mayor. You'd work in the local TV station. I'd run a little bookstore. Then Johnny came back to me. He came all the way back, Buzz. He's back to stay, I know he is. I don't know—maybe he was answering your prayer. You wanted to break things off—and I was too selfish to let you.

Durham Caldwell

"I know for sure you never miss anything. That's what makes you even more remarkable.

"I tried to hide it, but I was a mixed-up little girl those first weeks. Maybe the campaign kept me going—the campaign and the way you stayed by me, not asking a question, not saying a word, giving above and beyond the call right up till Election Day and even till now.

"I told you once before, Buzz darling, when we became lovers, you made it easy for me. This wasn't easy—I wanted so badly not to hurt you. Not easy—but so much easier than it could have been. And Buzz, don't ever think for a minute that what we did was wrong. At the time, it was the right thing for both of us."

"Oh, Buzz!" He could see tears glistening in the corners of her eyes as she embraced him. "I can never thank you enough for being such a kind, patient, and loving man."

He held her there for a moment, her tear-dampened cheek against his chin, as memories of other embraces flooded through his mind.

When he finally released her, she gave him a light daughter-in-law kiss on his left cheek, got into the car without another word, and drove away.

As he walked slowly to his own car, he had the same mixed feeling of elation and deep down pain that he had experienced that first night when Johnny was away but she didn't invite him in. Elation at hearing from her own lips that their long and loving affair was really over, something he had known for many weeks, and at the same time pain at the end of a romance that had been as warm and real and beautiful as it had been unlikely and, yes, wrong.

For a moment, he felt as lonely and as empty as the sidewalks surrounding the deserted City Hall. But far ahead of him, he could see the strings of colored lights on Main Street and hear the faint lilt of carols from the loudspeaker at the front of the record store. He picked up his pace. It was almost Christmas. He was lonely, but he was at peace.

32

Buzz was full of the Christmas spirit as he strode through the falling snow to resume the weekly dinners with Johnny and Judy which they had suspended in the hurly-burly of the campaign. He was looking forward to seeing them both. In a way, he felt like Scrooge when he threw open the window on Christmas morning. He had always loved Johnny, always been begrudgingly proud of him and proud of the things he accomplished, but now, he told himself, he genuinely liked him. He liked the way he had cast aside a big job with a Fortune 500 company out of renewed loyalty to Judy, how he had rolled up his sleeves in the campaign and trudged door to door never complaining about fatigue or about the weather, and how—he had Judy's word for it, but he could also see it in Johnny's eyes—how he had once again become a loving husband.

The snow had cut down on the Heidelberg's usual Friday evening trade. Buzz spotted Johnny in a booth at the far end of the dining room, away from most of the other diners. He was surprised to see that he was alone.

"Judy begged off tonight."

"Doesn't she feel well?"

"No, she's fine." He paused. "I think she just wanted to give you and me the chance to be alone together."

Buzz slid into the booth.

"Dad, the bookstore business is going very well. Judy did an A-One job of running it while I was off helping Money Bags earn another three hundred million. Since Election Day, I've had a lot of time to sit and think—and to look back.

"Dad, I've been a real asshole most of my life. And I want to tell you, it doesn't make me feel good to realize it. I don't remember too much about when you came home from the Army—I was too little. About all I remember is this guy is coming in and stealing my mommy.

"By the time I finally started growing up and began to appreciate my dad and realize all the good things you and Mom together did for me, I got a kick in the face. A girl I was sweet on in high school—your boss's daughter, Millie Baker—wouldn't let me take her to a dance. Can you think of anything more stupid to get upset about? I started to take it out on everybody, especially Baker Broadcasting. I became Mister Smart-Ass Bastard."

Buzz started to say something.

"No, Dad, let me finish. Looking back, I even wonder how Mom put up with me. This one girl put me down, so I became Mister Chip-on-My-Shoulder Know-It-All. Nobody could tell me anything.

"And Dad, the worst thing—you introduced me to the prettiest, smartest, sexiest woman in the Commonwealth of Massachusetts. I married her. And I cheated on her—not once, not twice, but for three whole goddam years. Why the hell would any man in his right mind cheat on the most beautiful, most intelligent, most loving woman in Massachusetts—or probably in the whole goddam United States? Why, Dad, why? To sell more toys for Money Bags? Ego? Just plain old adventure?

"Dad, I've learned one thing these last few weeks: when the choice is between love and adventure, take love every time."

"Sometimes, son, you can be lucky—and find love and adventure with the same woman."

Johnny cocked his head for a moment and looked at his father. "Is that the way it was with you and Mom?"

"Yes, it was," Buzz said, although to be truthful with himself, it hadn't been Elaine he was thinking of.

The waiter came and took their orders, apologizing for not seeing them "way back here in the corner."

"That's okay," said Johnny. "We had things to talk about. About thirty years of things." The waiter took their orders with a puzzled look on his face.

"Dad, I was so busy being a playboy and a big salesman these last few years, I wasn't paying much attention to what was happen-

Tumultuous Affairs

ing at home. I don't know why Judy didn't divorce me. She had every reason to. She had all the grounds. But somehow, some way, you were there for support, there for her to lean on. I can't imagine a woman anywhere who is as fond of her father-in-law as she is of you."

"You married a very wonderful girl, Johnny." He felt a Gibraltar-sized lump in his throat as he said it, and there was moisture in the corner of his eyes that he hoped Johnny wouldn't notice.

Almost the only sound as they ate was the clink of silverware on china. The waiter clearing the table must have concluded their appetites were off. They each left more food on their plates than they ate. As they waited for the check, Johnny broke the long silence. "Dad, I've made only one promise in my life that I've kept. That's the promise to Mom when she was dying that I'd get together with you for dinner on Friday nights.

"Dad, I make you another promise right here and now. I still may be an asshole in five thousand ways, but I'm going to be the best husband to Judy that I can possibly be."

The waiter came with the check. Johnny went for his wallet, but Buzz held up a hand. "Tonight it's on me."

As he waited for his change, Buzz cleared his throat. "Son, what I'm going to say is just as hard for me as what you said tonight must've been for you. I've been doing a lot of thinking—and a lot of thinking tonight while you were talking and afterward. It's not easy to admit. I know I wasn't much of a dad when I came home from the Army. And I wasn't much of a dad after that either. Your mom held the family together. A lot of the things you blamed yourself for—a lot of the things I blamed you for—were most likely my fault."

"Dad—"

"No, my turn. Let me finish.

"Something else. And this'll probably shock you." He delivered the next line with a half smile. "I haven't been an angel all my life. That's all you need to know. But I hope you won't think the worse of me for it.

"One thing we can agree on. That's Judy. Love her. Cherish her. She'll make you the happiest goddam bookseller in North America—if she hasn't already."

243

Durham Caldwell

Buzz counted out the tip, and they slid out of the booth. The handful of diners at the tables up front might have been surprised if they had looked up at the rear corner of the dining room where two grown men were locked in a long embrace.

Nothing can surprise me any more. That was Buzz's reaction to Richard Nixon's choice of House Minority Leader Gerald Ford as the new vice president. Gerry Ford, so much a nobody they almost hadn't covered him when he spoke at one of the local colleges—and now the vice president? No, no more surprises after that.

He was wrong.

When he swung by one morning to pick up Judy for the ride to the transition office—her car was in the shop again—she met him at the door in one of her tailored suits.

"Come in for a minute."

She sat him on the same brocaded sofa where so long ago she had advised him that she was about to seduce him.

She plunked herself down on the coffee table that stood in front of the sofa. On her face was the delighted look of someone about to spring a big secret that is guaranteed to take the listener by complete surprise—the kind of look Buzz hadn't seen since the day Big Jim McCann sprang the news that he was not running for reelection.

"Buzz, I'm pregnant."

His jaw dropped the requisite distance to ratchet the look on her face up another notch on the scale of delight. She was waiting for him to recover from his shock, but all he could think was: Pregnant? Inauguration the first week in January, and she's pregnant? A pregnant mayor?

Finally he recovered enough to stammer, "That's wonderful! Is Johnny happy about it?"

"He's delighted! We're both delighted." She was bubbling over with exuberance. "We tried so hard to have a baby, and nothing worked. Now elected mayor and getting pregnant all at the same time! I can hardly believe it!"

Tumultuous Affairs

She was so pleased with her news—her face was glowing—and even more pleased to have taken him by such complete surprise. But then she turned reflective.

"Johnny and I didn't want to rush into being parents. We faithfully used contraception for the first couple of years. Then we decided we were ready. But we couldn't conceive. He wanted very badly to give you a grandson. We tried everything—even that second honeymoon to the Caribbean. Doctor Connors had us take tests. Johnny passed with flying colors. I was the one who was infertile.

"We both took it very hard. Maybe that's why he started sowing his wild oats—because his wife couldn't be a complete wife. I guess for a man it can be a real downer to find out your wife can't have children. I know, Buzz, it's a real downer for a woman to find out you're infertile."

"What changed it?" He remembered how long it had taken Judy's mother to get pregnant.

"Doctor Connors isn't sure. It sounds far out, but he speculates it could be something as crazy as falling downstairs. I did. Remember?"

Her tumble on the cellar stairs, he thought, was as good an explanation as any. He thought back. That had happened while he and she were still lovers. Unlike Mar, who had always used a diaphragm, Judy had never seemed to take any precautions. He had just assumed she was on the pill, like so many modern women. But if she was convinced she was infertile, she wouldn't have been taking birth control pills. He wondered how sure she was that Johnny was the father. But he said nothing.

"I never was very regular, so I didn't think anything of it when I missed a couple of periods. Figured it was just the stress of the campaign. But I went in this week for a checkup. The doctor confirms: I'm going to have a baby, sometime in the summer."

His brain shifted into high gear. Johnny had come back to her—when was it?—in the fall. "Sometime in the summer" told him nothing. He wondered if the question had crossed her mind. If it had, she wasn't letting on. And what difference did it make? Johnny would be the father, Buzz the grandfather. It was a role he'd often imagined

245

Durham Caldwell

during the early years of Judy and Johnny's marriage. It was a role he could be content with. No, delighted with.

As they drove to City Hall, he asked her, "Do you want a boy or a girl?"

"Johnny very badly wants a son. I'm not particular."

"Can you be mayor and have a baby at the same time?" Buzz asked Judy seriously as he pulled a chair up beside her desk in the transition office. It was his initial thought, back there in her living room—but had been pushed aside by the realization that he and not Johnny could be the baby's actual father.

"Johnny and I talked about that last night. I think so. But it won't be easy. This racial imbalance thing is hanging over us like the Sword of Damocles. But if I concentrate on that and get that resolved, and concentrate on the budget, and carry the baby to term, I can take a little time off with a clear conscience. Most mayors take time off in the summer anyway.

"I talked with my folks last night. They're thrilled. They've been praying for a grandchild for a long time. They'll move east—a nice thing about being retired—and Mom'll help out with the baby. One of the great things about having a pediatric nurse for a mother.

"But Buzz, this makes the election for council president really critical. The president is acting mayor when I'm not here. Chairs the School Committee. And even if it's only for a little while, the wrong guy could really gum up something as delicate as racial balance."

The mayor's office traditionally kept hands off the perennial jockeying for the council presidency. But Judy and those close to her had been watching with concern the way this year's jousting had been proceeding. Neither of the two declared candidates had been able to muster enough votes to clinch the election. And neither was a special friend of the new mayor.

Judy and Buzz went down the list of council members, eliminating one after the other for various reasons. Then, "Rowdy!" their voices rang out simultaneously. Rowdy Hennessy was the man. He had the experience. He was an independent thinker, but his heart

Tumultuous Affairs

was in the right place. And control a meeting? He would jam a gavel down somebody's throat if he got out of line.

"He won't take it though," said Judy after a moment's reflection.

"Why not?"

"We tried to get him to take it when Max was elected mayor and again the time I was elected president. He wouldn't have any part of it. Said it was more fun being a member of the rank and file and being able to jump into the heat of the debate without worrying about where the chips would fall. Claimed he didn't have the temperament to be president."

"Let me try blindsiding him."

Big Jim McCann was in a rest home. The former mayor was making a good recovery from a mild stroke a few weeks earlier. He had lost some weight, but his face was still a healthy pink under that immaculately groomed mane of white hair. He had fully recovered his speaking ability, but his left side, which had been partially paralyzed, was still a little weak and he leaned his remaining bulk on a cane as he came across the room to thrust his hand out to his visitor.

"You know, Buzz, when I woke up after that stroke, I couldn't talk. That's the scariest thing in the world for an old politician. They told me I started talking in the cradle. How was I to present my side of the case to Saint Peter if I couldn't talk? But those therapists, Buzz, they do wonders. Not wonders, miracles!"

With that touch of a brogue, he made the word "therapist" sound as if it belonged right up there among the cherubim and seraphim.

Could he convince Rowdy, "that old rogue," to take the council presidency?

"During my years, Buzz, he could have had it any number of times. I figure he just didn't want the spotlight. But he always had a reason for turning it down. He could be more help to me talking his blarney out there as a backbencher. Or it wouldn't do for two boys from the Patch, him and me, to be the top two officials at the same time. Or it would take too much time, and Mrs. Hennessy was feeling poorly. Always a reason. But those reasons are all gone, Buzz. As

247

you know, poor Abigail Hennessy, rest her soul, passed on three years ago. Let me talk with him.

"And Buzz, you tell that little lady how pleased I am with the news that she is going to be a mother as well as a mayor. Tell her the secret is safe with me until she is ready to tell the world about it. I know if it's a boy, they'll name it John J. Buckley IV. But you tell her if it should be twins, I would be very proud for her to consider James Garfield McCann Buckley for the second one.

"Yes, Buzz, tell her the secret is safe with me—except I'll have to tell Rowdy.

"You know," Big Jim said as Buzz got up to leave, "I'll never be able to figure it out. I led a life of moderation—ate well of course—but I gave up smoking at the age of seventeen, drank spirits only on very special occasions like weddings and wakes, exercised regularly, went to bed early.

"My old teammate probably never went to bed in his life before midnight, except on his honeymoon—three days in Boston. Probably never did heavier exercise than bending his elbow at the Hibernian Club since we played our last football game at the Brickyard. Still smokes a pack of cigars every day of the week except during Lent.

"And now I'm in here, bent over and hobbling with a stick. And he's out there as mean and rugged and physically fit as ever. He could take out DDT with one arm tied behind him. I'll talk with him. If he gives me any guff, I'll ask him to take pity on an old man making a final request of an old friend."

Buzz never found out just what Big Jim McCann said to his old friend, but on New Year's Day, 1974, Rowdy Hennessy's picture was on the front page of the paper, and he was on the television news between bowl games announcing his candidacy for City Council president.

"It'll be—what do they call it?—my valedictory. That's it, my valedictory," he told Jerry Finnerty. "I hope I'm pronouncin' it right. I mean, this is my last term on the council. And I can't think of a better way to go out than by honorin' the friends who've supported me for so long by takin' the presidency. If I can be of assistance to the lovely lady who is to be our mayor, that will just be frostin' on the cake."

Tumultuous Affairs

When councilors caucused on the eve of their first official meeting, Rowdy was their unanimous choice.

The higher gasoline prices touched off by the OPEC oil embargo—forty-five-point-three cents per gallon for regular in Massachusetts, forty-nine-point-three for high test—the limited hours at many service stations, and the long lines at others may have encouraged more carpooling than in previous years. But it appeared that everybody who wanted to get to Judy's inauguration got there. Some people kept their coats on because the thermostat was set so low—part of the Nixon administration's embargo countermeasures, along with the nationwide fifty-five-mile-per-hour speed limit. But the big Civic Auditorium was nearly filled.

Max had more or less forgiven Jimmie Shoemaker for running against him in 1965—but never to the point of asking him to take part in any of his inaugurations. Judy rehabilitated the deep-voiced pastor by inviting him to deliver the invocation at hers. She showed her gratitude to Timmy McCann and Big Jim by asking Father McGonigle of Blessed Sacrament to give the benediction.

The police and fire chiefs—in gold-braided dress uniforms and white gloves—led the 1974 inaugural procession into the auditorium and onto the stage. Everyone stood at attention—some even tried to sing the words—as the Lincoln High band shook the ceiling with the National Anthem.

Rowdy as senior member of the City Council was to open the proceedings even though his formal election as president would not come till later. Just before he stepped forward to the lectern, Judy whispered something into his ear. He nodded.

Rowdy had bought a new suit, probably his first in a decade. It was a three-piecer with a gold watch chain across the bulky vest and a white carnation boutonniere. He looked as dandified as Big Jim used to.

Rowdy rapped a gavel on the lectern. After extending a greeting to his colleagues in city government who were behind him on the stage and to the audience in front of him, he announced, "Judge Louis Goldsmith will now come forward to swear in Mayor Buckley."

Durham Caldwell

There was a small murmur in the crowd. He's made a mistake, Buzz thought. Buckley instead of Ferguson. Rowdy must be nervous.

Rowdy took a Bible from the lectern and held it out for Judy to touch with her left hand. It was customary to have a judge administer the oath to the new mayor—Judy asked Judge Goldsmith because he was Max's uncle.

"Madame Mayor, please raise your right hand and repeat after me: I, say your own name, do solemnly swear . . ."

"I, Judy Ferguson Buckley, do solemnly swear . . ."

". . . that I will bear true faith and allegiance . . ."

Buzz and Johnny looked at each other.

". . . that I will bear true faith and allegiance . . ."

". . . to the Commonwealth of Massachusetts, and will support the constitution thereof."

After the ceremony, reporters crowded eagerly around the new mayor—not to ask her about her well-received inaugural address or her new administration but about what appeared to be her new name.

"Is this going to be the Buckley administration rather than the Ferguson administration?" Roger Davis of the local paper wanted to know.

Buzz was also curious to hear the answer. He and Johnny pushed into the little group surrounding Judy.

She smiled gaily at Roger and the other reporters, linked her arm through Johnny's, and said, "Actually I've been Mrs. John J. Buckley III for almost nine years." She linked her other arm through Buzz's. "And I'm very proud to be a member of the Buckley family."

"Yeah, but you've always campaigned under Ferguson," said Happy Hooper. "Why change now?"

Judy glanced at Buzz and winked.

"Well," she told Happy, "I've promised the taxpayers of this city a frugal administration. This is just an example of my frugality. When I was first elected to the City Council, I had a whole bunch of business cards printed. Judy Ferguson, City Councilor. So I told my husband I wouldn't change my name till I used up all those cards. And I've just run out of the Judy Ferguson cards."

Tumultuous Affairs

"Ah, come on, Judy—you're pulling my leg," protested Happy.

"Yes, I am. Actually the cards ran out in October, but we were just preparing those 'Forward with Judy Ferguson' campaign commercials. And 'Forward with Judy Buckley' wouldn't fit the music. Not enough syllables."

Everybody laughed except Happy. He thought she had pulled his leg again, but he wasn't sure.

Judy sat behind the big mahogany desk in the mayor's office beaming at Johnny and Buzz and at Max and his wife with the pleased air of someone who has planned a big surprise and successfully kept it a secret right up to the moment of breaking it. It was the same look she had the previous month when she announced to Buzz that she was pregnant. Except this was something she must have planned for a long time.

"When did you decide to be Mayor Buckley?" Johnny asked.

"When I got up there on the stage and saw you and Buzz down in the front row."

This time it was Buzz and Johnny who had to wonder whether they were having their legs pulled.

After a little small talk, Max's wife excused herself to "do a little shopping while I'm downtown."

Max stayed a few more minutes to show Judy how to lock and unlock the big mayoral desk, caution her on how to adjust the thermostat to comply with President Nixon's energy conservation rules, and how to close the window curtains to keep from being blinded by late afternoon sun. Then he, too, took his leave. Buzz escorted him to the door.

At the door, Max grasped Buzz by the arm, guided him into the empty hallway, and closed the door behind them.

"Buzz, old friend, I'm very relieved that you and the mayor have finally come to your senses."

"Is that what she told you?"

"She didn't have to tell me. I can still see the electricity in her eyes—but I can see it's directed at your son, not at you. That's the way it ought to be." Max smiled a thin smile. "Buzz, that makes me almost as happy as seeing her get elected—happy for both of you."

Buzz tried to smile back. "Max," he said, "this is hard to put into words—but your friendship has meant an awful lot." He paused, and this time he managed a real smile. "Even when you were reading the riot act to both of us."

The two men shook hands. Max walked toward the stairs to street level. Buzz silently reopened the door to the mayor's office and silently closed it when he saw the new mayor and her husband locked in a warm embrace in front of a portrait of the city's gimlet-eyed first mayor. He walked down the hall to the outer office and sat down at his own new desk.

When Johnny came out, he grinned at his father. "She's come up with another reason for changing her name to Buckley. Says she doesn't want to confuse the baby."

33

Judy's first School Committee meeting as mayor was routine until it reached the section on the agenda labeled "Reports from the Superintendent."

"Madam Chairman," began Rod Berry, "the commissioner informs me that the Board of Education is taking us back to court because of our failure to comply with the board's order. That's the order to submit specific details on our planning for next September."

"Is there any way we can keep this out of court, Mister Berry?" asked Judy.

"I would imagine that the only way, Madam Chairman, is to submit a report on the planning that school administration has done since the board issued its order—along with a projection of when we'll complete the various phases of the work".

"I will not vote to submit a plan—in fact, I'm incensed that school administration has allowed planning to continue!" exclaimed Lucille Cournoyer.

Committeeman Chester Zemba protested, "The commissioner and the board are trying to blackmail us into instituting a massive busing program!"

Committeeman Henry Doane shouted, "I agree with Lucille—I mean Mrs. Cournoyer. I won't vote to submit anything. It's time for civil disobedience."

Domenico DiTotola spoke up. "Dis is my foist meetin'. But I'm wid you guys. I'm sick an' tired o' minority people tryna tell da majority what t'do. I'll go t' jail foist!"

Larry Sidney, the only black on the committee, ostentatiously counted four fingers. Buzz took it to mean he was conceding that his side would lose, four to three, even if the other committee liberal, Mary Williams, and the new mayor joined him in trying to force the issue. He contented himself with remarking, "I hope you folks will get me a cell with an outside view when they haul us in for contempt."

Committeewoman Cournoyer told the meeting, "We've been maneuvering since the law was passed in 1965. We'll just keep on maneuvering."

Rowdy Hennessy grinned at Buzz and Judy when he caught up with them leaving the building. "I may hafta rethink this acting mayor business. These people make the City Council look like statesmen."

City Solicitor Herb Mason shrugged his shoulders when Judy called him in for a conference the next morning.

"Judy," he said, "I'm bound to do what my client wants. In this case, my client is the School Committee—or in practical terms, the School Committee majority. I can fight this again right up to the Supreme Judicial Court, just like I did for Max. But I'll be candid with you—I don't think I'll win unless they change the law."

"Tell that to the committee at the next meeting."

With the September school opening still more than eight months away, there was suddenly rapid movement at the state level. The office of Attorney General Robert Quinn backed the state board's demand for a planning timetable from the city. A Superior Court judge ordered the plan submitted "forthwith." And a justice of the Supreme Judicial Court rejected the city solicitor's bid for a stay of the lower court order.

Herb Mason gave it to the School Committee point blank: "Either submit the timetable, or be prepared to be cited for contempt."

"That's not fair," claimed Committeeman Doane. "You said yourself the plan doesn't comply with the law. How can they push us into a plan before the court's even ruled the plan is valid?"

"I've asked the attorney general's office the same question," replied the solicitor. "But Superintendent Berry has said it will take six months' work to implement the plan. The attorney general is fearful that waiting for a court ruling may not give Mister Berry the six months he needs before the opening of the next school year."

Tumultuous Affairs

Herb assured committee members that voting to submit the plan would not prejudice the committee's legal case. That cut no ice with Cournoyer, Doane, and DDT—they were all ready for jail. Chester Zemba voted with the mayor and the two liberals but told the meeting, "Just because I'm agreeing to submit the planning doesn't mean I'll agree to implement it."

The TV stations had their sound cameras set up just outside the meeting room. Lucille Cournoyer told both stations, "The state board and the attorney general are trying to bulldoze us, trying to bulldoze us into accepting a plan we don't like."

Lenora Clark volunteered a rebuttal for Baker Broadcasting's Whitney Garland. "How can it be bulldozing when this committee has had nine years to prepare a plan? We've had nine years of stalling tactics. A whole generation of school children has gone through segregated schools in the Central City during these nine years.

"We're glad the committee at least voted tonight to submit the timetable. But we'd like to see some stronger leadership from the new mayor. This city must eliminate every vestige of segregation in its schools."

The Reverend Doctor Shoemaker told the other station, "The School Committee has been playing the politics of evasion for over ten years. It's time for our public officials to display positive moral leadership in the integration of our elementary schools."

Vintage Jimmie Shoemaker, thought Buzz, as he listened to the interviews. And Lenora Clark does okay, too—she doesn't need Bobby to make speeches for her.

"That burns a little bit," said Judy when apprised by Buzz of Lenora's remark about the new mayor. "But what's the profit of getting into a skunk fight with DDT, Lucille, and Henry? The important thing is to prevent an explosion."

Spring brought with it two important pieces of news from Boston. The Supreme Judicial Court upheld the validity of the Board of Education's order to put the five-district Berry Pie plan into effect with the September school opening without ruling on the plan itself. And Governor Sargent, faced with dwindling popularity and a tough

255

Durham Caldwell

fight for reelection, backpedaled in his support for the Racial Balance Act. He said he would submit "modifications" to the Legislature which would "rely heavily on voluntary compliance."

Lucille Cournoyer and Henry Doane testified at the State House in favor of the governor's legislation which, among other things, would offer a five hundred dollar per year incentive for every black student accepted by a white majority school.

Lenora Clark told the legislative hearing, "The governor's so-called modifications will emasculate the Racial Balance Act. They will return black children to the status of chattel, offering a bounty of five hundred dollars to any white school which accepts a black student. Mister Chairman, the days of slavery are over!"

In accordance with the court ruling, Superintendent Berry sent letters to parents of elementary school children informing them of their youngsters' probable assignments for September. He and his Research Department had concluded that splitting the elementary schools after fourth grade, instead of after third grade, made more sense educationally than Johnny's "three and three." These "Johnny Cake amendments," as Judy and the superintendent referred to them jokingly, mollified some of the public opposition to the plan by assuring parents their youngsters would be in their neighborhood schools for at least two years—plus kindergarten. But some unhappy white parents began picketing school headquarters.

Mayor Buckley was quoted regularly in the paper and appeared frequently on television to explain the status of the racial imbalance situation: that the School Committee is appealing the state board's order on two-way busing, that City Solicitor Mason will argue the School Committee's position forcefully before the Supreme Judicial Court, and that all parties should be prepared to accept the court's decision and to get on with the business of making Riverbridge a good place for everybody to live and a good place for all kids to go to school.

Privately, she used her contacts in the League of Women Voters and other women's organizations and with both black and white clergy to hold a continuing series of low-key small-group meetings, many of them interracial, to smooth the way for the busing program which, she told them, was almost certain to go into effect in September. She urged those attending the meetings to serve as ambassadors to their own neighbors and families and friends to build acceptance for whatever the court might rule. She accepted invitations to speak in churches all over the city until the advanced stages of pregnancy made it difficult for her to waddle up the steps to the pulpit.

Buzz, listening to his car radio or through his earpiece as he ate lunch at his desk, or catching the TV news when he was home in time, absorbed a steady stream of Watergate headlines. Judge Sirica ruled that President Nixon must turn over sixty-four tapes to Special Prosecutor Jaworski and to seven defendants being tried on cover-up charges. The Supreme Court agreed to make a quick decision on the president's appeal of the Sirica ruling, the unusual speedup in court procedures bypassing the Court of Appeals. And U.S. District Judge Gerhard Gesell said Nixon's refusal to surrender subpoenaed evidence for former aide John Ehrlichman's Ellsberg break-in trial bordered on obstruction of justice and might put the president in contempt.

There was also news from Boston. The Massachusetts House gave initial approval to Governor Sargent's bill modifying the state's Racial Balance Act. The bill would prohibit mandatory busing to end *de facto* school segregation and rely instead on voluntary programs.

The governor's legislation was pending in the Senate when Judy's baby was born on the Fourth of July. "A few days early," said Johnny as he led Buzz in to Judy's bedside, "but he still weighed over eight pounds."

More likely a few days late, thought Buzz.

Judy was radiant. Tired, but she had never looked more beautiful, Buzz thought. She held up her hand for Buzz to take in his. He leaned over and kissed her cheek.

"When I realized what day it was, I wanted to name him George M. Cohan Buckley. But Johnny insisted on John James Buckley the Fourth. He's an old traditionalist."

Buzz felt Johnny's hand on his shoulder.

"But Dad, we're going to call him Buddy."

Durham Caldwell

Buzz turned away. His dead brother's nickname. The name he'd tried to impose on Johnny. Tears filled his eyes. He dabbed at them with his handkerchief. When he put the handkerchief away, Judy took his hand again. Johnny was smiling broadly. Buzz noticed for the first time that Johnny still had on the surgeon's gown he had worn in the delivery room.

"Did you come through okay?"

"Dad, I was so confident after all those childbirth classes that I almost told the doctor to take a coffee break so I could do it myself."

Judy dropped Buzz's hand and grabbed for Johnny's. "It was comforting to have you there with me."

"You were just lucky you picked a holiday. If it was tomorrow or yesterday, I'd have to be at work."

She dropped his hand and gave it a playful slap.

A nurse brought in the baby and put him down in the bed beside Judy.

"Not as much hair, Dad," observed Johnny, "but I think he looks like you."

Buzz blushed.

Judy smiled a wide smile at Buzz and turned her head to look at the baby. "You know, I think you're right."

Everyone was quiet for a moment. Buzz's eyes took in the baby. He was beautiful. But even more beautiful was the affection he could see in Johnny's face as he looked at Judy and the affection in her face as she gazed at Johnny. Enough electricity was passing between them to light the city. It so moved him that he turned his back on them to wipe away more tears.

He felt Johnny's arm around his shoulders.

"Emotional experience becoming a grandfather?"

"Yes," he answered as he thought to himself, that too.

34

There were parts of his City Hall job that Buzz found rewarding, especially the chance to watch the new mayor in action. Even though they had put behind them the chapter of their lives in which they were lovers, they remained warm and affectionate friends. He had admired her energy, her candor, and her unfailing good humor even as her pregnancy had worn on into its fifth, sixth, seventh, eighth, and final month. He had marveled at her work in the open and behind the scenes to maintain Max's coalitions and to build new ones, the calmness and confidence with which she had assured the frightened that lowering racial barriers posed no threats to their own lifestyles, and the evenhanded way she had lobbied with educators, politicians, civil rights activists, and parents of all colors to gain acceptance for "a fair and reasonable plan" for racial balance. He was proud to be part of such an administration.

On the other hand, he was finding it restricting to be chained to a desk so many hours of the average day. There had been desk work in the newsroom, but he had always been able to escape it by getting out into the field to cover a story. Now his only escape was the tedium of meetings, meetings, and more meetings—sometimes accompanying the mayor but more often attending them as her representative, sometimes taking part in the discussion but more often sitting like a bump on a log listening and taking notes.

Another part of the executive assistant's role was becoming increasingly aggravating. He was the mayor's designated point man for citizen complaints. And although he had fielded many calls from outraged people during his years as a news director, he'd had no inkling of the number of whiners who telephoned or visited the mayor's office on a daily, almost hourly basis. Nor was Buzz Buckley famous for his patience.

Durham Caldwell

There were complaints about barking dogs, about property assessments, about garbage collection, about people dumping trash where it shouldn't be dumped, about rowdy kids, about noisy motorcycles, about aggressive cops, about never being able to find a cop, about discourteous treatment from city departments.

"If the other departments hear half the whining I do," he told secretary Ginny Bruce, "it's no wonder there's some discourteous treatment."

Ginny, who had been in the mayor's office since the days of Big Jim, merely smiled.

Buzz tried gamely to resolve each complaint, or to make sure that the appropriate department head resolved it. But the process was wearing him down. He had stayed on this long because of Judy's pregnancy and because of the continuing furor over balancing the schools. How could he tell Judy he wanted to bail out, especially when she knew he had nothing lined up to move to and when the school question remained unresolved and as delicate as ever?

Rescue came from an unexpected quarter. H.B. Baker phoned him at home one morning while he was still shaving.

"Buzz, I want you back. Hooper finally got that job in Boston he started angling for ten years ago. Jerry can't handle managing things. We tried a new guy from out of town. He drove east to get to the West End. I knew you were the heart and soul of the department, but I never realized how much everybody else depended on you. They've been trying, but the news has been flat ever since you left. No, not flat—sliding. Whaddaya say?"

Buzz wiped shaving cream off the telephone mouthpiece as he tried to frame a response.

H.B. didn't wait. "Same setup as before, with an extra twenty a week. I know that's better than you make at City Hall." It was—fifty a week better.

"Make it thirty, and you've got a deal."

"Isn't that what I said? An extra thirty! And Buzz, as much as it hurts you, I know you'll be fair and objective about reporting on city government."

Tumultuous Affairs

He felt like a heel doing it, springing the news on Judy only a few days after she'd become a mother. She was more understanding than he had anticipated.

"Buzz, I owe you so much that I can't put it in words. Our little fling may be over, but our love affair, that's forever. Much as I want to keep you with me at City Hall, I don't want to stand in your way. The people I feel sorry for are the competition. You'll knock 'em dead!

"Besides"—her till-now serious face brightened—"I have to find a job for Timmy McCann. He just got laid off at his company."

"Bless him! He'll be a lot better at it than I've been."

An even bigger surprise for Buzz was the warmth of the welcome his first day back in the newsroom. Jerry Finnerty, who he worried might be resentful, greeted him with a bear hug.

"I don't know how you kept your sanity in this goddam job. I was only handling half of it, the TV half, and the paperwork alone was enough to make a male rabbit give up sex. I kept telling him, 'Goddammit, H.B., my name is Jerry not Jesus,' but he never gave me a break.

"And the broad he told us would be the next Barbara Walters. You'd think he was using an audition couch. Built like a brick shithouse, and just about as brainy. Name's Helena—Helena Sanborn. I call her 'Helena Handbasket'—that's sure as hell where she's been taking us. One day she's downtown in the news car, opens the door into traffic, and gets the door ripped off. Another time they put the camera on her in the studio for a standup report, and she's powdering her nose. Thank God she wasn't scratching her crotch. Been here eight months and still screwing up.

"Boy, am I glad to see you!"

Close newsroom friends whispered other stories: slipshod planning, dwindling coordination between TV and radio, nobody coaching the new people, failure to follow up, and so on. But Benny Goodreau provided Buzz with probably the key reason for H.B.'s phone call. "I saw the new TV rating book the other day in Al Maroney's office. You know they usually play the numbers close to the vest. But he

Durham Caldwell told me the news ratings have gone downhill with every book since you left the job."

To cheers in Boston and mixed reviews in Riverbridge, the Massachusetts Senate added its okay to Governor Sargent's bill drastically modifying the state's Racial Balance Act. In agreeing to rely on voluntary transfers to end segregated schools, the Senate ignored its Ways and Means chairman, James A. Kelley, who warned colleagues, "What we are doing eighteen years later is what Orval Faubus did in Little Rock." Faubus was the Arkansas governor who forced President Eisenhower to call out federal troops to accomplish the racial integration of Little Rock's Central High School.

Governor Sargent signed the bill into law five days later, adding an emergency preamble "to give Mayor Buckley and her city as much time as possible to plan for the opening of school in September."

With Judy on maternity leave, Rowdy presided over a noisy meeting of the School Committee. Buzz, just getting his feet wet back at the station, assigned Whitney Garland to cover the meeting but went along himself as a spectator.

Lucille, DDT, Chet Zemba, and Henry Doane were crowing over the new legislation. Lucille had asked the city solicitor to attend the meeting.

"This new law gets us off the hook, doesn't it?"

"Maybe," said Herb Mason, "but you're still under court order to implement the busing plan in September. You can ask the court to vacate the order."

"I so move, Mister Chairman," declared Lucille. "No one has proved to me that putting kids on a bus is going to make them better educated."

Lucille's motion carried over the token protests of the two liberal members. Rowdy banged his gavel to silence the mixture of applause and groans from the audience.

"An' Mister Chairman," shouted Domenico DiTotola, "I make da motion dat we open in September widout da busin'!"

Tumultuous Affairs

More applause and groans. Another bang of the gavel as DDT rose from his chair and made a mock bow to the spectators.

This time the opposition was more than token. Larry Sidney reminded his colleagues, "We're under court order. Mister DiTotola, your motion is premature."

"We're going to leave parents confused on where their kids will go to school," protested Mary Williams.

"We'll be confused, too," volunteered Superintendent Berry. "We've moved some furniture already. Do we move it back? What do we tell parents?"

"Jus' tell da parents dat Ol' Domenic's lookin' out for 'em!" responded DDT.

Rod Berry continued, "What do we tell teachers? What do we tell the bus company that's already bought new buses? This is such a big job to make all these changes that the state is letting us postpone the opening of elementary schools for twelve days. We start reversing things, we may not open till Columbus Day."

Despite the arguments against it, DDT's motion passed on a four-to-three vote with Rowdy joining Larry and Mary in opposition.

"Bad move," Herb Mason confided to Buzz as they left the meeting room. "Our claim that changes in the law make the state board's order invalid is one thing. The commissioner claims the new law is unconstitutional. And there's a long-accepted principle in most jurisdictions: new legislation doesn't supersede a court order based on previous law. By our jumping the gun and voting to ignore the order, the court is likely to take the School Committee as thumbing its nose at the bench.

"Rowdy got outvoted," he added, "but at least he kept the meeting from blowing up."

Suddenly Buzz found racial balance being crowded out of the news by rapid-fire developments on Watergate. The United States Supreme Court ruled unanimously that President Nixon must hand over White House tapes despite his claims of executive privilege. The White House released edited tape transcripts linking Nixon to the Watergate cover-up as early as June 23, 1972, six days after the

Durham Caldwell

break-in. Congressman Eddie Boland told Jerry Finnerty that the president "deceived the American people." House Republicans previously supportive of the president deserted in droves. Three senior Republicans—John Rhodes, House minority leader, and Senators Barry Goldwater and Hugh Scott—visited the White House and told Nixon if he didn't resign he would be thrown out.

The president got the message. He arranged to speak to the country on television, presumably to announce his resignation.

"Larry O'Brien's around. Probably at his sister's house in Longmeadow," Buzz told Jerry. "You go for him." O'Brien, a Western Massachusetts native son, was Democratic national chairman when the Watergate burglars broke into his office.

"O'Brien won't go on camera. He's even stiffing the networks," Jerry reported. "He'll do a phone interview if I call him back after he finishes dinner."

Waiting in his office for Nixon to appear on screen from the White House, Buzz doodled on his desk calendar with a blue ballpoint. He circled the date—August 8, 1974.

"This is a date we'll remember," he told Tommy Goldman, who was waiting with him.

Buzz was surprised to find Tommy so relaxed on what had to be a black day for Republicans and especially for those who had worked for "R.N."

After watching the resignation speech together, Buzz asked Tommy on camera, "What went wrong? Wasn't Nixon supposed to be a smart politician?"

"He was. Probably one of the smartest. But he had a paranoia. Sort of like the guy who's walking down Main Street on a sunny day at high noon with a cop on every block, and he's looking over his shoulder to see if somebody's gonna mug him. Nixon—even after finally making it to the White House—was always afraid he'd be victim of a political mugging.

"You know, Buzz, Nixon didn't order that Watergate break-in— that I'm sure of. But the atmosphere at the White House, he created it. They already had the precedent of trying to get Ellsberg's psychiatric records. That paranoid atmosphere is what gave those cuckoos their license to burglarize Larry O'Brien's office." Daniel Ellsberg was the former Defense Department official who had leaked the Pentagon Papers, a compendium of previously secret documents tracing U.S. involvement in Vietnam.

"You could've worked in that Nixon White House, couldn't you?" Buzz asked.

"The Germans didn't want me there."

"You mean Haldeman and Ehrlichman?" Bob Haldeman had been Nixon's chief of staff, John Ehrlichman his chief domestic adviser.

"Right. We called them the Germans. Not just because of their names. They also had that Prussian mentality."

"So you worked under Attorney General Mitchell at Justice?"

"Way under. A flunky job. But John Mitchell—despite that pipe smoking, easy-going image—was just as paranoid as Nixon and the Germans.

"Too bad. Nixon could have gone down in history as one of our greatest presidents. But he blew it—just like Johnson."

Larry O'Brien, who could have been forgiven for gloating, instead was somber. He told Jerry in his gravelly voice how he resented the break into his office by the Watergate burglars. He called it espionage and violation of his civil rights. He recalled how disturbed he was that it took so long to get Congress and the public to understand the seriousness of the break-in. "But," he said, referring to the day's events, "I had no inkling it would come to this. Until maybe the last six months, I had no idea myself of the depth of White House involvement. When it finally came out, Nixon had no choice but to leave.

"What really appalls me is the attempted use of government agencies—the FBI, the CIA—to destroy people. We were on the brink of becoming a police state."

Then the man who had been the very partisan chief political operative for John F. Kennedy, for Bobby Kennedy—and, in the 1968 campaign, for Hubert Humphrey—turned apolitical. "President Ford

Durham Caldwell

needs bipartisan support over the next few months. We have to overcome what's been a tremendous drop of confidence and a growing cynicism about government."

35

Judy was back at City Hall now almost full time. Buzz had stopped in to check for news. Secretary Ginny Bruce's voice came over the intercom: "City solicitor to see you."

"Send him in."

Buzz got up to leave.

"No, stay—you might get a story."

Herb appeared agitated. "Judy, I'm not sure whether this is good news or bad news. The attorney general is joining the School Committee in asking the court to vacate the busing order."

"But he represents the state board."

"Judy, he says the new law has 'presumptive validity'—something about the Legislature and the governor in their wisdom seeing fit to supersede the court decree by the new act. He says the state board has no right to challenge it."

"What does that mean?"

"It means," offered Buzz, "that Bob Quinn is in a tough fight for governor. And with the big foofaraw in Boston, he figures he can't afford to look tougher on racial imbalance than Governor Sargent does."

"You're probably right," said the solicitor. "He won't even let the state board be represented in court against us."

"Does that mean the School Committee wins by default?" asked Judy.

"Not necessarily. Remember, what the committee is bucking is an order of the court. Even if the court upholds the new law, it could rule that it doesn't apply retroactively. My advice to the School Department would be to keep moving the furniture—regardless of Attorney General Quinn and regardless of Domenic's motion."

Things on the Boston end began to move swiftly. Story after story chattered into the newsroom on the UPI wire. The state board

Durham Caldwell

found that the School Committee violated the court order when it approved the DDT motion. A judge ordered work on implementation of the Berry Pie plan to continue. Boston schools meanwhile faced their own two-way busing edict, this one from a federal judge.

Back home, the white Unitarian minister told Jerry Finnerty in an interview, "Our School Committee members are orchestrating a race riot by pretending schools will not be integrated this fall!"

Then came the hearing before the full bench of the Supreme Judicial Court. The mayor herself phoned Buzz from Boston to give him a fill-in. She had taken good notes. The Civil Liberties Union lawyer representing Lenora Clark argued, "Neither the state nor the federal constitution permits the shabby and petty conduct of the School Committee in denying the rights of thousands of children to an equal education under the Racial Balance Act."

One justice rapped the attorney general for refusing to supply counsel to the Board of Education. The chief justice noted, "The language in the new law seems to make it possible for school committees to promote segregation."

"Sounds like the handwriting is on the wall," Buzz observed.

"That's what Herb says," Judy agreed. "He expects the court to move fast, maybe give us a ruling in a week or so. He's sure the ruling will go against the School Committee."

The court did move fast—lightning fast. It issued a unanimous decision four hours after the hearing. It ordered the city to proceed with the two-way busing program as directed by the state board with the opening of schools in September.

As soon as the bulletin from Boston hit the UPI wire, Buzz mobilized his troops to chase down reaction.

Jerry Finnerty caught up with Lucille Cournoyer. He radioed in to Buzz. "She calls it a travesty on justice, says she's in complete disbelief. But Buzz, she says the city's got no choice but to abide by the court order."

That's a good sign, thought Buzz.

Tumultuous Affairs

Whitney Garland tracked down Henry Doane. "Mister Doane says he's disappointed," Whitney radioed, "but he says he'll comply with the law. Same with Mister Zemba."

Jerry was on the two-way again. "I found DDT, Buzz, but he won't comment." He put on an exaggerated version of the DiTotola Bronx accent. "He says he ain't gonna have no comment for no news medias on what dem judges said till he sees it in writin'—and somebody wid brains intoiprets da writin' fer 'im."

Well, thought Buzz, at least he's not threatening riots in the street.

Whitney brought back an interview with Lenora Clark. Buzz watched the screening of the film in the editing room. She did not appear as jubilant as he expected. She was pleased with the decision, but said there was still a lot of work to do. "The mayor," she told the camera, "seems to have been on the fence on this issue. She enjoys great popularity in the city. I hope she will use that popularity to unite the city during the integration process."

Buzz got Judy and Rod Berry, the school superintendent, to come on the newscast live. Rod called the SJC ruling "quite clear" and said the school system would move ahead to implement the five-district plan.

"You mean the Berry Pie plan," corrected anchorman Finnerty.

"Well, some people call it that, but there's no pride in authorship. It's just a way of getting the job done. Fortunately, the court ruled quickly. We have just a little more than three weeks to get everything in place for the opening of classes on September sixteenth. And there's still a lot of work to do."

"Wouldn't this have gone easier, Doctor Berry," Jerry asked, "if the School Committee hadn't thrown roadblocks into the planning process?"

"Jerry, the members of the committee took positions which they felt were correct to take. It's time now to move ahead."

A real diplomat, Buzz thought, as he watched from the control room. He saw Judy lean forward.

"Jerry, I think the interviews you just showed with Mrs. Cournoyer, Mister Zemba, and Mister Doane make it clear the School

Durham Caldwell

Committee is going to do everything it can to make the integration program work smoothly. And I assure Mrs. Clark that the mayor's office will work with all people of good will toward uniting what has been a divided community. The mayor, the School Committee, the superintendent—we have two things uppermost in our minds: the safety and the education of the city's children."

Domenico DiTotola wouldn't talk to Jerry Finnerty, but he did comment to the paper. "Judges who make decisions like that," the paper quoted him, "should be forced to live in the community that will be affected by their decision."

"Christ," observed Jerry, "I bet it took the reporter and two deskmen to make DDT sound that literate."

"At least," noted Buzz, this time out loud, "he's not calling for rebellion in the streets."

But Buzz spoke a day too early. The next day, DDT was back in the paper invoking the spirit of Mahatma Gandhi and Martin Luther King and suggesting, "Civil disobedience has become a traditional response to injustice."

"Sonuvabitch must have a ghost writer," observed Jerry.

DDT's remarks provoked the old firebrand, Bobby Clark, he who had once gone limp on the City Hall steps, to urge the School Committee "to restrain one of its members from making inflammatory statements."

"To accept tyranny is to condone tyranny!" a young white mother told the School Committee at a special meeting called to provide information to the public and iron out last-minute details connected with the opening of schools. "I'm damned if I'll let my kids go to Miller Street School! I'll keep 'em home first!"

There was a round of applause and a smattering of boos. Buzz, who was covering the meeting himself because it was Whitney's day off, could feel the tension in the room.

Judy rapped the gavel. "Please. We're under a court order. Let's listen to each other without any demonstrations. The superintendent wants to respond to the lady who just spoke."

Tumultuous Affairs

"Madam," said Rod Berry in a calm voice, "I assure you your children will have fine teachers and get a good education at any of our schools. I also want to remind you that school attendance in Massachusetts is compulsory for all children ages seven to sixteen unless the child is being taught at home in an approved program. If a child is found to be truant, the parent is subject to fines, quite substantial fines."

A man stood up in the back row. "It's a shame all you School Committee members have caved in—all except Domenic. You know as well as I know, there's gonna be trouble here when school opens—real trouble!"

Applause mingled with cries of "sit down!" Judy banged the gavel again.

A man Buzz recognized as a neighborhood civic leader got to his feet. He turned first toward the young mother who had threatened to keep her children at home, then to the man in the back row. "I know how you feel, Mrs. Dickson, and you, too, Mister Riley. I've fought against busing for better than four years. We fought, and we lost. School opens in two weeks. I don't want to see one kid hurt. And I don't think anybody else does. We've got to stop predicting trouble, stop giving excuses in advance to anybody who might be thinking about doing something violent. If we and these people up here"—he indicated the School Committee and the superintendent—"work together like ladies and gentlemen, we can pull it off without any trouble."

There was enough applause this time to drown out any dissent. Encouraging, Buzz thought.

Judy might have used the gavel again, but she was distracted by the white-shirted gold-badged deputy fire chief who strode into the room, went directly to the committee table, and bent over to whisper in the mayor's ear. Buzz could see her responding with a whispered question. The deputy chief nodded.

Judy turned back to what had become a hushed meeting room.

"The deputy chief tells me we've had a bomb threat. In the interest of prudence and public safety, he's asked that we evacuate the building."

Durham Caldwell

A murmur went through the room.

"No reason to panic. Just walk down the stairs and out the front door."

People began standing up. Judy put a whispered question to Rod Berry, then turned back to those in the room, speaking in a loud voice to make herself heard over shuffling feet. "We'll reassemble in the bleachers up the street at the high school athletic field." She rapped the gavel. "We stand in recess for fifteen minutes."

Reporters gathered around the deputy fire chief who was standing on the sidewalk watching the exodus from the building along with a squad of firefighters waiting to get inside.

"Some jerk claimin' to be a Navy demolition expert. He called nine-one-one, said he'd planted a bomb in the meetin' room. Somethin' about gettin' even with the turncoats."

The deputy glanced at his watch. "Still got half an hour before he said the place would blow up. Fifty to one it's a crank call, but with all the tension over this busin', you don't wanta take chances."

Some members of the crowd went to their cars, but most of them walked up the hill to the athletic field and filed into a section of the bleachers. A custodian had turned on the floodlights. Buzz could see people talking earnestly together in small groups. He saw Mrs. Dickson, the young mother who had denounced tyranny and threatened to keep her children out of school, sit down beside the neighborhood civic leader who had spoken inside.

"Well," asked Judy as she reconvened the meeting, standing in front of the bleachers with other committee members and the superintendent in a semicircle behind her, "what else can happen?"

There was a flash of lightning and a distant roll of thunder. Everybody laughed.

"Maybe the good Lord is sending us a message," suggested Judy.

There was more laughter and a round of applause. Buzz sensed a change in mood.

Mrs. Dickson stood up. "My friend here is right," she said, indicating the neighborhood leader sitting beside her. "None of us want any kids to get hurt. But I'm still worried about sending my kids to a new school in the Central City. How do we know they're gonna be safe?"

There was another flash of lightning. The thunder sounded a little closer.

"As mayor," Judy answered, "I can assure you..."

"Can't hear you!" shouted somebody from the top of the bleachers.

"I can assure you," Judy shouted back, "that the mayor's office is already working with Superintendent Berry and with the chief of police to make certain the school environment is safe. Any troublemakers on or around school grounds—or on the bus routes—will be dealt with severely!"

Applause and cheers. A light rain began to fall. Judy looked up at the sky. "I think the good Lord may also be telling us it's time to go home. Mister Zemba moves we adjourn. Mister Doane seconds. All in favor say aye! The meeting's adjourned!"

Max Feigenson's rules of order, thought Buzz. Chet Zemba and Henry Doane hadn't moved or seconded anything. But it began to rain harder, and nobody challenged the chairman's call. School board members, parents, and reporters all began to run toward the gate and down the hill toward their cars.

As he drove back up the hill, Buzz noted two forms huddled in a doorway talking earnestly to each other: DDT and Chris Riley, the man who had spoken up from the back row to predict "real trouble."

When Buzz stopped by later in the week to see his grandson, Judy seemed pleased with the progress of preparations for opening day. And she was convinced that DDT and Riley, although they were still mumbling about "civil disobedience," were not attracting any substantial support.

The Friday before the local elementary school Monday opening, Buzz could read concern on Judy's face—and he knew why it was there: school integration trouble in Boston.

While waiting for her father and mother to arrive for dinner, dinner that Johnny had come home early to fix, they made a little small talk—Buzz and Judy and Johnny—about how the young upstart

Durham Caldwell

Michael Dukakis had knocked off the old pro, Attorney General Bob Quinn, in Tuesday's Democratic gubernatorial primary. And how Dukakis had polled nearly fifty-eight percent of the vote!

But it was the Boston school story that was uppermost in the minds of all three of them. The story had broken on radio and TV the day before. The Friday morning newspaper headlines read, "Whites boycott Boston schools," "Eight black students hit by rocks." The story continued throughout the day on the UPI wire: "NINE PEOPLE HAVE BEEN ARRESTED IN THE SECOND STRAIGHT DAY OF INTEGRATION-CONNECTED VIOLENCE IN BOSTON SCHOOLS"; "ONE BLACK STUDENT WAS SLIGHTLY INJURED IN A MELEE"; "ANGRY WHITE YOUTHS SHOWERED POLICE CARS WITH BRICKS AND BOTTLES."

Boston had instituted two-way busing to integrate its high schools under a federal court order. Predictions of violence had turned into reality.

"We knew Boston could be setting us a bad example when we postponed school opening," conceded Judy, "but Rod said he needed the time to get everything in place. Now the question is, will the bad example be contagious?"

"People here have got too much sense," Johnny said hopefully, "at least everybody but DDT."

"I hope you're right," Buzz said. He turned to Judy.

"Are you set with the police?"

"The chief's been very cooperative. He's canceled days off on Monday. He's holding over the dogwatch, calling the eight-to-four in early, so there'll be double coverage plus. There'll be officers at every school, cruisers patrolling the bus routes. You can't stop a real nut, I suppose, but he'll intimidate a few of them."

"Okay, and you're going on television again Saturday and Sunday to calm people's fears? And in the Sunday paper?"

"I'm tired, but yeah, I guess I should."

"You think you could get Lucille or Henry Doane to go on with you—or that guy who spoke up at the School Committee meeting? You know—longtime foes of busing joining the mayor in a last appeal for a peaceful opening day?"

"Worth a try."

"Judy," said Johnny, "why don't you ask DDT to go on with you?"

Buzz wondered if his son was joking, but Johnny looked serious.

"He may not be a complete nitwit," Johnny continued. "He must have some concerns about what's happening in Boston."

Judy pondered for a moment. She looked at Buzz for guidance. He shrugged his shoulders.

"Can't tell what a guy like DDT will say."

"Hey, Dad, I thought you were a TV man. You don't have to put him on live. Stand him up in front of the sound camera and film him. If he demagogues it, you lose the film in the processor—or you never put it in. If he says something positive, you get it on the air quick—before he changes his mind."

Buzz realized again how his son had moved ahead so fast while he himself had plodded through life. Johnny was the brainy one.

"Next question: who calls him," asked Buzz, "the station or the mayor? Neither one of us is on especially buddy-buddy terms with him."

"It's a long shot either way," answered Judy. "I'll call him. Tell me where you want him to be and when."

Domenico, Judy reported, was surprised to get a call from the mayor. He also allowed that he was "boddered" by what was happening in Boston and didn't want to be responsible for anything like that happening here. He appeared jointly with her the next afternoon in front of the sound cameras for both TV stations.

"I don' wanna see us become anudder Boston," he told the TV news audience. "Anybody who plans t' disrupt t'ings Monday on openin' day is no friend o' da kids an' da parents o' dis city—an' no friend o' mine." And then the real shocker: "Ol' Domenic's gonna be out on da street wid da mayor and da chief on Monday doin' whatever I kin do t' make sure we got a peaceable openin' an' alla da kids get t' deir schools safe an' sound."

Judy told Buzz after the filming, "This is off the record, but there's another reason besides Boston for Mister DDT's change of heart. He'd told his daughter to keep her two younger kids home rather than put them on the bus to Miller Street. The daughter told me the two kids went to him and said, 'Grampa, we want to go to school. We don't care if there are black kids, we want to go to school.' I think those kids had more impact on him than Boston."

On Sunday, the school story played second fiddle to a big story from Washington. The new president, Gerald Ford, granted Richard Nixon a full and unconditional pardon to spare Nixon and the country additional grief, he said, in this "American tragedy."

Buzz didn't mind the spotlight turning back to Washington—even though after DDT's turnaround, he believed there was a better than even chance Riverbridge could open its schools peaceably.

Tension on Monday was running high. Scores of parents drove their kids to their new schools instead of putting them on the bus. Scores of kids still walking to neighborhood schools had parental escorts. Buzz saw Chris Riley and a handful of other adults holding up signs at some of the schools: "BUSSING UNFAIR" and "KEEP YOUR KIDS HOME," but most parents accompanying their children to school ignored them.

Buzz was at Miller Street School when a police cruiser pulled up and disgorged five white youngsters.

"Trouble?" Buzz asked the officer at the wheel.

The officer laughed. "Bus forgot to pick 'em up. Happens every year first day of school. Probably a lot more this year with all the route changes."

Buzz noted that the principal of every school he visited was at the front door to give a smiling greeting to children getting off the buses and to parents escorting their kids. In most cases, the PTO president was there with the principal to add reassurance that this was a school where the parents played an active role. Just another example, Buzz thought, of Rod Berry's thoroughness in getting the school system ready for mammoth change.

At one school, Buzz saw the principal intercept a mother trying to sneak two children into the building who had been transferred to another school. The principal politely but firmly turned the mother and the youngsters away.

Rod Berry reported opening day attendance a little below normal but expressed confidence it would pick up as more parents became satisfied their kids were not in any danger. DDT, true to his word, rode with Judy in her city car as she drove from school to school to check how things were going and to offer encouragement to parents and to teachers. She told Buzz later how relieved she was that all the traffic on the police radio in the car was routine with nothing more alarming than bus route mixups.

Back at the station, the news wire told of "VIOLENCE IN BOSTON SCHOOLS FOR THE THIRD CONSECUTIVE DAY" and, later in the week, "A RIOT HAS FORCED THE CLOSING OF A BOSTON HIGH SCHOOL." Fights and confrontations in Boston continued into mid-October. Governor Sargent, locked in a tough fight for reelection, mobilized four hundred and fifty National Guardsmen and asked President Ford, unsuccessfully, for federal troops to help maintain order.

"Why the difference between us and Boston?" Doctor Ferguson wondered as he and his wife joined Judy, Johnny, and Buzz around the dinner table for a meal that Louise and Johnny had teamed up to cook. Young Buddy Buckley was sleeping soundly in his crib upstairs.

Buzz took it that the question was addressed to him.

"The commissioner of education credits the leadership of the superintendent and his staff. The governor says it's because we had a locally developed plan designed to meet our particular situation, not something imposed on us by some court-appointed board of experts."

"Dad," interjected Judy, "we had tremendous community cooperation. After they realized we couldn't stall any more, everybody pulled together. Lucille, Henry, finally even DDT. And Rod did a fantastic job of preparing the principals and preparing the teachers. If they hadn't been determined to make it work, it could have been a mess."

Durham Caldwell

"The superintendent, of course, is very modest," said Buzz. "He passes the credit around—the community, the teachers, even the news media for the way we played it. We had less inflammatory rhetoric from public officials than they had in Boston. They were integrating high schools. With us it was elementaries—none of our secondary schools was imbalanced—and that probably made a difference. Plus, and Rod Berry and the governor and the commissioner are unanimous on this"—he raised his vodka collins and tipped the glass toward Judy in a toast—"the leadership of our mayor. Doc, Judy made a big difference!"

"Hear! Hear!" said Johnny, raising his glass. "To the mayor who made the difference!"

36

Buzz hadn't realized until the year he was away from it how much he enjoyed the challenge of running a news department—of teaming up the right reporters with the right camera people, of putting politicians including the new mayor on the spot by asking the right questions, of sifting breaking stories out of the *mélange* of routine transmissions on the police scanner, of encouraging reporters to use the right words and to write compelling leads and short sentences and to develop their stories coherently and of knowing when to let the visual material speak for itself, of watching youngsters like Whitney Garland hone their skills, of encouraging photographers to let their lenses linger on scenes with visual impact and to mix up their shots to give the viewer an unending stream of visual surprises, of encouraging the radiomen to weave in taped voice reports and interview segments in a way to make their newscasts move and not slow them down.

Buzz was cracking the whip again, but with a mellowness and a good humor that were sometimes in short supply during his earlier tenure in this same newsroom.

There was plenty of work to do. One of the immediate jobs was interviewing people to fill a new morning news anchor opening that H.B. had reluctantly agreed was necessary if he really wanted to overtake the competition.

Buzz was in early. He was there late more times than not, except on Friday when staff members knew he had a standing dinner obligation at his son's house with Johnny and the mayor. And don't call him weekends unless a major story was breaking. Those were his days to give the Fergusons a break and help with his grandson's diaper changes. Work late on the other days? Why not? The later he worked, the longer it put off going home to an empty house.

Durham Caldwell

One afternoon after the day crews had come in off the road, and just before the night crew went out, the whole staff gathered in the middle of the newsroom. Jerry came into his cubbyhole and said, "Buzz, come out a minute—we've got a problem."

He went out to find that the problem was a birthday cake—a birthday cake for him. He was moved. He had spent a lot of birthdays in this newsroom, and this was the first time the gang had brought him a cake.

After an off-key chorus of "Happy Birthday," Stan Wlodyka asked the important question: "Buzz, how does it feel to be an old man?" God, he was fifty-four!

"Nothing's different except I'm a little stiff when I wake up in the morning."

"Me too," said Jerry Finnerty, "but it goes away when I pee."

Buzz kept marveling at how easy it had been to get back into the newsroom routine. But there was one thing he was finding it difficult to get used to: the attention certain females appeared to be paying him. At first, he thought maybe it was his imagination, but Linda, H.B.'s secretary—the friendly and curvaceous brunette whom Jerry called "the Employee Benefits" and who again was newly divorced—seemed to be finding more and more excuses to visit the newsroom. Even though she had typed H.B.'s memos, it seemed she would always lean over Buzz's shoulder to read them with him, putting her cheek very close to his and brushing his back with her ample bosom.

He wondered if it was his long-ago invitation to dinner—which came too late, just after she'd gotten engaged. Or perhaps his straight arrow reputation intrigued her or challenged her. His undeserved straight arrow reputation, he thought, remembering his many trysts with Mar and with Judy. Or had Linda decided he was harmless and was only teasing him?

He almost told her one day, "If you don't get your tits off my back, I'm gonna complain to H.B. and put a sign on the newsroom door, 'Off limits to Linda Kokoski.'" But he knew that in company politics there is nothing more debilitating than making an enemy of the boss's secretary. He adopted the substitute strategy of getting up from his desk and walking out to the center of the newsroom to meet her whenever he spotted her flouncing in with a new memo.

Maybe it was his imagination, but Helena Sanborn—the new girl that Jerry called Helena Handbasket and was "built like you know what"—seemed overly eager to visit him in the cubbyhole news director's office. She wanted critiques on her stories, critiques on the way she dressed. She commented on how empty her social life had become since she moved to the city. She invariably would close the door when she came in, explaining, "I want to talk about personal things."

One day when she hovered over him, practically inviting him to put his arm around her to console her, he whispered with a knowing glance toward the newsroom and the new night reporter, "Harry Vermelli has a very empty social life. Why don't you get to know him a little better?" And he changed her hours to dovetail with Harry's.

Again it might be his imagination, but the eyes of at least two of the eager young women applying for the new morning news anchor slot conveyed the unspoken message that he might claim any reward he wanted if he chose her for the opening. Pretty girls, too. Their bedroom eyes didn't interfere with his determination to add another woman to the station's news team, but he bypassed the two cuties in favor of a candidate with a more neutral gaze. That she happened to be a young black woman was a bonus. Protection from the FCC, thought Buzz, in case Whitney leaves.

One night as he was driving home, Buzz tried to explain to himself why he had brushed off these come-ons without asking even a single one of them to lunch or dinner or even a trip to the Coke machine. Pressure of work? Hell, he had time for a lunch date or a dinner date, to say nothing of a Coke, any time he wanted to take it.

In a rare moment of introspection, he thought maybe it was the sweet memories of the happiness he had shared for so long with Elaine and so briefly with Judy—and the certainty that nowhere in the world could there be another woman who was the match for either of these two.

Whatever it was, for the first time in his adult life—not counting the period right after Elaine died—there was no longing for female companionship. Women just didn't interest him. His time as Judy's lover hadn't been so long ago. Maybe she'd been keeping him young, and now he was showing his age. That must be part of it. He was getting old, and the fire was out.

The fire out? He searched for a different metaphor. How about: is the battery run down? He smiled a sweet memory. Or is the battery dead? Yes, he thought, the battery must be dead. Too bad I'm having so much fun in the newsroom, he told himself. Otherwise I'd be a pretty good candidate for the priesthood.

When Myra Hot-Pants—that was the only way Buzz could think of her after Jerry gave her the name—saw him downtown, smiled a flirtatious smile, and invited him to dinner, he almost said, Sorry, Myra, but I've got a dead battery.

What he did say was, "Gee, I'm sorry, Myra, but between H.B. and my new grandson, I'm so darned busy I don't even go to dinner any more."

She stalked off in a huff.

It was exciting to be broadcasting elections again. Democrats won the governor's office in 1974 for the first time in ten years with Michael Dukakis beating incumbent Francis Sargent by more than two hundred thousand votes. Former lieutenant governor Francis X. Bellotti, out of elective office for a decade, was elected attorney general as Massachusetts Democrats scored a clean sweep of offices voted on statewide.

Too bad Mar isn't here, Buzz thought to himself as he drove home after he and Jerry had wrapped up the Election Night broadcast. It would give me a chance to needle her a little bit about all those winning Democrats. But why the hell am I thinking about Mar? It's been more than five years.

At least he could think of her now without the anguish that enveloped him for so many months after they parted. Christ, he thought, the battery must really be dead.

It was late one afternoon in the spring when a call came into the newsroom.

"Buzz, for you."

He almost didn't take it, he was so wrapped up with Jerry trying to shoehorn two more stories into the lineup for the six-thirty news.

"Buzz, this is Mar. Mar Antonelli," she added, as if he could have forgotten who Mar was or could have forgotten that throaty voice.

"Buzz, I'm in town overnight on a story. I was wondering if you were free for dinner."

His first impulse was to say "no," not to give her the chance to hurt him another time. But there was something in her tone, coupled with his own natural curiosity at least to look at her again, that impelled him to say "yes." He gave her directions to the Heidelberg and told her he would meet her there at seven-thirty—after the news and after he had cleared his desk.

The restaurant wasn't crowded. They were able to get a booth at the back away from most of the diners. They sat awkwardly at first, looking at each other across the table, each it seemed waiting for the other to start the conversation. She's aged, he thought. She's probably thinking the same thing about me. The skin did hang a little more loosely from her neck and face. A few strands of silver lightened her sandy hair. But she was still a pretty woman—still an eye turner even in a tailored suit.

She broke the silence. "How've you been?"

"I've had my ups and downs," he told her truthfully.

"You and I had a lot of nice ups and downs," she said, with just a hint of dimple. "I think I enjoyed every one of them."

She hasn't lost her sense of humor, he thought. Still hasn't seen the chance for a *double entendre* without taking it.

He had been tense when they sat down. Now he relaxed a little bit.

"You've been doing some good work for the paper," he volunteered. "I see your byline almost every time I pick up the *Globe*. And congratulations on the awards you've gotten. You deserved them."

"Buzz, I have to give a lot of the credit to you for what you taught me—leads and pronouns and God knows what else."

"Nothing a good *Globe* deskman couldn't have taught you."

"But that's the point. When I got to the *Globe*, the deskmen didn't have to teach me. They turned me loose to go after the stories."

"And you've done well."

Her voice turned very serious.

"Buzz, my daughter came up from New York last week to spend a few days with me. She used almost those same words. She said, 'Mom, you've done very well. Why aren't you happy?' Jenny saw right through me.

"Buzz, I lead a very empty life. I come home at night wanting to share my little triumphs, and my pratfalls too, with somebody who's dear to me. But the apartment's empty. Just me and the goldfish."

He knew the empty feeling well. Not so much now. But certainly after Elaine died—and then again after the breakup with this woman sitting across the table from him.

"It's nice to get an award," she went on, "but how much nicer it would be to come back to sit down and see the face of someone very special beaming up at you."

Oh-oh, Buzz, watch out, he told himself. Here it comes. Don't let her hurt you again.

"Gotta be a lot of nice guys in Boston. A woman pretty as you shouldn't have any trouble meeting them."

"Buzz, I've met some. Trouble is you spoiled me."

She tried to smile, but Buzz detected the glint of tears in the corners of those beautiful gray eyes.

Watch out for the tears, Buzz, old boy; don't get washed away by the tears. What was it Dad used to say? The most effective water power in the world is a woman's tears.

"I'd go out with somebody, and I'd compare him with you. Buzz, they never measured up.

"Buzz, I guess what I'm trying to tell you is that I made a big mistake letting you get away. I miss you terribly. I've wanted to call you for so long." Her voice seemed on the edge of breaking. "I finally got the courage to do it.

"If by some major miracle you're currently unattached, this very lonely little girl would like one more chance to be part of your life. I can't imagine any award, any recognition, I would rather have than the name 'Mrs. John J. Buckley, Jr.' I feel so stupid that I had the chance and booted it." She paused. "Can we start seeing each other again—see if it works out—see if the magic is still there?"

My God! he thought as the full impact of what she was saying hit him.

She stared expectantly across the table. The thoughts were churning in his brain. He didn't want to be hurt again, didn't want to take a chance, couldn't stand being hurt again. But this proud, accomplished woman had thrown pride to the wind—asking him for another chance. This lump in the throat was bigger than the Rock of Gibraltar. He couldn't trust his voice to say anything.

He put a hand across the table and rested it on hers. The sober, almost pleading look on her pretty face dissolved into the old saucy, dimpled smile. If any resistance lingered within him, it crumbled in the joy and the warmth of that smile.

"Let's try it. I've been very lonely. And I don't even have goldfish to come home to."

There was a waiter standing over them. "Are you folks ready to order?"

His voice was almost apologetic. Buzz wondered how long he had been standing there.

When the waiter went back to the kitchen, Buzz and Mar sat there for a few moments just smiling at each other. The lump had disappeared from his throat. Suddenly he felt as relaxed with her as he was in the old days. And he sensed stirring within him old feelings he hadn't felt for a long time. He stretched a hand back across the table and rested it again on hers.

"Mar," he said, and the smile carried over into his voice as he remembered the way she had teased him so long ago in Atlantic City, "I know the importance you put on ups and downs, but I've got to warn you. I'm not forty-four years old any more . . . "

"Neither am I."

" . . . and I may very well have atrophied from disuse."

She put her other hand on top of his and answered very seriously, "Buzz, darling, when we were together before, the ups and downs were wonderfully exciting. But the important thing then, the important thing for me now, is just being with you."

The saucy smile enveloped her face. "I'll take my chances on the other part."

"Okay," he grinned, "but you were warned."

They chatted happily with each other all through dinner. Chatted as easily as though they'd been apart for only a weekend rather than six long years. Chatted on a potpourri of topics: funny things that had happened to them, books she'd read, things they could do together while getting reacquainted.

Then there was one of those lulls that happen in the most spirited of conversations—each participant waiting for the other to pick it up. After perhaps half a minute of silence, just looking at each other, she said softly, "A penny for your thoughts."

He laughed. "I was just thinking of that first kiss in San Francisco." A pause. "And yours?"

She smiled that special smile and said in that throaty voice, "I was thinking about the same thing." The smile vanished, replaced by a wistful, lonely look. "And all the ones we've missed since we stopped seeing each other."

He stretched his hand across the table and again rested it on hers.

"I could make it up to you," he offered.

She gently held his arm as he walked her to her hotel.

"You have a beautiful grandson," she told him.

"You saw him?"

"I went to see Judy. I met her at the office. She broke off early to take me home so I could meet Buddy.

"Buzz, I almost called you up so many times over the years. At first I blamed you for walking out on me. Eventually I realized how shabbily I'd treated you. I wanted to call you, but I kept losing my nerve. Judy gave me the last bit of courage I needed. She even insisted I use her phone. I figured she might know if you were romancing anybody."

Tumultuous Affairs

Yes, Judy would know. He wondered if Judy had told her anything else but dismissed the thought. What he and Judy had meant to each other was their secret—theirs and Max's.

"Does Judy know how close you and I used to be?"

"Not unless you told her. But Buzz, she certainly thinks the world of you."

"We think the world of each other."

"And not only did she encourage me to call you, she told me you needed a woman in your life—said you have so much love to share. Oh, Buzz," she squeezed his arm, "I want so much to share it with you! I hope you'll let me!"

As they waited for the traffic light across from the hotel, Mar resumed the conversation.

"As somebody once said, I've been to the big city and seen the bright lights. I'm ready to take another shot at being a housewife. As you may recall, I have a certain expertise with the vacuum cleaner."

"The dust has been accumulating ever since you stopped coming to see me. But Mar, you've worked too hard to get where you are. You're too good at it to give it up. Can't hide talent like yours behind a vacuum cleaner."

"Buzz, if things work out for us, I could look for a job in Riverbridge. Or I could free lance. Or maybe the *Globe* would want a Western Massachusetts correspondent. Getting to know you again is my priority."

"I might even look for a job in Boston," he volunteered.

"No, Buzz—you belong here. And I want so much to be here with you."

As they entered the lobby of the hotel, she asked him softly, "You'll stay a while, won't you?"

He nodded.

As the elevator door closed, he embraced her. The scent of that subtle, intoxicating perfume filled his nostrils just as it had on the airplane to San Francisco and so many times after that. As they kissed and as the elevator rose, he silently pondered this new turn of events. His marriage with Elaine had been so warm and so satisfying, but so traditional, that he couldn't have imagined the wild adventure that had come to him since. And now for a third time in these few years since Elaine had gone, a pretty woman was throwing herself into his arms, begging him to take her. First Mar. Then Judy. Now Mar again. Warm, witty, wonderful Mar. It would work out—and this time it would be for keeps. He knew it would. Thrice blessed, he thought. No, four times blessed. Elaine would always rank first and dearest. He was remembering one of the last things she had said to him—"You live for today, not yesterday"—when he felt the elevator stop and he and Mar reluctantly broke their embrace as the door slid open.

"You should've gotten a room on a higher floor," he chided her as they walked down the corridor toward her room. Interesting thing about a dead battery, it came to him—sometimes, with the proper equipment, you can recharge it. As Mar pulled her key out of the lock and pushed open the door, Buzz swept her up in his arms and carried her into the room. She struggled and kicked and pummeled him with her fists, but not too hard. He turned on the light switch with his wrist, closed the door with his elbow, and dropped her on the bed.

THE END

Made in the USA
Charleston, SC
03 February 2011